À J*ONATHAN*

un coeur immense, un ami sans égal et le plus vieux témoin

d'Isandor.

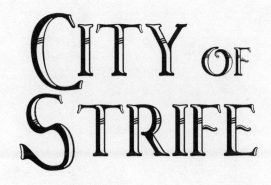

CITY OF STRIFE

CITY OF STRIFE: An Isandor Novel
Copyright © 2017 Claudie Arseneault.

Published by The Kraken Collective
krakencollectivebooks.com

Edited by Brenda Pierson and Jess R. Sutton.
Cover by Gabrielle Arseneault.
Interior Design by Key of Heart Designs.

claudiearseneault.com

ISBN: 978-1-7753129-2-5

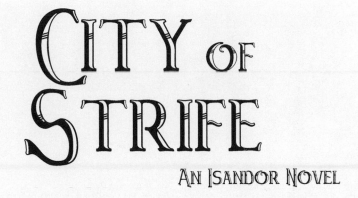

CITY OF STRIFE

AN ISANDOR NOVEL

CLAUDIE ARSENEAULT

Kraken
Collective

CHAPTER ONE

ARATHIEL pulled himself out of the water, kicking and heaving, his fingers latching onto the uneven wooden planks of Isandor's docks. He stared at his hands, afraid his grip would loosen once more. Last time, it had let go without his permission, without even warning him it had given up. Drenched and exhausted, Arathiel flopped on his back the moment his entire body was safely out.

What a wonderful homecoming.

After more than a hundred thirty years of absence, his city greeted him with a long swim through glacial water. At least, he assumed it was glacial. Late autumn chill must have settled over Isandor, turning the Reonne River coursing at its feet into a deadly frozen trap. Not even that cold was strong enough to pierce the numbness of his senses, however. Arathiel sat up, a sudden thought constricting his heart, and raised his hands. Shivering. Nausea gripped him. Just because he couldn't feel the cold didn't mean it wouldn't affect him. Or kill him. He couldn't stay put, unmoving.

Arathiel sprang to his feet. A wide circle of careful onlookers jerked back, surprised by the sudden movement. Their gazes remained fixed on him as he gained a tentative balance, arms spread and dripping. It would have been easier if he could have felt the docks under his feet, but that too had been stolen by the Well, sapped away through the decades. Arathiel had adapted since he'd escaped the magical trap, but his peculiarities still set many ill at ease. Not hard to imagine, really, once you put yourself in their shoes.

They had seen a black man clamber out of the icy water wearing nothing but a strange patchwork of multiple outfits, sewn together from scraps. His hair had turned as white as the snow which would soon fall on the city. By all rights he should be a useless and shivering mess on the ground, but instead he'd jumped up with the energy of a youth—and indeed, he couldn't look older than thirty despite the white hair. A bloodied red line ran along his forearm, obviously recent, yet it didn't pain him. A gift from the crew that had forced him to jump overboard, so close to his destination. The sailors must have figured out he couldn't taste, smell, or sense what he touched, and it had scared them. Arathiel didn't blame them. The world was full of dangerous mysteries, and one of them had been travelling on their ship.

He didn't want to wait and see what fear could trigger in the dock workers, however. Arathiel wrung his clothes, and cleared his throat. "Sorry about that."

"Go away!"

Arathiel wondered who had yelled that, but his muffled hearing made it hard to pinpoint the source. Before he could hurry on his way, a second voice called to him. "Hey, are you all right?"

A petite woman pushed through the crowd, brown hair held by a triangular scarf. She stomped up to him, high leather boots contrasting with her flowery skirt, and glared at the wide circle that had formed around them. When she reached for his forearm, Arathiel withdrew.

"F-Fine, yes." Were his teeth chattering from the cold, or from the stress? He swallowed hard. "Thank you."

"Are you new in town? Do you need somewhere to stay? Help to get there?"

Arathiel stared, reeling from her concern. Around them, the ring of dockers and other workers dissipated, moving along. Several still threw wary glances his way. Caution and threats were more frequent reactions to him than the insistent helpfulness Arathiel now faced. "I'm … not sure." After all, he wasn't new, but the prospect of knocking home—at the Brasten Tower, where he'd not set foot in a hundred thirty years—didn't excite him. Not yet. "Any suggestions?"

"You bet! I'm the queen of suggestions!"

She motioned for him to go first, and after a hesitant step, Arathiel moved forward. Although she needed almost two steps for each of his long stride, her vibrant energy allowed her to keep up with ease. Arathiel's new companion listed potential inns to greet him, most located in the Middle City—the buffer section between the poor neighbourhoods of the Lower City, and the rich noble towers of the

Upper City. After a while, Arathiel stopped her.

"I can't afford these."

This time, she turned to take a good look at him. Her lips pinched. "Of course. Should've known, with rags like these ..." Something in her tone indicated the state of his clothes irritated her more than anything else. "Respectable establishments turn you away, don't they? But I wouldn't recommend most of those in the Lower City. They're as likely to steal what you have left as to house you. Except—oh, I know!" She clapped her hands, and Arathiel's heart leaped at her enthusiasm. "You should find the Shelter!"

"The Shelter." He liked the sound of it. One would hope the place meant to live up to its name.

"Rumours say they let anyone in, and offer free meals. Kind of a last resort, but I've yet to hear a single bad story about it. Its patrons boast the food is miraculous—so good whoever owns this place must have been a high-class chef."

Arathiel allowed himself hope. Perhaps they wouldn't be as welcoming as rumours promised, but he had to try. Where else would he go? He didn't have the courage to face his family—or, well, their descendants—yet. "Sounds like what I need," he said. "You have my thanks, um ..."

"Branwen. Lady Branwen Dathirii, to be exact, but don't let it bother you."

His breath caught. A Dathirii? Of course the elven noble house would still hold power in Isandor. Their natural lifespan covered several centuries. His throat raw, Arathiel belatedly realized other elves he'd known before leaving would have survived. He stared at

Branwen, trying to remember, but he doubted he'd met her. Too young. As a human, he'd have put her in her mid-thirties, which meant she must have been born within a decade of his departure from Isandor, either before or after. Temptation flickered through him, gone as quickly as it'd come. He could tell her who he was, ask to speak with the older members of the family. House Dathirii had always been welcoming. The idea twisted his gut, however, and Arathiel discarded it.

"I'm Arathiel. Thank you."

"Can you get there by yourself?" she asked.

He nodded then parted from her without another word, barely hearing her wish him luck. Once he'd left her behind, he turned his attention to Isandor.

The city Arathiel remembered no longer existed—not to him, at any rate. Once, the cluster of sharp spires perched on a cliffside had been stunning in their irregular shapes and bright colours, each building an attempt to outshine the others with beautiful glasswork, forests of pinnacles, or cascading waterfalls. Now the colours were mostly gone for him, the towers a greyed blur to his damaged eyes, their life and beauty stolen from him. In a way, his city had become a reflection of himself: half-alive, a pale imitation of what it had once been.

At least the Upper City had changed beyond that. He'd noticed blooming gardens from the ship and, even down here, he could spot luscious vines hanging from every bridge. He wondered how many new archways had been built, connecting the towers hundreds of feet above the ground, forming an intricate network of paths. He would have ample time to discover. He was home now.

The thought brought nothing but a tightness in his chest. It had been a mistake, returning. A lot would have changed. His family would be long dead, taken by time or illness. He should have said goodbye instead of promising to return. But now, so many decades later, his home would be taken over by their descendants. Would there even be anything left for him? Would they believe he hadn't perished a century ago, as should have happened? Improbable. But where else could he go? Arathiel had grown tired—tired of not feeling rough wood under his hand, tired of not smelling the salty sea or earthy autumn air, tired of not tasting even allegedly spicy meals. Tired of being alone, a shadow, always one step removed from the world. One day, he would need to face his family.

He pulled his hood up and hurried into Isandor proper. Passing through bustling areas of a city was like standing behind a glass wall, looking into the world. Dock workers pushed large crates around or sorted the latest loads of fish, but he could smell neither the sweat of the former nor the pungent stench of the latter. Their yells sounded muffled and distant, as though hands pressed against his ears. Sometimes Arathiel's gaze caught a cloak snapping in the wind, but the gusts weren't strong enough for him to feel their push. He could guess what he should perceive, which made the dull absence even harder to bear.

He was glad to reach the Lower City, all sloped streets and alleyways snaking at the feet of Isandor's towers. The stench of refuse and unwashed bodies should be stronger here, choking him, but his throat wasn't even a little raw. Half of Isandor's population crammed into tiny apartments around him, and Arathiel couldn't smell a single one of them. He hated this. He was home, but here the distance and numbness hurt more than anything. Home, yet not all there, not really. Arathiel took a deep, steadying breath, fighting off the creeping doubts. He had grown up in Isandor. If he couldn't find himself here, he never would.

❧⌘❧

TOWERS blocked what daylight remained by the time Arathiel reached the recommended Shelter: a tiny wooden house, built in the nook created by two towers at the very heart of the Lower City. Branwen Dathirii's promises echoed in his mind, a glint of hope in an otherwise difficult day. Arathiel wished someone with such reputed culinary talent could prepare a meal even he would taste, but studying the building now, he suspected a gross exaggeration.

Years of downpours and wind had battered some of its planks while others seemed new, nailed on top of the spaces between old ones. The roof was also a sloped mismatch, all cracks and quick fixes, barely holding together. Rain must slip through and drip inside. At least they had a chimney, which meant a fire to keep everyone warm. Arathiel approached the door—heavy and solid, newer than most of the building, but a little too small for its hole. A perfect entry for the cold wind to sneak in at night. In fact, it probably did now, even if Arathiel couldn't feel the gusts on his bare arms.

Arathiel stood in front of the door in silence for several minutes. He shook the mud off his boots, wrung his wet clothes again, glanced around. What if they turned him away, despite promises of accepting anyone? What if he remained too bizarre even for them? But what other choice did he have? If they didn't accept him here, he might never find a room. This was his best bet. He would freeze outside, even if he didn't feel the cold creeping up on him. Arathiel straightened his outfit as much as he could, then put his hand on the door. A distant pressure on his palm bypassed his numbness as he pushed and entered the Shelter.

The buzz of conversations enveloped him right away, closer and warmer than at the docks. Dozens of people sat around small tables or on the floor with bowls and mugs before them. Many huddled near a tiny fireplace, the only stone feature in the room. Arathiel had expected the floor to be in as bad of shape as the walls and roof but instead found brand-new wooden boards, clean except for the day's mud. Nothing a sturdy mop wouldn't wash away. Was this where people slept? They'd have warmth, protection from the elements, and clean ground. Luxuries, for most of them. No wonder they seemed so upbeat. Conversations were carried in loud voices instead of shady whispers, and laughter replaced the insults more common to lowly taverns. On the other side of the room, three musicians gathered around strange instruments: wooden spoons attached together, a metal rod and empty crates, and a rundown violin. The spoon-wielder sat on a chair, nodded to her companions, and snapped her heel against the ground. The sharp sound surprised Arathiel, carrying across the crowd so loud and clear even he caught it. Then they were off, lively music dancing in the air, bringing cheers from other patrons. The atmosphere dragged a smile out of Arathiel. He spotted an empty table and sat, searching for a waiter, wondering if there even was one.

A startling cheer caught his attention, and Arathiel turned his gaze to a section near the back of the Shelter. They'd pushed four tables together, forming an uneven surface. At its centre stood a large dessert plate covered with caramel-and-nut apples stacked atop one another. Several customers had gathered around. They all raised their mugs except the young half-elf who presided over their table. His brown cheeks turned a deeper shade as the circle of friends downed their drinks. Amid the mostly human crowd were a wary dark elf—not full-blooded, if one judged by his smaller ears, but with the same obsidian skin as others of his race—and an overweight halfling. As everyone lunged for their apple, the halfling's gaze met Arathiel's, then widened. He nudged the dark elf, pointed his way, then climbed off his chair. They looked worried. Arathiel ground his teeth and forced himself not to dash for the door.

As he wove his way between the tables, the halfling spoke to other customers—a few jokes, a laugh, an encouragement, then he moved on. Sometimes Arathiel lost track of him. Small even by his race's standards, he vanished behind tables and slipped between everyone's legs with remarkable ease. He eventually reached Arathiel, and his smile diminished after a quick inspection.

"Are you okay? You must be freezing. It's too cold for a midnight bath, you know." Concern shone in his stark blue eyes, adding a layer of seriousness to his quip. "I'll bring you a towel to dry yourself, and you should move to that table there, closer to the fire. It just won't do to have you—"

"I'm fine," Arathiel blurted. How did one deal with so much concern after the wariness everyone treated him with? "All I need is a room. A meal, too, perhaps."

"And warmth." The halfling smiled, an encouragement to accept, a promise Arathiel could trust him. "I'll get you the meal and room, but please take the towel and dry yourself. As a favour to your host." He motioned toward the half-elf being celebrated—the one who'd lived at most twenty years and certainly shouldn't own a place like this. "It's his birthday. Can't refuse that to him."

"This place belongs to him?"

"You're really new, aren't you?" He laughed, then extended his plump hand, standing on the tip of his toes to reach higher. "Let's start from the beginning. I'm Cal. That's Larryn, and yes, he's the owner and cook. Did anyone tell you how things work around here?"

The notion that he was new to Isandor when he'd lived here more than a century ago amused Arathiel, but it wasn't wrong. He'd just arrived. Nothing like this Shelter had existed before. Arathiel shook Cal's hand, ignoring how his own trembled from cold he couldn't even feel.

"Arathiel B—" He bit back his family name. House Brasten might still stand, and impersonating a member of Isandor's noble families would get him imprisoned. He had to be careful whom he told, and find a way to support his claims. Records from a hundred thirty years ago might not suffice. Curiosity lit Cal's gaze, so Arathiel hurried to the next topic. "I was informed you offer free meals and beds and allow everyone inside."

He tried to make it sound like the 'allow everyone' hadn't worried him, but from the sad expression passing over Cal's features, he'd failed.

"You have to pay for rooms," he explained. "We take what you can give. If you have no money at all, you can sleep on the floor. You'll have a blanket and we keep the fire warm, and tomorrow morning there's a free meal for everyone."

Arathiel reached for his coin pouch. When his fingers closed over thin air, his heart clenched. Gone again. Had it sunk in the Reonne when Arathiel had jumped ship? Or did a thief snatch it? He'd never know, like he'd never found out what had happened to the last six. He didn't feel the weight of his purse, nor most people bumping into him. With a sigh, Arathiel reached for a second pouch hidden close to his heart. After the first two thefts, he'd learned from his mistakes. He was home now, in the city for good. He poured the few emergency coins he had left on the table.

"How long does that get me?"

"Long!" Eyes wide, Cal counted the money then scooped it off. "Don't worry about days. That's a fortune by our standards and you'll have your room until winter's over."

A wave of relief washed over Arathiel. They might be trapping him—they could take his money and throw him out after—but Arathiel found it hard to distrust Cal or the Shelter as a whole. He'd often slept in low-class inns since leaving the Well, sometimes even curling up in the dark corner of an alley. He had seen people fight for a stale loaf of bread, get caught stealing half-rotten fruit, plead and beg for scraps and bones. Here they had an abundance of food and drink, but no one quarrelled for it, like they all knew that for once, they would survive without stepping on others. Instead they celebrated the young owner who no doubt made it possible.

"I'm glad I came here."

Arathiel had been talking mostly to himself, but Cal brightened at the words, as if the praise had been addressed directly to him.

"You'll have room number six. No locks anywhere, but you have a chair inside to bar it, if you're worried about thieves. Take that corridor over there," he said, pointing. "Numbers are painted on the doors. Welcome to Isandor, Mister Arathiel! I'll be back with a warm meal and a towel to keep you dry and cozy."

Arathiel knew he wouldn't feel the food's warmth whether down his throat or through the bowl. Yet Cal's concern sufficed to draw him in, erasing much of this distance he perceived between himself and the world. He watched the celebration at the back of the Shelter continue, envious knots forming in his stomach. Larryn had a home, knew his role in life. Arathiel wondered if he would ever find his. At least he had somewhere to sleep, and the first genuinely kind contact in a long while.

One step at a time, Arathiel promised himself. One step at a time, and he would find meaning to his life again.

CHAPTER TWO

HASRYAN didn't mind the cold night if it meant he escaped the Shelter's cheering crowd. Every occasion to mingle with the patrons brought mixed feelings. On the one hand, they never commented on his jet-black skin and included him in all discussions. On the other, Hasryan always detected a hint of reluctance at his presence, and he disliked large groups. Too hard to keep track of everyone. He preferred to know where others' were and most importantly, who stood right behind him.

The Shelter's roof might threaten to collapse, but to Hasryan's over-cautious mind, it would always be safer than a mass of people. Besides, he'd shared a drink with Larryn in more dangerous locations before. They'd initiated their friendship on a balcony of House Allastam's tower. It hadn't threatened to give in under their weight, but had any guards found two half-elves—including a dark-skinned one—sharing life stories in their home without permission, it wouldn't have ended well.

Larryn let his legs dangle over the edge of the roof, mug stuck between his knees, rubbing his hands together to keep them warm. They'd come up together, Hasryan sitting on Larryn's right as always—his friend's left ear had never entirely recovered from an infection. Larryn had spent the last five minutes in silence, chin tilted up as he glared at the criss-cross of bridges above their heads. Between the bridges and the rising towers, they could barely see the sky. Hasryan didn't speak. The quiet didn't bother him. They could let it stretch for over an hour at times, especially if Larryn had his hands busy preparing the next meal for the Shelter. Strange, how different Hasryan's two friendships were. Cal couldn't endure more than a few minutes without anyone speaking.

"What did Cal say about the newcomer?" Larryn's voice shattered the silence. He turned his grey eyes to Hasryan, not bothering to hide his wariness. He extended the same protectiveness to his Shelter as he did to children, and Larryn could always sense when someone didn't come from Isandor's streets. He could tell from their smell, their demeanour—from a lifetime of experience inhabiting the Lower City.

"He declared him trustworthy."

"Which means shit coming from Cal. He'd call an assassin trustworthy."

Hasryan stiffened. He'd shared so many stories and silences with Larryn, he often forgot how much more he'd kept secret. "He also said it sounded like most places didn't want to serve him. Funny how that happens to people with dark skin and white hair, huh?" Not that this Arathiel possessed any elven blood. His facial structure wasn't angular enough, and he had round ears.

"Point taken." Larryn raised his mug and drank. "As long as he doesn't cause problems, I don't mind him here. Same rules as anyone."

Rules Hasryan inwardly thanked him for. It helped to have a safe haven, and he often wished Larryn had entered his life sooner. He might have been too young for such a building, however. "So ... Are you ever going to reveal how old you are, or is it some kind of state secret?"

"Secret. Best to let everyone believe they're dealing with a responsible adult, well into his twenties."

Hasryan's clear laugh covered the hint of conversations below. "No one thinks you're responsible. Do you take us for fools?"

"Shut up." Larryn grinned and shoved him. "I'm more adult than all the assholes living in towers above, prancing about with fancy silk underwear and commanding dozens of servants."

"Not a high standard."

Larryn snickered, then downed the rest of his beer. "Tell you what," he said with a substantial slur to his speech, "I'll give you my age when you reveal what it is you do, exactly. For work."

Hasryan had to force himself to laugh. A lifetime of lies made it easier than it should have been. "Me? Just a trustworthy assassin."

He regretted the words as soon as they left his lips. Some things should remain unsaid, even as a joke. When Larryn snorted, reiterating how ridiculous the idea was to him, Hasryan focused on his drink and struggled to ignore the painful stab in his heart.

"I can live without knowing your age," he said.

More importantly, Larryn could never learn of Hasryan's job. How did one tell his best friend—his only friend, aside from Cal—he was a trained assassin? Oh, nothing much, Larryn. I just kill people for money! No way, especially now. They joked about the mystery around Larryn's age, but to Hasryan, secrets were a matter of life and death. Larryn and Cal knew he worked for Brune, the head of Isandor's tentacular mercenary organization, but Hasryan had never slipped a word about killing anyone. He had found people who trusted him despite his dark elven blood—actual friends!—and refused to risk that. What could ever be worth more?

"Plans for the coming year?" Hasryan asked, eager to push the topic in another direction.

"Some. Fix the Shelter even more. Force the merchant prick using the second floor as storage to sell it to me." He motioned at one of the two towers between which the wooden Shelter had been built. He sketched a smile and ran a hand through his hair. "I'd love to dedicate an entire level to the kids. They could have a safe space to play and sleep. Efua would have company her age."

"You just want an excuse to adopt them all."

Larryn's sheepish grin was all the answer Hasryan needed. He laughed, then clapped his friend on the back. "I could help with the merchant. Bring my parentage's terrible reputation to bear, make him piss his pants."

"I'd love to see that." But Larryn was shaking his head. They'd had this kind of conversation before, and Hasryan guessed what

Larryn would add. "You know I try to stay as legal as possible with the Shelter. Wouldn't take much for the guards to decide to shut it down and then everyone would be on the streets with no food and no roof over their head. Winter's about to roll in. I can't inflict that on them."

Hasryan might have laughed earlier, but Larryn's behaviour, though reckless, exceeded the typical maturity of others his age. At least when it came to the Shelter. Not even in his twenties, he'd said, and yet so many people depended on him already. They relied on him and his Shelter in a way very few had ever relied on Hasryan.

"Not much we can do, then. I doubt our new friend has large enough funds to buy you a whole floor." Not if Hasryan judged by his paper-thin clothes, sewn over and over, and the lack of coat despite the chilling weather. Besides, he'd emptied his purse in front of Cal. They knew how little was available there. A cold wind swooped through the Shelter's alley. Hasryan blew on his hands. "We ought to go back inside. I wouldn't mind the fire, and there might even be some cheese left."

"With Cal around?" Larryn snorted. "Don't count on it. He'd share just about anything in his life, but not cheese."

Hasryan laughed as he stood and stretched, blood warming his frozen limbs. It really was getting too late in the year for long discussions outside. Or even short ones. After shaking his legs and arms awake, he moved to the side of the roof and leaped off, glass still in hand, onto a large crate below.

"Just a warm fire, then, and maybe a quick game if you're all up for it?"

"You bet."

Larryn jumped after him, his landing less graceful than Hasryan's. More alcohol and less practice. Hasryan steadied him, then smiled as they ambled to the door. Cheese didn't matter. Neither did the fire, in truth. He only needed an evening with real friends to fulfill him.

CHAPTER THREE

NEVIAN'S back and knees hurt from scrubbing the floor. The soapy water had wrinkled his skin, and the nerves in his wrists screamed every time he clenched the minuscule brush given to him to accomplish his task. It was shorter than his index finger—not at all appropriate to clean the large storage room. If only he could use his magic to mop the floor in seconds. Master Avenazar's orders were clear, though: no spells and no bigger brush than the one Jilssan had created. Nothing but long hours on his knees, supposed to teach him discipline. As if Nevian needed the lesson! Discipline had carried him through the rigorous training required to become an apprentice to knowledgeable Myrian masters. Discipline allowed him to tolerate Master Avenazar's ridiculous and time-consuming demands and Master Jilssan's subtle mockery without a word of complaint. Discipline meant that when Avenazar unwound his frustration on Nevian, shooting waves of agonizing magic into his mind, he endured the punishment then managed to crawl to his room and study through the night.

In the long run, only the studying mattered. No matter how much he hurt at the end of the day, Nevian opened his books, picked up his quill, and learned what Avenazar refused to teach him.

Nevian scrubbed harder. Discipline would transform him into the best wizard in the Myrian Empire, all odds be damned. He had laboured for too long to let anything stop him. Especially not a floor. Nevian straightened to evaluate how much remained to clean and smiled. Three-quarters done! Not so bad. He stretched his fingers, easing his cramped hands, when a shadow fell upon him.

"Is this the tiniest brush ever created? What a cutie."

Nevian recognized the chirpy voice and withheld a sigh. Isra, the enclave's only other apprentice. The one person who could strain his self-control even more than Avenazar's abuse. He didn't know why she pierced his defences so easily. Something in her constant good mood, in the simplicity of her entire life. Isra didn't need discipline. She hadn't struggled. Whenever he thought of all the opportunities offered to her, of how she wasted the gift of her circumstances, sharp and bitter pain stabbed his stomach.

Isra reached for the brush with a grin. She fit Myria's beauty standards perfectly, as if her parents had followed a chart upon her conception. Every strand of her dark blonde hair was placed with calculated care, her nose was round and small, and cherry makeup highlighted her lips. Nevian didn't know who she was trying to impress with that. Not him, he hoped. He had no interest in these things—not with her, and not with anyone. The thought had always made him recoil a little. Nevian gripped the tiny brush, certain she'd never give it back.

"I have Master Jilssan to thank for that," he told her.

Jilssan was Isra's tutor and a specialist in transmutation spells. Unlike Avenazar, Jilssan cared about the success of her apprentice and did her best to teach Isra every day. Nevian avoided attending their training sessions. They reminded him of his first Master. Sauria would buy him fancy quills or new tomes to celebrate his achievements. She'd shown him her secret spots outside where she both studied and caught some sun. If only she had never offended Master Avenazar, she might still be alive, and Nevian wouldn't be paying for her mistakes. How powerful would he already have become, with her help? Better not to think of it, to just focus on the present—on what was rather than what could have been.

Isra favoured him with a bright smile. "Jilssan's really talented, isn't she? But why use the brush? Snap your fingers, cast a spell, and finish the cleaning, no?" Isra touched her chin, as though an important idea had occurred to her. "You can cast spells, right? I've never seen you wield magic."

Nevian's fingers clenched around the brush. He lumbered to his feet, straightening until he stood almost a full head taller than Isra. "Master Avenazar forbade the use of magic to teach me the value of hard work and perseverance."

Isra snorted, then scanned the partly-cleaned floor without bothering to hide her disdain. "Nevian, no one knows the meaning of hard work better than you do. Just do a spell."

She lifted a hand, readying herself to cast without waiting for him. Nevian's heart skipped several beats. He grabbed her arm and pushed it down, stopping her before she could ruin his life.

"Don't! He ordered no magic!" His voice squeaked, high-pitched and out of control.

"He'll never know." Isra peeled away his fingers one by one, her nose pinched into an exasperated expression. "Come on, Nevian. This is called initiative. It's a very useful skill for wizards, and you've yet to learn this one."

"Master Avenazar doesn't care for initiative." Nevian's throat tightened, and the blood drained from his face. Isra was too carefree. No one had taught her what happened when you disobeyed. He had to make her understand. "He'll punish me."

Isra's eyebrows quirked, then she drew back with a fit of giggles. Energy swirled around her hands, and she kicked the bucket of soapy water, spilling it across the still-dirty floor. Nevian rushed to interrupt her, but this time Isra pulled her arm out of his grasp. His heart clenched as the water fizzled, shone for a second with white energy, then vanished. The floor beneath sparkled, stainless. Nevian suppressed a groan as Isra stood with her hands on her hips, studying her handiwork. She looked so proud of herself. Didn't she realize she had condemned him to hours of pain?

"I'm doomed," Nevian whispered.

Isra laughed and slapped his shoulder. "You're always so dramatic, Nevian! Don't worry. If he asks, I'll tell him I did it. You're safe." She wrenched the tiny brush out of his grasp and flung it next to the upturned bucket before grabbing his hand and pulling him toward the exit. "Now come on. I don't like visiting Isandor alone."

"No way!"

Nevian snatched his hand away and stopped in the middle of the room. He wasn't going anywhere with her! Isra turned to him, and the corners of her lips lifted in that arrogant half-smile she wore whenever she accomplished her goals.

"You don't want to be alone if Master Avenazar realizes magic was used, do you?"

His lips parted to answer, but no sound followed. Trapped. Isra winked and tugged him along, and Nevian wondered if she'd had it planned from the start. Her bubbly exterior lured others into becoming complacent, and he had fallen for it. She had wanted company for her escapade into Isandor. No choice now. All he could do was follow and pray Master Avenazar never found out.

❦

ISRA dragged Nevian all the way to Isandor's Lower City, where the poor and the stinky gathered. A risky area for a teenage girl. Wanting company made sense, but Nevian wished she'd set her sights on someone else. Located in a town plaza shadowed by the criss-cross of bridges above, the apothecary's shop was one of many sleazy establishments catering to the local lowlife. Its door led to a cobblestone square erected twenty feet above ground—not high enough to be part of the Middle City, but avoiding the utter filth of the ground level. Nevian kept his nose scrunched up in an attempt to block the stench of unwashed bodies and waited by the door of the dimly-lit shop. Isra rummaged through shelves of ingredients, squinting to read the labels, slowly filling her arms. Nevian wondered what the purchases were for. Maybe she'd found recipes for fancy potions and intended to waste time on them. He'd never understood the use. Not when spells required no materials and could be stored by experienced wizards into single words of power, easily shouted in a bind.

Regrets surfaced as he watched Isra's shopping. He should have stayed at the enclave and continued to scrub the already-clean floor, to prove he had nothing to do with her use of magic. He couldn't even enjoy this exceptional visit to the city. Too nervous. By the time Isra paid for the ingredients, he was aching to return to the tentative security of his room.

"Come on," he said, pulling her through the entrancetoward square outside. "We've been gone long enough."

Nevian stopped dead after his first step outside the shop.

In the middle of the area stood Master Avenazar, waiting with his arms crossed. Most residents gave him a wide berth, perhaps sensing the danger packed into the Myrian's small stature. Nevian's fingertips grew cold, his stomach heaving. Avenazar had known. Of course he'd known. How could Nevian ever think this would go unnoticed?

Isra bumped into him. Nevian didn't budge.

"What's going on?" she asked.

"Master Avenazar."

Isra cursed behind him, healthy fear underlying her voice for once. Nevian spun as her body shrank. Wings sprouted from her back, her fingers turning into talons barely large enough to hold her purchase bag. Wide pupils narrowed into a slit, her round nose and mouth lengthened into a beak, and her hair shifted to a great brown mane before changing into feathers. From human to hawk in a few smooth seconds … then she took flight. Ditching him. Nevian followed Isra's animal form as she rose to the nearest bridge, too shocked to say a word. She was supposed to shoulder the blame!

A strong hand grabbed his wrist and pulled. Nevian's surprised yelp died on his lips as he met Avenazar's dark and angry eyes, which promised painful retribution. Energy accumulated in his master's palm, ready to be released.

"I hope you have an excellent explanation, you ingrate."

No justification would satisfy Master Avenazar, not from him. Nevian struggled with his growing panic, reining in his urge to jerk out of his master's grasp and run. What would be the point? Instead, he cast his gaze down and stopped moving, knowing any other reaction would make his situation worse. His jaws worked until he could utter a single word.

"Isra—"

Avenazar unleashed his magic before Nevian could say more. The energy dug into his nerves, sending a wave of searing pain up his arm and into his brain. Nevian gasped, and his legs gave out. He fell to his knees, allowing Avenazar to look down on him. Might have been the point, Nevian thought in his daze. Avenazar preferred not to be reminded of his height.

"I said no magic, yet here you are. You used a cleaning spell, disobeying my express orders and opting instead for frivolous gallivanting in the city. How can I trust you with dangerous spells if you cannot follow simple instructions?"

Nevian choked. Had Avenazar really suggested something as ridiculous as him 'gallivanting'? He had no time to waste on light entertainment. Even without Avenazar's endless tasks, Nevian would use every minute of his day to study. Not all apprentices flung golden opportunities to become masters away.

"I cast nothing," Nevian said. "I swear Isra came and—"

Once again, Avenazar cut his explanation short with a jolt of energy. The magic coursed through his muscles. Bright spots obscured his vision. It hurt. Every inch, every fibre, every ounce of him. A long whimper escaped Nevian's lips despite his best efforts. His ears rang, making it hard to hear Avenazar's shrill voice.

"She doesn't decide for you. I don't care what she did, or when. You were in charge of that floor, of cleaning it with the brush I gave you, and instead you came here." He crouched a little, bringing himself eye-to-eye with his apprentice. "I expected better, Nevian, and you know how I hate to be disappointed."

Tears rolled down Nevian's cheeks. Everyone had cleared the small square, too afraid to intervene. Avenazar wore his Myrian robes, and Isandor's residents knew not to mess with a powerful spellcaster from their Empire. In the two years since the enclave's crew had arrived as envoys, they had gained major political influence and a fearsome reputation. Nevian would get no help from citizens. Or from anyone. Who would dare to antagonize Avenazar? The young mage clenched his teeth, steeling himself. He had to weather the torture without provoking Avenazar any further. His master enjoyed sneaking into other people's minds and sifting through memories, but that might spell Nevian's death. The wrong flashback witnessed by Master Avenazar, and he'd expose Nevian's nightly activities.

If a clean floor could cause such fury, what agony would Master Avenazar inflict on him once he discovered Nevian slipped out of the enclave and traded information for magical training?

So he endured, knowing he'd pass out from the pain eventually, knowing he'd be unable to study tonight, knowing Avenazar might decide to make him clean again out of spite. None of it compared to what awaited him should his master learn the secrets Nevian hid from him.

"Master Avenazar. What an unpleasant surprise!"

The pain stopped, interrupted by a melodic voice. It had barely pierced the haze of Nevian's mind. He crumpled to the ground, gasping for air, shaking and confused. Who? They'd said 'unpleasant'. What a terrible idea. Nevian wanted to warn them, beg them not to push the matter, but Master Avenazar was still holding his wrist, ready to start again anytime.

"I must agree, Lord Dathirii," Avenazar said. "What could possibly bring an important elf such as yourself to these lowly parts of town?"

Nevian knew better than to trust Avenazar's pleasant tone. His master disliked interruptions even more than he disliked disappointments. The young mage glanced at the fool who had committed this horrible mistake. A middle-aged elf stood in the plaza, hands clasped behind his back. He wore a forest-green doublet, and his golden hair tumbled to his shoulders, kept out of his face by two braids. Instead of worry, he displayed confidence, his smile bringing about small crow's feet at the corners of his eyes.

"My business is my own. I am glad to have stumbled upon you at this moment, however." The elf's green eyes caught Nevian's for a split second—the time it took for Nevian to lower his gaze, his heart hammering. Lord Dathirii was an important noble in Isandor. What if Avenazar believed they knew each other? How much worse would everything get? Nevian wished the elf would disappear. Leave before it ended badly. Instead of listening to Nevian's silent wisdom, Lord Dathirii dared to order Avenazar. "Let him go."

Sudden magic jerked through Nevian's body. He gasped, sparks flying before his eyes. His apprentice's robes clung to his sweaty back.

"Absolutely not," Avenazar said, firm but pleasant.

Lord Dathirii's footsteps grew closer. He stopped a single stride away and stared down at Avenazar, using his height to make the Myrian wizard feel even tinier. Another bad idea. Would this lord ever leave them be?

"Isandor is a civilized city, and its laws forbid such an assault. You may have convinced the lords and ladies of the Golden Table to declare the enclave grounds Myrian territory, ruled by Myrian laws, but as long as you stand in our streets and bridges, you will abide by our laws. Let him go or I will have you jailed."

Avenazar cackled, then he grabbed a handful of Nevian's hair and pulled on it, forcing him to look up. "Hear that, Nevian? The good lord doesn't like to see his precious city sullied and wants us to go play elsewhere."

The elf's horrified gasp drew an irritated groan from Nevian. Had he really believed he could stop Avenazar? Every delay Lord Dathirii imposed on the punishment would make it worse. He couldn't help— which didn't keep him from trying.

"No, I—"

"You were quite clear, milord," interrupted Avenazar. "As long as I'm not in your precious city …"

He forced Nevian to stand. The elven lord straightened, his jaws tight. Nevian almost pleaded him to let it go, but he didn't dare speak in front of Avenazar. Or even in front of Lord Dathirii. A dangerous fire lit his eyes, a scary determination to see this conflict through to the end.

"You're an affront to decency."

"Again, Lord Dathirii? How often have we discussed this in the last two years? Always, you go on about one's moral obligations to other human beings, as if I cared for your naive admonitions. The Myrian Empire doesn't thrive on goodwill."

"No, it prospers through the widespread and inhuman trading of slaves." Angry red coloured Lord Dathirii's cheeks now. "How many do you keep hidden behind your enclave's walls?"

A dozen, Nevian thought, if not more. All of Isbari descent, their skin golden to brown, keeping out of sight as much as work would allow. High Priest Daramond—the only free Isbari in the enclave— might know how many. Nevian wouldn't be surprised if he could name them all.

"They're not hidden," Avenazar said. "You can visit them anytime, milord! I'm sure your concern will please them."

"I've had enough," Lord Dathirii said, and indeed Nevian could hear the anger boiling under his tight voice, barely restrained. "Don't think you're safe. We've tolerated your presence for too long."

"Is that a threat, Lord Dathirii?" Avenazar asked.

"It is." A weight sank to the bottom of Nevian's stomach. He didn't know the elf, and now he never would. This lord had a death wish; for himself, his entire family, and anyone else he loved. He would end the same way Sauria had: tortured and broken by Avenazar. Yet Lord Dathirii kept going, adding one layer of insult after another. "I don't care if you have the economic might of Myria behind you. Isandor isn't part of your corrupt empire, and I will die before I let you crush us under your boot."

Master Avenazar clapped his hands together with another sharp laugh. "What a wonderful challenge! Who knows, you might get your wish. Thank you for the warning, Lord Dathirii. I will look forward to your pathetic attempts at hindering us. For now, however, I must go on with my disgraceful life."

Nevian closed his eyes as he heard the first arcane words of a teleportation spell. An invisible force pulled at his body, and his surroundings blurred. Lord Dathirii seemed to blink in and out several times, but the apprentice knew better: they were the ones fading. Isandor's shadowed plaza vanished, replaced by the very floor Nevian should've been scrubbing. Before he could utter a word, Avenazar flung him to the ground.

"You and I have to talk, my dear apprentice," he said. "Something about assault and abuse, I believe."

Avenazar shoved his palms against Nevian's chest, unleashing his power with renewed rage. The magic went straight to Nevian's head, ripping through his consciousness as he sprawled out with a scream.

CHAPTER FOUR

J AEGER glanced up from the redaction of his formal letters when the door to his office slammed shut. As Diel Dathirii's personal steward and secretary, he sometimes stood outside to ensure unwelcome visitors never reached the Head of the Dathirii House. Diel had gone into the Lower City, however, and Jaeger had hoped to use the spare time to knock a few things off his long list of tasks. The brutal sound snapped his concentration, but as he noticed who had walked in, Jaeger's stern reproach died on his lips, his mouth turning a little dry.

The door slammer was Diel himself. He stood at the entrance, panting, his fists clenched at his side. Wild strands of golden hair escaped his braids' hold, crowning him, and his cheeks had a rosy colour. Either it was windy outside—nothing surprising there, for a city perched on a cliff and built ever-upward—or he had been running. The latter, Jaeger guessed. Diel's short breath, fiery gaze, and grimace convinced his secretary something had happened. The longer Jaeger stared, the more he ached to kiss the smile back onto his lips. Diel pinched his nose, then let out a frustrated groan.

"How do such horrible people live with themselves? This is ridiculous!"

He threw his hands up with another angry cry, and Jaeger struggled to maintain his neutral expression. He wanted to stride to Diel, wrap his arms around him, and hold him until he simmered down. After a hundred years with him, however, Jaeger knew the other elf would go from silent, frustrated huffing to emptying his heart. The steward clasped his hands behind his back and waited.

"How can you stay so calm, Jaeger?" Diel paced forward, sharp movements punctuating his words. "He mocks our laws, our lifestyle, the core principles toward which I'm trying to push this city! He thinks he can bully us until we give in! He won't stop at worming his way into financial control of half the Golden Table. I'm not going to let him piss on everything I love anymore. 'Naive admonitions'? Listen to him, using words bigger than he is! Don't you want to throw him out, too?"

Jaeger allowed a moment to slide by. Most of the time, Diel did not expect answers to his rants. When you offered him a chance to go on and he stopped, however, it meant his enquiry warranted a response. This one obviously did. Diel was staring at him, hoping Jaeger would share in his fury.

"Hard to say, milord," he said. "I have my suspicions, but perhaps if you told me who we're talking about …"

"Oh." For a moment Diel seemed confused, then a smile curved his lips. He laughed and ran a hand through his hair, shaking his head. "I did it again, didn't I? You're so often by my side, silent and faithful, I imagine you witness everything."

Jaeger wished he did, but if he followed Lord Dathirii to all his appointments, he would never get the paperwork done. Someone needed to keep track of schedules, organize the household, and write the official letters while Diel met with nobles and merchants. They formed an efficient team because they could rely on each other, trusting their counterpart to do their job.

"Then I apologize for not being present this time."

"Don't be silly."

Jaeger frowned. He was not being silly. Something had upset Diel, and Jaeger hated when he missed an occasion to support him. Seeing Diel distressed sent tiny needles through his stomach. Jaeger went around his desk and put his hand on Diel's upper arm. The other elf's shoulders sagged as he relaxed.

"Tell me what happened, milord," Jaeger said.

A mischievous smile curved Diel's lips. "Only if you stop calling me that."

"Milord?" Jaeger hadn't needed to ask. They'd first had this argument a century ago, and it resurfaced every now and then, more as a joke than a real conflict. Despite Jaeger's adamant insistence on proper titles, Diel always tried to make him stop. The discussion unfolded the same way every time, but Jaeger enjoyed the banter too much to give in. "I'm afraid I'll have to live on without knowing, then, milord."

Diel laughed, the clear and melodic sound music to Jaeger's ears. It eased his worry, spreading a warm feeling inside him. The steward smiled, certain he had won again, until Diel surprised him by sliding his fingers across Jaeger's cheek and into his dark hair. "You always go on about what's proper and what's not, but ..." Diel pulled Jaeger closer, green eyes shining with amusement, and kissed him. The steward relaxed, enjoyed the slight spice of Diel's cologne and the caress of fingers on his neck. "I'm not hearing any protests now."

"I was unaware my kisses constituted an insult to your station, your family, or your person." He kept his tone contrived, despite knowing that wasn't Diel's point at all. Horror flashed through his companion's delicate features.

"Of course not! I didn't mean—"

"Oh! Then I see no contradiction in my actions, *milord*." Jaeger squared his shoulders and allowed a victorious smile to peek through his otherwise professional mask. "Besides, I enjoy the twitch in your eyebrows every time I use the proper title too much to let it go."

Diel gave him a playful shove. "Damn you. You always win these arguments. And I need your help with this, so I have to tell you what happened."

"I know."

Jaeger clasped his hands behind his back, and Diel rewarded his little smirk with another push. The truth was, Lord Dathirii never worked alone. He had hired Jaeger before he became Head of the House, but even before the steward's arrival, Diel had relied on his sister and cousins a lot. He was at the heart of a close-knit family where every member had a role to fulfill. The Dathirii elves formed one of the six founding merchant Houses of Isandor, and while most human Houses rose and fell through the decades, they had endured with substantial wealth and influence. They had all been playing the games, trades, and politics for longer than most nobles stayed alive— even the youngest Dathirii had almost twenty years of solid experience. They were a team, and if every elf was a different muscle in the body, then Jaeger was their nerves, transmitting the signal.

And what a signal it was.

Lord Diel Dathirii had inherited the mantle from his father and promptly broken from his conservative ways. It had taken a lot of arguing with other family members, immense passion and stubbornness, but he'd put an end to trade agreements exploiting labour in distant regions of the world—a staple of most of Isandor's powerful families, even today—then developed new partnerships with local merchants. Their considerable wealth had stalled, but Diel preferred his money clean. It wasn't rare for certain cousins—always the same—to complain that they could be at the top of the city's hierarchy and own more than half the Golden Table without this nonsense. The rest of the family agreed it was better to have fewer seats if it meant resisting immoral practices, however. And so when Jaeger asked again who had ruined Diel's afternoon, he was not surprised by the answer.

"Master Avenazar, from the Myrian Enclave."

Jaeger's stomach churned anyway. They had watched the Myrians get a foothold in this city with dread, knowing this confrontation would come. The Myrian Empire needed to go through Isandor to trade with most of the northeastern regions, and two years ago, they had sent Master Avenazar to establish an outpost on the outskirts of the city. The wizard had confirmed the Empire's reputation: ruthless enemies, shrewd tacticians, unapologetic slavers. He'd concluded several substantial trade deals with major houses in Isandor, using the Empire's wealth to rise as an important economic power. Lord Dathirii would only tolerate them so long before he provoked a trading war.

'So long' had lasted two years—a record for Diel.

Three sharp knocks at the door interrupted their conversation. Diel called for the newcomer to enter, and in walked Lord Kellian Dathirii. One of Diel's cousins, Kellian had inherited the golden hair typical to the Dathirii family and kept it tied in a loose ponytail. He could barely claim two inches above five feet, but his muscular build and cat-like agility made sure no one mistook him for a harmless soldier. Most days he wore the Dathirii ceremonial armour, but this time only the sword hung by his side. It bore the family crest: a silver *D* on a green background. Kellian stopped after two strides, then stood straight and waited for permission to speak. Jaeger enjoyed his discipline and respect of etiquette—qualities sorely lacking in most others.

"You sent?" Kellian asked at a sign from Lord Dathirii.

"Drop everything you're working on," Diel answered.

Kellian's lips became a thin line as he struggled with the order. "Milord, we're just about to catch the thief who—"

"I don't care about one robber, Kellian," Diel said. "You tell me he's been stealing for years, and yet we never really missed anything he took. Let him be. You'll have more pressing concerns."

That gave Kellian pause. His brown eyes settled on Lord Dathirii, then narrowed. As captain of their guard, he was well-acquainted with how Diel's idealist impulses could stir trouble.

"Pressing concerns?" he repeated without hiding his accusatory undertone. "Can't it be delayed long enough for my partner and me to catch this thief?"

Diel exchanged a quick glance with Jaeger. Kellian had been spending a lot of time with Detective Sora Sharpe over the last month, and they both agreed his interest in her had outgrown professional matters. Not that it moved very fast. They had worked together for a year now, and neither had pushed for the relationship to develop. Either Diel and Jaeger were mistaken, or Kellian preferred to take extra care with his heart—understandable, considering how long he'd needed to recover from his first wife's death. Whichever it was, however, it would have to be postponed.

"I'm afraid it cannot wait," Diel said. "He won't, after the threats I made."

"Who, Diel?"

"Master Avenazar."

"You—" Kellian stopped, clacked his tongue, shook his head. "Of course you did."

"Of course." Diel's tone had no trace of guilt or shame. He never apologized for standing up to wrong-doings, even if it put the whole family in danger. "He was torturing his apprentice."

Jaeger imagined the scene without a problem. He had seen this same scenario happen time and again. Diel spotted an injustice, flushed red, then called the perpetrator out. It didn't matter if he was jumping into the middle of dangerous business, unguarded and unprepared. He always interrupted. His name often sufficed as a shield, but he had been wounded in the past. Jaeger wouldn't change that for all the gold in the world. Judging from Kellian's annoyed frown, however, he might. The guard clacked his tongue again.

"Has anyone ever told you, Lord Dathirii, that you are this family's greatest peril?"

Diel's laughter once more filled the room. He put a hand over his heart in mock hurt, then met Kellian's gaze with a confident smile. A strange light burned in Diel's eyes, like a man about to jump down a high bridge, certain he would survive the fall. Despite his chirpy disposition, Lord Dathirii knew what he had just unleashed.

"Greatest peril? You do me a disservice, Kellian." He leaned forward a little, grinning. "I'm its greatest challenge."

Jaeger couldn't tear his gaze away. Diel's wild confidence when he threw himself at a trial entranced him. This was the man he loved. The one who laughed as he put his entire life on the line to defend others, the daring noble who relentlessly pushed back against horrible acts and damaging systems. Kellian grunted, but Jaeger noticed a hint of a smile on his square features. Diel must have seen it, too. He spread his arms with a chuckle, then settled his hands on his hips. He breathed out slowly, as if exhaling his desire to joke.

"I have no fear that everyone will be up to the task. Kellian, please brief your men on the new circumstances. We'll build a list of potential targets to defend as soon as possible. Jaeger, we'll need everything we know about the Myrian Enclave. Activities, members, allies—everything. See Garith about it. At this hour he shouldn't be with a lady yet. I'll contact the other families likely to lend us a hand. The Myrians might have an empire behind them, but if Isandor stands together, nothing can stop us."

Lord Diel Dathirii inhaled, eyes closed and gathering his focus, then his gaze went from Kellian to Jaeger. Under the determination Jaeger loved hid a hint of fear. The steward doubted anyone else could see it, but it was there, in his expression and in the slight tension of his shoulders. Master Avenazar's reputation described a violent and unpredictable man. Rumours said the wizard had brought down an entire block of houses in Myria before being sent here. Isandor's trade wars most often resolved themselves through deals and bribes, but this one might turn into a bloody exception. Yet the more dangerous Avenazar was, the more necessary throwing him out became. Diel lifted his chin, perhaps following a similar train of thought.

"Gentlemen," Diel Dathirii said, "it's time to clean our city."

⟨∘⟩

JAEGER knocked on Lord Garith Dathirii's door with more than a little apprehension. Despite Diel's belief that he wouldn't have company at this hour of the day, Jaeger expected the young lord to answer half-clothed, his golden hair tumbling down his shoulders and back. Many instances of Garith opening in a hurry were followed by a woman's voice asking, "Is it important?" or worse, "Should I dress?" It seemed to the steward that he was always interrupting one bout of lustful pleasure or another. There was no avoiding it, however, because Garith refused to keep a regular schedule. Sometimes he worked in the middle of the night, sometimes early afternoon. Yet at the end of the day, House Dathirii's accounts were always up to date.

Long minutes passed as Jaeger waited at the door. He pressed his lips together, his dread increasing with every additional second. The more time Garith took to answer, the more likely it became that the young elf was putting clothes back on. As the handle turned, the steward offered one last prayer to the gods.

When Jaeger's gaze fell upon the lord's clean, wine-coloured outfit, sporting more buttons than he could've reasonably fastened since he'd knocked, he heaved a sigh of relief. Garith wore his round optics and had tied his hair into a half ponytail, both signs he had been working. Excellent. With his current attire, Jaeger was once more struck by the resemblance between Garith and Diel. They shared a similar build along with the wide green eyes, the luscious hair, and the pointed chin. Garith's face was rounder, however, his nose smaller. And as charming as the ladies found the young lord's half-smile, Jaeger preferred Diel's honest grin and how it drew out the little crow's feet at his eyes. He was, however, horribly biased when it came to Diel Dathirii.

"I'm sorry," Garith said. "I was finishing a calculation. You need anything?"

"Indeed. Did you have company?"

Jaeger preferred to ask, on the off-chance Garith had cracked the finance books while a naked lady slept in the bed behind him. He would still let him in, if that was the case. It had happened once, and

Jaeger didn't intend to ever repeat the experience. Garith laughed and pulled the door wide open.

"No woman with me, I'm afraid. I'm all yours." He sighed as Jaeger entered, faking heart-broken desperation. "You're lucky, too, because I was supposed to dine with Sora—you know, Kellian's charming partner? She had questions for me but cancelled. So here I am, buried under endless strings of numbers instead of enjoying a glass of wine with an amazing and witty lady. What a waste."

"Her time is better spent now."

"You wound me, Jaeger!"

The steward's eyebrows arched. If it took so little …

"Your time will also be better spent," Jaeger answered. "We have work."

"You always prioritize duty over dinner." Garith moved back to his desk, removed his glasses, and set them down. Although Garith's quarters were a mess—clothes strewn across a luxurious rug, half-read books scattered on every surface, even an empty bottle of wine—he kept his workplace neat and organized. "What can I do for you?"

"You hold a detailed account of trade deals in this city, classified by which noble families are involved, don't you?"

"Well, detailed …" Garith made a dismissive sign with his hand. "Branwen puts a lot of time and energy into following the flow of coins, but such information is guarded." He strode to a bookshelf, stretched to reach a fair-sized crate, and pulled it down. "Who are our lucky fellows?"

"The Myrian Enclave."

Garith paled and raised his gaze from the dozens of rolled-up scrolls inside the crate. For all his flights of fancy and wild nights, the Dathirii bookkeeper did have a drop of common sense. After his initial shock passed, his smile returned. Nothing dampened his mood for long. He plunged his hand into the scrolls and lined the ones tied by a black ribbon on the table. One colour per noble House, all with their corresponding symbols for Jaeger's benefit. A code easy to remember, and easy to share. Jaeger had developed the habit of marking his notes in a similar fashion. As the number of scrolls on the desk grew, the steward's eyes widened.

"How much information do we have on them?"

"Lots." Garith put the crate down, returned to his library, and scanned it. He retrieved a leather-bound notebook, half an inch thick, and set it next to the scrolls. "Diel fumed when the Table voted that Myrian laws would govern the Myrian Enclave instead of ours. Branwen and I knew he'd try to run them out of Isandor one day. It's not a surprise to anyone, is it? So we prepared."

Jaeger cracked the notebook open, then flipped through the pages to get an overview of the information within. Names, positions, rumours about the enclave's members, their contacts and relationships in town—everything they could unearth, waiting for this occasion. Branwen's work, while the scrolls would be Garith's tally of their trades. He unrolled one to confirm and smiled at the numbers lined in a perfect column. The amount of information varied depending on the trade deal, but they had decent estimates of their values, as well as when they'd been agreed upon. In Isandor, a profitable trade meant a solid alliance, and the precision behind Garith's work might save them all.

"I'm impressed."

Garith laughed as he stored the crate once more. "Now those are words I don't often hear from you. Glad to be of help. Come back if there's anything you don't understand."

Jaeger gathered the precious information in his arms. He wanted to start reading right away. It would mean hour upon hour of deciphering the web of trade deals, half-secret agreements, and allies and enemies, but he liked to sift through the information and reorganize it for Diel. It would help him get a good grip of the situation, and decide how to approach the Myrians.

It might take them until dawn, but the idea only made Jaeger smile. He knew how such nights went: they would sit on the floor like teenagers, Diel leaning on him while Jaeger placed the scrolls in organized piles. Diel wouldn't stop talking, sometimes bending forward slightly to retie his golden hair. He'd ask a question to Jaeger, and while the steward went diving through the information for an answer, Diel would outline the beginning of a plan. Hours would fly by as they refined the idea. Jaeger's great organizational skills provided Diel's keen political instincts with a more concrete form, and by dawn, the elven lord knew which orders to give but was too exhausted to enact the plan. He often fell asleep with his head in Jaeger's lap long before the steward finished his notes.

Jaeger loved his work, and he loved Diel even more. A night with both was his idea of perfection.

"Thank you, Lord Garith," he said. "I advise you remain available tomorrow afternoon. Lord Dathirii will want to discuss these with you."

"Don't worry, my friend, I'll be right here until he needs me." He tapped the desk and wished Jaeger a good day. "Close the door, will you?"

Jaeger nodded his agreement. As he left, arms full of scrolls, the bookkeeper put his glasses back on and dipped his quill in dark ink. Garith might not pull an all-nighter, but with the dangerous task of taking down the Myrian Enclave, he could kiss a lot of his free time goodbye. Jaeger shut the door with his heel, leaving the young lord to his duties, then hurried to his own.

CHAPTER FIVE

EVERY evening, High Priest Varden Daramond tended to Keroth's sacred fire. The brazier never died, but it always lost strength during the day. Varden arrived with three dry logs, then crossed the temple's ceremonial hall. It was small, one of the handful of buildings in the Myrian Enclave, but Varden preferred it to the grand temples in Myria. The hall had a rectangular shape, with a circular end instead of a flat wall. Ramps curved up around the end of the hall, embracing the brazier's stone platform like two large arms. At the top of the ramps were two corridors, one leading to the acolytes' quarters, the other to Varden's. Long windows allowed sunlight inside the hall, and two rows of columns traced a path to the entrance. Their tops arched toward the end, carved to resemble flames licking the vaulted ceiling. Varden wished they had fireflowers to decorate them, but the bright red flowers would never survive

Isandor's winters. To Varden's artistic eye, the temple lacked a touch of life without them.

He promised himself he would find a substitute as he climbed the stairs to the fire's dais. Even diminished, it burned well over five feet high. Varden focused on the warmth against his skin and the energy within. After a deep breath, he stepped into the flames. The logs in his arms gave a familiar crack as fire enveloped them, blackening the wood but leaving the priest unharmed. Other temples delegated the brazier duty to new acolytes, but Varden loved the sensation of warm currents dancing in his brown curls. The design of his High Priest outfit allowed air to flow through, snapping it about as Varden sat down, smiling, and placed the three logs around him. The fire bath eased his spirits, and he began the Night Watch Prayer. He asked Keroth to grant him Their brilliant flame to push back the night and permit him to witness the world's beauty, in both light and shadows. Varden's fingers curled around a piece of charcoal as he prayed. His urge to draw something grew with every passing second.

Master Avenazar's snide voice broke through his concentration, speaking directly into his mind. *Blondie needs your help.*

Varden's eyes snapped open and his heart sank. He managed to finish the prayer, but the message had wiped out his serenity. When had peacefulness ever lasted in the Myrian Enclave? This particular sentence pained him more than others, however. Its meaning never changed. 'Blondie' was Nevian, and 'needs your help' meant Avenazar had tortured him again. The wizard always refused to tell him where to find Nevian, though, leaving Varden to search for him. Once, before he'd understood the kind of man he dealt with, Varden had asked where to look for the apprentice. Avenazar's cackle and noncommittal shrug were the only answers he'd received.

Varden emerged from the brazier, wisps of smoke trailing behind him, then hurried out of Keroth's temple.

He stopped at Nevian's tiny bedroom first and pushed against the piles of books blocking the door from opening, cringing when one collapsed to the ground. Nevian was always sneaking tomes out of the library, using the countless books to conceal a number of Avenazar's magic manuals. Varden doubted anyone other than him had noticed. Most knew better than to get involved in Avenazar's business, and the way the Myrian wizard treated his apprentice—as property, mostly—made it clear he was also off-limits. No one would inspect his room, but Nevian still risked a lot. Not his worst decision in that regard, Varden knew. Another secret he intended to keep.

When Varden didn't find Nevian with these books, he moved to the library and searched it one alley at a time. Every passing minute worsened the tightness in his chest. One day, Varden wouldn't reach the poor teenager in time, and Avenazar's cruelty would leave a permanent mark on Nevian. Well ... a *more* permanent one. Varden didn't doubt it had already left scars in the young man's mind. How could it not, after two years of such treatment? The High Priest checked the courtyard—nothing. He stifled his disgust of the dank underground corridor lined with prison cells and peered inside them but found no trace of him there either. Panic settled into his gut, nauseating him. His mind sped through other possible locations as he half-ran down the hallways.

A hawk flew through an open window, forcing Varden to skid to a stop. Its talons straightened into legs while brown feathers transformed into pale skin and a prune-coloured dress. The wings stretched into delicate arms and hands. The head shifted last, its beak flattening into Isra's small nose while the eyes recovered their blue hue. Isra stood still an instant, shaking the transformation's daze away. Varden called to her.

"Miss Isra!"

She shot him a haughty glare and Varden ground his teeth, steeling himself. Isra hated all Isbari. The moment she had noticed his tanned skin and thick hair, she'd treated him as an inferior. His people were slaves in Myria, and Isra clearly wished he was, too.

"I'm looking for Nevian," Varden said.

"I am not your personal information centre, Isbari. Find him yourself."

As Isra lifted her chin, Varden's fists clenched at his side. On another day, he would have let it slide. Some fights weren't worth his limited energy, and he disliked pulling rank on anyone, let alone a prideful Myrian who might seek revenge later. But Nevian didn't have time for her little power plays, and in theory he followed Avenazar and Jilssan in their hierarchy. Varden grabbed her forearm and yanked her close, his grip tight around her tiny wrist.

"I am your superior by rank, and this kid might be dying. If you have any clue, tell me now."

Anger flashed through her expression, and she wrenched out of his grasp with a huff. For a moment, Varden glimpsed fear too, but she pinched her lips and straightened into a dignified position.

"He was tasked with cleaning the storage room floor."

Varden spun on his heels, walking out on Isra without a thank you. He lengthened his strides, forcing himself not to run despite his urge to get there as fast as possible. *Please, Keroth*, he thought. *Let him be there.*

☙❧

VARDEN found the young apprentice curled on the floor, unconscious. Blood trickled from his nose, forming a minuscule pool on the otherwise clean wooden floor, but he sported no other visible injuries. He rarely did. Avenazar favoured mental pain over anything physical, although on occasion, he'd combine both and leave the kid in a horrible state. The priest's insides twisted as he approached the prone form and rolled him onto his back. Even out cold, Nevian clutched a tiny brush, as though holding onto it could save him. Pain warped his features, and his short blond hair stuck to his forehead. Varden sighed and tried not to imagine what he'd endured in the last hours.

He placed his fingers on either side of the apprentice's head and began a low chant. The room's chill made it hard to feel Keroth's presence beside him, but Varden focused, and a soft orange light emerged from his hands. It flickered like a thousand tiny flames and slid off his fingers to wrap around Nevian's head. Varden had trained as a healer for years, dedicating himself to tending to his fellow Isbari's wounds, but the two years in Isandor's enclave had taught him even more, especially about mental injuries. Avenazar destroyed or twisted memories as a pastime, but Varden had learned to reconstruct them before the damage turned permanent. He didn't want to discover what would happen if he couldn't fix it in time.

Nevian's muscles relaxed as the priest eased his mind and soothed his migraine. The teenager stirred but didn't wake. He wouldn't for another hour, at least—long enough for Varden to move him elsewhere. Varden picked him up, eager to be in his quarters, in the temple. Avenazar never went there. Too hot, the wizard complained, and Varden avoided admitting that was on purpose. He deserved a haven—if any location within the enclave's walls could be called that. With quite a distance to go, however, Varden soon found Nevian's long and dangling legs unwieldy. He was glad to put him down at last.

Despite Varden's position, his quarters weren't fancy: a heavy curtain across the middle of the small room hid his bed. On this side stood his beloved fireplace. Nothing decorated the walls, except over his desk. Varden had dared to expose a handful of his favourite drawings—those that wouldn't get him in trouble, at any rate. All were portraits of the Isbari who'd come to his service in Myria, who'd looked up to him for guidance, even though some were twice his age. These were his people, his flock, and he knew the Myrians had sent him far away from them on purpose. An Isbari leader gave them cohesion, determination, and hope for better circumstances. Inadmissible for most Myrians. Every time Varden looked at his portraits, his resolve hardened. He would survive Avenazar and this temporary exile, return home, and help his enslaved kinsmen.

Varden's gaze went from his sketches to the teenager. Nevian took the brunt of Avenazar's dangerous mood swings, but not a day passed without Varden expecting his turn to come. How horrible for someone so young to suffer so much. Yet Varden couldn't help but thank Keroth it wasn't him instead. One day he would fail to save Nevian, or Avenazar would grow bored with him. And when that happened? Varden would be next.

At least Nevian's body had accustomed itself to the frequent exertion. He recovered faster and quickly returned to his secret studies. How long could he keep it up, though? Between the torture sessions, the hours learning magic on his own, those spent completing Avenazar's tasks, and Nevian's nightly escapades in Isandor, it was a wonder the apprentice slept at all. Perhaps he didn't. He always seemed exhausted. Varden sighed. He wanted to help, but every time he tried to reach out, Nevian shunned him. So Varden kept his secrets and healed him when necessary.

As he sat there, tending to the pale teenager, a new idea surfaced in Varden's mind. It might get him in a world of trouble, but he had to try. Sitting still and bemoaning his fate didn't sit well with Varden. Besides, Nevian's audacity made him feel less lonely. When the apprentice woke up, Varden would have a proposition for him. In the meantime, he retrieved his sketch pad out of his desk and traced the general contour of the teenager's body shape. Tall, lanky, bony. Nevian had no muscles to speak of. Just a firm square jaw and a prominent brow—features most often associated with brutish savages, not logic-addicted teenagers. They granted Nevian an appearance of constant irritation, which suited him just fine.

After some time, Nevian's breathing changed, and he moaned. Varden set his sketch pad aside as the apprentice's eyes fluttered open.

"Welcome back," the priest said.

Nevian glanced at him and tried to dab his nose with his sleeve even though it no longer bled. Once he realized that, he squeezed his eyes shut and remained still, breathing in and out slowly as time passed. One minute. Another. Then he pushed himself up. Varden's eyes widened as Nevian sat, threw the blankets off, and slid his legs out of the bed.

"What are you doing?"

Nevian swallowed hard. His pale skin turned a sick and sweaty white, and he fell back with a grunt. Varden tilted his head to the side and stared at him, unimpressed. Nevian met his disapproving glare with unflinching determination.

"I'm leaving," he said. His weak voice siphoned all credibility out of his statement.

"You can't. Your body needs rest."

Nevian's fingers curled into the blankets, and he fixed his gaze on his knees, no doubt gathering strength for another attempt. Varden withheld a sigh. They went through this routine every single time. And indeed, Nevian tried again a few seconds later, only to fall right back. He grabbed the edge of the bed and managed to retain a precarious sitting position.

"Nevian, please," Varden said more softly.

He would have gently pushed Nevian back into bed, but Varden had learned to touch him as little as possible, even in a supportive manner. Nevian flinched away from it every time, even when Varden gave advance warning. He couldn't heal without contact, so they'd worked around it as best as they could, and Nevian's forearm was an absolute forbidden zone. No need to ask why; Avenazar always grabbed him there.

The apprentice shot him a glare. "I need to work. I can't waste my time here. You're the healer. Make me better."

Another frequent discussion. Nevian only ever wanted to leave as fast as possible, whether or not he should. Varden had given in on countless occasions before. He could saturate Nevian with enough energy to carry him through the day, and the teenager would collapse in his bed as soon as night came. Except Nevian wouldn't sleep until forced to, and energizing him could lead to serious health complications.

"No. I won't wash your exhaustion away."

"But—"

"This is the third time this week. Your body cannot sustain it." Varden crossed his arms. He needed Nevian to understand that he wanted to help. Cramming energy into him wasn't the way to go. "What imagined slight triggered Avenazar this time?"

"Master Avenazar did nothing I did not deserve."

"I'm sure."

Varden let the obvious sarcasm float in the room for a moment. Nevian always shot down conversations about Avenazar, as if the wizard would hear them. He avoided Varden's gaze and tried to straighten his fluffed blond hair and apprentice's robes. He smoothed the folds, never using more than one hand, keeping the other clamped on the mattress for support. Varden let him stew in the awkward silence for a while. Perhaps it would make him more receptive to his proposition.

"If you stay here and allow me to take care of you, I promise I'll help you make up for the lost time."

And just like that, he had Nevian's attention. The apprentice sat a little straighter, lips parted, eyes bright. He studied Varden, not bothering to hide his suspicion, but the hook must have been too intriguing. He bit.

"How?"

Varden smiled as he transferred from the bedside to his desk. Nevian wouldn't agree to anything without details, but his offer would be irresistible. The priest withdrew a wooden box from the last drawer. Long and flat, it sported fire-like carvings in its dark wood. Varden slid the top off with reverent care then retrieved the black bandanna within. Its only distinctive features were the two burnt orange designs at the front, stitched in the shape of Keroth's flame symbol. Varden traced the sleek fabric with his thumb, remembering his first time wearing one of them. It had felt like Keroth had expanded his mind a thousand times.

"What's that?" Nevian asked.

His wariness amused Varden. What did he imagine? Mind-controlling headgear? Avenazar performed enough of such atrocities for the entire enclave. But Nevian was always suspicious, by nature and by necessity. Varden regained his seat near the bed and showed him the piece of clothing.

"A rekhemal. We use them during the Long Night's Watch ceremony—the night of winter solstice, when Keroth's light and protection are gone the longest. It amplifies awareness and sensory input, drawing power from fire. You feel ... more present, and also more awake." Varden enjoyed the warm fabric a moment, then offered it to the young wizard. "I won't need it until the winter solstice. We wear it over our eyes, but you could tie it on your forearm. A candle is sufficient for its magic to work."

Nevian did not move. He eyed the bandanna, then Varden, then the bandanna again. "Why would you give me that?"

"I am naively hoping that if you are more efficient, you will allow yourself well-deserved rest. The rekhemal cannot replace sleep. It helps one remain awake, nothing else." It was a gamble, with Nevian. The apprentice might ignore his warnings and never lay in bed again. Varden needed to contribute however he could. If only he could tell Nevian he knew about the nights of studying, or ask what he did when he left the enclave! But that would throw the teenager into a panic. It might be best if Nevian believed Varden had something to gain from this. "You become distracted and irritable when tired from an all-nighter, which makes it more likely you'll provoke Avenazar. If you don't get hurt, I don't have to heal you. We both benefit."

Nevian's nostrils flared when Varden mentioned the sleepless nights, but his breathing remained level. He examined Varden with care, his expression at a calculated neutral. Perhaps he wondered how much Varden knew.

"You have keen eyes," Nevian said.

"It always pays to watch others. Take it, but please keep it a secret. The rekhemal is a holy relic. Purists would condemn me for lending it to someone outside the church."

Nevian was about to close his fingers on the bandanna when

Varden asked for secrecy. Instead he snatched his hand back and
glared at Varden.

"You can't do that. You're Isbari. Master Avenazar is waiting for
an excuse to snap chains around your wrists. If they catch you, they
won't just retrograde you to a lower rank."

Varden's stomach clenched. He'd heard enough snide comments
from Avenazar to know Nevian wasn't lying. None of this was new
to him. From the moment he had entered Keroth's acolytes, he had
been one false step away from returning to slavery.

"There is always someone waiting for that excuse, Nevian. Take
the bandanna."

"You have no reason to risk this." Nevian hesitated but finally
picked up the rekhemal. "Where's the trick?"

Varden couldn't help but mock his unrelenting doubts. After a
guilty cough, he answered. "Once you wear it, your soul belongs to
the Fire Lord."

A horrified frown passed through Nevian's square features.
"You're joking."

"Am I?"

"You are."

Varden was glad the conversation had moved away from the
danger he put himself in. "Then you won't hesitate to wear it. Not
now, however. My one condition is that you sleep, at least tonight.
It's early evening—you'll feel better in the morning."

For a moment it looked like Nevian might refuse. He had raised
his chin with the usual stubborn expression, but he instead let himself
fall back in Varden's bed, his arms spread out. The way he flopped

down reminded the High Priest of moody teenagers throwing a fit, and Varden's smile widened. Only Nevian would get so angry about being unable to work.

"All right, I'll sleep," the apprentice said. "At least until Master Avenazar comes calling again."

"I'll buy you until late morning," Varden promised.

Nevian grunted in approval, and the High Priest rose from his seat. He grabbed his charcoal and sketchbook, intent on finishing his earlier piece. This deal felt like a huge victory. Nevian might never allow him any closer than this, but with the sacred bandanna, he would fare better. He could progress faster, which might mean more to him than any amount of healing.

He had his confirmation a moment later, just as he was about to cross the curtain and move to the other room. Nevian's voice rose from the bed, low and hesitant.

"High Priest?"

Varden stopped and waited for the rest. Nevian stared at the ceiling, and spoke two words he'd never offered in years of Varden tending to his injuries.

"Thank you."

CHAPTER SIX

LADY Camilla Dathirii didn't have a wide array of talents. Unlike her grandson Garith, numbers slipped through the threads of her mind, blurring together in a confusing mess. Her two serious attempts at sword fighting had ended in a sprained wrist and a broken leg, to Kellian's great dismay. She couldn't lie or disguise herself as Branwen so often did, nor could she sway the hearts of many, the way her nephew managed when he assumed his role as Lord Dathirii and addressed a crowd. Even the youngest Dathirii had a speciality: the family hadn't seen such a healer in centuries.

No, Camilla Dathirii couldn't claim any such skills. She was, however, without a doubt the best listener in Isandor, and it suited her just fine. When trouble knocked at a Dathirii's door, they always came to her. She settled them down with tea tailored to their taste, and they poured their hearts out while she poured the comforting brew into their cup. With time, Lady Camilla had extended her skills to the often-forgotten elderly of Isandor. At six hundred something years, she could hardly be called youthful anymore, but she did not age as humans did. So she helped however she could, cleaning their houses and chatting, strolling outside whenever the weather allowed.

Today she met with Mister Stillman, a retired haberdasher who clung to her arm with surprising strength. Lady Camilla could usually pay the utmost attention to his rants, answering with the appropriate exclamations of offence and rectifying his thoughts when he went too far. Yet she found it hard to focus since Diel had made an irruption into her quarters last night, requesting strong tea and advice, but bringing dire news in return. While it wasn't in her nature to call any story trivial—she hadn't earned the trust of Isandor's old folks by mocking their daily concerns—Mister Stillman's tale failed to retain her attention on this particular morning.

Her gaze wandered across the busy bridges, tracing the beautiful towers rising around them. She always strolled the Upper City with Stillman, even though his knees suffered from the many stairs to get there. He enjoyed pretending he belonged in the middle of all these riches, and Camilla saw no reason to deny him this pleasure. So far above ground, railingscarved from white marble lined the bridges to keep everyone safe. They arched from one noble tower to another, sometimes changing style midway to match the spire they approached.

Camilla loved to survey Isandor from a high vantage point. The city started at the bottom of the cliff, where its extensive docks formed the last navigable port on the Reonne River. From there, it curved in a slow spiral around the steep incline, and the closer to the top one climbed, the more eccentric the towers became. Isandor's founding families had almost all been Allorians, and the region's cultural love for drama and exuberant shows of wealth had translated into a strange architectural competition. A tower needed to reach higher or be stranger than all the others, or it was unworthy of respect.

She could mock them, but the Dathirii Tower wasn't all that different. Her grandfather—the first Lord Dathirii—had marked their elven heritage by building it entirely of wood, crafting the spire to resemble a trunk while the bridges extending from it became branches. Elegant rather than whimsical, and outlandish enough to attract attention. The elven family had chosen to settle with humans, which meant participating in competitions and traditions. Now they were so involved in the conflicts inherent to Isandor's lifestyle that Diel had struck a war of his own.

As Camilla's mind drifted back to the present, she noticed a strange figure standing in front of the Brasten Tower. Lord Arathiel Brasten. He'd changed, yet the man staring wistfully at what was once his home could be no one else. His dark hair had turned whiter than hers, but he still kept it in cornrows, although the style had gone out of fashion decades ago. Camilla wouldn't have thought much of his peculiar appearance, if not for the indisputable fact that this man shouldn't be in the city at all. He shouldn't even be alive!

Lord Arathiel Brasten had left Isandor more than a hundred years ago. Time should have killed him, yet he hadn't aged at all. He still looked like the sprightly, late-twenties weapons master that had gone in search of a cure for his diseased sister.

Camilla raised a hand to interrupt Stillman and led him toward Arathiel. She would apologize later. Her curiosity demanded she investigate.

"Excuse me, Lord Arathiel Brasten?"

Her soft voice startled the lord, and he spun on his heels, shoulders tensed and eyes wide. While he eased when he recognized her, Camilla sensed he wanted to bolt.

"Lady Camilla Dathirii." His greeting was deep and smooth despite his initial shock. "Pardon my surprise. I didn't expect to hear my full name."

"Colour me pleased for this chance to utter it, Lord Arathiel," she said.

Stillman shuffled, then leaned forward to squint at Arathiel. He had never been the most patient person, and she suspected he wouldn't grant her the long conversation she desired with the elder by her side.

"Would you care for tea, milord?" she asked.

She offered him her best 'sweet old lady' smile. To Isandor's human population, Camilla had always been the aged elf who prepared cookies and tea or strolled around the bridges, caring for those whose age or illness had stolen their autonomy. Her golden locks had gone grey decades ago, and in the city's psyche, she had never been young—an amusing fantasy. Arathiel studied her, wary and hesitant, but his expression soon softened.

"I would be grateful for one of Lady Camilla's legendary tea chats," he said. "I have been gone too long and feel a little lost."

The brimming nostalgia in Arathiel's voice sent needles at her heart. The last century had changed more than his physique. Camilla remembered an energetic young man, always volunteering for difficult tasks and very protective of his sister. The kind of person friends relied on. Something about him now was … unsteady. Frail.

"Meet me at the Little Square in an hour."

Before he could agree, Mister Stillman let out a loud cough. "Can we go now? I need to pee, and I don't like the looks of him."

A soft chuckle escaped Camilla's lips, but it died as she caught Arathiel's haunted expression. He said nothing about the insult so casually flung at him, stepping aside to let them pass. Camilla thanked him.

"Don't worry, Mister Stillman. We'll be at your house in no time."

She continued on her way, even deeper in her thoughts than before. One thing felt horribly wrong about her short encounter: Lord Arathiel had been staring at the Brasten Tower—his home—with the nervousness of an introvert about to give a public speech. By all means, he should have strode inside without hesitation. After so many years, however … Every Brasten he knew would be dead. No wonder Arathiel had been so surprised to hear his name. He was a ghost to this city. A ghost only a handful of elves could recognize.

❦

LITTLE Square was a small park at the frontier between the Lower and Middle City, in the eastern part of Isandor, where the land rose more abruptly. The large elm tree clinging to the steep ground, half its roots protruding, used to be a pathetic and desperate piece of vegetation, and the small platform built around it a mockery of the glorious plaza Upper City folks enjoyed. After a hundred thirty years, however, it had grown into a solid and majestic tree, and mages had helped grass and flowers blossom into a beautiful garden. Arathiel waited on a bench park alone. He watched couples huddle close and rub their hands together as they strolled through the neighborhood, and a dog barked at him for long minutes before his owner managed to control it. Had the animal sensed his difference? He'd done his best to remain inconspicuous—putting on proper winter cloaks despite his inability to feel and sitting rather than walking—but animals detected things no human could. Arathiel tried not to let it bother him, but it made him feel like he no longer belonged.

"Why is it that whenever I find you, half of you seems in another world?"

Arathiel started as Lady Camilla Dathirii slid onto the bench next to him. He hadn't spotted her, one colourless blur among many others, unimportant to his tired mind. She'd thrown a shawl over her shoulders, concealing part of her wealthy dress, but her Dathirii House brooch was displayed plainly. Arathiel met her gaze, uncertain how to answer. Camilla hadn't wasted time getting to her interrogations, yet they didn't threaten him the way strangers' enquiries so often did.

"I feel like it, truth be told." His fingers went to his sleeves, to pull them even though he couldn't quite feel the fabric. He'd never lost that nervous habit. "It's unsettling to be an outsider in your own city."

"I can't imagine," she said. "There is a teahouse nearby you might enjoy or, if you prefer privacy, we can return to my quarters in the Dathirii Tower. I assure you, however, that the establishment is well-reputed for its discretion."

Arathiel's stomach churned at the idea of meeting any of the Dathirii. He'd avoided giving his full name to Branwen when he'd arrived, and felt no more ready to do so now. If they recognized him, he would have to explain over and over. Once with Lady Camilla would be more than enough. She had a calm sweetness about her that invited confidence and long-winded tales. Perhaps that was the magic of Lady Camilla Dathirii, so reputed for listening to everyone: she made you feel at ease.

"I can deal with the tea house."

Twenty minutes later, they sat in a semi-private booth, hidden by curtains from the rest of the customers. The employees knew Lady Camilla and had this table ready for her in an instant. Without a single question about her companion, they had taken her order then slid out of sight. Their attitude relieved Arathiel. He hadn't realized how hard on his morale the stares had become. In the tea house, the only gaze to withstand came from Camilla's sharp blue eyes, and they brimmed with compassion.

"You haven't entered the Brasten Tower, have you?" she asked.

"No." Arathiel set both his hands on the table and stared at them. "I've been in town for a week, but I can't bring myself to knock. They're my family but … at the same time, they're not. No one's left."

He knew Camilla would understand the void that left in him. Blood ties mattered in every noble house in Isandor, but the Dathirii elves were more tightly knit than most. They lived together for decades—centuries, even. When one of them died, it created a permanent hole. Arathiel watched the sadness settle on the old lady's expression as she reflected upon his words.

"I'm sorry for your loss. So much has changed since you left us. How long has it been, exactly?"

"A hundred thirty-two years." He leaned back in his chair. Time had no significance in the Well. A century had vanished and he hadn't noticed. Was he supposed to have aged and died in there? The magic had drained colour from his hair and broken the rest of his body, yet Arathiel had retained the strength of his youth. Perhaps his skewed perception of time was only because of the added longevity. "Is it normal, for more than a century to feel like a single year?"

Camilla's breath caught in her throat and her eyes widened in horror; Arathiel didn't need another answer. He regretted asking. The waitress arrived, and an awkward silence settled between them. She poured the pale yellow infusion into their cups, then left the teapot on the table and withdrew. Camilla leaned forward and wrapped her wrinkled fingers around her steaming teacup.

"I'm afraid not. Passage of time doesn't change when you live longer. Some elves have excellent memory and can recall with precision most of their lives, but most lose entire decades, remembering only key events. Really, you just forget more."

Arathiel's mind whirled as he tried to buffer the blow, and he spread his fingers on the light wood. If only he could ground himself with that gesture! The Well had stolen more than a century from him, however. The table under his hand was but a dull pressure, and the tea Camilla had chosen with such care would never smell or taste like anything to him. He struggled to find a way to continue their conversation and eventually decided to change the topic. It would help to talk about something other than himself.

"How is Lord Dathirii?"

"Lord Dathirii is no longer Lord Dathirii," she said, a hollow to her voice. "My brother died more than a century ago—some twenty years after you left. His son, Diel Dathirii, took up that mantle. You two were of an age. You might remember him?"

"I do." Diel was a carefree idealist who spent more time goofing around the city with friends than learning about politics and history. The last Arathiel had heard, he'd ditched his family to go exploring the world with a servant. Not the most serious of leaders, but very handsome nonetheless. "So he returned from his trip, at least."

Arathiel's expression must have revealed his doubts because Lady Camilla chuckled. "He did, and has since grown into a fine man—the kind who puts actions behind words, even when it brings his entire family on the frontline."

Something in her tone made Arathiel examine her—a hint of fear behind the pride. Arathiel had always been good at picking up on others' moods. He used his talent in battles to predict his opponents' intentions and in conversations to understand what was left unsaid. This sounded more like a specific reference than a general comment on her nephew's behaviour.

"Has something happened?"

Camilla didn't bother to hide her surprise at his question. Her thin smile created a ripple of wrinkles on her face. "I'm afraid we'll be very busy running terrible people out of the city, but you shouldn't concern yourself with it. You must have so much on your mind already. Do you have somewhere to stay, at least? Enough funds to be comfortable? We could accommodate you."

Arathiel shook his head before she had finished her offer. "I have a room inside a shelter, in the Lower City. I gave them what I had left and they will house and feed me for as long as I want. They've treated me well since I've arrived, and I would not dream of going elsewhere at the moment."

At first he'd thought they wanted to trap him. They were too trusting, too nice. In the Lower City's hostile environment, Cal's cheerfulness felt out of place. If neither he nor this Larryn were wary of him, perhaps they were trying to lure him in. Except they invited the one with dark elven blood without hesitation, playing long card games with him despite his ancestors' terrible reputation. As he'd watched them, Arathiel had understood. They didn't care. In Larryn's Shelter, he would always be welcome, no matter how different. Smiling, Arathiel reached for his cup. As he grasped the handle and raised it, Lady Camilla's eyes widened.

"Don't drink it yet, it'll be—"

Too late. The tea slipped through his lips and he swallowed.

Liquid ran down his throat, tasteless, barely noticeable.

"Scalding hot," Camilla finished. "Are you okay?"

"It ... hurts." Arathiel tried to reassure her with a brief smile. "I'll be fine. I was distracted."

His voice trailed off under Camilla's piercing stare. She didn't believe a word of it. Arathiel put down the cup, his hands shaking a little. He must have burned his tongue but couldn't tell. All he'd wanted was to keep himself busy as his mind wandered, and now he'd drunk steaming hot tea right in front of her. No wonder she would have none of his 'I'm distracted' excuse. Fighting the panic swirling at the bottom of his stomach, Arathiel pushed the topic in another direction.

"There is something else you could do for me."

He hesitated. Now might not be the best time for strange requests. This could become a matter of life and death, however. How could he phrase his needs so they seemed normal?

She leaned forward and put her hand on his. She must have squeezed, or he wouldn't have felt the pressure. "Won't you tell me what happened? You should be dead."

"I'd rather not." Arathiel avoided her gaze. "I don't truly know and never will. I'm alive, for no reason I can fathom. Perhaps some things are best unquestioned."

Camilla didn't answer, allowing his words to sink in. Then she once more wrapped wrinkled hands over her tea. "Very well. Tell me what you need, and I won't ask why. It would be a pleasure to help, no matter what happened to you. Just ask. It pains me to think you would deal with this alone."

Arathiel's throat tightened, and he met her gaze. He'd believed himself without allies, isolated in a city he no longer recognized, but here was Lady Camilla Dathirii, offering unconditional help. Returning to Isandor had always been a gamble—a last resort. If Arathiel couldn't find a home here, he never would. After his plunge in the docks' water, he'd doubted his decision and despaired at his chances. Camilla's concern shed a ray of hope on his future. He had to try.

"A mirror. A tiny hand-held mirror. It's a lot of money, I know, but it could save my life."

"Consider it done." She blew on her tea and finally sipped it. The slight pain in her expression told Arathiel the drink was still too hot. She set it down with a disappointed frown. "My door will always be open to you. To talk, or for anything else. And if one day you wish to return to your family, I will vouch for the veracity of your claim. We all will."

Arathiel nodded, slow and solemn. "It means a lot to me, milady."

More than the offer, her willingness to help without prying warmed his heart. He clung to it, gathering the courage to ask his most painful question yet—the one he needed answered, even though he feared the knowledge it would bring.

"Milady, if you heard of what happened to my sister ..."

Lindi was dead, of course. She was human, a century had passed, and she had been deathly sick when he'd left. Widespread tales of a magical well that could cure all ailments had reached him even as he despaired of seeing her recover. Her illness had been eating her body fat away and killing her lungs, and no healer, priest, or mage in the city could help. Lindi hadn't wanted him to go, but he had been too stubborn to listen.

"Healers eased her pain. She died within a year of your departure. I'm sorry, I don't know a lot. Lady Brasten will."

Arathiel thanked her in a whisper—he couldn't manage more at the moment. He'd started grieving as soon as he'd learned how much time had passed while he was imprisoned in the Well, yet he didn't think he'd ever stop. He should have been by her side. That had been his place. Home with Lindi. Now she was gone, and he didn't know what to do.

Camilla shifted the topic to the city's politics, allowing Arathiel to both wrangle his grief in silence and catch up with the most important changes. It amazed him how few true transformations the city had undergone. Names had switched, certainly, but everything else remained similar. House Allastam had grown enough to rival House Lorn's power, House Balthazar's wealth had risen like a shooting star—it was expected to burn out just as fast, leaving behind nothing but vines of gold crawling across an empty tower—and Arathiel's family had managed to carve out for themselves a monopoly over alchemical components and rare magic items. Trades changed, power shifted from one family to another, but in the end Isandor was mostly the same: bickering lords fighting over the Golden Table's limited seats, flaunting their wealth and letting as little trickle down as possible. The Myrians were new. They had stepped into the game like any up-and-coming House, but the power of an empire backed them up. Camilla detailed how they'd wormed their way into major Houses' finances, leaving a bloody trail whenever they deemed it necessary. Their influence reached everywhere, yet they didn't even sit at the Golden Table, and the fear in the old lady's voice was unmistakable. She worried about her family.

By the time they emptied their teacups, the sunlight outside had dimmed. Dark clouds still hung in the sky, promising rain, but nothing had fallen yet. Camilla finished the tale of Lady Allastam's gruesome murder a decade ago and the feud between House Allastam and House Freitz that had followed. The bad news far outweighed the good, and she heaved out a sigh.

"Often I feel as if there is little this old lady can do about anything important. It's a balm on my weary heart to see you alive, even if my mind has trouble believing it still. I must return to the tower, but we should talk again. Maybe with me doing less of it, and you more?"

Arathiel laughed. As their conversation had stretched on, he had grown more and more comfortable. He'd dared to ask questions, make a few jokes, connect events to others that had happened while he was still in Isandor. It wasn't much, but it seemed easier to be himself around Camilla now.

"Most certainly. You are too hard on yourself, milady. A long conversation with a kind lady was exactly what I needed today."

She thanked him with a small laugh, then stood up, using the table for support. Lady Camilla wished him a good evening before leaving the tea house. Arathiel watched her go, a strange daze settling into his mind. He hadn't planned on meeting anyone he knew when he'd awoken this morning, but it was pleasing. The kind of pleasing that spread all the way to his fingertips and made him smile despite everything else.

CHAPTER SEVEN

JILSSAN leaned on the balcony next to Master Avenazar, keeping a careful eye on Isra practising spells and on the dark grey sky above. How long before the rain broke out? Dead leaves covered the small grassy area, taken from their branches by the night's howling winds, and humidity thickened the air. She loved how autumn's colours shifted from vivid green to bright yellows and oranges, but the rotting brown that always followed killed her enthusiasm. Nothing escaped the transition from living to dead, not even peoples' moods. Or most peoples' moods, anyway.

Avenazar must have had an excellent time yesterday. He had an extra skip to his steps and unlike most days, it didn't bother him to be unable to lean on the tall railing without looking ridiculous. He usually demanded they walk to another spot that didn't underscore his height. Not today, however. If Jilssan was to venture a guess, this abnormal pleasantness tied into the long screaming session he'd inflicted upon his apprentice the previous afternoon.

At least hers had escaped. Isra had taken a ridiculous and unnecessary risk, and Jilssan worried that despite her admonition to be warier of Avenazar, the teenage girl might pull off such a dangerous stunt again. Master Avenazar was staring at her now, examining her as Isra transformed a carrot into an apple.

"I heard you haven't punished your apprentice yet," he said.

His casual tone gave her goosebumps. Careful, Jilssan, she told herself. If she messed this up, Isra might be next on his list. Or her, even. In theory, Avenazar shouldn't be involved at all in Isra's education, and unless Jilssan betrayed the Myrian Empire, he had no right to attack her either, but they lived a long way from home. In the two years since their arrival in Isandor, Avenazar had demonstrated his love for retribution, his disdain for rules, and his unwillingness to let any slight slide. Jilssan hadn't thrived in Myria's nasty political environment by provoking dangerous and volatile men. She gave a noncommittal shrug.

"What for?" she asked.

"Don't play this game with me. I saw her fly away yesterday. She was in Isandor with Nevian."

Jilssan kept her gaze on the thin girl now planting her apple into the ground. Isra focused on the fruit, palms on the packed dirt. Years of practice had attuned Jilssan to magical currents, and she followed their movement as they gathered around her apprentice. Isra always struggled with this part, and the swirl of magic deviated from the norm, bumpy instead of smooth. She eventually managed to sprout a tiny tree from the ground, right where the apple had been. Jilssan suspected she'd have no trouble casting the spell if she put her heart to it, but Isra didn't care about basic transmutations. If she could ignore Jilssan's assignments, she'd try to skip over them and specialize in shapeshifting right away.

"I never forbade her to visit the city," she said. "Once she finishes her daily tasks, Isra is free to do as she will."

Which shouldn't have included pushing Nevian to go against Avenazar's orders. Every now and then, Isra got those terrible ideas she couldn't resist. Without her father's reputation as one of the best transmuters in Myria, she would've paid long ago for her recklessness. How could it last, however? Avenazar's good mood was ephemeral at best, and Master Enezi couldn't protect his daughter from so far away.

"She wasted my apprentice's time," he said. "Ruined his important character-building task."

Jilssan called upon every ounce of her willpower not to roll her eyes. Forcing Nevian to clean the floor with the minuscule brush she'd downsized for him might amuse Avenazar, but it held no training value. Master Avenazar enjoyed keeping up the front, however, and why would she contradict him? It would only anger him. She remained silent in the hope he would leave it at that—a naive impulse.

"Oh yes, she's been a naughty girl," he said.

A shiver ran up her spine and stuck in her throat. She dared to glance at him, and her grip tightened on the railing when she saw how he detailed her body, his gaze trailing down the small of Isra's back. Jilssan imagined his hand crawling up the girl's leg, under the apprentice dress, and she fought to keep herself calm. Did he really think he could get away with that? Myria was far, but if news reached Master Enezi ... Yet as long as Isra's father didn't learn of it, Avenazar could do whatever he wanted. No one here possessed the influence or raw power to stop him.

And right now, what he wanted to do ... was Isra. One more way to assert his control and dominance over the Enclave. Jilssan swallowed hard. She couldn't let that happen. No way—some prices were too high.

"I'll remind Master Enezi's daughter not to interfere with others' schedules."

She hoped the name-dropping would kill his desire. Avenazar turned to her with an excited cackle, the lustful spark never vanishing from his eyes.

"Oh no, allow me! As an important future member of our community, I feel I must be involved in her education. Besides, I'm curious about why she wanted Nevian to come. Perhaps they have a little something going, you know?"

"Doubtful."

She'd once found Isra kissing a servant girl, most of their clothes unbuttoned or otherwise loosened. On the one hand, it always comforted Jilssan to discover she wasn't the only one who preferred women. On the other, Jilssan had a lot of experience with what happened to same-sex partners in Myria. She'd made Isra's mistake of being caught with another girl when she was young. Her lover had been executed for debauchery—she was Isbari, and thus beyond any forgiveness to most Myrians—while Jilssan was forced to swear she would not kiss a woman again. At least Jilssan excelled at vows she didn't intend to respect. They never caught her after that day, and her occasional interest in men helped alleviate suspicions. Bisexuality had its advantages.

Isra liked girls, though, and girls only. It would be harder to hide, and Jilssan knew better than to suggest Isra should find a nice boy for cover-up purposes. The teenager did what she wanted, how she wanted, and never bothered with what needed to be done.

Unlike Jilssan, who'd learned the hard way that what needed to be done should always come first, no matter how distasteful. Today it meant keeping Isra out of Avenazar's grubby hands. Master Enezi had entrusted his daughter to her. If anything happened, she would be blamed, and she needed his approval if she hoped to gain influence in Myria. Not to mention the very thought of Avenazar touching her apprentice—or any young girl, especially one who disliked men— made her stomach churn.

She considered drawing attention to herself. Though petite and flat, Jilssan had mastered the art of perceived cleavage and outfits tailored to amplify every curve. Between those, short skirts, and skillful innuendos, it wouldn't be the first time she led a man to bed for political reasons. Avenazar, however … She feared once she started, he wouldn't allow her to break it off. Besides, as good a liar as Jilssan was, this particular ploy might be beyond her. A last resort, she decided. Better her than Isra, but she didn't have to choose yet.

"Nevian has never shown interest in anything but his studies. You're lucky to have such a dedicated apprentice." Avenazar snorted.

Everyone knew he wanted Nevian to fail. The poor boy would always be Master Sauria's apprentice to him—a target for his continued revenge against the wizard who'd dared to insult him. He'd killed her, and now Nevian buffered the rest of his anger. He'd already punished him for going to the city, however, so Jilssan needed another distraction. "Don't trouble yourself with Isra. We have a war coming! Our favourite elven lord needs all your attention. Someone has to teach him not to intervene with Nevian's education, or to disrupt our social climb in Isandor, and who better than you?" Avenazar perked up, and his eyes finally left Isra to focus on Jilssan. She thanked Keroth and all other gods watching for his good mood, then continued with forced enthusiasm. "I can't wait to hear your plans for him!"

Jilssan never thought she'd find Avenazar's mean cackle reassuring, but when he laughed and clapped his hands, she knew she'd diverted his attention. Relieving warmth spread through her. With Avenazar's ire, redirection was often the only solution.

"I figured we should start with a splendid fire," he said.

Fire. He'd involve Varden, then. Not a surprise. High Priest Varden steered clear of Myrian wizards to the best of his ability, focusing on his temple, his duties, and the dozen Isbari slaves on the enclave's premises. He would not want to take part in this, which in turn meant Avenazar would use every opportunity to shove him in the middle of it. Which was his right as designated leader of their mission. Varden could not refuse.

Before she could reply, Jilssan noticed Isra had stopped spells that transformed objects and started those which reshaped her body. Of course. She never wasted an opportunity to forego basic training, even though specialization shouldn't be on her mind so soon. Isra's hands grew into large claws, and she gave a playful swipe in the air.

"Isra!" Jilssan called. "I said no shapeshifting spells today!"

Isra turned to her with a pout. Her hands returned to their normal appearance: pale and delicate, with dark brown painted nails. "I don't care about the other ones!"

"Why not? They are versatile. Useful."

"Maybe they are, but they don't make me look fantastic! I prefer spells that let me be whoever I want."

Want. As always, she did what she wanted, not what needed to be done. And now she was drawing Avenazar's attention back to herself. Jilssan withheld a curse. "I fear I must go and talk some sense into the girl," she said, "but we should continue this discussion over a glass of wine. Especially the part about a beautiful brazier."

She apologized in silence to Varden. Focusing Avenazar's attention on him didn't please her. She'd rather have Varden's good will. In two years of subtle hints, however, Keroth's High Priest had never returned her clear interest in him. She wished he did. Who could resist his haunted, solemn stare? Or the righteous anger boiling inside, trapped by circumstances—raw power he could not unleash without dooming himself. When it came to men, Varden was the stuff she dreamed of. Instead of him, she'd get to spend the evening with Avenazar and dodge his potential desires.

"A fine plan," he said. "I'll expect you at my quarters later, Master Jilssan."

After a curt nod, she hurried down the nearby stairs and into the courtyard. Better not to prolong her time in Avenazar's company. Tonight would bring too much of him already. Once again, she would have to endure the needed before she got what she wanted. But to protect Isra from Avenazar's lust, it would be worth every minute of painful, dangerous conversation.

Chapter Eight

HASRYAN'S last assassination had been months ago, but he hadn't lost his touch. He wiped the blood of his latest victim from his dagger, satisfied by this simple truth: he was a killer. The best of Isandor. He needed to be—what else would Hasryan have to offer? Brune trusted him for his skills as an assassin, first and foremost. This city didn't house a lot of folks who needed killing—it wasn't really the way of Isandor, not like Nal-Gresh—but Hasryan wanted to be prepared. If someone crossed Brune, they would have to deal with him. Or, more specifically, deal with his trusty dagger.

Hasryan lifted his weapon to admire the beautiful patterns and wave-like curves of its blade. A small spark of electricity ran along its edge, crackling, only to die at the tip. A gift from Brune, ten years ago, as a seal of their new partnership. "As a reminder of what we owe each other. Always carry it, even if hidden," she'd said. "You can throw it as much as you want, and it will always return to your hand. Just keep it close. One day, having it with you will be a matter of life and death."

He had been a teenager then. Sixteen years old, shunned because of his dark elven blood, all based on some over-the-top stories about their ancestors Hasryan would bet had been invented from scraps. He'd entertained sneaking into the dark elves' protected lands once, to discover how many of the horror tales were lies. Too much travelling. Hasryan thrived—if any part of his life could be called that—in cities and dark alleys. Even as a teenager, he excelled at assassinations. Brune had noticed. She'd trusted him with difficult jobs. When the time had come to build her own mercenary empire, Hasryan chose to be *her* best, and followed her to Isandor.

A decade later, everyone in the city's underlife dreaded the waved-blade assassin. Rumours said he was half-shadow, emerging from the night itself—probably born from his jet-black skin. In his line of work, people's irrational fear of dark elves helped. Hasryan just wished it didn't make the rest of his life suck so much.

He sneaked out of the building where he'd cornered the now-dead merchant, then climbed down a few flights of stairs. Low and heavy clouds had hung in the sky all day, and he expected rain to imprison everyone inside for the evening. In the Lower City, the bridges lacked railings. Water or snow turned them into slippery traps, and most citizens without urgent business stayed safely home.

For Hasryan, this often meant a perfect occasion to move around unnoticed as he accomplished one shady contract or another.

Tonight, however, he had a more mundane activity in mind: a game of cards with the two precious friends he'd managed to make. Way more stressful than sneaking into an inhabited building during the day, locating his target, and slitting his throat before anyone noticed him. Not to mention, Cal wanted to invite a new player today. Worse, he wanted Hasryan to do it.

As he headed toward Larryn's Shelter, Hasryan tried to find comfort in Arathiel's own strangeness. He'd arrived drenched despite the cold weather and with a cut on his arm he seemed to forget, then he'd dumped every coin he had left on the table, asking for a room. After the first night, Hasryan had only seen him once. Larryn said he came out for dinner but otherwise hid away. No wonder. Hasryan had caught the wary looks thrown his way by the other patrons. They didn't make for pleasant meals. He would know; he'd received the same treatment at first.

Sympathy pushed Hasryan to give Arathiel a chance, but would he return the favour?

The first drop of rain fell as Hasryan reached the Shelter. Larryn owned the entire building, along with a floor in one of the two towers. Every evening, he handed out free meals to Isandor's homeless folk, and when night came, they cleared the tables so people could sleep on the ground. The chimney provided heat, even when cold autumn wind slipped through the crack in the door.

Hasryan had never questioned where Larryn—a street rat himself—had found the money to keep such a place alive. He had strong suspicions but didn't care to confirm them. It didn't matter how, only that at the very bottom of Isandor, where the streets stank of sweat and refuse, a small refuge existed where one could eat, drink, and sleep in warmth. One built by the best cook, a young talent unknown to the lordly nobles up in their pristine towers, who served delicious meals to everyone. No questions asked.

When Hasryan had first visited two years ago, he'd expected the rumours to be lies and exaggerations. 'Everyone' never included dark elves. Larryn and Cal had proved him wrong over and over, and they had been playing cards together for more than a year now. Hasryan worried about upsetting this delicate balance with another participant, but the prospect of adding a third friend to his limited roster excited him. How impossible even one friend had seemed three years ago! He'd only trusted Brune before, and that was a professional relationship.

Inside the Shelter, the aroma of rich cream sauce and apples greeted Hasryan. Whatever Larryn cooked, its scent drifted out, filling the common room and welcoming patrons in. The smell of acceptance—a little different every day, yet always warm and comforting. It didn't keep a lump of stress from forming in Hasryan's throat as he crossed the open area, snaking between tables toward the side corridor and private rooms. He stopped in front of door number six, where he knew Arathiel stayed, his knuckles more ready than his heart.

It would be okay. He'd dealt with rejection before. He could do it again.

Hasryan rapped the door with his knuckles three times. A surprised cry from inside followed, then the sound of a body collapsing to the wooden floor. He quirked his eyebrows, wondering what their mysterious newcomer was up to in there.

"Are you all right?" he called.

A brief silence preceded footsteps coming toward the door. Arathiel opened up, and as soon as his eyes rested on Hasryan, he frowned. Shameful and bitter heat rose in Hasryan's cheeks, and his tone turned sharp.

"Don't break anything. Larryn won't like it."

"I'm sorry, no. I haven't damaged the room. Yet." Arathiel paid less attention to Hasryan than to his own hands and arms. As if he checked for wounds? After a moment, he looked back at Hasryan again. "Is something wrong? We've never been introduced."

"The name's Hasryan." He leaned in the doorway and offered his best smile. "I'm a friend of Cal—y'know, the halfling who served you on your first night here? Small, overweight, laughs easily?"

Arathiel relaxed at the mention of Cal, then stepped aside to let Hasryan into the room, smiling. "I hadn't met anyone so welcoming in a long time."

"Don't hold it against him," Hasryan said with a chuckle. "He's always on the lookout for new players for our card games. Apparently you're his next target."

"Target."

Strong distaste tainted Arathiel's voice as he repeated the word. He pinched his lips together, and Hasryan regretted bringing the topic up this way. Too late now. An awkward silence stretched between them, and he sought something to restart the conversation. As Hasryan's gaze flicked around the room, he noticed a trail of blood on the ground. Footsteps, going from the bed's foot to the door, and then a few feet back again … to Arathiel.

"Are you sure you're not hurt?" Hasryan asked.

"Yes, thank you. I'm afraid you will need to find another player. I'm not interested in being the target."

Hasryan recognized the strange sadness in his voice immediately. Resignation. The powerful disappointment after expecting better, only to receive the same frustrating treatment as ever. Hasryan recalled his nervousness as he was about to knock, his bitterness when Arathiel had frowned. He'd interpreted it as an adverse reaction to his race, but just this once, he might have been wrong. Arathiel also lived with rejection on a daily basis. He must have been worried, and now Hasryan was confirming his fears. No wonder he didn't want to be a target.

"Look, I won't lie to you. Cal is a professional gossiper, and you caught his eye. But he didn't invite you just so he could ask questions, and if you tell him to back off, he will. I know him. This is his 'subtle' way of making sure you're all right and have a friend to talk to if things are bad on your end. I'll admit, I can't help but share his worry now." Hasryan's natural smirk slowly came back, and he added with a shrug, "After all, your foot is bleeding quite a bit on the floor, and that's twice you tell me you're fine."

Arathiel's eyes shot down, then widened. He mouthed a swear as he noticed the trail of blood around his room, pressed his lips together, and stood there, tense and ready to bolt, refusing to look back toward Hasryan. It reminded him of his many victims, when they finally understood they were about to die.

"I … couldn't feel it," he said.

Hasryan's eyebrows shot up. "Sure. As I said, I'm not going to ask. You ought to take care of it, though."

"Yes."

The words had escaped his lips reluctantly, and Arathiel sat on the bed's edge before bringing his foot over his leg. He had a fair-sized cut on his heel and clacked his tongue upon seeing it. Arathiel stretched to open his bedside table and removed a first aid kit and a handheld mirror from it. Hasryan wondered where he'd gotten the latter. The glass was clean, shiningly new. Their guest had more money than he'd let on.

Arathiel wiped most of the blood from the wound before shoving strong alcohol on a cloth to disinfect it. He didn't flinch as the liquid seeped into his cut, didn't really seem to notice it at all. Hasryan just stared, amazed at how stoic he was. Then he saw what was under the blood. Dozens of scars crisscrossed Arathiel's dark foot in a tight net of old cuts and scratches. Every inch had a handful of paler lines, connecting with one another. Hasryan's determination not to ask questions vanished as his mind tried to wrap around the sight.

"How the heck did you get all that? Walked a whole week in a deep forest without shoes on?"

"More like a month," Arathiel said.

His voice was soft and serious. Hasryan ran a hand through his hair, unable to imagine. He'd had his share of painful experiences and his own network of scars to prove it, but Arathiel hinted at a slow, daily attrition. A little more pain each day. Renewed stinging with every step. What was the story behind that? How had he been forced to walk for so long without shoes? His gaze went to the trail of blood, and another question surfaced.

"Did you feel it? The pain, I mean. Did you feel it back then?"

Arathiel stopped halfway through wrapping his bandage. A long pause followed, both of them holding their breath. Hasryan already had his answer; Arathiel's hesitation had betrayed him. Would he dare to admit it, however? To trust Hasryan with that information?

"No." Arathiel finished his bandage and tightened it. He straightened up, set his foot on the ground, and caught Hasryan's gaze. A hundred different things seemed to dance in his dark eyes. Thoughts he silenced, kept to himself, too scared to share. Too scarred to share, perhaps. How many secrets did Hasryan have? Reading the guarded, painful hesitation in Arathiel's expression wasn't hard. He'd lived the same whenever a stranger came too close. "I'm not a bizarre puzzle for Cal and you to unravel."

Hasryan smacked a smile on his face—the kind he used when people were insulting, or when a discussion became too awkward and personal. He'd promised Arathiel he wouldn't ask questions and refused to pry any further, curious or not. "Of course not. You're nothing but our future card partner! Ready to go?"

Their strange guest laughed, which stole all the tension from his shoulders. With a dramatic sigh, he gave in. "You got me. I'll make sure I have no other injuries, then head for the common room."

Arathiel picked up his mirror again and used it to check the back of his leg—a clear sign the conversation was over. Hasryan lingered, captivated by the process and the questions whirling in his mind. What a weird fellow. Hasryan liked that about him, he decided. Cal's trust hadn't been misplaced—it never was, even though Cal rarely expressed doubts about anyone's character. The kind of luck only a priest of Ren would have.

After wishing Arathiel a fun time with his inspection, Hasryan slipped out, musing on their short interaction. He'd expected the worst, and this peaceful chat left him light-headed.

Perhaps a third friend wasn't out of the question after all.

❧

"COME on, Larryn! There'll always be another patron to serve. Leave the barrel out and sit your ass at our table."

Arathiel's eyebrows shot up at Cal's assertive tone. He sat across from the halfling, waiting for the card game Hasryan had recruited him for, and clearly one did not mess with Cal's playing time. Arathiel pinched his lips, slightly intimidated by the energy Cal put into calling Larryn until Hasryan laughed.

"Yeah, Larryn. Cal just can't wait to win all your money! You have to come."

Larryn had been going around the Shelter, filling mugs and bringing warm meals to everyone, because "he didn't want anyone to miss out while he was busy." What should've taken a handful of minutes had been going on for half an hour.

"Is it always like this?" Arathiel asked.

"Every time we play in the Shelter, yes," Hasryan answered. "He can't help himself. Let me fix it."

Hasryan pushed his chair back and left their table. He split through the crowd, lined a dozen mugs on the counter, filled them to the brim, then headed for Larryn. "Look at this awesome reserve of alcohol!" He gestured at the mugs with a smirk. "You don't even charge for them, mate. Now come and meet our new player."

Larryn grimacedand rolled his eyes but followed Hasryan to the table. He sat with all the dignity he could muster. "Sorry about that," he said. "Arathiel, isn't it? Can I get you anything to eat before we start?"

"No!" Hasryan and Cal exclaimed at once.

Arathiel laughed. Their back-and-forth eased his stress, and he leaned into his chair. "I think I'll be okay. If I order anything, these two will kill me."

"Don't let it stop you." Larryn's tone stayed nonchalant, as if dying was nothing to worry about. "I'm great with food, in case you haven't noticed."

Arathiel frowned. Was Larryn fishing for compliments? Should he give one? He glanced at Hasryan and Cal, but their face offered no clue. "I ... heard a lot about it, yes."

"But you ate here, didn't you?" Cal's voice contained actual concern. Enough to make Arathiel squirm. What did they want to hear?

"Yes?" A heavy silence settled over the group. They stared in horror at his lack of enthusiasm. Arathiel cleared his throat. "Let's play?"

"No, no," Cal said, leaning forward and raising a hand to stop everyone. "What's wrong? Don't you love Larryn's food?"

This was exactly why he hadn't wanted to come. He couldn't taste it, and he'd missed his chance to outright lie and pretend he found it delicious. Arathiel gritted his teeth under their insistent stares, wondering at his options. Would Larryn later give him problems if he walked out now? Would their warm welcome vanish the moment he refused to answer? Maybe they didn't want to play cards with him, only with the freak. As he struggled to get coherent words past the lump in his throat, Hasryan jumped to the rescue.

"You'll have to live with the mystery, Cal," he said. "Maybe we found the one man who doesn't, or maybe it's something else. One thing's sure, however: Arathiel is here to play, not answer your endless personal questions."

At first, Cal pouted. He didn't protest, but instead fixed clear blue eyes on Arathiel. Studied him. Anxiety swirled at the bottom of Arathiel's stomach. Would it be enough? Would the otherwise kind halfling let him be, as Hasryan had promised? Could Arathiel ever feel at ease with the group? Then Cal smiled, his expression full of compassion, and relief pushed Arathiel's stress away.

"I get it," Cal said. "S'alright. Everyone has a topic they don't want discussed. I'm sorry for pushing it." He grabbed the deck of cards and grinned with a strange ferocity. "Let's play."

And play they did. One game after another, with everyone's meagre funds on the table. Hasryan had provided Arathiel with some coin, and as card draws went, that pile grew quickly. Arathiel wouldn't have given it any thoughts, if not for Larryn's and Hasryan's continuous exclamation whenever Cal lost.

"Are you sick, my friend?"

"Has Ren found a new favourite?"

"This is how we know the end is coming."

They teased, and Cal laughed it off with good grace. "Winning," he said in the solemn tone of someone older and wiser than he could be, "is not always about the money." His eyes glinted with pleasure. He glanced at Arathiel, then chuckled. "I'm having fun, am I not?"

In truth, so was Arathiel. After the initial questions about Larryn's cooking, they let him be. No one asked why he struggled to pass the cards, or why he held them so tightly he'd folded one. They allowed him to play and observe, saying as little as he desired, and listening in to his heart's content. The banter never stopped between the three friends. One moment they mocked Larryn's short temper, the other they poked fun at Hasryan's smirk—a sure-fire way to know he was bluffing, apparently. Lindi would have loved them. His sister had mixed into groups with amazing ease, adding to the banter as if she'd always been part of it. Arathiel preferred to take it slowly. His pile of coins continued to grow until the others had almost nothing left to play with. He stared at it, ill at ease.

"I wouldn't know what to do with all of this," he said. He didn't need it, not when the Shelter provided his bed and meals.

"Keep a fraction, and return the rest to the Shelter's funds," Hasryan suggested. "It's what we all do."

"Oh! That's a great idea." He grinned, slid a few coins off the table, and pushed the rest of the pile toward Larryn. "Here you go."

Larryn retrieved a pouch and stored them inside, one by one. "Isandor's Lower City inhabitants thank you. No one's ever interested in donating."

Arathiel tilted his head to the side. No one? "How do you even stay afloat, then?"

Heavy silence blanketed the group, and Larryn's expression darkened at his question. He finished storing the coins. "Another mystery we won't solve tonight."

No need to tell him twice. They'd allowed Arathiel to get away without explaining he couldn't taste Larryn's meals, and he would return them the favour. He'd never liked prying in others' business anyway. "If you need more funds, perhaps we ought to play somewhere else. You wouldn't have to watch over other patrons, and we might draw unsuspecting flies into our trap. Clean their pockets and bring them down here."

Larryn laughed, but his voice carried no mirth. "Not sure I want to endure rich assholes, even for the sake of retrieving their ill-earned gold."

"Let's play in the Middle City, then!" Cal suggested. "I like Arathiel's idea. We should test it out. You know I won't lose. I never do."

"You did tonight." Larryn huffed and pushed his chair on two legs as he thought. After a moment, his gaze sought Hasryan's. "You up for it?"

"Why not?" Hasryan smirked, but after hours of card games with him, Arathiel recognized the bluff right away. Something worried him about this idea—something he'd decided to keep silent. "We might lose an evening, but we'll know if it's a viable option or not."

"Awesome!" Of everyone around the table, Cal was by far the most excited by the prospect of hitting a Middle City tavern. "See, this is why we need new blood. One evening, and Arathiel's already opening new doors."

Larryn and Hasryan acquiesced within a heartbeat, and their immediate support stunned Arathiel. Twenty-four hours ago, Arathiel had known nothing but their names, yet now the three friends welcomed him. They didn't gape at him, or sling one intrusive question after another at him, the way so many had before. They just … chatted, listened to his suggestions, and even agreed with them. Such simple acts, when you stopped to think about it, yet Arathiel had forgotten how good they felt. Meeting Camilla had reminded him his old life hadn't entirely vanished, but this short night with Larryn, Cal, and Hasryan unveiled a completely different possibility: that of building a new life.

CHAPTER NINE

BRANWEN Dathirii leaned on the counter of a stuffy tavern, fingers wrapped around her now-empty mug. She trailed her cousin Garith with her eyes as he moved through the crowd, hailing a hot brunette who'd been dancing alone. Ever gallant, he had offered Branwen first dibs, but she wasn't in a mood to flirt with either boys or girls. It had been four days since Uncle Diel had provoked the Myrians. Word had gotten around the city. Tension had built. Her network of informers all brought the same story: everyone waited to see how Master Avenazar would react. They knew Diel was trying to garner support with important families, knew how ruthless the Myrian leader had proven in the past. No one wanted to get involved. Some had even turned Branwen away without another word. The more people she talked to, the more it became obvious that their greatest challenge would be to rally Isandor behind them. It had been rough, and tomorrow's tour of their allied shopkeepers to discuss protection promised to darken her mood further. Garith's offer to have a drink before the conflict exploded had seemed the perfect idea. A last night out, partying with her favorite cousin before they no longer had time to play.

Except even with two mugs of strong ale in her tiny body, Branwen couldn't lift her spirits. Alcohol made her heady, music filled her ears, and she'd chatted with a fascinating bard from Alloria, but none of it alleviated the weight at the bottom of her stomach. She left her mug on the counter and headed for Garith. He gave her a questioning look, but she ignored it until she was closer. The lady with him was staring, perhaps hoping she'd back off and leave her alone with this charming elf. Branwen touched Garith's arm to get his attention, then dismissed the brunette's concern.

"Cousin, I'm going home," she said. "Enjoy your night. I think I needed silence, not fun."

Branwen knew exactly what she wanted. She stretched on the tip of her toes, pecked Garith's cheek, then made a discreet thumbs-up at the other woman, behind her cousin's back. Her surprised laughter followed Branwen as she exited the tavern.

A freezing drizzle waited outside, and Branwen pulled her coat tighter around her small shoulders. She'd slipped into one of her favorite winter dresses earlier tonight. The heavy fabric kept her warm despite the increasingly chilly weather, and it came with a flowery hat that warded off the rain. A tight golden lace ran along the sleeves and in front of the corset, its design simple but elegant. As much as Branwen loved extravagant gowns with wide and flowing skirts, they were ill-suited to a night in Isandor's taverns. The high cut of this skirt was better. It not only made her seem taller, but also allowed her to flaunt her marvelous leggings, with flowers matching her hat. She ran her fingers over the very soft fabric under her coat, and the tightness in her stomach eased a little.

This was what she needed. Not the loud noise of a tavern, the heavy smoke hanging overhead, or the light-headedness of one drink too many. Branwen wanted to be among her gowns. Perhaps even modify one or two of them.

She hurried back to the Dathirii Tower, slowing only as she reached her quarters and shed the wet hat. Branwen lit every lamp in her room and held a single candle, protected inside a glass lantern. Her walk-in beckoned her. She pushed the large doors open.

More than a hundred outfits awaited her inside. The walk-in was her secret place, her little corner of paradise. On one side, Branwen's dresses—rich and elaborate gowns she could wear at princely balls, to impress nobles and uphold her rank as a Dathirii heir. The further in you walked, however, the simpler the outfits became. Branwen kept clothes better suited for scullery maids than a lady of her rank, as well as dresses of intermediate wealth a passing merchant could wear. Styles varied, reflecting many cultures: a bright orange gown with several layers of skirts from Alloria, a dark grey dress with a high collar from northern Mehr, and even a precious emerald qi'seng with a golden floral pattern after the fashion of the southeastern Phong Peninsula. She'd once pretended to be a traveling merchant obsessed with their culture and wished she had more excuses to wear the delicate one-piece dress.

The other side of the walk-in was filled with masculine outfits—pants and breeches, rich doublets, and hats of all styles and classes. Branwen had learned long ago to pitch her voice lower and bind her otherwise considerable breasts. She could pass for a young man of small stature with ease, which was always more inconspicuous than a woman. Hiding her elven ears to appear human gave her more trouble, but make-up did wonders to round off her features and mask her more angular traits.

Branwen often questioned her usefulness to the family. How could she compare to Garith's head for numbers, Kellian's swordsmanship, Uncle Diel's passionate speeches, or Vellien's mastery of both singing and healing? Even Jaeger, though family through Diel, could organize the entire world inside his head. Everybody knew their role. They knew who they were and how they fit within the Dathirii household while she wasted her life playing dress-up games.

Branwen pressed her lips together and moved through the rows of gowns and outfits. She let her fingers trail along the fabrics, sometimes smooth and soft, sometimes rough and layered with decorations. Every one of these had a history. The worn brown doublet with silver inlays? She'd tricked a noble into believing she was a merchant down on his luck. He'd let her in his office, and she'd flipped through his account books. With the wide-sleeved violet dress she'd attended a summer picnic down the river and charmed a young man into spilling secrets about his family's trades. Eventually, Branwen came to the Myrian merchant outfit, with its white cuffs and large pants. Intricate and rich designs covered every inch of the fabric. She traced it with her finger, remembering her brief but dangerous foray into the Myrian Enclave. She had posed as a merchant speculator who'd been in Isandor for over a year and had given them a handful of tips on the economy—nothing they couldn't have found by themselves. In exchange, she'd spoken with dozens of different people on the enclave's grounds, flirted a little with Master Jilssan, and wandered in the high temple dedicated to Keroth to offer a quick prayer. Her visit had convinced her these people were dangerous. Unpredictable. Master Avenazar gave her chills even today. Upon her return, she'd told Garith they needed to prepare.

She wasn't useless. She was the Dathirii spy, and she couldn't let her doubts get to her. Uncle Diel would need her at her best, starting tomorrow. Branwen gritted her teeth, pushed the Myrian clothes back among the others, then retrieved two gowns she'd bought last week. Every outfit she owned had been modified to fit a small dagger and lockpicking tools, except these.

Tomorrow she didn't need to disguise herself—she'd go as Branwen Dathirii, to warn local merchants and make arrangements—but she wanted to prepare her war outfits. Branwen settled in her work chair, needles in hand, and took a deep breath. Her stomach clenched again. She concentrated on the feel of the fabric under her fingers, the fibres threaded together, woven into a beautiful piece. Soft, with a hint of relief. It helped her stay focused, and she set to work. It was the middle of the night, but Branwen wouldn't sleep. Not tonight, and perhaps not until the rest of her family was safe again.

CHAPTER TEN

"**B**URN the place down."

Master Avenazar's instructions echoed in Varden's mind as he stared at the small tailor shop in front of him. Time for an offensive, according to the wizard. Wasn't it always with him? He'd selected one of the Dathirii's local partners, joking about the difficulty of choosing a first target. Like he would do the dirty work, and not Varden. The High Priest hated the thought of reducing an honest business to cinders. As he contemplated the task ahead, however, Varden understood why this task required his keen and intense control of fire.

The boutique was set on a middle floor of a long tower built entirely of wood. The previous night's cold rain gave a slick sheen to the black and green planks, but the wood would be dry—just waiting to catch fire. Any flames in the tailor's shop risked spreading above and below. If he wanted, Varden could create a brazier that would eat the entire tower. He wondered which Avenazar preferred. Burning a single floor would scare the Dathirii's allies, while destroying several might set the city against them. One was strategic, the other just the right amount of cruel to fit Avenazar's style.

Not that their illustrious Myrian leader would take the blame. Varden held no illusions about Avenazar's defence should things go sour. Between Keroth's priests' bad reputation for arson and the too-common branding of Isbari as savage criminals, Varden made a perfect target. Avenazar had requested he wear his full High Priest regalia to impress the locals ... and to better turn him into a scapegoat. After all, what could one do against an out-of-control, barbarian pyromaniac?

Yet Varden had accepted the mission. No choice there: refusal would be considered treason, and Master Avenazar's punishment terrified him more than anything Isandor could throw at him. Even death.

Jilssan stepped up to his side and glanced at the tower. Unlike him, she wore nothing to identify her as a Myrian. If guards arrived, she'd meld into the crowd, unseen. No one would notice her if he stood in the middle of the inferno, fire erupting from his hands, the burned orange and black outfit designed to mimic flames flapping in hot currents. Jilssan hadn't come to make an impression. She was here to keep an eye on him.

"You always look so sour," she said. "Like you bit into the world's biggest lemon as a kid, and the expression imprinted on your face. Don't you ever smile? You should. I bet it would melt every woman's heart."

Varden had no interest in melting women's hearts, and now that they'd forced him apart from Miles, he wasn't sure he wanted to melt any man's either. Two years had passed, and Varden knew they could never go back, but it was impossible to forget his teenage love. Not after a decade together. He refused to answer Jilssan's taunt and encourage her. Despite his continued polite disinterest in her, she wouldn't leave him alone. The enclave wasn't big, and time made her harder and harder to ignore. Varden stepped away and glared at her.

"We have work," he said.

"This particular task doesn't seem to please you. Strange. Burning things should be right up your alley."

"We're taking away someone's livelihood."

"So? Sometimes people are at the wrong place at the wrong time. Is it our fault if this merchant's ally threatened us?" With a sweet smile, she patted his shoulder. "I never thought you were a sentimentalist, Varden. How does an Isbari climb so high without stomping every competitor on the way?"

"He doesn't."

When it came to surpassing Myrians, however, Varden had no qualms. Why would he regret beating those who'd crushed his people for decades, reducing them to slaves and outlaws, taking their lands and destroying their culture? Isbar had been the first and most violent conquest of the Myrian Empire. They'd drained the narrow Bielal Sea between their countries and marched through while Isbari reeled from the loss. The water had never returned. Myrians called it the Victory Valley, but among Isbari, the vanished sea was known as the Bielal Scar. An ugly mark on the land. A century had passed, yet like the Isbari slaves huddling at night and retelling stories of their homeland, it, too, remembered the glorious life it once had.

Resisting sorrow and despair had become every Isbari's struggle. Varden took pride in Keroth's unwavering favour and the victories that came with it. How often did he have to stand by and watch Isbari get mistreated, though? It gnawed at his soul, this silence, this complicity. Without it, he wouldn't be High Priest. Varden had tried to make up for it and give back to his community, to help. He'd spoken eulogies and ceremonies dedicated to other Isbari in addition to his regular duties. By the time the Myrians had sent him away, all those who could attend did so. They came to him for guidance. But where they perceived a free Isbari who'd achieved something great despite Myrian prejudice, all Varden saw was the trail of those he'd abandoned before and the invisible chains still limiting him. Every morning, he prayed for forgiveness and the strength to do more.

"Well," Jilssan said, "think of it as another competitor to crush. It needs to be done."

True, even if it left a bitter taste on his tongue. Varden murmured a prayer to the Firelord, and Their presence filled him—infinite, warm, and hungry. Tiny flames danced at his fingertips as he strode into the boutique. Two customers browsed through the available gowns while the owner, a bony lady with curly hair, conversed with an elf.

A petite elf, with a slit skirt over comfortable pants and a vest-like top. A large barrette held her golden-brown hair pinned atop her head, decorated by a delicate peony. Varden's attention did not linger on the flower, too caught by the unmistakable brooch on her vest: a silver *D* on a forest-green background. Lady Branwen Dathirii. The family's ears and eyes, and Lord Dathirii's most likely heir. A wealth of knowledge for Avenazar, should he get his hands on her. He'd be inside her head in minutes, tearing through for the desired information. Varden's stomach churned. His gaze met Branwen's as he fought the rising nausea, his instincts screaming at him to stop. Stop. Varden ground his teeth. Branwen Dathirii's eyes widened as he aimed his palm at the ceiling and shot flames up. The powerful wave of heat struck panic in the few customers, and they threw themselves to the ground.

"Everybody out, now!" Varden called.

Nobody argued. Branwen Dathirii helped the tailor up, but as they passed him, Varden grabbed the elf's arm and stopped her.

"Except you."

Branwen wouldn't miss the intense warmth in his palms, even through her sleeve. Fire waiting to be unleashed again. She glared at him. Her free hand edged backwards. A hidden weapon. He didn't have long.

"And let you burn me down with the place?" she asked. "I'm not—"

"Hush." He released her, stepping away to be out of a quick strike's range. The shop owner had stopped at the exit. Despite her panicked breath, she seemed reluctant to abandon Branwen. Varden's mind whirled for a solution to his dilemma. "Is there a back door for her?" He jerked a thumb at the Dathirii, tense and close, one false move from pouncing on him.

The shopkeeper offered a confused frown and silence as an answer. Long seconds passed. Seconds Varden didn't have. Jilssan waited outside the tailor's shop, and any delays might make her suspicious. Large flames erupted from his hands with a puff and climbed up his arms. He let them dance around him, allowed the warmth to calm his frenzied heart. His voice, however, lashed out with resolve.

"Answer!"

"No! No back door. There's no bridge behind, so it's just the front."

Varden cursed his luck. No one would have known if she'd sneaked out. What now? Sweat ran down his forehead, and the growing fire wasn't the cause. Avenazar wouldn't forgive him if he let such a valuable source of information escape. He would finally inflict on Varden what he had reserved for Nevian so far. But if he brought back Branwen, she might get even worse.

Do what needs to be done, Jilssan would say. Another competitor crushed. Just one more sacrifice.

One too many.

"No one can know she was here," he told the shopkeeper. "No one. Or she's dead—or worse."

A small lie. If the truth spread, they were *both* dead, or worse. But Varden would reduce her shop to cinders. Why would she care about him?

"And … I'm sorry. For all this. Now get out."

His tone hardened and he shot a beam of flames next to her. With a startled cry she scrambled outside, where Jilssan would be waiting to deliver Avenazar's message. She could have followed inside, adding words to the fire, but Varden knew how smoke affected her lungs and turned her breathing into a wheeze. Varden turned to Branwen. He noted her tense shoulders and spread feet, to give herself better balance. One wrong word and she'd attack. He let most of the flames disappear and extended his hands, palms open, trying to appear non-threatening. Not an easy task after setting fire to a rack of pretty skirts.

"Listen. Please, listen to me." He didn't like his pleading tone but couldn't help it. Keroth's strength burned in him, pushing to be unleashed at last, and he ached to give in. Scorch everything. The power made him dizzy, and it became hard to concentrate. "Master Jilssan is waiting outside. They will take you prisoner. If I let you leave, she'll know I didn't capture you. We'll both be in trouble."

"What's your point? Should I stay and burn with the rest of the gowns? I love dresses, but not *that* much."

"No, no!" He groaned and ran a hand through his curls. New flames seeped out of his sleeves. When he had both feet in fire, Varden controlled it with ease. He couldn't maintain a conversation and lose himself in the blazing heat, though, and he struggled to focus. The flames burned the very thread of his consciousness, pulling him in. "I can get you out unseen."

"I don't trust you."

"If I wanted you captured, I would have let you leave, to run into Master Jilssan's arms. If I wanted you dead, I'd burn the hand and knife you're hiding, then all of your body. I'm not doing either. Take your chance."

Branwen didn't show any surprise at the mention of her weapon. She studied him from head to toe, as if evaluating his character. It reminded Varden of slave buyers as they judged potential acquisitions, and it left a bitter taste in his mouth.

He couldn't wait for her careful examination to be over, either. Now that everybody had supposedly cleared out, a tame fire would arise Jilssan's suspicions. Varden decided to offer Branwen a more convincing show and gave in to the tingling sensation in his fingertips. Keroth's strength coursed through him, a fiery and reassuring elation.

He evacuated the heat built inside. Large flames barrelled toward the door, then in a blast around the shop. Branwen let out a surprised yelp but crouched back into a readied position right away.

As the gowns began to burn, Varden enveloped himself in a shield of fire. Tendrils of flames shot in every direction from him, running across the floor, licking at the counter and support beams. When they circled around the Dathirii elf, Varden protected her from the heat with a flick of his hand. Raw power crackled inside of him, fuelled by the Firelord's presence—so close, so infinite. His throat was dry. The priest wanted to extend his hand, touch the power, get lost in it. Forget this world with its cold nights and even colder hearts, and forever be embraced by Keroth's warm grace.

"What are you doing?"

Branwen's voice pierced his daze and grounded him to the seared wooden floor. Shaky and exalted, Varden spun to face her.

"Choose. Leave with me or die here."

His tone had become hollow. He could kill her here. Burn her clothes and skin and flesh like he had everything else around. Leave nothing but blackened bones behind. A darker part of him wanted to try, just this once. He reined it back. Branwen raised her flimsy knife, and Varden let flames lick it as a warning, even as he quelled the heat.

"Choose!"

He stepped forward; she stepped back. Smoke rose between them and floated to the ceiling, obscuring the brazier. A wooden beam gave a plaintive crack. They didn't have long.

"Choose," Varden repeated, but this time he pushed the flames back from them.

She swallowed hard. "All right, fire zealot. Tell me what to do."

He didn't. Instead, Varden stalked to her and grabbed her wrist. Before she could wrestle out, the flames drew around them and formed an opaque cocoon. They didn't feel the heat, but an invisible force pulled at their bodies. The crackling fire turned into a blur of orange, red, and yellow. Varden passed through the plane between fires, and everything vanished.

No more smoke. No more roaring inferno.

They stood in his High Priest's quarters in front of the lit fireplace. Varden stared around, dazed, exhausted. Fire-striding drained his strength, and he no longer had the surrounding blaze to steal energy from. Branwen found her bearings faster than him. She smashed her elbow into his nose, then sprung on him and slammed his body to the ground, knocking his breath out. Stars flashed before his eyes, and her dagger's warmed blade pressed against his throat.

"Where are we?"

"My quarters. In the enclave's temple. Don't do this."

Her grip tightened against the front of his robes. Her weapon hand trembled, and the shaking dagger nicked his skin.

"You said—"

"I can't work miracles!" Every one of his muscles wanted to shove her off, but he never doubted Branwen's commitment. If he moved, he'd die. "I can't teleport to any fire. I need to be familiar with it, to have been there. My other option was the great brazier in the middle of our temple. Would you rather appear there?"

"How do I know you're not lying?"

She pressed harder, and a trickle of blood ran down his neck. A pathetic whimper escaped his lips. He didn't want to die. His whole life he'd known a single mistake would be the end, but that didn't mean he was ready. His stomach twisted and clawed up his throat. He had to convince her.

"You don't! By the flames, stop this, you're blowing what little cover we have by putting wounds on me. Nobody gets a dagger cut by starting a fire." Blood rushed to his head, made his own hand shaky. The longer he disappeared, the bigger the risk. "Please, miss. I need to go back. No one comes in here but me. You'll be safe."

Her lips tightened, her glare intensified; Varden's heart sank, dragged down by despair. She didn't believe him. She would slit his throat, then try to sneak out of the Myrian Enclave. Acolytes swarmed the temple at this time of day, and guards patrolled the walls. She'd fail. Maybe death wasn't so bad if that was her plan. Better to stand by Keroth's side than deal with Avenazar. Varden closed his eyes and whispered a short prayer.

The warm metal left his skin.

Branwen withdrew from him, her weapon ready, uncertain. He swallowed a big gulp of air and scrambled up, relief unknotting his stomach.

"Thank you." He shouldn't say that, not with the staggering risks he was taking for her. But she'd spared him, and his mind reeled from the kindness. Varden touched the blood at his neck. Their fates were sealed now. If either of them got caught, the other would pay. "I will return."

Under her silent scrutiny, Varden turned to the fire and set his hands in it. The heat prickled his skin, a telltale sign that his strength would run out soon. As the flames once more enveloped him, he prayed he'd have enough power to control his inferno before it consumed the entire tower.

CHAPTER ELEVEN

T HE fireplace's flames reached out like tendrils and enveloped their priest until he disappeared in a brilliant light. Branwen exhaled. Her fingers clutched the dagger's hilt so tightly they hurt, and her frenzied heart nauseated her. Heat and fear had turned her vest sticky with sweat. One moment, she'd been joking with the nice tailor lady about the latest fashion in sleeves, and the next, this wild fire monster had stormed in. Her skin still prickled from the intense heat inside the shop, and her throat clenched at the memory of the High Priest. He had stood in the middle of that brazier—whips of fire snapping in all directions, a warm current ruffling his curly hair and making his clothes flutter— and in that moment, Branwen had been convinced she was going to die. Too much power in a single man. Too much rage rippling under his golden skin.

Yet he'd brought her here.

She tried to focus on the way Varden Daramond's voice had broken when he'd said 'please', on how he'd apologized to the tailor, on his small whimper as she put a blade to his throat. The blazing cleric terrified her. The man squirming under her dagger? Not so much. Branwen took a deep breath. If he'd wanted her dead, she would be. Which didn't mean his intentions were pure. She needed to keep her wits about her and make sure she would have the upper hand by the time he came back.

Good thing he'd left her alone in his quarters, then.

She rotated slowly, giving the room a quick examination. How foolish of him. Two decades of sniffing around for her family had taught Branwen that everyone had secrets. While Branwen disliked using hidden weaknesses as blackmail, situations like these offered little choice. What other weapons did she have? Sneaking out of the enclave at this hour would be near impossible. She needed to ensure selling her out to Avenazar would be as dangerous to him as to her. She should also find a disguise in case a quick escape became her only solution.

As the beginning of a plan formed in her mind, Branwen's stress diminished. She rubbed her fingers against her skirt, the familiar fabric calming her nerves further. Step one, the disguise. You never knew when someone could open the door. Branwen spotted the closet and hurried over, opening it with unrestrained curiosity. Recreating a uniform required time and study, and she couldn't wear a High Priest's ceremonial robes. No one but this Varden held such a rank. Plus, he was half a foot taller than her, with broad shoulders.

She started by snatching a pair of black pants off the shelves and switched her skirt for them. The bottom trailed on the floor, so Branwen rolled them inward and took a mental note to search for a sewing kit. Then she flicked through the shirts and robes, looking for something that would belong to a fire acolyte without being an official outfit. She hadn't studied the details of their clothing and didn't want to be discovered for a small mistake. It would be easier to bluff that she'd hoped to join their cult. After all, the Firelord was one of the six original deities, and though Their religion mattered less here than in Myria, They were still honoured.

When Branwen spotted a light shirt with little flame designs at the bottom, she knew she had a winner. She snickered as she imagined the High Priest in it. Clichéd official outfits were one thing, but flames on an everyday shirt was kind of endearing. She changed into the shirt, her fear ebbing away. This top would've been loose even for Varden, and it hung around her awkwardly. She found a burnt orange belt and wrapped it around her waist, then pulled the heavy fabric down. It created folds under the line, which amplified the flames in what seemed like an intentional part of the design. The higher half also clung to her skin and revealed some cleavage. One could almost believe she wasn't wearing a man's shirt. Branwen completed the disguise with a threadbare travel cloak, which hid some of the imperfections and had a hood to conceal her ears. Close examination would unmask her, but she hoped never to risk it.

Branwen wished she'd paid more attention to the temple when she had first investigated the Myrian Enclave. Apart from Varden's status as High Priest, she knew little of their organization. They had at least two ordained priests and a bunch of acolytes. According to her discussions with the guards, almost everyone in the enclave had wound up here after causing trouble in Myria. Even their leader, Master Avenazar, had razed a neighbourhood in a fit of petty anger. Nothing reassuring there. She pulled at her shirt, swallowing hard, trying not to think of what he could unleash on her family.

Her emergency disguise finished—at least until she found a sewing kit—Branwen moved to the second part of her plan: gather information on High Priest Varden Daramond. She'd found nothing but surface details on him over the last two years. Her gaze went straight for the desk: a common hiding place, and Varden's already had the marks of a personal space. He had hung portraits of other Isbari above it, all done in charcoal or pencils. Branwen moved closer, amazed at the quality and life in them. Each stroke carried a powerful emotion, and the artist had managed to capture incredible details in black and white. On the old man it was every sun-baked wrinkle, on the pregnant lady it was the waves of her thick hair and the many tears in her worn robe. She extended her hand to touch but pulled it back in time. She didn't want to ruin them.

Branwen snapped herself out of the impressed daze. Artistic considerations weren't a priority. She sifted through the papers on top of the desk and found nothing of real use before starting on the drawers. In the second rested a sewing kit, and with a prayer of thanks to Ren the Chance Master for lending Xir luck, Branwen fixed her disguise. She sewed points to hold the sleeves and pants, then stored the kit back where she'd taken it. At least now it wouldn't fall apart at the worst possible moment.

When she pulled on the last drawer, it remained closed. Locked. Her heartbeat quickened at the excellent sign. Everyone kept the darker things behind a lock. She slid her lockpicks out of her sleeves, crouched down, and slipped them inside the keyhole. The poor mechanism was no match for her skills, and before long the *click-click* of her tools became the deeper sound of a latch giving in. Branwen held back a squeal and opened the drawer.

She found four thick sketchbooks and a box with charcoals. Branwen's breath caught in her throat. She glanced at the portraits on the wall. Had he drawn them? Were those the people Varden Daramond had left behind? She knew his church had sent him here. Branwen hadn't found ties to anyone in Myria, though—not that she could easily look into it from so far away. She brushed the cover of a sketchbook, then cracked it open. Her fingers shook a little. Invading a merchant's privacy never bothered her, but with art it felt wrong.

More portraits waited inside. Countless drawings, all of Isbari folks. Many had chains at their feet, others seemed too poor to afford clean clothes. They were old and young, men and women, skinny and fat. All had dark hair and tanned skin, often with broad shoulders and prominent noses. Sometimes, defiant pride shone in their eyes and their shoulders were squared. Most, however, stooped and didn't look in the artist's direction. Branwen's throat became tighter as she flipped through. Small dates were scribbled at the bottom—these were more than two years old, from a time when Varden had still been in Myria. She closed the sketchbook, shaken by the defeated sadness that permeated so many of the portraits.

The next was easier to browse through. Varden apparently

enjoyed sitting in front of fire and drawing it, over and over. His lines had more movement here, even she could tell. The third sketchbook was still empty. Branwen expected the same of the fourth and was starting to wonder if the lock had hidden any secrets at all.

Then she opened the last sketchbook to a random page and found herself staring at a quick profile of a naked man. A very hot naked man, with sculpted muscles drawn in precise details. One drawing might have counted as an anatomy study, but Branwen flipped the pages and realized male nudes occupied all of them. The sketches represented someone different every time, and she doubted they were models. Their shapes were too ideal, and she suspected they came out of Varden's imagination more than anything. Until she reached the last section.

He had dedicated a third of the book to a specific man—another priest, judging from the occasional images with clothes. Overweight, with a tuft of short blond hair and always the same shy smile. In the naked drawings, he often turned away from Varden, his legs folded, as if trying to hide what he could. Branwen smacked the sketchbook closed, her palms moist. It was becoming hard to think of the High Priest as an evil pyromaniac, and harder still to feel satisfied about unearthing his private life. She stored the sketchbook back in its place, locked the drawer, and sat staring at it.

This was exactly the kind of information she had needed. Myria did not look kindly upon homosexuality, and as an Isbari, Varden couldn't afford any mistake. The very idea of threatening him with this made her nauseated. She had nothing else, though. Her guts told her to trust him, but she couldn't risk being wrong.

Branwen remained sitting in front of the desk for the longest time, trying to come to terms with a decision, until she heard the doorknob turn.

She jumped to her feet, her dagger finding its way back to her hand as she sprinted for the door. By the time it cracked open, she waited behind it. The moment the High Priest stepped in, Branwen stretched to the tip of her toes, grabbed a handful of his hair, and pulled him down to her level. He didn't resist, letting himself fall to his knees, but when she put the blade back at his throat, he let out a little groan.

"Again?"

His voice mixed exhaustion and amusement. Branwen moved fully behind him and pushed the door closed with her foot. She wasn't sure what she was doing, but she needed to be in control. "Seems fair. You can toast me at any moment."

"No, I can't. I'm drained, and until I've had a full night of sleep in a warm room, I won't be creating the tiniest wisp of flame. Can't we talk face to face? Please, I'm … really tired." His shoulders slumped, which sent a stab through Branwen's heart. "I'm not an enemy. I let you keep your weapon, didn't I?"

"Something tells me you forgot to take it away."

A soft chuckle escaped his lips. Varden yanked his head, and she released his hair. "Perhaps," he admitted.

Branwen withdrew the dagger to give him room to breathe. Her mind screamed that she shouldn't, but her heart remembered the portraits.

"Why burn a well-loved shop while dressed in your full High

Priest uniform? Are you that desperate to have the entire city on your ass? I'd have expected vanity to be a sin in your holy gospel. Like, I don't know … take no pride in thy wealth or appearance, for our pyromaniac clerics will reduce you all to the same ugly, shrivelled, burned pack of meat and bones. Something ridiculous like that."

Maybe if she tested his limits, she could get a better sense of how dangerous he was to her—and a priest's faith was always a touchy topic, right? Except Varden answered with a long and genuine laugh. Branwen watched his shoulders shake with growing unease.

"Now that would be a sight," he said. "Equality through fiery death, huh? We do believe in fire's cleansing properties, but these rites involve protections from the flames, Miss Dathirii."

He put two fingers against her blade and pushed it away. Branwen waited for his next move, holding her weapon so tight her knuckles turned white. Varden had something fascinating she couldn't quite understand, a presence that was slowly getting to her. He had torched an entire shop and brought her to the enemy's heart, but she found herself drawn in, incapable of enforcing the prudence she knew she ought to show. He dusted himself off, then stood to face her. As his gaze took in her new outfit, the corners of his mouth quirked.

"You were busy."

"I unlocked your drawer." The words surged out on their own— guilt at snooping around, and the desire to let him know she was more dangerous than he thought. Branwen gritted her teeth and went all the way. "Nice taste in men."

Varden looked like she'd slapped him. Horror fought with

indignation as he struggled to remain calm. Though he made no flames with his hands, Branwen could feel the burn in his gaze. She swallowed hard.

"I'm not gonna tell, okay? I panicked and thought I might need to blackmail you to stay safe."

"I saved your life."

"You put it in danger to begin with." Not to mention she wasn't safe until she left Myrian grounds. "I just wanted to even the odds. Sorry about the whole privacy invasion."

Branwen could see his anger below the surface, simmering. He inhaled deeply, however, and as he exhaled, the tension in his body relaxed, and his shoulders sagged.

"How about we start over?" He sketched a smile, extended his hand. "I'm Varden—"

"Varden Daramond, High Priest of Keroth, Isbari." Branwen wasn't quite ready to let it all go. She wanted to remind him they were on different sides, but fear jumbled her thoughts, and all the information stumbled out. "Almost thirty, no known children, and until today I would've said no love affair. You're a great artist, and I have a feeling you never wanted to come here. Garith and I, we pegged you as our best chance to find an ally inside the Myrian Enclave because of how they treat Isbari. I always thought we shouldn't bother. You do everything Master Avenazar says. Too scared to disobey."

Varden snatched his hand back, and for a brief moment she noticed the flame within. He straightened, glared down at her, and Branwen had the distinct impression she'd said one word too many.

A bad habit of hers, that. When Varden spoke again, it was in a low, dangerous tone.

"I am not scared, Miss Dathirii, I am *terrified*. An Isbari in Myria has no defence. He walks with his eyes on the ground, praying no Myrian interprets his behaviour as defiance because he knows nothing will protect him or his family. It doesn't matter whether he's a slave, a successful merchant, or a High Priest. Titles are smokescreens, illusions. In the end, if you make one false move, you are an uncouth savage to be disciplined, an object that can be thrown away." His voice had grown louder. "And Master Avenazar? He combines this mentality with incredible fickleness, a cruel sense of humour, and the power to rip your mind into tiny shreds. And one day, I'll make a mistake, and it'll be my turn. It's inevitable. So yes, I'm scared, and yes, I obey."

He tried to capture Branwen's gaze, but she cast her eyes away, too flustered for even the briefest eye contact. These demanded so much out of her, and she already struggled for an appropriate answer, her mouth hanging half-open. There was really none she could give.

"S-Sorry …"

Varden raised a hand to stop her and shook his head. "You're also wrong. I did disobey. Avenazar would have wanted you. I couldn't do that, no matter the risk to myself. I've witnessed his torture before, and unlike Nevian, you would not need to recover. He wouldn't hold back. I could never let him peel off every layer of your mind that way. So you see, we really are in the same boat now. Either of us gets caught and the other goes down."

Varden heaved a sigh and sat at his desk, gripping his knees. His hands shook. The fire crackled. To Branwen, this felt like a second invasion, like witnessing a part of his life—a part of who he was—he could never show in the enclave. She stepped forward and set an awkward hand on his shoulder. He seemed so defeated. Burned out, literally.

"I was wrong about you." There had to be something else she could say. "Uncle Diel will beat him, though. You'll see."

He shrugged her off without answering. The silence stretched as he stilled his breath and calmed his shaking hands. "Winter solstice is in a week, and Keroth's followers will hold the Long Night's Watch. From sunset to sunrise, everyone will be in the main hall around the sacred brazier where I lead the ceremony. A growing number of wizards and soldiers attend the ritual, and it will be your best chance to slip out undetected. Until then, you'll have to remain here. I'll tell you what I know. Is that good enough for you?"

"I'll take all you can give me." What choice did she have? It would be wise to learn what she could while in the enclave. Besides, she had to admit she was fascinated by the Isbari priest. She wanted to know what his life had been like, who the chubby boyfriend was, how he'd wound up in Isandor. All in good time. She needed to settle one last detail first. "Can you get a message out? Send an acolyte into the city? I need to tell my uncle I'm safe."

Varden eyed her, then shook his head. "I don't trust anyone for this, and now that I've burned that shop, I won't risk going into the city. Anyone could spot me, and out of the enclave, I'm not protected by Myrian laws. I wouldn't even be surprised if they sought to arrest me. Your family will have to deal with its fears."

His answer dropped a weight in her stomach, but Branwen didn't protest. He'd done a lot for her already. "Understood."

"Good." Varden lumbered to his feet, groaning like an old man. It reminded Branwen of how her cousin Vellien had once slept for an entire day after they'd healed a dying man. Clearly channelling a god demanded tremendous energy. "I must rest. You can read on Myria, if you want. Don't touch my sketchbooks again."

Varden gestured to the half-empty bookshelf against a wall, then trudged to the other section of his quarters. He disappeared behind the curtain serving as a cut-off between them, not even waiting for an answer. She listened to him change and collapse to his bed, too shaken to move. A week. Her family would be worried to death.

Branwen turned to the handful of titles available and took one at random. You never knew what could help later, and at the very least, it would allow her to understand Varden better. She settled down, casting one last glance at the portraits above the desk, then began to read. Yet no matter how hard she tried, her thoughts always returned to Garith and the rest of her family. Her stomach clenched, and Branwen knew the sensation would become a constant companion over the next days. She slid her fingers over the unfamiliar texture of Varden's flame-decorated shirt and prayed she'd make it home alive.

CHAPTER TWELVE

HASRYAN regretted agreeing to this change in their card games' location. It had seemed a perfect idea at first, and they were glad Arathiel had felt integrated enough to propose it. Cal could meet new players and wipe their money pouches clean, and after accepting he'd have to endure their presence, Larryn had suggested an establishment catering to rich merchants and young nobles. That way, they'd acquire some of the wealth hoarded by Upper City folks and bring it down to the Shelter. All went according to plan ... except they'd scheduled this excursion into the Middle City on the rare night Arathiel couldn't. Perhaps they should've waited, taken his absence as an ill omen. Arathiel had played twice with them, adding his calm humour and silent bluffs to their noisier dynamics. As he sat at a smooth table with their worn-out deck of cards, Hasryan missed his presence and questioned the wisdom of their plan.

At least they hadn't chosen the wealthiest establishment. The Skyward Tavern thrived at the frontier between the Middle City and the Upper City, and it linked to a little inn for successful merchants. The floor was clean, the smoke drifting above came from high-class cigars, and nice vines wrapped around the supporting beams. Hasryan counted two exits: the front door and a large window he could climb down from—the tower's rough exterior featured enough handholds, and it hadn't rained today. A comfortable pub with an escape route and better beer than most of the Lower City's taverns. Plus, it was cheap, and they could afford it for one night, especially if Cal lured strangers into playing with them. The halfling's unnatural luck would cover for their expenses.

Their plan contained one problem, however: Hasryan himself. Ever since they stepped inside, people stared at him, sometimes pointing accusing fingers and whispering to one another. All he'd done was walk in, order a beer, and sit down with his friends. Too much for a dark elf, apparently. At least Larryn returned every glare tenfold. He sat on Hasryan's left, his grey eyes scanning the crowd, ready to answer any provocation. His high cheekbones provided him with quite the frightening scowl when he wanted to.

Either Cal was oblivious to the hostile environment, or he didn't let it show. He often acted casual and pleasant, even when angered. Perhaps because he was so small—a full inch under the halfling average certainly encouraged caution about provoking conflict. His friend's chubby fingers played with his cards, blue eyes admiring his hand. Hasryan tried to focus on the game. For once, he had a decent chance to win against one of Ren's priests. Beating Cal would make his day. With a confident smirk, Hasryan set his cards down on the table.

"Four Lorns," he declared.

In Isandor's slums, most cards had been renamed to fit the city's major noble families, and not in the most respectful manner. The lowest numbers were reserved for the biggest Houses, while Kings and Queens had been granted to deities. Using the slang so close to the Upper City was of questionable wisdom, however. Anyone looking over his shoulder would realize the Lorns were, in truth, lowly 2s. A tiny insult could spark a fight if the wrong noble heard it.

Cal chuckled and straightened in his chair. "Oh, I bet you're very proud of that Lorn House."

Hasryan disliked his tone. Cal sucked at bluffing. He didn't need to lie when he played these games: Ren's favour followed him, and somehow he always wound up with the best hand. For the longest time, Larryn and Hasryan had been convinced he cheated, but they both excelled at sleight of hand, and neither had ever caught him. It was all luck. Cheaty luck, but luck nonetheless. Hasryan glared at Cal.

"Don't you dare," he said.

His warning gave Cal a fit of giggles, confirming Hasryan's fears. His friend threw the cards on the table. "Sorry, mate. Got myself a full house of ... who were the 8s? House Serringer?"

"No one we care about, for sure," Larryn said.

He'd folded long ago, so he patted Hasryan's slumped shoulders as Cal raked the money in. It didn't matter who finished with the gold—everything returned to the Shelter, where Cal spent as much time as he did in his own flat. Winning was a matter of pride. One day, Hasryan promised himself, he would beat Cal.

"You really hoped to win against a priest of Ren?" Larryn asked. "Your powers of self-delusion are impressive."

"Why don't you shut your mouth and pass the next draw?" Hasryan answered. "I'm not giving up just yet."

He'd need more beer, though. His pint had remained empty, abandoned by the staff. They avoided him on purpose—yet another reminder of why they should always stay in the Shelter. Hasryan grabbed the mug and was about to stand when a nasal voice hailed them from behind.

"Well, well, well … look at that. Two half-elves and a halfling. They should call you the Halfies Trio. All halfway to being worthwhile."

That brilliant gem of wit emanated from a snide, twenty-something human noble—Drake Allastam, heir to the second most important House in Isandor.

The arrogant asshole had trimmed dark hair, a long straight nose and a pointed chin. He kept his hands on his hips and his chest puffed out, putting forward his family's crest for all to see. This little shithead had harassed Larryn for as long as Hasryan had known him. Whenever they ventured out of the Lower City and Drake caught wind of it, he followed them around, throwing uninspired insults and trying to provoke Larryn into a fight—which worked more often than not. The noble had his usual goons just a step behind, rippling muscles waiting to be put to good use. Between the glares of other patrons and his empty mug, Hasryan had no patience left to entertain him.

"You're right, O glorious Drake. How great would I become without a human half providing me with awful things like a conscience? Perhaps I should give in to my bloodthirsty, scheming impulses more often. Starting ... now?"

Hasryan's answer knocked Drake's smirk down a peg, but the young noble flicked two fingers, and his goons drew closer. Larryn's face had grown an ugly red, and his hands bundled into shaking fists under the table.

"Halflings aren't even half a race," Larryn said. "They're just small. Take your messy insults elsewhere and stop harassing me. Haven't you done enough?"

Drake leaned forward, his voice falling into a low pitch. "After the humiliation you put me through? My mattress still smells! Never. I do what I want." He straightened up and allowed his words to carry to the entire tavern. "But I guess you have a point about your friend. Wouldn't call him small, though, considering his girth."

Hasryan sprung to his feet, his chair falling with a thunk, and grabbed the front of Drake's rich doublet. Alone, he might have resisted the impulse. He knew Larryn, however, and his punch would've been a second behind. No one insulted Cal in front of them. This city didn't have a single person more generous with his time and luck, more open-minded and kind-hearted. Cal might be the luckiest soul to walk these bridges, but he shared every ounce of it. He had gone out of his way to earn Hasryan's friendship, to create a safe group for him, and Hasryan would never forget.

"Shut up."

"What's the problem?" Drake asked. "Don't think your friend can take a blow? He has all the fat he needs to cushion it."

Hasryan twisted his grip on the doublet with one hand, curling the other into a fist. Cal grabbed his arm right away.

"It's okay, Hasryan. Let it go. He's wrong and I'm awesome. I don't care."

Cal might not, but that was only part of the point. This little shit followed Larryn everywhere, mocking him, laughing at his rage. He believed his noble title made him invincible—that because he was Lord Drake Allastam, no one would dare touch him. Everyone knew he'd killed the Shelter's previous owner, even if Larryn never talked about it. Hasryan wanted to teach him a lesson. He inhaled deeply, unclenched his fist. A soft, self-satisfied laugh crossed Drake's lips.

Hasryan grabbed Drake's clothes with both hands again and yanked him close. He smashed his forehead hard into the noble's nose, enjoying the loud cracking sound. Blood gushed out, sprinkling red stains in Hasryan's white hair. His victim stumbled back with an outraged cry and tried to staunch the flow. Hasryan grinned. He could tell Larryn was struggling not to laugh.

"Get him! Call the guards! This is assault!"

The two goons surged forward and forced Hasryan to withdraw. He dodged the hands grabbing at him, but another customer smacked his wooden pint on the back of his head. Pain exploded behind his eyes, and Hasryan fell to his knees with a grunt. Larryn stepped between him and the goons, a small knife at the ready. Cal snatched the half-melted silver coin he kept as a holy symbol from his pocket, but Hasryan motioned for him to stay hidden. The wound didn't warrant healing—it would just turn into a bad headache. Hasryan lumbered to his feet and set his back against Larryn's, drawing out his blade. Not Brune's gift, not here, though it remained well within his reach should he need it. His other hand hovered near throwing daggers, half-hidden under his vest.

Holding his bleeding nose, Drake glared at them. "What a cute couple you make."

Larryn choked down a laugh while Hasryan gave the noble a long look-over. Was that supposed to insult him? They protected each other. Or tried to, at least. An overview of the room convinced Hasryan this fight wouldn't last. A dozen bar patrons circled them, ready to jump into a brawl, equipped with chairs, mugs, and fists. He doubted any would join his side.

"Not sure we've got the best idea here," he muttered, leaning on Larryn's left to make himself heard clearly.

"If I can land a punch on his face, it'll be worth it," Larryn answered.

Hasryan recognized that tone. Once you pushed Larryn past a certain point, he never backed down, no matter the consequences. Better not to waste time arguing. They couldn't take on a whole tavern by themselves, but Larryn was about to try, the rest of the world be damned. Hasryan tightened the grip on his dagger, then smirked. Cal would have to put his meagre healing skills to work after tonight.

"Let me open the way, then."

He flung two daggers at the goons near Drake, then dashed

forward and smacked the flat of his electrified blade against the left one's cheek. Head-on battle had never been Hasryan's forte, but his sudden burst destabilized their opponents. Larryn pounced on Drake with a wide grin.

He punched the noble twice before the crowd was upon them. Hasryan did his best to stay near Larryn and dodge, but he couldn't keep every strike at bay. Clubs connected with his shoulder, a glass was thrown at him from afar, then someone yanked his legs from under him. He fell on broken glass with a groan and tried to roll away. A kick smashed against his temple, and sparks flew before his eyes. Cal's voice called to them through the crowd. It seemed incredibly distant.

The clank of armour interrupted their brutal assault, and alarmed exclamations emerged from patrons. Everyone backed off. Hasryan spat blood on the ground. His split lip bled, he wasn't sure his left leg was still attached to his body, and his fingers clung to his electrified dagger despite being stepped on several times. A few feet away, Larryn held his side, panting. Four city guards surrounded them, swords gleaming in the tavern's light. Drake hurried to two of them.

"Arrest the dark elf. I want to see him pay."

Hasryan tried to scramble up, but they kicked his stomach again. The ground spun as his breath escaped. They grabbed his arms, snatched his dagger away, and lifted him to his feet. As they dragged him toward the exit, Larryn stumbled after them. He was grimacing, fists at the ready. Cal pushed through and caught his wrist to stop him from attacking the fully armoured guards. Hasryan met their gaze, touched by the worry in their eyes.

"It'll be fine. My boss will take care of it," he said.

The Crescent Moon Mercenaries dominated the landscape in the Lower City, and Brune would never have achieved this level of success without Hasryan. Together, they had crushed all competition and unearthed dirt on several influential figures in Isandor's guards, solidifying their position as *the* mercenary organization to hire and protecting themselves against the law. His friends knew that much, even if they'd never learned the details of Hasryan's role in it. Larryn gritted his teeth but nodded. Despite the pain in his muscles, Hasryan did his best to straighten up. He countered Drake's victorious grin with a smirk and winked at the young noble as they walked past him and into the night.

CHAPTER THIRTEEN

FOR the umpteenth time, Larryn yanked his hand back with a hiss. "What even is that shit? It hurts."

"Yeah, well, it'll save you two days of fever. Stop moving."

Cal grabbed his wrist and pulled it closer once more before dabbing the numerous cuts on Larryn's arms with his lemon-based solution. Every time he used this trick, his mind shifted toward Aberah Lake, far to the South, and the less-than-tender care of his mom. She didn't budge if it stung: you'd gotten yourself into trouble, and those were the consequences. A zealot had snatched control of the region at the time, and Cal had been too young to understand why bringing attention to their family was dangerous. But he'd learned, and it had hurt more than lemon ever could. Now all that was left of his parents were a few household tricks and a sadness that climbed like the tide every other month.

"I can't believe you're protesting this, and not the beating you just took. You didn't complain so much when you broke the bones at the base of your wrists to escape shackles!"

Cal had meant to tease, but he regretted it when Larryn's expression darkened. "Sorry, I was too busy thinking about how an asshole noble had just stabbed my father." He sighed, leaning back into his chair. "Can't you just call upon Ren and heal me?"

"Afraid not." Cal reached into his small kit for the bandages. He'd closed most of Larryn's wounds with magic, but Ren's power didn't lie in healing. Xe brought luck. Under Xir guidance, you avoided getting hurt at all, and thus never needed divine fixing. Larryn, on the other hand, still had a sizeable cut in his palm from a glass bottle. "You shouldn't have fought. Maybe it'll teach you."

Larryn straightened up, his attention snapping back to Cal. "He insulted you."

"So? I don't need Hasryan and you to prove you'd fight on my behalf. I know that already." In fact, they were a little too willing to do so. "You realize Drake used me as bait? It's bad enough to be mocked, but when you're the lure to provoke your friends into a brawl, it sucks double time."

"I couldn't let him get away with it."

"You should have!" Cal pulled on the bandages tighter than necessary, then captured Larryn's gaze. He needed him to understand. "I know you think you're helping me, but you're wrong. I asked you and Hasryan to stand down and ignore him, and you didn't listen. You weren't fighting for me. I'm just your excuse to land a few hits on him again.”

Cal tied the fabric in place and examined his handiwork. Few would try to treat people from the streets, and he’d learned a handful of tricks over time. Larryn’s propensity to get into fights provided ample practice.

“Well, if Arathiel had been there, maybe we—”

“Stop. You can’t blame those absent for actions you regret.”

Knocks interrupted them, and when Larryn called, Arathiel himself entered. He’d found a cleaner outfit than the mismatched mess he’d arrived at the Shelter in, but still wore short sleeves despite the cold nights. Temperatures outside dropped at an alarming rate, and the common room’s fire didn’t reach most of the Shelter, yet Arathiel continued to go around with inappropriately light clothes. He’d become sick before long.

Cal cast Larryn a meaningful stare. For all of Arathiel’s peculiarities, he’d proven a kind and warm new friend. From the moment Cal had spotted him waiting at a table, drenched and lost, he’d known Arathiel would be more than a patron. Cal might have no interest in romance, but he loved making new friends and spotted potential ones faster than most developed a crush. His instincts didn’t lie, and if Larryn scared Arathiel with ill-thought words, Cal would have a few choice ones of his own.

“What’s going on? The common room is so—” Arathiel stopped as he laid eyes on Larryn’s multiple bruises and bandaged hand. “Quiet. What happened?” He closed the door behind himself.

“Tavern brawl,” Larryn said. “They arrested Hasryan.”

“What? Why him?”

Larryn snorted, and Cal sensed the snarky answer long before it came. He interrupted. "He head-butted Drake Allastam. A lord."

"This asshole snapped his fingers, and they took him. Simple as that."

"What now? How can we help him?"

This time Larryn laughed. "We can't. Tonight they'll beat him up, but tomorrow his boss should bail him out."

"That's ..."

"Typical," Larryn said. "Typical is the word you're looking for."

"He'll be okay!" Cal added. "There's nothing you can do. He'll be touched to know you worried about him, though."

Arathiel half-pouted, half-smiled, as if he couldn't decide whether it irked him to have to wait or pleased him to learn Hasryan cared what he thought about him. Cal wondered how far that interest went. The bond between these two had forged quickly, but Hasryan had only ever expressed interest in women, and it always stopped at desire. When Cal had asked, Hasryan had shrugged it off as a potential trust issue, saying he'd never met someone he trusted deeply enough to have romantic urges. At the hint of anxiousness in his friend's voice, Cal had promptly answered, "If you ever get them, tell me how it feels, because I'm forever at a lost." It drew a smile out of Hasryan, and they let the matter rest.

Larryn lumbered to his feet with a groan and stretched his muscles. "We should return to the main room. The longer we stay apart, the wilder their theories will become. Cal, can you get the music started again? I'll prepare some quick snacks to distract them."

"And me?" Arathiel asked.

Larryn shrugged. "You're welcome to enjoy the fireplace and not freeze those poor arms off."

Fear flickered over Arathiel's expression, and he crossed his arms, trying to subtly inspect them. Questions burned Cal's lips. Their new friend so often seemed to forget the world, like he now had with the chill and his outfit. He never commented on the stink, and he hadn't noticed his wound, according to Hasryan. Larryn believed he couldn't taste anything, so he'd started cooking his meals with a wide range of textures for Arathiel, but the only reaction it had earned him was a suspicious stare when he'd brought a strange tomato jelly. And in Cal's modest opinion, that weird stuff had deserved the look. Despite his desire to ask about everything and promise Arathiel he could talk to them, Cal locked his questions behind tight lips. He wanted Arathiel to stay comfortable, and if that required intense willpower on his part, then so be it. Cal smiled at their new friend.

"Come with me. I'll introduce you to our musicians! Do you dance?"

And they were off, Arathiel surprising Cal with a wistful story of his sister, who had loved to dance.

⟨ᴏ❳ᴏ⟩

ARATHIEL tightened the cape over his shoulder. He kept thinking it would slip without him noticing, that the hood would fall off and reveal his features. Sneaking and sulking had never been his method of choice, but his other option involved sitting all night at the Shelter and doing nothing. Not much of one. After Cal had revived the music and introduced him to a few regular patrons, Arathiel had pretended he needed fresh air and left. He climbed through the city straight to the Sapphire Guard's headquarters and prison.

Arathiel's hand clasped over his emergency pouch, almost devoid of coins. It wasn't empty, though. Inside hid his family's sigil, the light blue tint washed away by the decades. Or perhaps Arathiel just couldn't see it anymore. So much looked grey to him now. He approached the two guards near the entrance. Their shoulders hunched and they rubbed their hands—must be cold, then. When they noticed him, however, they snapped to attention.

"No one goes in at night, sir."

"I need to visit someone. To make sure he'll be all right."

The guard scowled. "I said no one—"

"I heard you." Arathiel's soft tone vanished, and he recovered the commanding voice he'd used when training rookies. "He has dark elven blood. Your colleagues must have brought him in earlier, from a tavern brawl."

The guard snickered. "Ah, yes. You still can't get in, sir."

"It's milord." Arathiel had known it might come to this. Even on a good day, most people weren't permitted to enter the prisons. You needed influence, and his resided in his title. Voicing it felt wrong, however. Like an old relic trying to pass as modern art. He reached into his pouch and retrieved his family's sigil. It glinted in the torchlight despite its age, as if winking at him. Mocked even by inanimate objects. Arathiel gritted his teeth and extended his palm. "House Brasten."

The guard stifled a groan. He picked up the insignia and squinted. Perhaps in the darkness he wouldn't notice how old it was. "That's all good, milord, but he can't see anyone tonight. He can't even open his eyes!" Arathiel glared at them, and the two guards' snickers died. "Come back tomorrow."

"I will, and I expect him to be in shape to talk."

Arathiel turned on his heel and strode away. He'd maintained a firm tone despite his hammering heart and the doubts crawling into it. If he returned tomorrow, he'd have neither darkness nor his hood to hide himself. They'd ask for more than a sigil to substantiate his claim. Arathiel hurried down a flight of stairs, ignoring the risk inherent to his speed—he moved on instinct, the granite under his boots hard to feel through the numbness of his senses. He would fall long before he even realized his false steps. But the exertion helped clear his mind, and by the time he reached the ground, he'd spent his nervous energy.

He leaned against a nearby tower and closed his eyes. Cal and Larryn had assured him the guards would release Hasryan soon. He'd meant to lift his friend's spirit with a surprise visit through the night, but he didn't have it in him to return during the day. House Brasten was his family by name, a tool he'd accepted to use tonight, but he didn't have the courage to reconnect with them and drag his past into the light.

❦

BRUNE never did "take care of it." Not on the first day, at any rate. Hasryan lay in his cell for hours, muscles throbbing from the beating. The guards had added punches to those already distributed by the tavern's patrons until conscious thoughts slipped from Hasryan's mind. He tried not to move, but he couldn't escape the occasional spike of pain. He missed Cal. For his healing, yes, and also his cheerful company. A friend's laugh helped him deal with hatred. The guards had stated he would receive no visitors, however. They always said that. It had never kept Brune away before. Nothing could stop her. Her prolonged absence brought the inevitable question: Was this wait a lesson?

He could hear her in his mind. *Don't head-butt the nobles, Hasryan. You're wasting my time and money.* This stay in a cell wasn't his first, but every time before, Brune had reminded him he was lucky to be her best assassin and extracted him without delays. He liked that better. It meant she trusted him to carry out any job she handed to him despite how often he got in trouble. No one else relied on him that way, not even Larryn and Cal. The former had learned to handle his own problems, and the latter never had any. They were friends—a miracle in itself—but they didn't entrust their future success to him. Brune did, and would again. Not to mention no one else knew his real job.

She would get him out. It might take longer than usual, but she would.

When guards fetched him from his cell the following day, he wasn't scared. They dragged him to a windowless room containing a table and two chairs and shackled him to one of them. Its cold seeped through his pants, and Hasryan shivered. They hung the lamp on a wall, out of reach, and left him without explanation. Hasryan didn't need one. He had seen interrogation rooms before. What could they want to ask, though? He'd smashed that arrogant prick's nose with his forehead, and since the man had a title while Hasryan had black skin, he had landed in a cell. A straightforward story which he had no intention of denying.

A woman entered, clad in the Isandor Sapphire Guards' livery: a simple white and grey outfit with a light-blue cape behind. She wore no armour, but dark-blue threads decorated her collar, sleeves, and the bottom of her cape. Not a regular guard, then, but an investigator. He straightened up, more alert. Tavern fights should be below her. Her serious smile as she sat on the chair opposite of him didn't alleviate his stress. Deep-set eyes studied him as though she could parse out his soul from the get-go, and Hasryan swallowed hard. He needed to size her up, make the most of what little information she presented to him. Her confident bearing indicated she believed herself at an advantage, and her firm strides implied she knew what she wanted. She expected a quick win. Was she an outsider? Her darker skin and its rich ochre undertone marked her as a descendant from the Phong Peninsula—a land far to the southeast in which Hasryan had never set foot.

"Who's your friend in House Brasten?" Though her voice was sharp, her Allorian was smooth. From the region, then. She had probably lived in Isandor longer than him.

Hasryan tilted his head to the side. "No one? What do they even have to do with this?"

"Nothing, apparently." She shrugged it off. Hasryan didn't press the point. Good interrogators gave no more information than they meant to. "You're in trouble."

Hasryan crushed his mounting dread and snorted at her declaration. In trouble for that head-butt? They both knew better. Her smile didn't budge, and in deliberate movements, she leaned to the side, retrieved his wave-patterned dagger from her bag, and set it on the table. Hasryan's mirth died. The blade's specific shape was his trademark in the underworld. He couldn't resist using it even though it created distinctive wounds. Brune's trust mattered too much, and she usually arrived before they looked into the dagger or forced them to let it go. Her delay might complicate matters.

"Is this yours?" the investigator asked.

"Depends. Which gets me into more trouble? If I stole it, or if I had it all along?"

He smirked, but she tapped the blade again, sending sparks of electricity down its length.

"Is it yours or not?"

Hasryan spread his arms and shrugged. "Lady, I don't even know your name. Why would I answer your incriminating questions?"

Time to fool around and waste hours. Sooner or later, Brune would get him out. His job was to say nothing before then. Nothing important, anyway. Hasryan enjoyed a good banter, even more so with the city's guards. His ability to drag out a conversation infuriated them.

"It's Sora Sharpe. Please answer. I don't have all day."

She flicked her long black braid out of the way. Stiff tone, irritated scowl, angry glare: perfect for Hasryan.

"I do. A lengthy day in a dark cell. Although I'll admit, this hell hole isn't much better." Hasryan leaned back, his smirk steady. "You're a lady. You should find a nice decoration to brighten up this place."

"Charming. Your sexism is an appreciated change from my favourite colleague's repeated transphobia. I'm glad the bigot club is diversifying a little." Without missing a beat, she picked up his dagger and stuffed it back into her bag. "An interrogation room isn't meant for comfort, and I care nothing for decorations. Not everyone follows the stereotypes shoved upon them by gender or race, although you seem determined to excel in what dark elves are reputed for. Congratulations, Mister Fel'ethier: you are the prime suspect in a dozen murders, one of which is so old, it implies you were a killer before you were an adult."

Hasryan laughed, but his bitterness seeped through the mirth. How could she understand? He *had* become a killer long before he was an adult, or even a teenager. They'd forced the decision on him before he could have any grasp of the world and its cruel workings. Kill or be sacrificed. As far as he was concerned, Sora Sharpe could shove her righteous anger deep up her ass. She had no right to judge his life. Hasryan trailed his fingers on the table, keeping his cool.

"Which murder would that be, if I may enquire? I lose track, you see. Dark elves don't count their crimes."

His crimes, no, but he could name every assassination contract since arriving in Isandor. Brune didn't need people killed often, and even less now that she controlled the mercenary business. He asked to fuel her righteous anger, not satisfy his curiosity.

"Lady Ilyana Allastam, born Carrington."

"What?"

Hasryan jerked forward, pulling the chains on his wrists taut with a clang. Anyone who'd lived in Isandor during the last decade had experienced the scars caused by Lady Allastam's death. Her husband, the current Head of the Allastam House, had blamed everything on another family and launched the first bloody feud in over a century. Instead of attacking their opponent's trades, nobles outright killed each other and annihilated any lowborn remotely linked to the enemy house. Hasryan and Brune had arrived in Isandor less than two months beforehand. He'd been sixteen, eager to help. The feud had been an incredible boon to their business and had allowed the Crescent Moon Mercenaries to get ahead.

But he hadn't killed Lady Allastam. He had been planting evidence in another house, thrilled by this first job under Brune's command. How could they blame him for one of the rare assassinations he'd had no part in? A smile danced on Sharpe's lips. She enjoyed his surprise. The investigator caught his gaze and held it while she set her palms on the table.

"You heard me," she said. "You killed Lady Allastam with the very distinctive dagger we were discussing. The wounds match. You should use less conspicuous weapons."

Hasryan tilted his head to the side. Nice try, but her affirmation didn't hold. "I didn't even have it at the time."

"So it is yours."

Sora Sharpe straightened with a victorious smile and set a hand on her hip. Hasryan bit a curse back and forced a low chuckle out instead. He shouldn't have underestimated her. He was too used to angry guards with brains blunter than their clubs. Perhaps a little name-dropping was called for, to shake her confidence.

"Well played. Yes, it's mine. It's a gift from my boss. You might know her? Her name's Brune." And just like that, Sora Sharpe's mirth vanished. Everyone in Isandor's Sapphire Guards understood they couldn't touch Brune. Hasryan tapped on the table with his index finger. "You can ask her about the dagger. I'm sure she'll come by soon enough."

"Don't think you'll get out that easy. I'm not letting you go."

Hasryan's eyebrows shot up. Did she believe that for even one second? He'd received threats of justice from frustrated guards before. She could try to keep him inside, but in the long run he was safe. Brune would never abandon him. She relied on him, and he on her.

After a final glare and an unconvincing "You'll see," Sharpe headed toward the door. As she touched the knob, Hasryan cleared his throat. She spun on her heels, her expression a mix of anger and hope. He smirked.

"I'll enjoy your clinging to me!"

The energy she put into slamming the door warmed his heart.

Chapter Fourteen

J AEGER hated the slump in Diel Dathirii's shoulders, the nervous way he pulled at the skin near his nails, and the growing bags under his eyes. Since the Myrians had unleashed their High Priest on the local shops, burning one of them to a crisp and destroying merchandise in others, there had been a constant stream of urgent letters to the Dathirii Tower. Requests for protection and compensation, for the most part, but a growing number of them declared unilateral disaffiliation with House Dathirii. Local business owners rarely had anything to fall back upon. Their shops were their lives, their trades. Why would they risk them for a single partner? Jaeger had spent most of the morning separating the different types of messages to give them an idea while Diel paced around his office. As soon as the steward set the last letter down, Diel spun on his heels to face him.

"How many?"

Sometimes there were questions Jaeger wished he didn't have to answer. "Half of them are bailing out, milord."

"Half?"

Jaeger pressed his lips and nodded. When Diel plopped onto his desk with a groan, a pang of guilt stabbed at the steward. If only they had more positive news.

"We'll have to do better," Diel said. "First, let's write these partners and convince them we can, in fact, protect them. The Myrians caught us off guard, but Kellian's men are competent. They don't have to leave."

"I'll have drafts ready." Jaeger doubted they would change their minds, but he picked up the pile of letters. They had to try. Isandor had always put a lot of emphasis on the image you projected rather than the wealth you truly had. The founding families had rivaled in ingenious tower designs to demonstrate how well-off they were, and today the noble houses competed as to who had the most beautiful garden. In trade wars as in everything else, half the battle was in appearances. Defection by so many of their partners would be horrible for their image. "What of the noble families?"

"We've ... talked." Diel's lack of enthusiasm killed Jaeger's feeble hope. "None of them are eager to help."

He reached for the long black quill on his desk, picked it up, and started spinning it between his fingers. Diel stared at the feather, absorbed in his thoughts and refusing to look up at Jaeger. Not a good sign, if allies made themselves sparse so early in the fight.

"Traditional alliances won't work, then," Jaeger said. "Thankfully, you've never been inclined to stick with traditional methods. You'll find another way."

"Will I?" he asked with a soft scowl. "Myria is not one of us. It is an Empire, and its enclave has financial support well worth a hundred of our Houses. I cannot win alone against such a force. Neither will anyone else once their turn comes. And it will come." Diel lowered the quill and met Jaeger's eyes at last. "We're a stepping stone for them—the easiest way to access the East. Sooner or later, they'll want complete control."

"Appeal to their sense of independence."

"I fear they've lost the true meaning of the word. But perhaps ..." His gaze unfocused, he turned toward the window, muttering to himself, ideas churning behind his intense eyes. Jaeger waited, allowing Diel's thoughts to simmer and coalesce into a precise plan. "Pen a letter to the Heads of House Brasten, House Almanza, and House Carrington. Tell them I have a coalition proposal for them. A long-term one that could benefit Isandor for decades to come. I'll write up the details."

"A coalition?"

Diel smiled, the radiant expression washing away his lines of worry. A plan had taken form in his mind—another of his brilliant, out-of-the-box political schemes, perhaps. The kind Jaeger hammered into concrete steps and measures. He was about to ask for more information when a sharp knock at the door interrupted him.

Years of service had taught Jaeger to identify who sought entrance by the sound of their knock. Every Dathirii had a signature knock. Lord Kellian gave three taps, all the exact same strength, all separated by the same timespan. Branwen, on the other hand, enjoyed creating an almost musical sequence on the door. It varied from one day to another, but it always carried a certain lively quality. Garith's surprised with its soberness, considering who called: he never did more than two quick taps. Lady Camilla's was so inviting it made you want to come out, instead of letting her in, and Jaeger would readily admit it was one of his favourites.

As he turned toward the door, Jaeger wished this particular sequence of four snappy knocks belonged instead to Diel's aunt. Lady Camilla would never produce such a sound, however. Behind that door stood Lord Yultes, the family's second most despicable figure, who knocked as if the door should never have been closed, and it was a personal insult to have found it in such a position. Jaeger looked at Diel, half-hoping he would ask him to turn Yultes away. Instead, the Head of the House nodded.

Withholding a sigh, Jaeger crossed the room and let him in.

Lord Yultes Dathirii strode in without sparing a glance at the steward. His hands were clasped behind his back, and he tried to compensate for his short stature by squaring his shoulders and pinching his lips haughtily. Yultes had mastered the art of looking down at the world, no matter the actual angle of his neck. Unlike Lord Hellion, who directed his sense of superiority and arrogance at everyone equally, Yultes' animosity had targeted Jaeger since the steward's very first day within the family. Etiquette prevented Jaeger from a proper riposte most of the time—etiquette and his unwillingness to tire Diel, for whom the infighting was draining.

"Urgent news, milord."

Yultes should have waited for Diel to address him first, even if only with a simple greeting. Such a breach was unlike Yultes, and Jaeger found himself studying him more carefully. Unlike most Dathirii, his hair wasn't golden, but pale blonde, like sand too long under the sun. Yultes had joined the family through his brother's marriage and was one of the handful of Dathirii with no direct blood relation to others. His posture seemed strained, and although his high cheekbones had always created an organized set of judgmental angles, today his cheeks were even more hollow than usual. Diel must have noticed, because his expression shifted from barely-hidden irritation to concern.

"What is it?"

"These are grave tidings. Perhaps they'd best be heard in private."

Of course. Jaeger stiffened as Yultes implied he should leave the room. While Diel did have the occasional private audience, it was most often with lords of other families.

"Do they concern your personal life, Lord Yultes?"

"No, but—"

"Then Jaeger stays."

Diel met Yultes' gaze and held it. Grateful warmth spread through Jaeger's body, and he was careful to conceal his pleasure behind a professional mask. Leaving was a waste of time anyway. Diel always shared important news afterwards, a fact Yultes knew quite well. The other elf threw one annoyed glance at Jaeger but decided not to argue over his presence.

"None of this is official yet, but House Allastam was so shaken, I would lend credit to this rumour. It will be all over the city by now.

Yesterday evening, they arrested Lady Allastam's assassin. Formal accusations should be announced this afternoon."

The buzz in Jaeger's head seemed loud and intrusive in the silence that followed. Lady Allastam had been assassinated ten years ago, and her gruesome death had sparked Isandor's first blood feud since its establishment. No one spoke of it anymore, as if mentioning Lord Allastam's brutal retribution upon House Freitz could rekindle the fight. If Isandor's guards had found out who was responsible, the dead might finally rest, letting the city put an important part of its history behind itself.

"This assassin," Diel said at last, "is he …?"

Diel's voice was low and hesitant, as though he didn't dare ask the question on everybody's mind.

"Hired by the Freitz?" Yultes completed. "I'm afraid we have no idea, and may never do so. He is a member of the Crescent Moon, and it is unknown what Brune will do about this accusation."

"Were the Crescent Moon already in town a decade ago?"

"Freshly arrived," Jaeger answered. "These mercenaries began accepting contracts about a month before the feud, and much of their quick growth in the first years can be attributed to the efficiency they showed in completing the most brutal jobs offered by both House Allastam and House Freitz."

Diel frowned, and silence fell as they considered the possible repercussions. Brune had the influence necessary to make the guards drop their accusation before it became official, but it might cost her a lot if the Allastams were convinced of this find. Lord Allastam had never forgiven the world for his wife's death, and no one in the city would want to be the target of his bitterness, especially after a decade of festering. No matter her course of action, Brune and her mercenaries had caught his attention. Not an enviable position. Jaeger wondered if she might not cut her losses and leave her assassin to fend for himself.

After a while, Diel turned to Yultes. "What will Lord Allastam expect of us? Unwavering support?" Diel pinched his lips. "He is no fool. He knows I share none of his most violent inclinations."

"You cannot anger such an important ally and go against him." Yultes' voice had tensed. As the Dathirii elf in charge of that relationship, he would be the first to catch heat should Diel decide to clash with Lord Allastam. "Your war with the Myrians already strains our reputation and resources. House Allastam is a long-standing ally of ours, and they have agreed to help in our time of need, both through financial support and by pushing for anti-Myrian laws at the Golden Table. Milord, I have used every last ounce of my considerable skills of persuasion to get such an agreement. I beg that you don't ruin it with some personal moral qualm."

Jaeger's eyebrows shot up. He pressed his lips together, holding back a faint smile. Yultes could always dream, but if Diel found sufficient reason to call Lord Allastam's actions immoral, he wouldn't hesitate. And with Diel Dathirii, 'sufficient' wasn't a high standard to reach. Only the prospect of losing this alliance when they were in such a delicate predicament would hold him back. Public animosity between the Dathirii and the Allastams would be a hard blow to the other nobles' opinion of the Dathirii.

"Yultes, if I think it necessary to speak up, I will." Diel's sharp tone surprised even Jaeger. He usually tried to be more diplomatic with his family. "I trust your considerable persuasion skills will be sufficient to salvage our relationship from the wreckage of my unyielding ethics."

The scowl on Yultes' face was worth decades of aggravating arguments. Jaeger put all his training to bear in maintaining a neutral expression as the elven noble whirled around with a huff and strode toward the exit. "Not even I can work miracles, Diel!" he said over his shoulder, timing his declaration to give Lord Dathirii no chance to answer.

Yultes almost ran into Garith on the way out. The younger lord hadn't knocked or waited, rushing into the office without the slightest hesitation. He threw the departing Yultes a confused look, then rolled his eyes. Jaeger prepared for a little quip—Garith wasn't the kind to let Yultes' self-imbued attitude go unremarked—yet their coinmaster's expression returned to a frown. His hair hung unbound on each side of his face, and worry creased deep lines around his eyes and mouth. Jaeger's insides tightened. Only dire news would undermine Garith's carefree nature. Judging from the concern etched on Diel's face, the older elf had reached the same conclusion.

"What's wrong?"

Garith pushed strands of hair aside and looked up at his uncle. Slight nausea assaulted Jaeger. When had Garith ever needed to gather his courage to say anything? Especially to Diel? Most days, getting him to stop talking was the problem.

"Uncle, I can't find Branwen."

Diel tilted his head to the side. It wasn't rare for Branwen to disappear for a few days. "Isn't it part of her job?"

"She warns me when she goes into disguise. We were supposed to dine together yesterday, review everything we knew about the Myrian Enclave. She never showed up."

Garith fidgeted with a strand of hair, pulling and twisting it. Despite his apparent calm, Lord Dathirii's jawline and shoulders had tensed. His gaze darted from Garith to Jaeger, then to the parchments about the Myrians, before returning to Garith. They all knew what he was thinking.

"Two days ago, I asked her to make a round of our local merchants. She was to warn them they might become targets, but assure them we would do our best to protect them," Diel said. "Two days ago, those same Myrians reduced Sierra's shop to cinders."

"I know."

"And you haven't heard from her since."

Garith shook his head. "Not a word."

Diel Dathirii grabbed the closest chair and slumped into it. He leaned forward, head falling into his hands, skin paling. Jaeger remembered the panicked tales from their Dathirii guards. A pyromaniac cleric laying waste to the shop, great flames blazing around him. Nothing to comfort Diel there. The steward could almost follow his thoughts as they moved from one worst case scenario to the next. After a time, Diel cupped his hands around his mouth, breathed into them, then straightened. His gaze met Garith's, and his voice fell to a raspy whisper.

"If they've hurt her, I will have their enclave razed."

"No bodies were found within the shop's ruins." Jaeger worried someone like High Priest Daramond could incinerate others without a trace, but he refused to voice such thoughts before Diel.

Diel flicked his hair back and stood up. A fierce light burned in his eyes now, grim and determined, and this new energy washed away the slump brought by their earlier discussion about fleeing allies. Jaeger recognized that expression, having seen it hundreds of times. In every fight Lord Dathirii led, there came a point where Diel decided it was personal, when he could no longer raise a barrier between his professional endeavours and his private life. This was it. Jaeger's heartbeat quickened as the Head of the Dathirii House turned to him and deep green eyes caught his, burning with the very passion that had melted his heart decades ago.

"Jaeger." Diel said his name with the serious tone he kept for business, and the attitude brought the steward back to the present. As much as Jaeger loved indignant and determined Diel, now was not the time. "Trace her itinerary. Question witnesses until we know exactly where she went missing. If it's truly there ... send a missive to the Myrian Enclave. Make it public. Demand the safe return of Lady Branwen Dathirii, and make it clear that no respectable House of this city will stand for the kidnapping of one of our own."

Everyone knew worse than kidnapping could have occurred. None of them would say it out loud. "Right away, sir."

Jaeger hurried to his desk to carry out his task. He hoped Diel's dangerous wording would not come back to haunt them. In calling all of Isandor's nobles to his side, he forced the other families to declare their allegiance in this conflict. By framing the Myrians as outsiders, he turned them into invaders. Ignoring Branwen's predicament would be an affront to the Dathirii, and as good as an official alliance with the Myrians. Diel trusted traditions and decency would push them into action, but Jaeger had his doubts about the city's goodwill.

As Jaeger settled to write the missive, Diel pulled his nephew into a hug. His words stuck with Jaeger as he dipped his quill in ink.

"Don't worry," Diel said, "we'll find her. No one touches my family."

CHAPTER FIFTEEN

"**D**ID you read this? 'No respectable House of this city will stand for the kidnapping of one of our own.' How delightfully naive."

Avenazar brandished the public missive received from the Dathirii earlier that morning with a cackle. He'd stepped into Jilssan's quarters half an hour ago without knocking, interrupting her review of spy reports. Although he mocked the letter's content relentlessly, he'd yet to give Jilssan the chance to scan it. She bit back a bitter remark about it and the time wasted by his gleeful jokes and extended a hand, hoping he would finally share. Instead, he shook the parchment midair and read through it again, laughing.

"He has such a clean writing hand. It almost turns his passionate claim into a lie!"

His dramatic tone grated on her nerves. Since the start of this quarrel with the Dathirii, Jilssan had spent more time with Avenazar than she'd ever cared to. The insight into how deeply he loved violence and cruelty left her exhausted and scared. Pretending to care about the level of destruction she and Varden had wrought and how much more Avenazar intended to do demanded too much energy. Jilssan forced a smile to her lips nonetheless.

"Let me see." She would never get to if she didn't ask. Avenazar handed her the letter, pouting. She snatched it away before he changed his mind. "That's his steward's handwriting. They've been lovers for more than a century. Lord Dathirii is the impulsive saviour of the defenseless; Jaeger is the calm, organized rock on which he relies."

It amazed Jilssan how little Avenazar knew of their enemies. Two years living in Isandor, yet he'd never learned anything beyond who he liked, who he hated, and who he could easily crush. Jilssan provided information, giving what finesse she could to his blunt, violent plans.

While Avenazar rambled about how little he cared for Lord Dathirii's private life, she read through the message. Her mood shifted from mild amusement to confusion. They accused Myrians of holding their spymaster prisoner? Why would they throw such a baseless accusation around? Jilssan frowned, unable to find a rational explanation that fit Lord Dathirii's character. To pretend they'd used their assault on the shop to snatch Branwen Dathirii away seemed a dangerous gamble.

Unless it wasn't one. If he truly believed they had captured his niece, this letter would be his exact reaction.

Jilssan hadn't noticed Branwen at all during their tour of Dathirii allies. Not very conclusive evidence, considering her reputation for disguises, but still. What if she had been there? When could something have happened? Her mind turned to the posh boutique they'd turned to cinders, to the owner who kept glancing back, to Varden's slowness in starting a real, all-devouring brazier. Cold crept down her spine. What if indeed.

"What's with the frown? You don't think there's any truth to this, do you?"

"No." Her dismissive answer surprised her. What was she doing, lying to Avenazar? She folded the letter and handed it back to him, occupying her hands, trying to keep herself steady. "He's playing the victim, or he wants us to drop our guard and think his best spy is out of order." She hoped she sounded convincing, because she believed her words less with every passing second. "Deny everything. Say we abide by Isandor's tradition and would never touch someone of noble rank."

Avenazar scoffed. "How ironic. They trot about claiming superior morals, but you can kill anyone, and they won't bat an eye unless it's a noble. Then the public outcry is out of control."

Jilssan's eyebrows shot up. With the treatment reserved for Isbari in Myria, that was a rich statement. But Avenazar was a little different. He didn't care for human life, regardless of ethnicity. Slaves just happened to be the easier, more acceptable target.

"A great point, Avez. You're constantly ahead of the curve!"

Except when it came to information. Or plans involving finesse. Or self-control. In short, she was lying, but it paid to compliment

Avenazar.

"You don't need to sweet-talk me."

His honeyed tone indicated the contrary, and bile rose in Jilssan's mouth. He loved this. After his obvious lust for Isra, she wouldn't put it past him to get ideas. Perhaps she should slow down on the niceties and reestablish a healthier distance. She did not want him to take too keen an interest in her.

"Message received," she said. "Handle the nobles, and I'll see what our spies have to say about this declaration. I'll bet he's up to something."

She already knew he was. Those reports on her desk mentioned Lord Dathirii had sent several private letters at the same time as this public missive. She needed to get away from Avenazar and think this new situation through, however. Better to get her story straight before she lied again without an inkling of the implications. Jilssan strode out of her room, leaving Avenazar behind without another word. Questions jumped at her the moment she stepped out of the door, as if waiting for the dangerous mind-mage to be gone.

What had Varden done? He wouldn't hurt Branwen Dathirii, didn't have that in him. Which meant he'd protected her from the enclave. Hidden her from Jilssan. Where? Should she have checked the shop for survivors first? She knew he could shield himself from flames and wouldn't be surprised if his power extended to others. Varden's precise control impressed and scared her all at once. She was glad it didn't rest in the hands of a ruthless sadist like Avenazar.

This raised an interesting question: what could Varden do that none of them knew of? How much power did the High Priest conceal from them, out of reach of Avenazar's grubby hands? Her steps had led her to the temple, and she stopped in front of its large brazier, the source of Varden's strength. Never before had she considered how little she knew of his abilities. Jilssan let the fire warm her skin until it prickled—until unease nestled in the pit of her stomach. She had always thought of Varden as a pretty face with too good a heart, stuck in a hopeless situation. Until now, he'd never shown a sign of turning against them. She'd assumed it meant he was no match for Avenazar, but doubts crept into her. Perhaps he'd been biding his time, trying to endure, and encountering Branwen Dathirii had sparked the forest fire.

Jilssan stepped away from the temple's brazier, her face hot. She glanced around, searching for acolytes who might've been staring at her. She didn't often visit Keroth's holy site, and now it seemed almost hostile. She turned on her heel, hurrying to the exit.

Her first impulse was to search the library for more information. They'd brought a number of tomes with them to allow continued research into spells or to use as bargaining assets with some families. Knowledge was power, and Myrians had garnered a wealth of it through research and conquest, creating and stealing in equal parts. Even faraway outposts kept a core collection of tomes with them— copies scribed by the handful of slaves who could write. They might have records of divine magic granted by Keroth to Their priest, and then she'd have a better idea of what Varden could and couldn't do. She didn't want to confront him without a precise idea of his abilities.

Jilssan slowed, her strides faltering in the middle of the courtyard, cold wind slapping her face, prickling her skin in a way strangely similar to the fire. The thought of confronting Varden had sent a stab of fear through her stomach. A warning from her instincts, the certainty she was about to make a mistake, crawled under her skin. She breathed in deeply, freezing air shocking her lungs. Fear had gripped her mind and made her jump to the wrong conclusions.

෧⟩C⟨෧

IF High Priest Varden Daramond—favoured by Keroth, blessed with fire powers way beyond her current understanding or skills, fuelled by righteous anger he'd bottled up for years—if *he* wanted to go against Master Avenazar, Myria's wild enchanter, the wizard who destroyed entire neighbourhoods on a vendetta, who trampled through people's minds with relentless glee ... well, that was *his* business. Not hers. And she needed to stay as far away from the clash as possible.

Thriving in Myria's dangerous political grounds often didn't mean choosing the right side, but knowing not to get involved at all.

The best option now was to never confirm her doubts. She needed to stay safe if this showdown happened, no matter the outcome. If Varden truly wielded enough power to defeat Avenazar, then she could tell him she'd known from the start and kept his secret. But if Avenazar won ... She shuddered, as much from the cold as from the horrors he would no doubt inflict on Varden's mind. And in the process, he would stroll through the priest's memories, including any potential discussion with Jilssan about capturing Branwen. Once she knew the truth about Varden's actions, she would be forced to place a bet on one of these two men.

She grimaced and turned around, heading back to her quarters, hoping Avenazar hadn't lingered there. Branwen Dathirii could stay hidden, wherever she was. Jilssan was in no hurry to find her, risk Varden's anger, or allow Avenazar to unleash his sadistic impulses on the poor girl. She would read the spy reports instead and focus on her uncle. Lord Dathirii commanded no secret power, at least, and the choice between him and Master Avenazar was an obvious one.

CHAPTER SIXTEEN

L ARRYN looked down upon the pompous silver-trimmed doublet he had slipped on with a grimace. Sure, the outfit offered extra respectability compared to his sauce-stained shirt, but he hated having to wear it. He'd stolen it from the hypocritical elves during one of his many expeditions into the Dathirii Tower and used it whenever he had to deal with arrogant shitheads who preferred wealthy assholes to decent, normal folk. Most guards fell into that category, and Larryn hoped he'd cleaned up enough to get more than insults from them. As he dusted himself off one last time, a small voice called to him.

"You're dressed funny."

Larryn turned to greet one of the Shelter's youngest patrons, and his favourite. Efua was just ten years old, but she'd been on the streets for as long as he remembered. Her curly hair had grown into a huge sphere in the last years, and he loved the way it framed her round face and curious eyes. Very few others dared to enter his rooms without knocking, but Efua could get away with anything where he was concerned. Larryn never had it in him to stay angry at the kid.

She approached him and ran her fingers over the silver trim. "This looks rich. You don't like rich things."

"No, I don't. I need this to talk to Hasryan, though."

She frowned, and he watched her work through his statement, and Hasryan's absence yesterday. She would reach the right conclusion. No one could hide much from her quick brains, and Larryn had long ago stopped trying to conceal painful truths from her. Still, his heart twisted whenever she threw one back at him.

"Something happened, and the guards won't let you see him if you look like one of us."

In a better world, a girl her age wouldn't understand so thoroughly the dynamics between the homeless, the criminals, and the city's guards. This one sucked, though, and Efua lived through the worst of it. She already worked, delivering letters across the city—a job on which she'd been harassed before. Once, Larryn even bailed her out of jail after she'd been accused of stealing the messages. He couldn't shelter her from these events no matter how much he wanted to. Better to let her know her perceptions of injustice were spot on and comfort her as he could. He crouched next to her and squeezed her shoulders, withholding a tired sigh.

"Exactly. Do you have any deliveries today?"

She shook her head.

"Then I have a mission for you. I might be gone for some time, but breakfast is ready. Wake Cal and make sure he distributes it to everyone. Don't let him empty the entire pot! You know how he loves my cooking."

Efua chuckled, then her face became more serious, as though she wanted to scold him. "Everyone loves your cooking. Cal would never eat our food. He's too nice to do that."

"If you say so."

She was right, of course. Efua had seen Cal's generosity firsthand, when they had first met him. He had saved Larryn's life and offered his hospitality without question. Larryn couldn't name many Middle City residents who wouldn't sneer at the scrawny, shit-covered, dying teenager he'd been at the time. Since then, Cal gave everything he could to the Shelter, never asking for anything in return. Except the regular meals, that is, but how many did the shared gambling income pay for? Without him, the Shelter would've been impossible to manage the first few months.

At least people helped with that now. Every morning as he fixed breakfast up, the cacophony of tables rattling on the floor reached his kitchens. The night's residents arranged the common room for the coming meal on their own. Larryn had once needed to provide precise instructions on how to clear the floor for the night, then prepare everything in the morning. Now everyone from the streets knew the Shelter's rules. Those able had to contribute to the room's set-up. Sleeping spaces were split between first arrivals and late-night workers, and two rooms stayed available for those who couldn't stand a crowd. Stealing, fighting, and harassing were forbidden. Beyond that, Larryn served anyone regardless of background and encouraged those who could to pay to do so.

He'd spent many evenings watching Isandor's forgotten folk gather on his floor, curled under the threadbare blankets he distributed every night. Some held younger siblings in their arms; others cuddled with perfect strangers for the warmth. The luckiest had snagged a place near the fireplace, so close Larryn always feared they'd wake at the darkest hour of the night, their clothes on fire. One would be hard-pressed to find a single inch of free floor.

The sight brought him back to his own nights sleeping on the ground, shivering as the packed dirt's cold seeped into his bones. The Shelter was little more than a lean-to at the time, with no proper floor and more holes in the walls than he could count—not that Larryn could count very high anyway. He'd spent his youth half-protected by the Shelter's planks, working and begging to help the first owner, Jim, however he could. Now Jim was gone, and Larryn had inherited the Shelter. He liked to imagine his foster father lived in the floor's wooden boards, in the always-lit fireplace, and in every single meal Larryn gave away.

The Shelter was Jim's legacy. Upholding it had meant accepting charity money from his guilt-ridden, asshole father, but Larryn could make that sacrifice. It was worth it. Every time Efua's freckled face lit up with a smile, he remembered why he fought. Jim had been her foster father, too, and now Larryn was the closest thing to a family she had left. He refused to let her down—her, or anyone in his Shelter.

"Off you go," he insisted. "Cal is hard to wake, and people are moving about already."

Efua agreed with a high-pitched, enthusiastic exclamation, then scampered down the corridor. At least Cal had slept at the Shelter tonight. He often returned home, but he had known Larryn would need him this morning. With the Shelter in his friend's capable hands, Larryn left for the police headquarters.

Despite the necessity of it, Larryn wanted to tear his disguise off during his entire trek up to the Middle City. The clothes itched like a lie he feared would grow into a part of him. As if they could bring out his heritage, change him. Anything but that. Nobles could shove their golden canes all the way up their asses for all he cared. Better to be covered in piss and freeze every winter than to turn into the kind of person who could pretend to care about someone—pretend to love her!—then dump her on the city's most shit-ridden street the moment she became pregnant.

Larryn took a deep breath. Those were the people he needed to imitate. Arrogant and self-serving, with a false face of charming. He couldn't let himself grow too angry. There would be time for rage later. For now, he created his best sneering mask, channelling his disdain for guards, the law they represented, and the rich they actually served, then entered the headquarters.

The guardsman at the entrance led him straight to the woman in charge of Hasryan's case. He must have thought the Allastams had sent him because he was all yes-sir-of-course-sir with him. More courtesy than Larryn had received in his whole life, all in two minutes. Larryn gritted his teeth, battling his urge to punch the man or yell at him until he stopped treating him like his fake affiliation made him worthy of honours. If he grabbed him and spat in his face and told him he was just another nobody living on the street, however, he would never get to Hasryan. Larryn kept himself in check until he stood before Inspector Sora Sharpe. After one quick glance at him, she clacked her tongue. The derisive sound stung his nerves.

"Is this a joke?" she asked. "Don't tell me you fooled the guard with this ridiculous disguise. Highborn kids don't stoop their shoulders like you do, or have frayed sleeves. They stride in with their nose pinched from slight disgust, their back straight from undeserved pride, and they have none of that dirt under your fingernails."

"Your guard doesn't know shit, then." Larryn removed the hat and threw it on her desk, drawing immense satisfaction from the papers it knocked to the ground. He unbuttoned his collar next, breathing in with relief. If his cover was blown, there was no point to all the pretense. At least he'd reached the right person. "Better now. I'm here for Hasryan."

Sharpe stared at him for the longest time, wearing down his thin patience. She glanced at the fallen papers. "Of course you are." Larryn caught a whiff of disdain in her tone. He spread his feet and tensed, ready to pounce. When she motioned for him to sit, he snorted and stayed put. Sharpe's eyes narrowed. "No one is allowed a visit. Tell your boss money won't buy his freedom. I have questions for her, and won't accept anything but answers."

"My boss?"

What the heck was this arrogant, prickly investigator talking about? He wasn't going to let her order him around like a vulgar underling. Larryn stepped forward, jaws clenched. She raised her eyebrows and crossed her arms, unimpressed.

"You heard me." She threw the hat on her desk another derisive look. "I'm not sure what your goal here is, but please also convey my regrets to Brune. It saddens me that she'd think so little of me and put such slim efforts into reaching Hasryan. I expected men with a meagre amount of skill, not a street rat with some pathetic stand-in for classy clothes. My guard isn't the only incompetent person in this building."

"Look who's talking!" His cheeks turned red-hot, the last shreds of calm escaping him as he moved to Sharpe's desk. "I don't have a boss. Wouldn't take orders from anyone. You want messages carried? Do it yourself." He slammed his palms on the desk, his throat tight. She didn't budge, but her frown deepened. "I'm Hasryan's friend. I watched his headbutt reduce Drake's nose to tiny pieces. Let me see him. I know what you people are capable of."

Sharpe's lips tightened into a grimace. Her finger tapped the wooden surface, and her deep-set eyes studied Larryn. Her continued calm unsettled him, which in turn fuelled his anger. "Do tell," she said. "What are we capable of?"

"Like you don't know." Larryn's knuckles whitened. She wanted details? He would happily oblige. "Men die bleeding in your cells because the welcome beating was too much for their poor physical health. Women return home flinching whenever a man approaches them, a haunted look in their eyes. You pick up people from the streets for the slightest offence, and if we see them again, they're more dead than alive—they just don't have the rope mark around their neck! I had to save a nine-year-old girl out of your dirty prisons, and you want me to believe a dark elf is safe?"

She paled with every new sentence, her expression hardening into cold fury. Larryn waited for her denial. He knew the drill, had heard the words many times. Criminals were worthless and had earned every hit, and homeless people were a hideous stain on the city's beautiful gardens. He leaned forward, his anger growing at her obvious guilt.

"They beat him up, didn't they? How many broken ribs did he deserve because he smashed some pompous shit's nose? And now you'll let him rot into a dank cell to serve as an occasional punching bag until the day he dies, is that it?"

Sharpe's colour returned, indignation plain on her face. "He did more than break a nose. Your friend—"

"Let me guess," Larryn interrupted. "He 'resisted arrest'. Another violent criminal assaulting a heroic guard, only there to defend the law and respectable citizens. Imagine if something terrible had happened to him! The poor guard might be wearing solid chainmail to protect himself, but you never know with these dangerous dark elves. Isn't it heartbreaking, how your guard had to use brute force to neutralize the threat? How will he ever live with his guilt?"

"Are you done? Is the righteous fury over?" She paused, as though expecting an actual answer.

Larryn's fingers clenched into a fist. "No."

"Too bad. It's my turn now." She picked up Larryn's hat, flung it back at him, then scooped up the scrolls lying under it in a smooth movement. She unrolled one in front of his eyes. "Do you see what it says there? How many names there are under it?"

Larryn stared at the scrambled letters as though they held meaning. The symbols made his head spin. The more he tried to decrypt them, the more they seemed to merge with one another. He straightened up, bitter anger eating at his insides. Better not to let Sharpe know he couldn't read, or she'd have a free pass to lie about the content of her paper. Larryn flicked a finger into the parchment.

"I don't give a rat's ass. Hasryan—"

"Is an assassin." She tied the scroll back up. "He killed Lady Allastam ten years ago and is responsible for the deadliest feud in Isandor's history."

Shock silenced Larryn for an instant, then he burst into a mirthless laugh. How perfect! These people never ceased to surprise him. He thought he'd seen it all before, but no. They always came up with some new shit. "How much do they pay you to make such declarations with absolute conviction? I hope it's worth it, because you can't have much left in the way of dignity. Do you really think I'm that naive?"

"You're not listening," Sharpe said. "We have proof. I—"

"Invented it." Larryn scoffed and stepped away. His legs felt like tightly coiled springs, all compressed energy waiting to be unleashed. He would be running back down to the Shelter to vent his frustration. "You needed to pin this murder on someone to stop the poor, desperate nobles from killing each other, and the perfect scapegoat came along. How many horror stories are told about dark elves, after all? This one even attacked Lady Allastam's gentle son! Why would anyone doubt Hasryan's guilt when he so obviously holds a grudge?" Larryn glared at Sharpe. Blood thumped against his temples. Fury blackened the edge of his vision until he saw nothing but her impassive face, her cold disregard for this injustice. "You don't care if he did it. Some powdered-ass noble has a problem, and you're solving it by making a Lower City scum pay."

Inspector Sora Sharpe waited without a flinch, a grimace, or any indication of her mood. Only her fingers moved, straightening the ripples in her uniform's pants. Once Larryn finished, she clasped her hands behind her back. The motion sent a wave of bitter hatred down Larryn's spine.

"Whether you believe me or not doesn't matter," she said. "I can and will tie him to the other murders he committed, and he will receive just punishment. Your friend is an assassin. No visits will be allowed."

Larryn cried out in rage and threw his hat once more, aiming for her inkwell. It toppled over, but it brought him no satisfaction this time, and he made for the door. He couldn't stand her cool composure, how she hid her detached amusement behind it. This woman might not call others milord or milady twenty times in a minute, but she was just as corrupt as the guard who'd let him in. If he wanted to get Hasryan out, he would need other means.

Prison break was at the forefront of his mind.

CHAPTER SEVENTEEN

A DOZEN of Isandor's Heads of Houses sat around the small, square tables. They had trickled inside under Lord Dathirii's tense gaze, and most hadn't looked in his direction long enough to meet his eyes—a bad sign. Not quite as bad, however, as those who *had*, only to sneer and shake their heads.

Jaeger and he had hand-picked every noble invited tonight. They were Diel's best hope to form a Coalition, the ones who would benefit the most from his proposed arrangement or who tended to innovate more than others in their tactics. If he couldn't convince them this was an endeavour worth their time … Diel sighed. He had no idea what he'd do next. He wished he'd prepared more, and slept a few extra hours. Difficult political meetings required every ounce of concentration, wits, and smooth-talking he could muster. But all his efforts to focus had been thwarted by worry for Branwen and increasingly terrible scenarios about her fate. Diel berated himself for the lack of control. Similar thoughts must plague Garith, too, yet he'd managed to crunch the numbers for different Coalition scenarios despite the quick deadline. Diel needed to pull himself together. The family counted on him. With a deep breath, he returned his attention to the gathered nobles.

"You all received my proposition yesterday. Before we start, I thank you for attending the meeting on such short notice." His voice fell into a regular cadence, smooth and confident. Addressing groups and crowds came naturally to him, and Diel found his groove with ease. "This Coalition is a new idea and a strange beast, but I believe it can contribute to the continuous success of all those involved. At its core, it is an effort of cooperation and solidarity." Someone in the group scoffed. Diel swept his gaze over them but otherwise ignored the mocking sound. He couldn't let them get into his head. "The idea is simple yet efficient," he continued. "Every member of the Coalition contributes to a common pool of money. When trade falters and leaves a House in deep need, they can draw from the pool and stay afloat long enough to fix their problem. The more people join, the bigger the pool, and the less strain on an individual family."

"Giving an unfair advantage to anyone inside the Coalition in a trade war."

The first protest came from Lord Serringer, sitting in the back, still buried in several layers of fur. Jaeger had ensured the restaurant would be warm and welcoming for everyone, but the Lord didn't seem to notice. Perhaps it was a matter of pride: fur deals with northern lords had propelled his House into riches, allowing them a seat around Isandor's Golden Table. Without them, House Serringer wouldn't exist. Not as nobles, anyway.

"No more than what bigger Houses already have. It would give smaller players more endurance in a fight, but not the means to win it. These funds are meant for survival, not to climb the ladder of power."

That scoff again, and this time, Diel honed in on its source. Lady Almanza slouched into her chair, sitting at the front left of the crowd, her disinterest evident. Even her multiple layers of skirts sagged around her as if they, too, had grown bored with this conversation. "I fail to see the point of your proposition." She leaned forward, lively dark eyes meeting Diel's gaze. "Not every new idea is a good one."

"Stability is the point." For them, anyway. Much like House Serringer, several of his guests relied heavily on trade within a single market. Diel hoped to foster cooperation, unity, and a sense of community over time, too, but first he needed to convince them. "Our fortunes are tied to our trades. One slip—one unforeseen struggle—and we're liable to lose our power and be kicked out of the Golden Table. A single House cannot counter the fickleness of fate, but together we stand a chance."

Lady Almanza tilted her head to the side. Her fingers reached for the silver threads woven into her hair, tumbling down her shoulders alongside her springy curls. She played with them as she answered, her deep voice calm and secure. "Here's what I hear from you, Lord Dathirii: 'I don't have any allies, and the Myrians will crush me, so here's my new plan to get your gold.'" She laughed and shook her head. "Wonderful what one can do by switching a few words, isn't it? You're quite transparent, really."

"I would be a fool to deny an arrangement such as the Coalition would help my current situation." Her lips parted to answer, but Diel rose a hand and cut her off. He was not finished. "Who can tell which of us will need it next, however? The safety net doesn't vanish once the Myrians are taken care of. It's here for our future."

"*If* anyone needs it," Lady Almanza said.

"Are you willing to take the risk? Your family's place around the Golden Table might rest on your foresight."

"An ability I am quite confident in."

Several nobles chuckled, and a wave of frustration rose in Diel's throat. Did they think themselves gods? Nobody could predict the future, and sometimes one's provisions for emergencies didn't suffice. The Coalition would spread the impact of a financial crisis between many, but shouldering anyone else's troubles seemed beyond Isandor's nobles. Diel swallowed back his anger, his smile made solid through decades of political training.

"I hope you're right, for House Almanza's sake."

"There are other issues with your idea, Lord Dathirii."

Lady Carrington's voice rose from the crowd, and Diel turned toward the older leader with calm, despite the thundering in his heart. He had known tonight would be difficult, known his predicament added suspicious trappings to any of his propositions, but the unending stream of protests mined his morale. Even their curated list of Houses who would benefit the most from the Coalition pushed against it. What would it be this time?

"Please speak your mind, Lady Carrington," he said. "An

enterprise such as the Coalition will fail if we cannot trust one another. I called everyone together instead of requesting individual meetings to dispel all concerns."

A doubtful snicker punctuated his words. Diel once more pointedly focused on his interlocutor. Grey hair contrasted with her olive skin, and she held herself with poised grace. Lady Carrington had always combined deadly wits with a beautiful smile, and although age added wrinkles to her face, she'd never lost her two weapons. She used the smile now, captivating the group and stealing Diel's breath.

"Everyone here knows the tragic history of my House, and I will admit a safety net such as the one you suggest might have safeguarded our standing when sickness struck so many decades ago. We sit at the Golden Table by the good graces of our peers and in honour of our historical role in Isandor's foundation. Without these, House Carrington would be no more. Sometimes, one must fall to discover their own fallibility, or the value of a support network." She shot a meaningful look at Lady Almanza. "Yet I can't help but think, Lord Dathirii, that your Coalition is doomed to fail."

"Explain." Dread twisted Diel's stomach. Nice words often preceded the harshest critiques.

"You have used a similar idea with several local merchants. As a bigger force, you provide them with safety and stability. Yet the last few days proved it's never this simple. Your network abandoned you at the first sign of trouble. You couldn't protect them, and they won't risk standing by you." Lady Carrington kept her tone matter-of-fact. With or without mockery, however, her words brought a bitter knot to Diel's stomach. He could not deny them. "How can we ensure the Coalition won't fail in similar ways?"

"It is not the same beast. In the Coalition, we would be equals. We—"

"You couldn't even protect your niece!"

Diel flinched at the raspy voice. The words echoed in his skull, creating a buzzing pressure. Had they come from Lord Serringer? He couldn't quite tell. But the accusation rang between his ears, the sound twisting into a mocking sneer. Where was Branwen now? What were they doing to her? The questions seized his mind, blotting everything else out. Black spots crept in at the edge of his vision, and Diel blinked them away. Everyone stared at him. His mouth was dry, his legs shaky. Had he zoned out? How long? He needed to stay alert, to stay with the conversation. Fear and exhaustion ate at him, but he couldn't afford this kind of slip. Diel snapped his attention back to the small crowd, burying his gnawing doubts.

"Really?" He allowed a bitter smile to reach his lips. "Everyone tells me the Myrians are not a threat—that they don't see the necessity to fight against them. How many around the Golden Table believed they should be treated like any other House? Yet despite Master Avenazar's denial about Branwen, despite everyone insisting the Myrians aren't dangerous, you all conclude pretty quickly they *did* take her. So which is it? I'm asking you now, since you can't seem to make up your mind: friendly traders or ruthless conquerors?" He spread his arms, his exasperation growing. "Because if you believe they have her, if you think they are hurting her, then this is your chance to do something about it, to drive them out of the city!"

Resounding silence followed his words. Nobles shuffled in their seats and cleared their throats. No one looked back to him, or cheered, or even nodded. After minutes stretched on, Lady Almanza sighed and waved through the air in dismissal.

"I'm not getting involved. You make valid points, Lord Dathirii, but unless you can guarantee immediate protection, I want no part in this. You're right: the Myrians will attack us. I refuse to risk my family for yours."

She stood, and it acted as a signal for everyone. They rose, talking to each other, shaking their heads.

"You'll just be next," Diel said over the murmur of the crowd. He didn't like the desperation in his voice. "Sooner or later. Either we stand together now, or we all fall."

"Yes, so you keep repeating." She shrugged, dismissive and calm. "Find soldiers, and I will reconsider this offer. Many of us will, I suspect."

Her declaration provoked whispers of agreement, then his guests filed out. One by one, they left the restaurant, shoving winter hats over their heads and buttoning up their coats.

He had failed. The Myrians had painted a bright target on his family and no one wanted to risk stepping into its range. Yet fear wasn't the only factor here. If only! Diel could understand protectiveness and didn't blame others for placing their family's security above all. As much as Lady Almanza might dread Master Avenazar's attention, however, it hadn't motivated her refusal. Apathy had. She was convinced this war would never affect her and didn't care for the larger consequences of a strong Myrian presence. It wasn't her family before his, it was her family only. Worse, she'd convinced everyone to follow her short-sighted, individualistic path.

Soldiers, Diel thought bitterly. Isandor's Houses didn't have standing armies, only small private guards. With one exception. Since the start of their feud a decade ago, House Allastam had tripled the number of warriors at their service. After the recent capture of Lady Allastam's assassin, they might need a new occupation. He needed to speak with Lord Allastam.

As the last of his guests slipped out, Lord Dathirii was already forming new plans and arguments. Isandor's nobles might put more effort into protecting themselves from the cold than from hostile invaders, but he would not let that stop him. He couldn't. Without them, the Myrians would take over the city, then expand their Empire east. Barring their way required the strength of Isandor as a whole, not one or two houses. The silence left behind by the other nobles made one thing clear. Uniting Isandor would prove harder than defeating Master Avenazar could ever be.

⟨∽⟩

As sounds from the meeting died down, Isra shook her frozen wings and tried to shake herself from her torpor. Cold crept to her feathers and bones, casting a white daze over her mind. Had she fallen asleep? No, she could reconstitute most of what had been said. Enough to report back to Jilssan and make up for her escapade with Nevian. She didn't understand Jilssan's adamant statements that it had been a mistake, and that she should be more careful, but she trusted her master's opinion. If Jilssan believed Avenazar might hurt her, she didn't want to take the risk. Contributing to their little scuffle with the Dathirii would prove she was a useful member of the enclave, at least.

Even if these political meetings always turned out to be the most boring conversations to spy on. This task shouldn't have demanded so much energy of Isra, yet as she took flight from her windowsill, exhaustion weighed her wings down. She rarely maintained her hawk form this long, and concentrating on it *and* Lord Dathirii's pathetic attempts to convince other nobles to help him had drained her. Add the paralyzing cold, and Isra wasn't certain how she was even still awake.

She beat her wings faster, trying to push some life into them, soaring higher than necessary. High above the towers of Isandor, their tops gleaming in the fluorescent lights of modified gardens, as ridiculously fancy during the night as they were during the day. She wished she could fly all night, but her shapeshifting abilities wouldn't allow it. Her body strained to return to its human form, pushing at the magic holding it as if it were a cage. Stupid body. Didn't it understand the freedom of shapeshifting? Why did it want *normal*, of all things?

Or perhaps she was just bad at magic. Every spell she'd ever tried seemed to flee her, magic energy slipping between her fingers. Jilssan had no explanation. She had never heard of anything like it and insisted that Isra first master basic spells. As if those were any easier. If Isra had to spend hours struggling to cast any one spell, she didn't want to waste time turning apples into trees. She wanted to transform herself and fly.

Isra circled around Isandor's skies for few minutes, alone. No one to order her around. No one to judge her, mock her, or sneer at her. In summer, she could stay like this forever, hovering high above the city and taking in the sights. Sadly, she had a spy report to make and numbing cold to fight.

She dove back down with an internal sigh, zooming straight for the enclave's walls and gaining speed with every passing second. She let out a long screech—the closest thing to a cry of exaltation she could muster—then snapped her wings open and curved back up as she neared ground level. The thrill had washed her exhaustion away, leaving behind a frenzied heartbeat and an urge to take off once more. Isra reined her desire in and landed with a few lazy flaps at the top of the enclave's stone walls.

Time to be human again. Isra let the magic escape at last, sighing as it fled. Her wings became arms, her talons stretched into legs and feet. She pouted and ran a hand through her chosen short blonde hair, to make sure her transformation was complete. Sometimes she worried she'd get stuck halfway through. Isra gripped the amber amulet at her neck, and took a deep breath. Her father might be far away, but his magic remained with her, encapsulated in her necklace. As long as she had it, she would be okay.

Isra slid down the wall and onto the battlements, ready to seek out Jilssan. She had taken two steps when her eyes caught on a shadow across the courtyard. She squinted, regretting that she was no longer in her hawk form and missing the powerful vision it granted her, but she was too exhausted to shift back. Someone climbed the elm tree on the other side, branch by branch, until they could jump onto the walls. Isra's heart quickened.

They were in the middle of a war with House Dathirii. No one sneaking out at night would do so with good intentions. Her mind reeled from the thought—a traitor. They had a traitor in their midst.

It had to be Varden.

No one else would betray them. But he was always so angry at her and others, couching his words in fake politeness, waiting for the time to unleash his powers. If he was selling them out ... He'd turn on them. Destroy them from the inside. She had to warn Jilssan.

Isra ran off, scrambling down the closest flight of stairs. Cold night air hit her cheeks, and she suppressed a shudder. He had always scared her, but she wished her instincts weren't so right. At least she'd caught him. This would definitely erase Master Avenazar's ill thoughts of her, no? He had to be pleased with anyone bringing such a betrayal to light.

Anyone. She slowed at the thought. Perhaps she could let the credit for this slide to someone else. Nevian had avoided her since they were caught in Isandor. Would he forgive her if she brought him this information and let him report Varden? He had to! No one else was under twenty in the enclave, and even if Nevian spent all his time working, he was the closest thing to a friend she could get. She didn't want him to stay angry.

Isra grinned at her flash of genius. What a great night! She would make up to Jilssan with her report on Lord Dathirii and his need for soldiers, and when she next talked to Nevian, she would offer him the chance to wipe his slate with Avenazar clean. After that, Nevian could only like her again. Whistling to herself, Isra knocked on Jilssan's door, her exhaustion forgotten.

Chapter Eighteen

EVIAN hated coming to Isandor. No matter how often he'd snuck out successfully, the creeping sensation of being watched returned. Master Avenazar would find out. He always did. And this wasn't a benign excursion to the city. It was treason, plain and simple, and he would be punished accordingly. If defying pointless rules on his assigned tasks earned him hours of mind torture, what would Avenazar do once he discovered Nevian traded enclave secrets for magic training?

But Nevian could not be blamed. If Avenazar taught him *anything*, he would endure the abuse. Except he wasn't learning. He was losing years of potential improvement to Avenazar's insatiable desire for revenge. Nevian refused to fall behind other apprentices because his former master had provoked Avenazar. He had sacrificed too much to get this far. He would do whatever was needed to keep growing as a wizard.

Right now, this included a deal with Brune, the most prominent mercenary leader in Isandor and one of the only magic wielders in this city who might be able to stand up to Avenazar. Nevian met with her on a regular basis, always in the city, despite the express interdiction against leaving the enclave.

The leader of the Crescent Moon was a muscular woman—unusual for a mage—who did not enjoy smiling. Her wardrobe featured nothing but shades of brown. Pants, robes, blouses, shirts … everything was some variation of brown, including her long hair and eyes. Even her skin was a pale ochre, a fairly common tone in Isandor. More often than not, Nevian wished she were his real mentor. Brune had no patience for wasted time. She went straight to the point, both in her questions and lessons, leaving no room for banter. Nevian loved it. Every second he spent out of the enclave was a terrible risk. The faster they worked, the better for everyone.

He sat at their usual meeting place, a tranquil tea shop owned by the Crescent Moon that closed early in the evening. Minutes trickled by without any sign of Brune, and the location's usual soothing effect stopped working on Nevian's nerves. He tapped his middle finger on the table, biting his lower lip, until the mercenary leader finally walked in from the kitchens and slid into the chair opposite him, unruffled by his obvious displeasure.

"You're early," she said.

Nevian gritted his teeth. She was half an hour late, and they both knew it. If he'd learned one thing from Avenazar, however, it was not to contradict his superior. He forced himself to stop tapping on the table.

"It's not easy to sneak out of the enclave. I had no choice." He might roll with her lie, but not without reminding her he didn't have a lot of time, and she had just wasted a full thirty minutes of it.

Brune shrugged, a hint of irritation behind her bored mask. Instead of acknowledging his protest, she changed the topic to matters concerning her. "Has news of Hasryan's arrest reached the enclave yet?"

"The dark elf? Yes. What of it?"

"They will accuse him of Lady Allastam's murder, ending a long-lasting feud between two of Isandor's noble families. This could stabilize the political situation, and those closest to House Allastam and House Freitz might look more kindly upon Lord Dathirii's quest for allies. Who knows? Depending on how he plays it, he could garner enough support to stand a chance against your enclave." She leaned back into her chair. "It's unfortunate that this happens in the middle of your little war, and I would appreciate an indication of whether or not Master Avenazar intends to get involved, and if so, how."

Nevian stared at Brune, baffled by her question, struggling to encompass how Avenazar worked in a single answer. He ran a hand over his face and sighed. "You're trying to use logic to predict his actions. When our agents reported the arrest, Master Avenazar yelled at them for wasting his time with trivial matters. The enclave's mission might be to achieve control over Isandor's politics and assimilate it into the Empire, but Master Avenazar ... he doesn't care. He cares about Diel Dathirii, who made the terrible mistake of giving him personal offence, and added a layer of insult by accusing the enclave of kidnapping his niece and hiding her. Let me tell you, this elven lord has a death wish."

"You don't have Lady Branwen Dathirii?"

"No!" Nevian's heart hammered into his chest, painful and out of control. How could Brune not understand what it would mean? "If we had her, the entire city would know. No detail would be secret. Avenazar would rip every ounce of knowledge from her mind, mocking the Dathirii with the crunchiest parts, daring them to come rescue her. He'd wipe out her precious memories, maybe cut off a finger or two and have them delivered in special packages. Master Avenazar does not torture in secret. He likes his deed of vengeance to be gruesome and very public. If we held Branwen Dathirii at the enclave, she would be an example of just how far he is willing to go to crush those who defy him."

His voice shook, and he pushed his hands into his lap to keep them from trembling. He remembered the shrieks of his first master as Avenazar tore her mind to shreds. Sauria had writhed on the ground, clutching at the rug, reaching for him—only to have her outstretched hand promptly incinerated. He had remained frozen, back against the wall, the stench of charred flesh filling his nose and his ears ringing from the shrill screams. Not a sound escaped his lips, not even her name. Nevian tried to shake off the memory. He closed his eyes and took a deep breath.

"Once angered, Master Avenazar forgets the consequences of his actions. He will hunt every one of Diel's relatives, even if the elf is long dead and unable to see it. If he has to raze the entire city, he will. His last vengeance annihilated a whole block. He deprived his victim of all memories before he killed her, yet this didn't satisfy him. He claimed her apprentice, declared he'd train him to make up for the destroyed property, and he's still carrying out that particular revenge on him. So if you need to know whether or not Avenazar will do something … ask yourself if it'll hurt Lord Dathirii, or anyone he cares about. That's your answer."

He had said too much. Nevian gritted his teeth and lowered his gaze. He hated revealing anything about his past, but after three years of bottling it, the memory had tumbled out on its own. Brune didn't belong in Myria, had nothing to do with them, and for the first time, he'd felt free to explain. He had blurted it all out, and his cheeks burned from shame. How unprofessional.

Brune clacked her tongue. Her expression hadn't changed at all. "I feel obligated to remind you our partnership does not include any form of protection. If he finds out you are here, he is yours to deal with. I will defend myself, but nothing else."

"I know." Nevian's hand tightened into a fist. "I was not asking for it."

What would be the point? No one could protect him, and the consequences of trying were disastrous. Nevian wouldn't dare demand such a thing. Brune already taught him magic, and with her help, he could progress as a wizard despite Avenazar's best efforts. Once they returned to Myria, he would petition for a transfer or pass the exams, and this hell would be behind him. Until then, he needed to endure and survive—to never forget the end goal.

"Excellent," Brune said. "I'm baffled by their choice of leader, but the Myrian Empire is free to send brutes to Isandor if they're in no hurry to conquer."

"They think they don't need better." Nevian hadn't reflected upon Myria's politics, but Isra kept discussing them like an expert, no doubt using information gleaned from Jilssan. It might help Brune, so he endeavoured to repeat what he knew. "Sending Avenazar here was a form of punishment. They got rid of him before his volatile urges to destroy wiped out more than a neighbourhood. Isandor is an easy target to them, without glory or challenge."

Brune pinched her lips, and the slight hint of irritation surprised Nevian. She rarely allowed emotion to show. "Two years is a long delay for an easy target. Let me guess: Master Avenazar found out he loved to rule his little kingdom and is taking his sweet time."

"Yes. He plays with his prey. Once he grows bored or outraged, he'll bludgeon his way through any resistance and make them pay for the insolence."

"You are as insightful as ever, Nevian," she said, then she stood up. "I'm afraid this is all the time I have today, however. I have important business to attend to."

"What? You can't!" Nevian's stomach sank, and he jumped to his feet. "This isn't the deal. I need help with a spell."

"Not tonight, Nevian. Next time."

Panic slid into him, a clawed hand clenching tight. Next time should be good enough, but what if she kept pushing back? What if she meant to drag information out of him yet no longer helped in exchange? She couldn't! He needed these slivers of progress like a drowning man needed fresh air. He scrambled for his small sack, fumbled with the clasp closing it. His fingers slipped, but he managed to open it. Nevian rummaged inside until he found a neatly folded parchment. "Please … it's just one spell." He unfolded the notes, then handed them to Brune. "I can't understand where I'm going wrong with this protection charm. It should ward against the elements."

Brune sighed, snatched the notes, and scanned them. Her lips pursed, then she flattened his parchment on the table. "I'll point out your mistake, and you can look deeper into it on your own. If it's still a problem next time, we'll fix it."

"Please."

"Basic protection spells can defend one of three elements: body, mind, or spirit. As with all things, they work in one of two ways: either by creating a shield, or by destroying the source of danger. So right here?" She tapped the beginning of the runes scribbled on his paper, underlining a particular set of three. "You failed to define what you wanted to protect. Pick one, you're not powerful enough for more than that. Not to mention your runes on creation and destruction are a little off. These runes are your tools, Nevian. They let you craft magical energy into what you want. These are crude and blunt. Look all of that up, come back with a better version, and I'll make time for practice."

Nevian stared at the perfect cursive of his notes and the shapes of the runes. Now that she pointed out the one missing, it seemed obvious. He had browsed through so many different spells before trying to write this simple one that he had forgotten some of the most basic elements. The young wizard groaned, then picked up the paper and folded it back with extra care. Yet another revision. Would he ever get it right? Move from rune-casting to more flexible and powerful forms of magic? He had so much to learn, and so little time.

"Thank you." He might need a lot of practice to cast this one, but he'd feel better if he could defend himself. Nevian stored the spell back in his sack before looking up at Brune. "If you have nothing planned during the winter solstice, the Myrian Enclave has an important ritual related to Keroth's faith, and it would be easier for me to sneak out for an extended period of time."

"Let's do that." Brune straightened up with a slight shrug. She didn't seem to care, but Nevian suspected she had learned to hide what mattered and what didn't a long time ago. Calculated disinterest made aiming for her weak points harder, and he admired the ease with which she maintained her mask. "Good luck on your return."

Nevian nodded, though he believed in luck as much as he believed in Master Avenazar's good will. Perhaps because his own was horrendous. What rare positive things had happened to him had always come from skill and hard work, and that wasn't about to change.

CHAPTER NINETEEN

HREE days. Why was he still in this dank cell after three brutally long days? Hasryan had expected Brune's steady footfalls at any point during the first twenty-four hours. She would never abandon him. They had started working together before his voice broke, when he had yet to make a true profession out of killing. She had seen his potential, found him mentors, helped him climb the ranks of her organization at the time, and offered him a place by her side when she'd left them behind to build the Crescent Moon in Isandor. Where would he be without Brune's trust and support? Starving, hated, perhaps even dead.

Or in a cell like this one, maybe. Not that he would stay there. She would come. What were three tiresome days against a dozen years of collaboration?

In the meantime, he had for his sole company the ever-charming

Sora Sharpe and her endless questions. At this rate, Hasryan suspected she enjoyed the little banter surrounding his answers. First she went on and on about Lady Allastam's assassination and his dagger, and the dire consequences of her death for Isandor's political life. As if he cared about the latter. Soon, however, she moved away from the one murder he *didn't* commit to the many others he had accomplished for Brune. Judging by the bags under her eyes, she had spent entire nights digging through unsolved cases. Her dedication would be amusing if it didn't put dangerous pressure on him. When had the city guards become so efficient? Hasryan dodged questions and did his best not to incriminate himself, but sooner or later, he would slip. Brune needed to intervene before the quick and relentless Sharpe pinned enough murders on his head to make it impossible.

But where was his boss? By now, the entire city knew Lady's Allastam infamous assassin was a dark elf. She had to realize he'd be waiting for her, killing time by throwing a rock against the wall and annoying his fellow prisoners. Yet she was nowhere to be seen. Perhaps the importance of his supposed crime made it more complicated. He had to stay patient. To hold off until she extracted him from this mess. She counted on him.

His reward would be Sora Sharpe's bitter grimace when Brune finally showed up.

The lock on his door clicked, and once again, the investigator opened it. Hasryan pushed himself to his feet with a sigh. It amused him to watch Sora's irritation grow when her progress didn't, but the endless interrogations took their toll and exhausted him, clouding his mind. Oh, how he wanted to crash into a seat in the Shelter, devouring Larryn's incredible stew while junk instruments conjured impossible melodies. His stomach grumbled, then he caught a whiff of salty soup and discovered Sora held his meal. She brought the food now?

"Wow, they really do make you do the woman's job," he said. "Did you cook it too? Because if you're trying to impress me, you picked the wrong thing. I have high standards where my nourishment is concerned."

Anger darkened Sora's expression. He could feel her temptation to fling the soup at him in the way she jerked the bowl, lips tight. His smile widened.

"New questions?" he continued. "Trying to coax answers with an extra meal?"

"It's not extra." She shoved the soup under his nose, and he accepted without hesitation. Prison food left him in a constant state of hunger, and she was right: they had skipped one service, if not more. A thin smile returned to Sora's lips. "Brune came."

"Did she?"

Hasryan's heart leaped, but he kept his tone casual. Why was Sora smiling? This should be terrible news for her. The kind to infuriate or at least annoy her. Worry built at the bottom of his stomach, a knot tightening with every passing second. Hasryan forced his hand to remain steady as he brought the spoon to his lips. Never show fear to an enemy.

"When you're done eating, we will all go hear what she has to say. Along with a judge."

Hasryan stopped, the spoon in his mouth. Sora's current smirk had grown familiar over the last few days. She was withholding information from him, laying out a trap. Hasryan took his time with this spoonful, using the delay to calm his nerves.

"You look happy to see me go," he said. "I'm hurt."

"Oh, but I am sad. Our daily back and forth has taught me all I ever needed." The hint of sarcasm in her voice grew as she continued. "It's so different from the kitchen—like there's a whole new life for me! How had I never realized I could be doing a man's job? And so well, at that! Thank the gods you came along to enlighten me."

Hasryan couldn't suppress his laugh. Sora knew damn well she excelled at her work, and now she turned his jokes against him. One step ahead of him once more. "Cooking must have been terribly absorbing if you needed me to show you the way."

She wouldn't get anything closer to an admission of defeat than this. He met Sora's gaze, bent his head a little as a form of reverence. She let out a small scoff.

"You should try something different," Sora said. "Perhaps you'd have an epiphany about your life and drop assassinations."

Hasryan's mirth vanished. She couldn't understand. Killing was as much a part of him as his quips or his wariness of strangers. It had always been a part of his life, from the moment he'd first defended himself. He wouldn't apologize for something thrust upon him. They locked eyes for a long time, Hasryan's grip tightening on his spoon. It had taken Sharpe one sentence to remind him of where he was. Where authorities were concerned—nobles and guards alike—he would never be more than a criminal. Hasryan lowered his eyes to the soup and returned to it. He missed Larryn and Cal more than ever now. They treated him like an actual person. They had welcomed him in, just like Brune, opening a space in their lives for him. He needed his friends.

Soon enough, he promised himself. Brune had come at last.

SORA dragged him all the way through the guards' headquarters and to the judge's office, never letting go of his heavy shackles until they reached a cozy room with a wide window obscured by vines. A large painting covered the back wall, depicting Gresh as a slim and dark-skinned man, all sharp angles like jagged stone. This particular representation of the Earth Master was frequent along the Reonne River, where the deity had a strong following. In front of the painting stood a massive desk, dwarfing the scrawny old man slouching in the chair behind it. Bored. Used to the corrupt system snatching their targets before they could accuse them, probably. Perhaps actively benefitting from it. Hasryan didn't care. He sought his boss out.

Brune leaned on the bookshelves to the right, her arms crossed, her squarish features set into a serious mask. She'd tied her brown hair in a ponytail and wore her usual amber robes, cinched by a wide maroon sash. Hasryan smirked and waved, but it brought no smile out of her. Not that Brune ever showed signs of amusement. She distributed her smiles like they were precious gems, only offering them in meaningful instances. In that regard, she was Hasryan's exact

198 ～ CLAUDIE ARSENEAULT

opposite. He found reasons to grin even when there were none, in defiance of the never-ending hardships and the world beating down on him. Maybe if he smiled enough, the happiness he projected would stop being a lie and coalesce into his truth. Brune stared at him in silence until Sora Sharpe closed the door behind them.

"Let's make this quick," Sora said. "I want him to hear it."

Hear what? He knew what Brune would say. She'd clear his name and confirm his story. What else could she do? But why had Sharpe smiled, and what was this constant tug at his stomach, warning him, pleading for him to listen to the terrifying hunch hovering at the edge of his mind? Hasryan shoved it away, crushing it under the unwavering certitude that Brune would never betray him. She was the first person who had trusted him, and he trusted her in return.

Everything would be okay.

Brune's gaze flickered to him, then back at Sharpe. The corner of her mouth quirked into an irritated grimace. "Then ask your questions again. I don't have all day."

Neither did he. He was dying to return to the Shelter, sit down with a good pint of ale, and lose more money to Cal's ridiculous luck. Or even better, to devour Larryn's latest meal and wash out the taste of prison soup with the best cooking in the whole city. He wanted to hear his friends laugh as they recalled Drake's stunned indignation, his little cry of pain, and the way he'd held his broken nose. Soon, he could relax, the constant throb from his bruises ebbing away as Cal tended to the worst of his injuries. Hasryan settled against the wall opposite Brune's, ready for her sweet words. Sharpe stepped forward, a hand on her thigh. Business-like. She looked straight at Brune as she began.

"Hasryan Fel'ethier is your employee, is that correct?"

"Yes."

"When we arrested him, he had a special dagger in his possession." Sora withdrew his weapon and set it on the desk in front of the judge. The old man frowned and glared at Hasryan. "He says this weapon was a gift from you. Is that also correct?"

"Yes."

Brune's exasperated tone indicated she'd had enough of this charade. She'd always disliked repeating anything, especially due to long procedures. He would have to thank her for enduring the process. Perhaps he could find some of those caramel candies she craved and fuel her secret addiction.

"All right. One last question," Sharpe continued. "When did you give this dagger to Hasryan? Be specific."

Hasryan's smile widened and he crossed his arms as much as the shackles allowed. Brune's chocolate eyes stopped on him and for the first time in forever, her lips did curl up. Ever so slightly. His heart warmed; the knot in his stomach loosened. She was happy to settle this matter and get him out.

"Two days before Lady Allastam was killed."

Brune held his gaze, and Hasryan's heart stopped, his confident smirk frozen. *Before?* His ears rang, and his thoughts scattered like a thousand birds after a loud bang. What did she mean, before? After. She'd given it after. That's what she had meant to say. She must have gotten the dates wrong, misunderstood the question. He wanted to correct her, remind her how the dagger was a reward, how he'd framed Freitz for that murder, not committed it. It was his very first job in Isandor. Hasryan would never forget the pride swelling in his stomach as he beheld the waved blade, a symbol of their partnership, of her believing in him. His lips parted, a desperate protest forming in his mind. The words didn't make it past the lump in his throat.

She knew all that.

Brune didn't make mistakes.

Brune never smiled either, unless a long-standing plan came to fruition.

Sharpe had her repeat the information, then they discussed his other activities. Brune confirmed several of his crimes—assassination contracts he'd taken on her behalf. Without claiming responsibility or mentioning his affiliation to the Crescent Moon. He had finished those jobs for *her sake*. Except she didn't protect him. She sold him out.

This wasn't how the city worked. Employers took the blame, not executioners. Coherent sentences crumbled under the shock, words stumbling out of his blank mind, never crossing his lips. A dull throb covered the discussion, and he looked at Brune without seeing her.

Twelve years together, partners in crime. Yet she dropped him like a stinky sock. The perfect scapegoat. Had he ever been more? She had given him that dagger at their arrival in Isandor. *Always carry it, even if hidden*, she had said. *One day, having it with you will be a matter of life and death.* Had she planned it all along? Seen nothing but how easy it would be to deflect blame for heinous crimes on an assassin of dark elven blood? He shouldn't be surprised. What else would anyone ever see in him? He had walked into that one with a confident smile, glad to have found someone he could trust after years of struggle. In his mind, Brune sought a skilled and ruthless partner, without care for his race. They had built the Crescent Moons' influence in Isandor with careful planning and execution.

Or rather ... she had built it with the help of a perfect, naive, and willing tool.

He should have known. Why would she be any different? Everyone attacked him on sight, fled, or exploited him. No big deal. He was used to it ... right? Then why did he no longer feel the floor under his feet or the wall against his back? Why did a thousand needles poke at his heart all at once, leaving it a dysfunctional, bleeding mess? He was shaking, out of focus, throbbing in shocked pain. Hasryan closed his eyes, trying to wrestle himself back under control.

Sharpe put a hand on his arm, and he jumped. Brune was gone. When had that happened? Had he lost track? Hasryan forced a long breath in, then exhaled. He shouldn't space out like this, not if he wanted to survive. He was on his own again.

"Do you have anything to add?" she asked.

The judge was staring at him, unimpressed. Hasryan clenched his teeth together and pulled away from Sharpe.

"What's the point? Just convict me already."

"Lady Allastam's death anniversary is in five days," the judge said. "You will be hung over Carrington's Square then."

Of course. A short drop from the infamous archway, above the statue of the city's. A great show for the good people of Isandor. Hasryan turned his head away and allowed Sharpe to lead him out.

She seemed distant, like when she went over clues and evidence in her mind during interrogations. He remained silent, determined not to give her any more satisfaction. That's what she'd been so smug about. Brune had never intended to save him, and she had known.

When she pushed him back in his cell, she finally spoke up. "You really did expect her to lie for you."

Hasryan's hands curled into a fist. He'd trusted Brune with his life. What a mistake. How often had he been betrayed before? Did he never learn? All she'd had to do was confirm the guards' suspicions. Who would doubt the dark elf's guilt? "I expected her to tell the truth."

"Your truth."

Hasryan bit back his reply. No point in arguing, not when it was his word against Brune's, his empty hands against her full pockets. How he wished he had the chance to escape, find her, and ram that poisoned gift through her back! With that small pleasure before his execution, he would die happy. Happier. He'd have a meagre satisfaction to alleviate the empty burn inside, at any rate.

"I'm still not allowed visitors, I guess?"

He had to remember he still had Larryn and Cal. They were still his friends. The kind you fought with. The kind who didn't base a ten-year relationship on a plan to have you take the fall for one of the city's most famous crimes.

"Afraid not," said Sharpe. "You'll be allowed to write them letters on the last day."

Hasryan suppressed a bitter chuckle. Lots of good that would do Larryn. No one had ever taught the half-elf to read. But, well, Cal could always do it for him. He would have to tell them the truth, at least. He hoped they'd still like him once they knew what his job was. Hard to believe in it now.

"Better than nothing, I guess," he said. "Now why don't you leave? Go celebrate."

"I don't celebrate another death."

She seemed about to add more, then shrugged and left. As her footsteps echoed down the corridor, Hasryan wondered how many would, in fact, do exactly that. He had made many enemies through the years, most often by refusing to bend his knees to them and take their abuse. True to form, he longed to prepare one last retort for them, one last reason to hate him and celebrate his execution.

CHAPTER TWENTY

THE wax formed a solidified pool around Nevian's candles. Their light flickered, almost dead, but he didn't want to waste time finding new ones. He focused on the spell at the tip of his fingers and attempted to deconstruct it into smaller elements. Brune's clues had helped fix one major issue, but digging deeper into protective spells had brought more questions and almost no answers. What part of these arcane words stood for the range? How did one manipulate the web of magic to conjure a shield of force? Which of the creation runes was he supposed to use, and why? These runes were the key to magic—tools to channel power—but Nevian had no models to help him built his. Protection spells had never been Master Avenazar's favourites, and the enclave's library lacked tomes covering the basics. Nevian had dug through several books and found a dozen spells he might want to learn. He tried to make a chart out of them, to see what they had in common, and where the differences were. If he could identify every rune's role … The work demanded tremendous concentration, however, and induced a constant headache. Without High Priest Daramond's magical bandanna, he'd have collapsed long ago.

Nevian reached for his arm, touching the rekhemal under his robes. Snatched his hand back right away. No one could know. The High Priest had risked too much in helping him, and now Nevian regretted the responsibility. He would have returned the bandanna, but every time he considered seeking High Priest Daramond, he remembered the mind-numbing exhaustion of late-night studying. How often had he collapsed in his books, unable to continue the endless deciphering of runes and spells? Every time he slipped the artifact around his forearm, Nevian's mind lit up. His surroundings came into sharp contrast—he could see farther, hear the tiniest scuffle, bask in the old book smell around him—and the fatigue that turned crisp runes into foreign scrawls vanished. He accomplished twice as much in a day as he had before. The constant progress made the risk worthwhile.

Nevian cast a glance around the library. No one spying on him in the darkness, not that he could tell. Everything was fine. For now. Sometimes, he wondered if the Isbari priest had known how useful his gift would be. He had seemed to act on a hunch, drawing his conclusion from keen observation, but it was difficult for Nevian not to distrust Varden. He'd been watching, that much was certain, and his willingness to help Nevian might have a limit. Who would risk Avenazar's wrath, after all?

With a sigh, Nevian returned to his spells. Better not to worry about that. He'd need to bring back the rekhemal for the Long Night's Watch. He ought to make the most of it before Master Avenazar filled his schedule with petty tasks to frustrate him. He had half an hour before the candles gave out, and he intended to make the best of it.

Nevian dipped his quill in ink and started writing, linking spells through their similarities while scratching off possible connections between others. The back-and-forth of his quill quickened, brush-like, as a pattern began to emerge. His heart sped, his fingers tingled, and he bent over the table. Every new note brought him closer to an understanding of these spells, to practise and mastery. Closer to becoming a true wizard. His throat tightened, and he couldn't keep the smile from his lips. All the spells protecting from physical harm, whether through a force field or by dispelling elemental magic, had a single rune in common. It had to be the body rune. Nevian fumbled for the draft he'd shown Brune. If he added the rune at the start …

The light vanished, his last candle dead. He slammed his quill on the table.

"No! Curse it."

A brownish glow flickered at the library's entrance in the form of a tiny ball of luminous energy. It hovered above Isra's hand as she strode to his side, a slight skip to her steps. Nevian stared in silence, teeth ground together. What did she want this time? Hadn't she caused enough damage already? Isra brought her fingers near the candles and blew on the light, and the small globe stayed above them when she withdrew her hand.

"You ought to learn this spell if you intend to spend entire nights studying."

"Then give me its script and leave."

Isra pouted and instead took a nearby chair, flipped it, and sat down, wrapping her arms around the back. Nevian withheld a sigh. He wanted her to disappear, not get comfortable.

"Can't leave you in the dark, can I? Besides, I wanna know what you were doing. It looked so intense."

"I'm working. Studying." Nevian glanced at his almost-complete set of notes. He'd been so close to rewriting his protection spell. "You interrupted."

"I didn't. Your light source dying did."

True. Whether Isra had arrived or not, he would have been forced to seek out new candles. Nevian put the cork back on his ink bottle. He could finish in his room.

"So you're done now?" She settled her chin in her hands. He couldn't tell if she was disappointed or not.

"No," he said, "but I'll finish later. Elsewhere. Alone."

"Leaving because of me? You shouldn't!" Isra's lips stretched into a large smile. "I'll be silent, I promise."

Nevian blew on his notes to dry the ink, then folded them. He was careful not to crease the delicate paper at the wrong places. He wanted to be able to reread them. Isra watched his every movement, as if studying him. Nevian wondered how much she would repeat to Jilssan. "Leave me alone, Isra."

"Why?"

Nevian gritted his teeth and caught her gaze. She had that silly smile, like she had no idea why he would want her gone. He breathed in slowly and gathered his ink bottle and quill with trembling hands.

"All you ever bring is trouble, and I don't have the time or inclination for it. I'm done. You cleaned that floor on my behalf, without my permission, then ran instead of taking the blame as promised. I could have died. This is over. You play your games with someone else. I refuse to waste my precious free time talking to you."

He lifted a heavy tome on protection spells, set his notes on top, and prepared to depart. Isra jumped to her feet and grabbed his forearm, stopping him.

"Nevian, I—"

Her fingers burned through his sleeve.

"Don't touch me!"

His breath quickened, and a jolt ran up his arm, straight to his mind. It wasn't real—he knew it wasn't—but he almost dropped everything. Nevian grunted and stepped back. He could hear Avenazar's cackle, foreshadowing intense pain. Isra let go with a gasp and withdrew. Her light globe flew to her head and hovered there as Nevian continued to stumble back.

He hit a bookshelf and stopped, breathless, his chest tight. It felt like a dozen bugs were scurrying out of it and up his arm. He wished people would quit touching his forearm, or that he had some self-control. The throb in his arm wouldn't vanish anytime soon, now. No more than the scratching discomfort at the back of his mind, an alarm bell constantly ringing, waiting for the worst. Nevian hoped Isra would go away without another word. That, too, was asking too much.

"I'm sorry, Nev," Isra said. "I didn't mean to … Maybe I can make it up to you?"

"No."

"But—"

"I said no!"

As if repeating a refusal had ever kept Isra from doing anything. Her disappointed pout turned into an insulted frown.

"Fine! Be like that. I thought you'd enjoy telling Master Avenazar that there's a traitor in our ranks. Maybe he'd like you more after."

"A what?"

His anger drained away, and Nevian stared at her, his head empty. Dazed. A traitor. His legs threatened to give out under him. Her showing up now couldn't be a coincidence, not after his recent outing to Isandor. How did she know? His throbbing arm had grown numb, but the alarm bell seemed stronger than ever.

"You heard, you stubborn fool," Isra said. "A traitor. That Isbari cleric."

"High Priest Varden?"

Nevian's voice stuttered, weaker than he'd have liked. It didn't make sense. Why would he do such a risky thing? He had what he needed here. Varden wasn't the one selling information in exchange for magic lessons.

Isra beamed at him, proud of his sudden interest. Once again, she'd laid a perfect trap to force her topic into the conversation. "Who else?"

Isra leaned forward and fell silent, as if expecting a string of questions. Nevian devoted his energy to keeping a neutral mask instead of either collapsing to the ground with a whimper or running away. This conversation couldn't lead anywhere safe for him.

Faced with a definite lack of enthusiasm from him, Isra apparently decided to fill in the blanks. "Last night, I flew over the courtyard, coming back from the city. You know what I saw? A man, cloaked, climbing the big oak to get over the enclave's wall! He had his hood on, but it had to be him."

It wasn't. Nevian had almost fallen off that very tree the previous night, trying to get to Brune. Could Isra really have mixed him up with Varden? The High Priest's pale brown skin couldn't be confused with Nevian's pasty white. He had more muscles and was two inches shorter than Nevian. Not to mention Varden's hair was brown and curled, while he had a flat blond mess on his head. How did you confuse the lanky teenager with the broad-shouldered Isbari? In the dim moonlight and with his hood, however, she might not have seen the differences—especially if she had expected to see Varden.

"Why would he do that?"

Nevian regretted asking. He shouldn't question what she had imagined. If no one figured out he was the traitor, he would stay safe. As safe as this enclave could be, at any rate.

"Oh, silly Nevian. He's Isbari. He can't be trusted." She lifted herself onto the table and dangled her legs. The light floated above her head, slowly spinning around. "If you visited the city every once in a while, you would hear all the tales about him."

He did visit Isandor, in secret. Officially, however, Master Avenazar had forbidden him to go to Isandor unless under his direct orders. His forced trip with Isra had put him through hours of torture, and yet here she was, suggesting he should take a stroll on the city's bridges to listen to gossip more often. Like there would be no consequences to that. It took a moment for Nevian to get an answer past his stunned disbelief.

"I don't care."

"They say flames whisked in and out of existence with every step as he exited the tailor's shop." Her voice fell into a hushed whisper, and she punctuated her description with twirls of her hands. "His face and hair were covered with soot, and smoke swirled around him in a cloak of darkness that couldn't conceal his evil gaze."

"Don't be ridiculous. High Priest Daramond was raised among Myrians. He's not a pyromaniac, and I don't think he's a traitor either."

He tried to push past her, but she slid off the table and set her hands on her thighs. "You don't know him. I've watched him manipulate fire, and he gets that gleam in his eyes, like he's possessed or something. The thing about Isbari is, they're predators. It doesn't matter where and how they're raised; it's always there, waiting. Maybe the flames call to his inner instincts."

Nevian almost choked. Straight out of the *Myrian's Handbook to Racism*. He'd had enough encounters with Varden to believe the High Priest might be the gentlest soul stuck in this damned enclave. No point in arguing this with Isra, though. She lived in a world of her own, romanticized to include a fire-happy Isbari traitor and a girl's heroic discovery of his heinous acts. Some days, she behaved like she was still twelve and the universe belonged to her. A powerful father and the notable absence of a sadistic and controlling mentor might have contributed a lot to her illusions. One thing was certain, however: Nevian wanted no part in her game.

"You enjoy the retelling of your discovery to Master Avenazar. I don't want to be involved."

Her smile turned once more into a disappointed pout. What did she expect? He didn't have time to waste on convoluted storylines meant to satisfy her sense of drama and self-importance. And he didn't want to be anywhere nearby when Avenazar discovered Varden had nothing to do with this mess, and Isra had no idea who did. As she began to protest, he pushed her aside and plunged into the darkened library. He needed no light to find the door and left without another word. When he heard Isra's footsteps behind him, Nevian sped up. She exited the library as he reached the nearby corner.

"You're no fun!" she called.

Nevian couldn't help but smile, glad she'd learned that much about him tonight.

CHAPTER TWENTY-ONE

EVERY fibre of Larryn's being hated what he was about to do.

He had climbed all the way to the Middle City, almost turning back with every step, and now waited on a thin bridge stuck between two large towers. Far above, lush plants hung from a balcony and cast a green glow on the marble beneath his feet. Dark smudges marred the grey stone—years of unwashed grime, protected from most of the rain by the two giant towers on each side of this high, suspended alley. The dirt's brown and plants' green mixed into a sickly hue, like the bridge itself wanted to puke on those below. Larryn watched a thin rivulet crawl across the stone at his feet, focusing all his anger and unease on the water slowly making its way for the bridge's edge. It would fall into the Lower City, carrying this bridge's filth with it. Nothing new there. Gold moved up and shit moved down. Such was Isandor's way. Yet the slums were Larryn's favourite part of the city. They stank, but they were his home, and they housed his people. If this were only about him, he would never leave the Lower City. Especially not to talk to a noble.

Especially not to plead for his father's help.

Three years had passed since Yultes Dathirii had first sought him out, eager to alleviate his guilt with money, but when the elven noble appeared at the alley's entrance, Larryn's urge to smash his knuckles into his father's thin nose came back in full force. He couldn't help it. He and Yultes looked too much alike—same high cheekbones, same eyebrows, same frown. The obvious resemblance struck bitter anger in his throat. Anyone walking by would assume Yultes was his father—as if blood ties de facto earned him that position. As if Yultes hadn't abandoned him long before his birth, throwing Larryn's mother to the streets. Heat flushed his cheeks, and he pushed himself off the wall, straightening up. No matter how much Yultes tried, he would never be his father. He would always remain a hated relative with enough remorse to offer unwanted but necessary help.

Yultes stopped a few steps away from Larryn. He had learned to keep his distance. "You look … better. Healthier."

"Eating helps. Give people enough money and they won't look so famished anymore. A true miracle."

Not the entire story, but Larryn had no intention to share the grief that had kept him awake and unable to eat when they had first met. Yultes had landed in his life right after his *real* father had been stabbed. The worst trade possible. It still hurt to think Jim would never see the Shelter, never hear its music or taste its food, never know how much he'd meant to Larryn and how they honoured his passing every year. Larryn tried to pull his thoughts out of the dark pattern and to the business at hand. Yultes always brought these memories back, striking his grief raw again.

Yultes scowled at his acidic tone. His voice turned thin and tense. "I'm glad to learn my gold is put to good use."

"It's not yours, it's mine." Larryn crossed his arms. "The deal is that I can do whatever I want with it."

"Yes."

Larryn remembered that first and last conversation with great clarity. The moment was burned into his mind, the last of trying events. It had taken every shred of his willpower not to kill Yultes on the spot. Too much to gain. Even through the rage and grief, he had seen that. Larryn had allowed him to fund the Shelter for everyone else's sake. He had let Yultes bribe the guards and mark him as untouchable, even from Drake and noble shitstains like him, to be certain he would always be there to cook. Larryn had thought that would be the end of it and had sworn never to speak with the hypocrite again.

Yet here they were, and Larryn had called this meeting. Just looking at Yultes sickened him. His heart hammered against his chest, his stomach shifted about in a strange, nauseating dance, and his head hurt from a dull throb. This man had killed his mother, as surely as Drake had killed Jim. He had almost killed Larryn, too—all because a half-breed child wasn't good enough for him. Larryn reined in his urges to hit or spit on him again. Hasryan needed him to stay calm.

"I need your help."

Every word had to be torn from Larryn, and 'help' came out in a resentful whisper. Saying them was like a punch to his gut, and when Yultes leaned forward to examine him, Larryn's gaze fled to the ground. He clenched his jaw so hard it pained him, angry that life had brought him here, ashamed to hurt so much. He shouldn't care. He knew he was better than this asshole, knew he owed him nothing. But it felt like begging, and Yultes was the last person in the universe he wanted to beg to.

"Anything, Larryn. Please. You only need to ask."

Larryn's head shot up at the barely-restrained enthusiasm in Yultes' tone, and his shame washed away. What was Yultes thinking now? That Larryn had forgiven him? Forgotten how he'd almost never had a mother because of him, how he'd grown frail, easily sick, bones breaking at the slightest hit? It didn't matter how much Yultes said he wanted to help. Larryn wanted none of it. He was several years too late to play the good father with him. Larryn stepped forward and grabbed Yultes by his way-too-clean lapels.

"Don't get your hopes up, asshole," he said. "This is a one-time demand, and only because I can't let a friend die because I hate your face. You're his best chance."

Yultes pinched his lips, flushing red. After a few seconds, he put his hand on Larryn's forearm. Larryn hoped the filth in his clothes would dirty Yultes' manicured fingers. "Just ask."

"Hasryan head-butted Drake's nose and ruined it. It earned him a stay in prison. They beat him up—I know they did—and now that inspector lady wants to frame him with all their unsolved murders.

Get him out."

Colour drained from Yultes's cheeks as Larryn explained, his eyes widening in horror. He stumbled back, licking his lips. Larryn's stomach clenched as his useless father started shaking his head.

"You were with Lady Allastam's assassin when they arrested him?"

"He's not an assassin!" Larryn stepped forward and glared at Yultes. The noble drew back. "Listen well, you piece of shit, because I'm about to tell you how they get their culprit. They take an unlucky bloke from the street—anyone who made the mistake of defending himself or trying to live his piss-poor life—they put him in shackles, and they work up a case after. They don't give a rat's ass if it's true or not. We're all criminals, and to you people we're all expendable."

"His boss—"

"Is a lying hag," Larryn finished. "All I want is for you to wave your cute little title around, make a few threats, grease some palms, and *get him out.*"

"I can't, Larryn. I wish I could, but I can't!" This time when Larryn advanced on him, Yultes didn't back down. "You're safe because you're a nobody. Only two nobles care about what happens to you in this city—Lord Drake Allastam and myself. The guards have no love for Lord Drake Allastam, and some strange fascination with your ... notable escape method. They think it's funny, how you break bones to get out of shackles. And now they know the Bonebreaker is under a Dathirii's protection, and that's enough for them. But your friend Hasryan is in over his head. The entire city has its eyes on him. He's not going anywhere, and I'm not burning my good graces and the Dathirii's reputation by trying."

Of course not. Yultes was happy to help when it didn't affect his position, but the very moment his precious title might be scratched, he bailed out. Larryn didn't know why he'd even asked. Yultes' aid had never been more than charity meant to make his pathetic conscience feel better. He didn't care about Larryn himself. With a scowl, Larryn met his father's eyes.

"I should've known. Forget I asked."

Larryn whirled around before Yultes could answer. The elven lord started protesting behind him, stammering excuses and apologies. Larryn raised a dismissive hand, never looking back.

"I still expect my money next week!"

Yultes would never be good for anything else. Larryn hurried away, angry he'd wasted so much time and energy. Fury burned his reserves, and tears threatened to resurface. Larryn kicked at a rock with a cry of rage, venting the pent-up emotion, but his mind was slipping into the past. Jim's hearty laugh echoed in his head, his never-ending optimism, his resilience. Jim never gave up. He'd spent his entire life trying to save others, only to have it brutally shortened by Drake. Larryn's fingers clenched and unclenched—they needed to hold a spoon or a knife. Any kind of cooking tool, really. And with a dozen onions sliced under his blade, perhaps memories of Jim and the vague memory of his mom would finally pass, giving his mind enough room to come up with a new plan to save Hasryan.

CHAPTER TWENTY-TWO

D ESPITE his best intentions, Nevian couldn't study after Isra's visit. He sat at his desk, staring blankly at his notes while her story ran through his head. How could he have been so careless? A tall man climbing the oak tree? With a little more light, she would never have mistaken him for Varden. His secret would be out, and he'd be dead. Or worse. Nevian's nighttime expeditions now seemed downright suicidal. But what else was he supposed to do? Stay trapped in the enclave at the mercy of Master Avenazar's whims, unable to progress with his magic? Nevian could endure a lot of abuse when he put his mind to it. He needed to know when it would end, however. To have a goal. He had no choice, not if he wanted his life to get anywhere, but he couldn't stop thinking about how close he had come to being discovered.

Luck had redirected the blame on Varden. Pure luck—a luxury he couldn't rely on. It never lasted. Nevian shuddered to imagine what might happen to him once it gave out. Varden's very fate, soon. For him it would be brief, at least. Long enough to figure out Isra's accusations were baseless, that he'd done nothing wrong. Then Master Avenazar would turn his attention to Isra. Perhaps his retribution for the time wasted would grant Nevian a few hours of peace to study more, free of his master's constant ridiculous demands.

Nevian frowned and reached for the bandanna tied around his forearm. He hated that it had to be Varden first. Who would heal the priest once Avenazar trampled through his memories and turned him into a wretched ball of pain? Wasn't right to let him take the fall, however briefly. Avenazar would have too much fun. Nevian should warn him as a thank you for the rekhemal. It'd give him a chance to flee.

Except he couldn't do that.

No one escaped Master Avenazar. Sauria had tried. She'd run halfway across Myria, Nevian in tow, before Avenazar found her. Nevian had heard every inn they'd stayed at during their flight had been razed to the ground. After witnessing the destruction Avenazar had left at her last hideout, Nevian had no trouble believing the stories. Once the wizard set his sights on someone, there was no escape. Nevian was already trapped with him by virtue of being Sauria's old apprentice, and Varden would be no different. Avenazar would find him, and once he had his hands on him, he would rip through his memories and discover Nevian's warning. If he tried to help Varden, he would condemn himself. He couldn't save the priest. Nevian's best option was to sever all ties with Varden. He had to think of himself first.

The next morning, Nevian found his way to the High Priest's door. He knocked twice to warn of his presence, then turned the knob. He needed to be fast, before guilt overrode his good sense. *Tell Varden*, the burning shame in his stomach said. *You owe him.* But he had never asked for Varden's help. Nevian refused to get himself killed because the priest was nice to him once. He had to go in, return the rekhemal, and leave. Nothing else.

As he pushed open the door, he heard swearing and scrambling. A foot blocked the movement from the other side.

"A moment, please!"

Panic seeped into Varden's voice. Nevian frowned and stopped pushing.

"I don't have one."

"Nevian?" Behind the priest's nervousness was a hint of relief. "You can't come in, not yet. I'm sorry, I'm … naked."

Nevian jumped back as if the door had burned him. Why was the High Priest naked in the middle of the day? Then he heard a woman's stifled giggles, and Varden hushed her. The door snapped shut and they shuffled inside. Nevian would never understand that kind of desire—he had never even experienced attraction and doubted he one day would—and physical proximity unnerved him. He waited, wishing people were more reasonable about this whole sex thing. Because, really? The middle of the day?

After a minute or two, Varden reopened the door. He wore black pants and was buttoning up the front of his dark orange shirt. His official robes had been thrown on his desk's chair, in disarray, and the curly hair seemed more a mess than usual.

"I didn't expect you." His cold tone indicated he didn't want him either and left a strange taste in Nevian's mouth. Varden had never made him feel unwelcome, building in his person one of the rare sources of safety in the enclave. The subtle rejection hurt more than it should have. When had Nevian grown attached? This was bad, very bad. Good thing the priest had decided to play in the middle of a work day, then. His irritation at being interrupted reminded Nevian of what their relationship truly was, and had to be. In Avenazar's enclave, no one had room for tentative friendships. Nevian gritted his teeth and prepared to underscore the ridicule of Varden's annoyance considering the moment of the day, but the High Priest cut him short. "Be quick."

The apprentice bit back his previous comment on timely recreational activities. He was supposed to get in, give Varden the rekhemal, and get out. Not lecture him. "Tomorrow is the Long Night's Watch," he said. "You should have this back."

Nevian lifted the bandanna but couldn't meet Varden's gaze. What a pointless gesture. What if Avenazar went overboard and Varden was dead within a week? Perhaps Nevian should keep the artifact and continue using it. It had done such amazing things for his productivity! But Varden had said it bordered on heresy. Best not to give Avenazar another excuse to attack either of them.

"Thank you, Nevian." A smile brightened Varden's face as he retrieved the bandanna, all of the usual warmth flooding back into his tone. Had the cold treatment been a fluke? Could he still count on Varden? Yearning tugged at Nevian, but he hushed it. Things would get bad now. He needed to stay away. Varden folded the rekhemal with great care. "Will you want it again?" he asked.

If only. Nevian tried to hide his desire. If he could, Nevian would wear the rekhemal every day, every hour. Only Varden's warning about sleep had stopped him. As desperate as he was to progress, Nevian knew better than to disregard instructions.

"No." When he saw Varden's eyebrows shoot up, Nevian struggled to find a good justification. He didn't want to appear suspicious. Just in case Avenazar searched through Varden's memories, noticed anomalies, and wondered if Nevian had known beforehand. And even though the apprentice wasn't warning Varden, Avenazar might resent him. Better not to take the slightest chance with him. He needed a credible excuse. "I rely on it too much. It won't always be there."

"True, but—"

"I'll manage," Nevian interrupted. "I don't need your help."

Varden flinched, and the reaction twisted Nevian's stomach. People were always trying to use him or destroy him, yet Varden had been nothing but helpful. Friendly, even. The apprentice could give it back, allow Varden closer. Right now, with just a few words, he could tell him to flee. Help. Nevian closed his eyes. He focused on the terrible punishment that would follow, and the dull throb it brought to his arm kept him silent.

"Sometimes, Nevian, it shouldn't be about what you need." Varden lowered his gaze and ran his finger over the bandanna's soft fabric. "If you change your mind ..."

"I won't. I'm sorry."

Nevian realized he was apologizing for much more than refusing the rekhemal. He forced himself to look straight at the man he was about to sacrifice for his own safety. Nevian's mouth went dry, and Isra's story almost crossed his lips. Then Varden sighed and leaned against the doorway.

"If you say so," he replied with a slight smile. "Good luck, Nevian. We'll see each other when Master Avenazar again decides to vent his anger on a helpless target."

Nevian's stomach churned. Varden *was* the next helpless target. Isra had it all wrong. The High Priest was no savage. His smiles hid concern for Nevian's safety, and his jabs at Avenazar reeked of ill-concealed outrage. But if Nevian didn't correct Isra's racist mistake, was he any better? Letting Varden take the fall was a cruel decision made by a terrible human being. Nevian gritted his teeth. He needed the respite. A pause in his painful life. If that made him a horrible person, so be it. His arm burned at the very thought of getting involved. This couldn't be tracked to him, not if he wanted to live. Every extra hour he was spared from Avenazar's wrath would allow him to learn new spells and become a full-fledged wizard.

"One day, I won't be helpless anymore."

He let the promise hang in the hair and spun on his heels, hurrying down the corridor. Bullets of sweat ran down his forehead and neck. He could feel Avenazar's hand on his forearm, the imaginary pain coursing up. A scream swirled at the bottom of his lungs and wound its way up, only to get stuck in his throat and choke him. Nevian broke into a sprint as he emerged from the temple and onto the enclave's ground. His vision blackened at the corners as he fought for control over his wheezing. The imaginary pain had crawled all the way up to his shoulder and neck, reminding him of a very simple fact: nothing was worth facing Master Avenazar. Varden would have to fend for himself.

⊙ϿᎧ⊙

VARDEN stared at the door as it closed behind Nevian, the soft rekhemal in his hands. He'd expected Nevian to take it back after the Long Night's Watch. Varden had seen the change in the young apprentice through the last week. It was subtle, but Nevian had grown more alert and healthy, prompter to complete Avenazar's tasks and vanish. More determined to see things through. There had been a new spark in him—one gone from the scared and distrustful teenager who had just left his quarters.

"Was that his apprentice?" Branwen asked. "The one he attacked in front of Uncle Diel?"

"Yes."

Varden set the bandanna atop his desk, then slipped back into his official attire. He tried to flatten his hair into a more respectable appearance and destroy the quick disguise he'd created to explain Branwen's presence if needed. *One day, I won't be helpless.* He wondered how long it would take Nevian to escape, and whether Varden would ever have that chance. Nevian might learn to defend himself and become a full-fledged wizard, protected from Avenazar's wrath by fellow Myrian mages, but as long as Varden lived among Myrians, he would need to watch his words. No magic could make the power imbalance between Isbari and Myrians vanish. Sometimes, he daydreamed of fleeing Myria entirely, but guilt locked him down. He had managed to carve a space for himself in Keroth's church and help so many other Isbari. Varden couldn't resolve himself to abandon them. He had to hope he would eventually move somewhere safer than around Avenazar.

"We'll trounce him," Branwen said, as if she'd been following his train of thought. "My uncle is the best, you'll see. He'll find a way to crush Avenazar and send this whole enclave running!"

Varden answered with a bitter smile. Branwen's absolute conviction in the Dathirii's success warmed his heart, but it was naive and pointless. Master Avenazar wouldn't pack up and leave. If things became bad enough, even a direct order from Myria wouldn't keep him from inflicting his wrath upon the Dathirii.

"Lord Dathirii made a mistake. Skilled politician or not, this is too much for him. He should have stayed out."

Branwen jumped to her feet, her wide grin transforming into a serious grimace. The sudden shifts in her moods always took Varden unaware. One minute she was a cheerful companion, the next a ruthless professional. He wondered if she did it on purpose, to keep others on their toes. Or maybe she didn't even notice.

"You don't know him," she said. "Uncle couldn't have stayed out. This enclave has bothered him from the very first day you arrived. It's a surprise it took two years before he acted, really, but that's good. I gathered a lot of information on you guys, and Garith had an almost complete financial portrait. Everyone except Uncle Diel himself knew this was coming. Sooner or later, we'd have had this conflict.

We're ready."

She leaned past Varden and pulled a blank parchment out of his pile, then handed him the cooled charcoal he used to sketch. Branwen was so close her hair tickled his skin, but he didn't say a word about the sudden proximity. He'd learned quickly that she had little concept of personal space.

"You're helping me," Branwen said, "so you don't believe this is hopeless. Don't be a defeatist and draw me a map of the enclave."

"A map?"

"I'm leaving tomorrow, right? We've covered a lot of things together, but a map will be precious information if I need to infiltrate again. Be precise."

A small laugh escaped Varden, and he picked up the charcoal. It seemed they were back to her badgering him for every tidbit of knowledge about Myria and the enclave. Once Branwen had accepted she wouldn't leave the enclave before the winter solstice, she had decided to make the most of her time. Every evening, when Varden returned and closed the door behind him, she assaulted him with an endless string of questions. He suspected she spent her days thinking of a list then waited to ambush him. The interrogation carried late into the night—her sitting cross-legged on the couch, him lying in his bed. Sometimes he'd try to cut it short. "Can I sleep?" he'd ask, but Branwen would laugh and reply, "I'm not done yet."

Varden answered everything he could. Why not? Lord Dathirii was his best chance to get rid of Avenazar, no matter how little Varden believed in it. He'd already crossed so far into traitor territory he doubted this information would worsen his fate.

Last night, the tone of her questions had changed. Varden had tried to coax Branwen into silence or toward other topics with a bottle of wine. Not the best idea. At first, it had worked. They had drunk most of the night, occupying their usual seats, their posture getting more and more relaxed as the level of wine in the bottle lowered. Branwen talked about what it was like to grow up with the Dathirii family. Her parents had vanished before she could commit them to memory, and Diel Dathirii had done his best to be an adequate substitute despite his other duties.

"He didn't really have the time, so he let me braid his hair while he worked and did mine on occasions," she'd said. "But there were the others, too. I spent entire days playing tricks on Vellien with Garith, being scolded by Kellian, or eating Aunt Camilla's cookies. Sometimes I wondered why my parents left. If it was my fault. When Uncle Diel talks about them, he makes it sound like they were the most romantic couple he had ever seen. But anyway ..." She'd swirled the wine in her glass, thoughtful. "I'm glad I have everyone else. Parents matter less when you have a family like mine."

Varden had stared at the flames burning in his fireplace. A supportive family must have been nice. Having anyone to catch you when you stumbled made life a lot easier. Growing up, he'd learned not to expect praise, had taken his victories in the disapproving glares of rivals and masters as he constantly managed to do better than them. As long as he succeeded, he knew Keroth was with him. The strength of his power over fire—his incredible control even when older priests struggled—became his best guide.

Branwen had stretched out on the couch, taking as much room as she could. "Do you have anyone back in Myria? I could never find anything on your family."

Her question had shattered his relative peace of mind. "A fire took them. We were slaves locked in a wooden barn. I was six."

Varden didn't remember a lot of it. Chains and iron bars had kept everyone inside. He'd buried the events away, trying to ignore the holes in his memory and the flashes of recollection haunting his dreams. Branwen cleared her throat and emptied her glass of wine. She turned to face him.

"You survived."

"I'm here, am I not?"

"How?"

"Because somehow, even at six, I could stand in the middle of a brazier and not die. Just me. No one else, and I couldn't protect anyone." The fire had blinded him, but human screams had pierced its roar. He still dreamed of his mother's hand, blackened by the flames, grabbing his wrist, crying. He didn't know if it was a real memory or not. He hoped he never would. "One of Keroth's priests found me. They control major fires in Myria, extinguishing them safely. He told me I was standing in the middle of the building, flames still dancing around me like a cocoon, and he stole me away. Before someone could claim me as a slave again."

Branwen had tilted her head to the side and propped herself up. "Fire put your entire family through a horrible death, so you decided to become a priest of Keroth?"

Her reaction had knocked his breath out. A little 'I'm sorry' before the insensitive questions would have been welcomed. He'd slammed the glass on the ground, almost breaking it, and straightened into a sitting position. His fingers had dug into the blankets to keep his hands from shaking too much.

"I love Keroth, but I did not choose Them. Isbari don't choose, not in Myria. You take what life grants you and make the best from it. And at this?" He gestured toward the fire, and flames leaped into his palm, forming a swirling ball. "I *am* the best. Keroth destroyed my previous life—one of slavery and fear—to grant me another, where I control at least some of what happens to me. It hurt—it still hurts— but I've moved on. Creating one thing requires the destruction of another. When I draw, I use the leftovers of wood I burned. Such is the nature of the universe. Call me a fool, but I accept that while my life wasn't without trials, I have at least been able to accomplish a lot already. Including saving you."

His tone had hardened at the end, and he'd released the fire in his hands. Branwen had bitten her lower lip and stretched to set the empty glass on the ground.

"Sorry, Varden. I—I'm really glad for that, and my comment was horrible. After everything you've told me about Myria, I should've known better."

Varden had barely refrained from agreeing with the last statement. Branwen wouldn't stop berating herself for the mistake. She often spoke out of turn, and the stress of having her in his quarters or sneaking around the temple thinned his patience, but her apologies were quick and sincere. Varden had no desire to hold a grudge. He snatched his glass of wine and emptied it.

"To answer your original question, however, I did have someone. First, I had my people. Other Isbari looked up to me, sought my guidance and blessings, and I did my best to help. Then there was Miles." He had smiled, breathed in. He could almost smell Miles' light cologne, even so long after leaving Myria for Isandor. "You saw him in my sketchbook. Someone tipped the Myrian wizards to us, however. He arranged to be transferred far away before it got me into trouble. I think it contributed to my forced assignment to this mission, though."

"How was he?"

"Really sweet." They had shared so many secret routines. Every year on what passed for their anniversary, Miles had brought him fireflowers—the flowers under which they'd first kissed, almost a decade ago. "Shy, too. The first few years, we'd see each other all the time. It grew into a calmer relationship, but he helped me get through a lot."

They'd discussed Miles for a while longer, with Varden recalling their first meeting. Branwen had stayed clear of the heaviest topics for the night, and after some time, she became drowsy. Varden had trouble remaining awake too—the wine and fire's warmth enveloped him, soothing some of his worries away. They had fallen asleep still dressed.

Varden pushed the memories of last night away. He had dreamt of his parents again, crawling through the flames, trying to grab him. He hoped they would go away soon. He couldn't afford to be distracted during the Long Night's Watch ceremony. He finished the sketch of the enclave's map for Branwen, then pointed to the eastern gates.

"You should leave through there. They put guards on the wall but not at the door itself. Time yourself between their patrols to sneak out. If Nevian manages it every other week, you should be fine."

"Nevian?"

Varden realized his mistake too late. This wasn't his secret to share, but the difficult night had dulled his wits, and he'd said too much. Varden had caught him once, and since then, he kept an eye out for the apprentice and sometimes helped him leave. Nevian had no idea, and perhaps that was for the best. He would push him further away, as he had whenever Varden attempted to get closer and make his life a little better.

"Nevian isn't the docile and enduring apprentice he'd like us all to believe." Varden smirked, then changed his charcoal for a quill. He began marking areas of his map, moving the conversation away from Nevian. "The prisons are here. Avenazar's quarters are in the northern side of this building, here. This is my temple, and the guards' quarters are near the enclave's main door. If you can't leave through the eastern gates, there is also an oak tree here, which might be tall enough to climb out from."

He blew on his writing, then threw a bit of sand on it to dry. Branwen examined the map while they waited, her eyes darting about the rough plan as she committed it to memory. After a few minutes, she rolled it up. "When should I leave?"

"An hour after sunset. You should have enough light to navigate the enclave, and everyone will be either in their quarters or at the temple for the ceremony."

"Perfect!" She slid the tiny map in her bosom, then lifted herself onto his desk. "This might be the most productive information gathering I've done in years. To think I believed it was over when you flame-jumped here with me. I ... Thanks, Varden. You're great. Not at all what I expected."

"What did you expect?" he asked. "A sadistic pyromaniac hell-bent on setting the world afire and crushing it under his foot? I hear that's the new rumour in town these days."

Branwen laughed—until she noticed his bitter expression. Varden couldn't help himself. Her compliment reminded him of what others believed. Her mirth vanished. "They'll forget. It doesn't matter. They couldn't be more mistaken."

Varden shrugged. It did matter to him. Even if they hadn't cared about his race, they had pegged him as a dangerous maniac. How was that any better? But perhaps with time, they would forgive and forget. He hoped he could prove them wrong one day.

"Let's take care of Avenazar first. We'll figure out something about my reputation after."

"You bet we will!" Branwen smiled at him and set a hand on his forearm. "You're a Dathirii ally now, and my friend. We don't abandon either."

CHAPTER TWENTY-THREE

IEL Dathirii strode into the Allastam Tower's top garden with his chin high and his back straight. Great trees with white bark flanked the pathway, and their branches extended over his head, intertwined into a thick, natural roof. Their dark blue leaves matched House Allastam's colours, and it gave Diel the impression night had fallen despite it being the middle of the day. Phosphorescent vines wrapped around their trunks, their pale blue glow compensating somewhat for the lack of sun. They didn't help with the stuffy atmosphere, like the air itself had grown warm and heavy, but perhaps that was all in Diel's heart and mind.

It seemed so long since he had last slept that Diel had forgotten what rest felt like. Horrible torture scenes featuring Branwen haunted Diel's nights, keeping him wide awake. If only he had his Coalition! The other Houses' refusal had poisoned his mind with bitterness.

This city didn't have a soul anymore. It welcomed invaders with an open heart, thinking only in terms of individual houses and profit. He wished he could make them see how horrible the Myrians were, but they were all too scared, and too obsessed with the dark elf about to be hanged for murder. They would make him pay for assaulting a noble house a decade ago, declare justice done, and ignore the much bigger threat now torturing Diel's family under their nose.

He wasn't done fighting, however. Diel intended to use every resource at his disposal. They had demanded soldiers, and he had come pleading for them.

He hated asking for Lord Allastam's troops, but what other options were there? He needed them for the Coalition, and he needed them to extract Branwen from the Myrian Enclave. Kellian was already planning an assault. They would move after the winter solstice. Hit and run, if possible. Too many would die at the hands of the wizards as it was. Diel prayed Lord Allastam would agree— sending the Dathirii guards alone would result in a catastrophe. Diel didn't often see eye-to-eye with the Allastams' leader, but their respective families had been tacit allies since Lord Allastam's grandfather had been Head of the House. Diel hoped it would be worth something today.

He reached the end of the pathway, where Lord Allastam waited as a king would on his subject. The subtle hint of superiority annoyed Diel, but he refrained his urge to stand taller, as his equal. The bigger and richer houses weren't better despite what they often liked to think. Diel didn't have the time and energy for power plays today, however, and he didn't want to irritate Lord Allastam. He glanced at the other lord, meeting his eyes. His grey temples seemed to absorb the ambient blue light, giving them a darker shade. Perhaps that was intentional, to make him appear younger, but nothing could hide the angry wrinkles at his mouth. Decades of frowns and sneers had marked his skin. Diel nodded, then bent his head and looked down. The submissive position left a bitter taste in his mouth, but he endured. What was a little begging in exchange for Branwen's life?

"Milord, thank you for the audience," he said.

Lord Allastam answered with a derisive snort. "Cut to the chase, Diel. What do you want?"

Diel flinched. Allastam didn't even grant him the courtesy of a title. He knew he was in a position of power here, and he seemed intent on enjoying every moment of it. Diel closed his eyes, breathed in deeply. The Allastams were the only House in Isandor with a decent standing military, and he didn't have the funds to hire mercenaries. If he didn't get their help, he would have nothing.

"Soldiers." His voice was a whisper.

"You want to attack the Myrian Enclave."

"Yes." Diel spoke louder this time, his resolve hardening.

"They haven't broken any laws."

"They kidnapped my niece!"

He lifted his head and met Lord Allastam's gaze. The other noble didn't bother to hide his amusement. He clacked his tongue and shrugged.

"You have no proof of that. Master Avenazar was quite adamant in his denial, and I'm certain you'd have shown us anything that could support your claim."

"You can't be serious. I cannot find her. She was last seen at the very shop they burned to the ground. Where else could she be?"

"Dead."

The possibility was like a punch to his gut. She wasn't dead. He didn't even want to consider it. Blood rushed out of Diel's head, and the world blurred. *Focus.* He couldn't let fear and exhaustion take over, couldn't lose control like he had at the Coalition's meeting.

"Then they killed her, and my point remains." Diel squared his shoulders. "I need your help. You know I'd offer whatever support I could if they had your children. Please, milord. All I want is for Branwen to return home unharmed."

Silence followed, and with every passing second, Diel grew certain he would be rebuffed. Lord Allastam had never intended to help. He was staring down at him, his sneer only half-concealed, enjoying his little power trip. Diel tried not to think of all the times he had cracked down on one of Lord Allastam's immoral propositions at the Golden Table, of how often their opposing senses of ethics had put them at odds. How had Lord Allastam once expressed it? *It's not worth helping those who can't help themselves, Lord Dathirii.*

"I would never be in such a position," Lord Allastam said. "I know not to make powerful enemies for the sake of a meaningless boy. You brought this on yourself, and I will not put my family at risk for your foolishness."

"Ah, yes, my foolishness." That's what they always called it when he stood up for someone who wasn't Dathirii. The despair building in Diel shifted, transforming into roiling anger. "If you had even an ounce of foresight, you'd realize the Myrians aren't going to stop at a few influential trade deals. They own half the western lands, and we sit on a key position to move east. This is only the beginning. Once they're done with my family, others will be next. Have you looked into what happened to other cities they conquered? We would lose all control, become puppets or be wiped out. We have to act now, but it seems I am foolish for trying to stop them before it is too late."

"You are. Sometimes it's best to bend rather than break." Lord Allastam stepped forward and pushed Diel's chest with his gold-tipped cane. "You never learned that lesson, and I'm glad I deal with Lord Yultes more often than with you. He's more amenable to logic. I agreed to stay out of this affair rather than side with the Myrians and gain a great ally, so I suggest you quit your self-righteous lecture before I change my mind."

Diel wrapped his fingers around the cane, his mouth dry and his head buzzing. Yultes had omitted to mention Lord Allastam had considered joining the Myrians. Did the Allastams want to upstage the Lorns, their biggest rival family and the holders of an invaluable trade deal with the enclave? How pointless would the Golden Table become if both of Isandor's most powerful Houses sided with the Myrians' interests? They wouldn't need to have a seat of their own to dictate the city's laws. Lord Allastam was too savvy a politician not to notice … which meant he didn't care he'd be selling Isandor out. Diel lowered the cane with a sigh.

"You may be right. I'm wasting my time here."

He cast a look around the beautiful garden. He remembered a time when the blue-leaved trees didn't cover their heads entirely and sunlight shone upon the pathway. Lady Allastam had been alive, and she had spent many hours caring for the flowers spreading beyond the trees. He had visited once to find her slipping a crown of blue leaves onto her daughter's head. Mia was a toddler at the time—they'd yet to learn chronic pain was what caused her to cry a lot and tire quickly—and Lord Allastam wasn't as bitter and aggressive. Arrogant, yes. Self-serving, yes. But he still listened and smiled, and the household hadn't seemed as dark as today. House Allastam had nothing left in it for Diel to ally himself with despite what Yultes might think.

"Let's not make this meeting into a complete waste, then," he said. "You have my personal congratulations for finally resolving your wife's murder. I'm glad your loss can be put to rest, and this city can move on."

The corner of Lord Allastam's mouth stirred upward. "Ah yes, I bet you're happy I won't be attacking your friends the Freitz anymore. I hope we'll see you at the execution, Lord Dathirii. Erik will be there."

Diel wasn't surprised to hear Lord Freitz would come. After a decade of enduring Lord Allastam's violence on the assumption he was behind the murder, he must thank the gods that someone else took the blame. How ironic that Isandor's bloodiest feud had relied on Lord Allastam's baseless accusation, yet the very same lord had berated him for concluding Branwen was detained in the Myrian Enclave. But you couldn't ask Lord Allastam to hold himself to the same standard as everyone else.

"Of course, milord. It must be an immense relief for Lord Freitz to see his name cleared, and to contemplate the reparations sure to come his way." Diel almost regretted the last sentence. Almost. The anger flashing across Lord Allastam's face erased any misgivings he had about infuriating him, burying them under intense satisfaction. "If you'll excuse me, I have my own family to see to."

He didn't wait for approval and turned on his heel, striding down the blue-tinted garden without another word. It was a meagre victory, but he would not let Lord Allastam dismiss him like a vulgar servant.

Diel's shoulders slumped the moment he left the Allastam Tower. That had gone worse than expected. He had no soldiers, almost a new enemy, and he had never felt more disconnected from Isandor before. His throat tightened as he hurried through vine-covered bridges to the tree-like tower of his home. Panic and exhaustion were crawling into his mind, turning his thoughts to dark torture again, and he needed Jaeger's arms to keep it at bay. Stave off his rising despair long enough to prepare their last-resort attack on the Myrian Enclave.

Chapter Twenty-Four

H IGH Priest Varden Daramond stared at his temple's brazier, amazed by its strength. Several tree trunks formed a tent, and acolytes had fed the fire large logs throughout the day, building a tower of flames that reached to the high roof. Varden stood just a foot away. The heat would have been unbearable to anyone else, but he had shielded himself. The fire didn't burn, it caressed. He watched it dance, marvelling at the shifts in colour and intensity, dazed by its beauty. If only he had an enormous canvas and large chunks of charcoal. He would draw until exhaustion crawled into his muscles and killed the urge, until he could only collapse to the ground, satisfied by his art. One of these days, he would start a massive project like that. Something so big he would need week upon week to finish it.

This was neither the time nor place, however. The Long Night's

Watch would begin in an hour, and he had to be in shape for the demanding ritual. Varden glanced down at his ceremonial outfit. The heavy multilayered garb seemed hotter to him than the blazing fire nearby. Thick black fabric was sewn in a triangle pattern with a lighter, pale orange material. The robes fell in waves around him, more orange than black, moving almost like flames. Varden closed his eyes and relaxed his breathing. Tonight, the triangles would become more than an illusion of fire. He allowed his mind to wander, soaking in the heat, reaching for Keroth's blessed strength. Through the roar and crackle of flames, he heard a small *puff*—or perhaps he felt it more than anything. He peeked down. The orange triangles had lit with real, tiny flames.

His personal light, to carry them through the darkness of the night. He was ready.

Varden turned and watched acolytes shuffle into the temple's large hall. They had arrived early, but he wasn't surprised. Every member of the Firelord's faith waited for this night with great anticipation. Their collective strength would be required tonight. Each of them carried a small black torch. One of the elderly priests had remained at the temple's main gates, distributing them to any newcomers from the enclave. It took longer for the other Myrians to arrive, but they filed in as the sun set through the large windows. Keroth's faith was widespread throughout the Empire, and while they were far from home, no one would miss such an important ceremony.

They lined up along the aisle. Everyone wore dark robes, a thin sash around their waist, and held small bandannas to cover their eyes.

Theirs weren't enchanted like the rekhemal, however, except for two triangles of the same orange fabric from which Varden's robes were crafted, meant to be put before their eyes. The High Priest studied the group. All of the fifty or so gathered in the temple's hall were Myrians—pale-skinned, most of them with blond hair, all proud of their heritage and their homeland. The other Isbari in the enclave were slaves and no doubt had their own smaller ceremony, honouring both Keroth and other deities. Varden wished he could be with them instead of with the Myrians who scorned him.

He knew his reputation in the temple. He was the oddity, the one who had broken through their crushing oppressive structures and succeeded, the one who flaunted the natural talent so common among Isbari right in their faces. From his youngest age, he had defied their expectations and walked with Keroth's blessing. Varden had spent two decades within the church, and he'd met his equal only once—a priest whose gender flickered like the flames, elusive and changing. Varden remembered the raw power emanating from them, the way flames seemed drawn into them, a part of them. Others looked at him with the same envious awe he'd had for this priest, but with an added layer of resentment. Isbari were not supposed to have that kind of power, and it didn't sit well with most Myrians to see him exist.

Yet here they were, ready to follow and support him through the Long Night's Watch. The whisper of their conversations died, and irregular crackling from the fire behind Varden filled the expectant silence. Time to begin. He withdrew his rekhemal, brushing his finger over the fabric once. He prayed that Nevian would ask for it again one day, and that Branwen would make it out of the enclave. He had done all he could for both of them.

High Priest Varden Daramond straightened up, squared his shoulders, and spread his arms out to call for attention. Every eye turned to him.

"The Long Night is approaching. Light dims and darkness grows, but still the sun shines upon us. Bathe in its last rays, and partake in their strength to better face the struggle before us."

His voice boomed through the hall, powerful. Varden always surprised himself when he began a ceremony. He preferred to speak in soft tones, to measure his speech and use kind words instead of threats. Yet when he stood before a crowd, his chest seemed to grow larger. The confidence permeating his voice bolstered him. The last minutes of sunlight filtered through the glass windows on each side of the temple's hall, imbuing them all with its warmth. Varden waited, the brazier at his back and the crowd in front, until the last ray vanished.

He knew the very moment it happened. Keroth's presence weakened during winter solstice as They took Their annual rest. It was up to Their priests all across the land to defend the world against the night's illusions and dangers.

"The Long Night has come."

Varden tied the bandanna around his eyes, and the acolytes followed suit. They hated this part, the long minutes when nothing was visible to them and they had to rely on their other senses. Only Varden's rekhemal had been enchanted with awareness, enhancing his senses—hearing, smell, and touch. Everyone else stayed in the dark as Varden led them into the first chant, about the blindness of men, the danger of illusions. His heart wasn't in the verses tonight. He repeated them without thinking, his mind on Branwen sneaking through the enclave. Had she made it to the gates yet? Was she safe? Was *he* safe? As he reached the end of the psalm, he forced his thoughts back to the ceremony.

"Keroth, bless us with your eyes, grant us your wisdom, let us see each other as bright flames, illuminating the enemies lurking in the dark. May our faith shine bright. Raise your torches!"

Through the bandanna's magic, Varden could hear every shuffle, every breath from the crowd. A flurry of heavy fabric indicated arms brandishing torches. Varden shifted his focus to the fire behind, and the flames leaned into him. He didn't need to see. With the rekhemal, he became one with them, his awareness spreading through the fire, expanding far beyond anything he could have otherwise dreamed. The bristling energy made Varden feverish, tense, as if on the verge of bursting. He took a deep breath, focused on the heat running across his arms, then exhaled.

Balls of fire sprouted from the flames whipping about him. They spun over his head, more and more numerous, until Varden lowered his extended arms and brought them back in front of him, palms still open, facing out. The balls hovered for an instant, as if confused, then zipped through the main hall. Each of them hit a torch, lighting it bright and clear. A few audience members gasped, but most remained stoic. The sashes around their waists gave a soft glow, as did the triangles set before their eyes. They would all see one another now, and Varden's robes would be a beacon at the front. Maintaining their sight during the night would exact a powerful toll on him, but relief spread through the crowd. Varden allowed the sentiment to settle.

"Steady, my friends. Though darkness is unrelenting, we are strong and we will hold. We are candles in the night, warding off shadows."

"We are candles in the night."

Fifty enthusiastic voice repeated his words, lending Varden their strength. Tonight, he was their beacon, their guide, and they followed with eagerness. The trust filled his chest with warmth, and he launched into the second chant, his determination renewed. Psalms and meditations succeeded each other during the Long Night's Watch ceremony, acolytes taking strength in them and in the large fire behind their High Priest. Time lost its meaning and flew by unheeded as Varden led them through the rites, his concerns for Branwen giving way to his duties.

They crashed back as the temple's main doors swung open with a plaintive creak. Varden's heart caught in his throat. His awareness still resided in the crowd's torches, and he could sense the newcomer. Avenazar's snide voice called his name with terrifying joy.

"High Priest Varden Daramond!" The chant died on everyone's lips. Panic crushed Varden's insides, and for a moment the torches' lights wavered. Avenazar continued, and the sound of his voice helped Varden pinpoint him. "What a marvellous ceremony. But perhaps I could make it into an even better show?"

Hushed whispers ran through the crowd, and the acolytes shifted aside as Avenazar moved among them. Part of Varden screamed at him to douse the torch and fire, limiting Avenazar's sight, but the thought nauseated him. Keroth relied on them to keep the light steady, to stay strong through the night. He would hold as long as he could.

"What a pleasant surprise to have you here, Master Avenazar," Varden said, his tone smooth despite the tightness in his throat. "Please, settle among the acolytes. Your strength can only bolster ours."

"I'll show you some bolstering, you traitorous scum!"

The crowd gasped. Varden stepped back, focused on the torches. Avenazar pushed acolytes aside as he advanced on him. The wizard knew. Somehow, he had found out. Varden prayed for Branwen's safety and took another step away. Where could he go? Did it matter? Avenazar had called him a traitor. His life in the Myrian Enclave was over. Varden turned his attention to the remainder of the great brazier, a terrible pain in his chest where his heart hammered. Go. Flee. All he needed was to stride back into the fire and jump. Yet his muscles refused to budge, frozen against his will, a cold spell binding them. A hundred torches wavered as power slipped from his control.

Fingers touched his neck, long and slim. Not Avenazar's. Varden could still track his progress up the aisle. Then Jilssan's smooth voice whispered in his ear:

"I'm sorry, handsome, but you'll have to warm yourself another way."

Intense nausea spun Varden's head. He couldn't even twitch under her grasp. Had she turned him into stone? How had he not felt it? Jilssan untied the rekhemal, and the artificial vision of orange triangles vanished, replaced by the diminished glare of real torches. The binding spell relaxed as Avenazar reached him. All at once, the acolytes tore off their bandannas to watch. Varden noticed Isra at the temple's entrance, wide-eyed. Scared? He had no time to determine. Master Avenazar clasped his hands around his forearm, and Varden flinched. This was the very spot he always grabbed on Nevian. Energy gathered in the wizard's palm, a preview of the immense pain that awaited him.

"Varden, my friend," Avenazar said, his voice smooth once again, "did you really think you could sneak out at night, betray us to the Dathirii, and not face the consequences? Someone was bound to see you. Like a brilliant young apprentice, returning from a mission."

Varden's gaze shifted to Isra, confused. Sneak out at night? He would fire-stride if he ever needed to do anything like that. Had she invented this to get back at him? He had talked down to her when looking for Nevian—always dangerous when dealing with a Myrian. Even the most tolerant ones could turn your life into hell. All it took was a little lie about an Isbari traitor, sneaking out …

Sneaking out like a certain apprentice, leaving the enclave in the dead of night, skipping sleep in order to study. Living his double life with the secret help of the temple's High Priest. Varden's breath caught as he understood. Isra *had* seen someone, without a doubt. Had Nevian known yesterday as he returned the rekhemal to Varden? He'd seemed so … terrified. He must have. And he'd said nothing, instead getting rid of what he thought was their only connection.

Avenazar discharged his power into Varden's arm, and the pain shot right to his mind. The High Priest screamed and collapsed to his knees, panting. Every torch in the temple flared then died. Avenazar laughed and dug his fingers into Varden's flesh.

"Not so proud now, are you?"

Varden stifled a bitter chuckle. Public humiliation couldn't touch his pride. He'd had to stoop to Myrians every day, obeying disgraceful orders, enduring whispered insults until his position offered some leeway. And even then ... Overt pride got Isbari killed. You had to seal it off, keep it secret. The discharge had blown his wits away, however, and when Varden tried to answer, only a pained mumble came out.

"I ... no. I didn't—"

"Don't bother." Avenazar grabbed his chin and pulled him close. Varden's skin sizzled under his fingers, and the priest moaned. It shouldn't. Fire had never burned him before. But Keroth was far away tonight, resting. Avenazar's magic wasn't fire as much as raw power. The wizard chuckled. "I can check myself."

The world darkened as a bloated presence forced its way into Varden's head, flattening his mind against his skull, squishing everything into a bloody pulp as it occupied every inch of space available. Varden cried out but barely heard himself. He fought for control, clawing at Avenazar's immense power. The wizard browsed through his memories with childish glee, wrenching those of interest from their rightful place and bringing them to the forefront.

Varden found himself standing on the cobblestone road leading through the eastern gate, frowning. He'd noticed a shape slink along the walls while returning to Keroth's temple, but now that he moved closer, he couldn't spot anyone. Had he imagined it? Who would try to avoid detection? The priest retreated behind a nearby building, crouching into the shadows to spy upon the entrance. He waited, more and more convinced his mind was playing tricks on him, until he noticed movement again. Varden tracked the shape with his eyes, his palms sweaty.

His heart skipped a beat when he recognized the lanky teenager Avenazar tortured every day. Nevian. And he was acting against orders, heading toward the east gate to sneak out? A slight smile reached Varden's lips at the unexpected defiance. It vanished when he spotted a soldier on the wall, moving at a leisurely pace. He would catch Nevian soon. Had the young apprentice not noticed? Nevian kept creeping forward, unaware. They would find him out. The Myrian Enclave had only been settled for a few months, but Varden understood Avenazar's punishment would be dire.

Varden prayed to Keroth for guidance and forgiveness. Getting involved put him and perhaps the whole temple at risk, but how could he stay out of this? He opened his palm, cast his awareness forward until it settled on the guard's torch, and closed his fist to douse it. The soldier cursed as the flame went out. Nevian ducked into hiding, then edged out and made a dash for the exit while he had the cover of shadows.

Varden's memory faded, and his eyes fell upon the temple's stone floor under him. Avenazar's outrage swirled, gaining strength, pressing against Varden's mind and inflicting on him a terrible nausea. *Nevian dared!* Avenazar's rage coalesced into a resounding scream, thousands of times worse than when he'd thought Varden had betrayed him to the Dathirii. He ripped through the priest's memories, tearing apart two years of life at the enclave to uncover every single time Varden had helped the young apprentice. Shreds scattered in his broken mind. He tried to cling to these moments, but they slipped through his fingers, fuzzier with every attack from Avenazar. The priest fought, desperate to keep these memories intact. A soft moan escaped his lips. Helping Nevian was one of the rare good things he'd done while at the enclave. Helping him and—no. Varden tried to stop himself, but too late. The fleeting image of Branwen Dathirii, sitting in his quarters with a glass of wine, had crossed his thoughts. Avenazar pounced on it.

What's this, Varden? An elven friend?

Avenazar released him. The sudden disappearance created a hole in Varden's mind, an emptiness impossible to fill. Pain exploded as his consciousness reclaimed the space that was his, and he crumpled to the ground with a final scream. His head throbbed. He rolled over, shaking. *An elven friend.* Varden stared at the ceiling above, with large arches climbing alongside like flames licking the dome. His temple? He tried to gather his mind, to remember where and when he was, but the jumble of confused memories refused to cooperate. Two years had been stacked and mixed inside his head, leaving writhing fragments behind. He needed more time.

An invisible hand grabbed the front of his ceremonial garb and pulled him up. Varden's muscles throbbed as his feet lifted from the ground. Avenazar stood beside him, palms extended in his direction. He made him rotate until the priest faced a gathering of acolytes. The ceremony, Varden recalled. Tonight was the Long Night's Watch. Their torches had died. No one held watch for Keroth while They rested. Varden's gaze scanned the crowd, slow and dazed. The fire behind cast a flickering light on horrified and enraged faces.

"Our good Isbari priest hides a lot from us, it seems," Avenazar said. "Would you believe he'd secreted away a Dathirii elf—our enemy—in his quarters?"

An angry whisper ran through the crowd. Varden squeezed his eyes shut. He hung midair before a group of Myrians who had always had more fear than respect for him. They had trusted him to lead the ceremony, but Avenazar would destroy that sentiment. The wizard cackled.

"The Long Night is difficult for many of Keroth's flock. It is filled with dangers, sometimes from within. We should be thankful the Firelord showed us the truth about this traitor. Should we learn more? Make him pay?"

"Make him pay!"

The chorus sank his heart. Unanimous decision. Varden searched for a friendly face, desperate for a little comfort. At the back of the crowd, Jilssan cast him an apologetic look before slipping away with Isra.

Another woman stepped forward as the door clicked behind them—Kira, the temple's second-highest-ranking member. She threw him a savage grin. "In this darkest of nights, we must stand strong and united. We cannot let past sentiment stay our hands. The Firelord wouldn't. The High Priest has deceived us. Let him pay."

She lifted her hand, and everyone's torches lit again, shining brighter than ever. The gathering cheered. With just a few words, she had cast Varden as the outsider to defend themselves against. Cries of "burn him" and "traitorous scum" rang through the hall, each a stab to his stomach, cutting deeper than Avenazar's magic ever could.

"You heard them," Avenazar whispered as he dropped Varden to the ground. "Let's see what else is in your beautiful mind."

A scream escaped his lips as Avenazar trampled back into his head, harder than before. The pain spiralled out, tendrils of shock running down his spine. The world blurred once again, but the cheers of his fellow priests echoed in Varden's mind, clear and loud, as Avenazar ripped through the recent memories of his time with Branwen.

CHAPTER TWENTY-FIVE

NEVIAN didn't dare escape the enclave through the oak tree tonight. He hated sneaking out so soon after being spotted, but what choice did he have? He had a rendezvous with Brune, and they had so little time together, he had to see her. Plus, skipping out would anger her, and he couldn't risk it. He approached the eastern gates gingerly, keeping an eye on the pathway above. This place brought back memories of the one time, early in his nightly outings, when he'd almost been caught. If the guard's torch hadn't flickered out, causing him to swear, Nevian wouldn't have made it out. The warning had sufficed for him to dive under the cover of shadows and escape unseen, however. He had never repeated his mistake.

At least tonight was the winter solstice, and a large part of the enclave would be praying in Keroth's temple or in their personal chambers. Nevian cast another glance around the empty courtyard, then hurried through the gate. He had have to stop sneaking out for the next few months. He had to let them think blaming Varden had solved the problem or they'd realize Isra's mistake and start looking for the real culprit. Nevian would need to lay low. It unnerved him to stall his magical progress this way, but 'better safe than sorry' was a saying he very much agreed with.

One last night out, then he would bide his time again. He hurried down the cobblestone road, his mind turning back to his protection spell. He had almost figured it all out, and he expected to spend the night practising with Brune. If he could nail this one, he might be capable of mastering the others on his own.

He should look into invisibility, too. The area between the enclave and Isandor proper had a few choice pieces of cover—a large rock, a clump of gnarly trees, and the rather tall grass on the left—but otherwise it contained little to hide behind. It wasn't a long stretch of road to the city, perhaps half an hour's walk, but late at night, anyone would appear suspicious. He kept to the side as much as he could, ready to duck away should someone else come along.

If they spotted him tonight, while Varden led the Long Night Watch's ceremony in front of fifty acolytes, they would know to search for another traitor. Letting him take the fall shot bitter pain through Nevian's stomach, but he saw no way out. Surviving Avenazar meant allowing others to sink. Still … he let his mind wander, seeking a solution. What if he convinced Isra not to tell yet? He could argue he'd thought about her words some more, and she was right, he wanted to bring it to Avenazar himself. Only if he witnessed it first, however. She owed that much to him, didn't she? Then they would waste entire nights waiting for this nonexistent traitor to sneak out again. When no one showed up, he could tell Isra that if she'd wanted to spend time with him, she should have invented a better lie.

Nevian couldn't help but smile. She might even be angry enough to leave him alone for a while. This plan's only flaw was that he would need to endure all those nights with an annoying brat rather than studying, but Varden deserved the sacrifice. Nevian might even manage to make up for the lost time by borrowing his magical bandanna again.

As Nevian finessed his future talking points for Isra, a rock rattled on the road behind him. He spun around, eyes wide, heart threatening to burst through his chest. No one. He scolded himself for letting his mind wander and scanned his surroundings. Nothing moved but a few dead leaves in the wind. Perhaps it had been a small animal. He might even have imagined the sound. He didn't think so, though. Every other step Nevian glanced back, certain he would notice someone, certain he would be attacked. Yet he reached Isandor without anything happening.

Nevian wiped his palms on his cloak, which didn't quite hide his apprentice robes. He wished he had something subtler to wear. Perhaps that should be his first order of business once he started returning to Isandor in a few months. For now, though, he had to remain calm. Take normal steps. *Not* look suspicious.

Despite his best efforts, anxiety sped his heartbeat and lengthened his strides. He hurried through the Lower City, unable to slow himself. Something was coming. He could tell in the shiver creeping up his arms, the lurching of his stomach, and the lump tightening his throat. Nothing rational about the way his mind spun out of control, dragging his body along with it, but he couldn't help it. The lack of logical reason was the worst part to him. He could not justify his urge to get to Brune before it was too late, before—

Master Avenazar materialized in front of him.

It was too late.

They stood on top of one of Isandor's many bridges, halfway to the Middle City and Brune's tea shop. A cold wind buffeted Nevian's cloak. Avenazar hadn't bothered with extra layers—he intended to make this short. Nevian's mouth went dry. There would be no Lord Dathirii to save him this time.

"Good evening, Apprentice," Master Avenazar said. "I don't recall sending you out for a bout of nightly shopping."

Words froze in Nevian's throat before they could escape.

"I'm disappointed, Nevian. I used to think I could break this streak of disobedience in you—that given time and patience, you would learn to do as told, without questions. Yet what do I discover tonight? You are too much like your old master. She lied to me, too. Humiliated me. What am I going to do with you now?" After a noncommittal shrug, Avenazar's voice dropped to a dangerous growl. "One meaningless escapade, I could forgive. More than a year of betrayal, however ..."

Dead. He was dead. Nevian stumbled back. How had Avenazar discovered? How could he know how long Nevian had been with Brune? Did he know about her? Had she told him? Did it even matter? He had seen what Avenazar was capable of—had lived through it. His hands shaking, his voice a desperate whisper, he launched into the only protection spell in his repertoire. Kind of. If one counted his scribbled notes and untested beliefs of how to cast it. But Nevian had to try *something* at least, even if he didn't stand a chance. Terrified obedience wouldn't cut it, not anymore. A shimmering barrier appeared around the apprentice as he finished. What little satisfaction Nevian drew at his success vanished when Avenazar cackled.

"Is that a shield against elements? Fantastic! Let's test how good you became while I wasn't looking, shall we?" Avenazar tilted his head to the side and clapped his hands. "I say we start with fire! It'll be an homage to your Isbari friend. Watch out, though. If your spell fails, he won't be there to douse the flames for you."

His Isbari friend? Avenazar had to mean Varden. Why was he talking about Varden?

Nevian had no time to think further about it. Great flames burst from Avenazar's hands and crashed into his meagre protection. His spell deflected the initial blast of heat, but the shield cracked, and fire leaked inside. Sweat rolled down Nevian's forehead as he tried to hold. He poured all his willpower into that simple spell, praying for it to survive Avenazar's assault. It felt like a hammer pounding on his thin defence. It burst in a handful of seconds, and fire crashed through.

Flames seared Nevian's flesh and skin as he stumbled backward and fell with a scream. He raised his arm to protect himself, curling up. Avenazar dropped the magic and strode closer. Laughing. Of course he was laughing. Exactly like he had three years ago. Nevian crawled away, still on his back, tears rolling down his cheeks. He wanted to hide, to disappear and be safe, just this once. He whispered the start of another spell, but Avenazar stomped on his ankle, and Nevian's casting morphed into a cry of pain.

"Poor Nevian. Did you think you could resist?"

Avenazar snatched his forearm, and Nevian's nausea hit before the first wave of agonizing energy. His muscles stiffened as the pain reached his mind like a powerful hand crushing everything inside his skull. Nevian almost welcomed the familiar sensation. He knew how to deal with it, could endure the mental assault more easily than the burns. No matter how long it would take to get back on his feet from it, he would. All he needed was to survive.

The painful flare shifted as Master Avenazar's presence slipped into Nevian's mind. Raw pain became a throbbing crush, and Avenazar withdrew the last memory of studying. He forced Nevian to remember his evening at the library, dissecting the different types of protection spells, classifying them, searching for common ground. The longer Nevian watched himself, the fuzzier the details became. He sat there by the flickering candlelight, writing a flurry of notes, but what had sparked such enthusiasm? What had he understood? What was he even studying at the time? Nevian recognized Avenazar's touch with growing panic. He was washing the knowledge away, leaving nothing but the hours of work. The memory faded, and Avenazar called forth another one.

"N-no!" Tears ran down Nevian's cheeks as Avenazar browsed through his mind. He felt their distant coolness, a stark contrast against his burning skin. "*Please.*"

Master Avenazar kept going. He found every sleepless night, every moment snatched away to learn new spells or acquire new tomes, and he wiped the result clean. All the risks taken to become a competent wizard, all the information given by Brune ... Hours upon hours of back-breaking work, erased one by one as Master Avenazar careened through his memories and destroyed them.

You will die without the spells you worked so hard for, Avenazar warned. *When I'm done, the most basic knowledge of magic will have been wiped from your mind.*

Nevian squeezed his eyes shut and set his forehead against the bridge's cool stone. He didn't want to die, not like this. Working day and night was the story of his life. Even in his early years in the large classes, when the other kids created small sparks and read scrolls while he couldn't name basic runes, he had persevered. He had found the time and discipline to catch up to what their rich or talented parents had taught them and earned himself a spot with one of the capital's best wizards. And when Avenazar had exterminated Sauria and forced him to be his servant? He had created time in the dead of night for his studies. Nevian didn't give up. He didn't even slow down. He found a way to make it work, because he knew he could become an incredible wizard if life gave him the chance.

It wasn't going to, though. He would die with nothing but the memory of his sacrifices and the certainty they'd been useless.

The grip on Nevian's mind vanished, and his eyes flew open as Avenazar stumbled back, a slim dagger embedded in his shoulder. A single dagger—nothing that would stop him for long. The sudden release in his mind created a vacuum, and some of his memories flooded back in. He groaned against the blossoming pain. Avenazar gave the surroundings a quick scan, then advanced on him.

"Seems you'll have to die now after all," he said.

No. He still remembered tiny glimpses of knowledge. He had to preserve them. Nevian took the only escape offered to him. He brought his legs back underneath him and swung his weight to the side, rolling off the bridge's edge. Throwing himself into a lethal fall. Perhaps he would survive. He hadn't climbed so high in the city yet. Wind whistled in his ears, half-covering Avenazar's cry of frustration. The ground of the Lower City rushed to meet him, faster than he had expected or wanted it to. It would hurt. Snap his spine. But that was okay.

Even if he died, he would at least remember something of his magic. He would remember himself.

Nevian hit a bridge with a bone-crushing crack.

⌾⟨⟩⌾

MANY had told Branwen that her curiosity would get her killed—a silly statement in her opinion. As House Dathirii's spy and main source of information, curiosity was a job requirement. Her work was by no means safe, so they had a point: it might get her killed. She wouldn't stop, though, so they might as well cease warning her.

She wasn't sure tracking Nevian could be called work, however. It could lead her to useful information, true, but she mostly wanted to know what made the teenager tick. His master was a sadistic maniac, yet this kid sneaked out of the enclave on a regular basis. What could be worth the impending torture? Nevian endured Master Avenazar's wrath more often than not, and Branwen couldn't think of a good reason to risk it, but she'd learned long ago that didn't mean one didn't exist. She would find her mark's motivation if she followed him.

Not a hard feat. Branwen might be rusty from a week of nervous pacing in Varden's warm quarters, but Nevian was so nervous and distracted even a beginner could've made it. He kept glancing back, so Branwen made sure to stay ahead, half-hidden in Varden's overcoat. In Isandor proper, she used the crisscross of bridges and stairs to track his movements without ever following from behind. The city was her playground. One would need to know it by heart to ditch her, and Nevian certainly didn't. The renewed freedom heartened Branwen, slowly unwinding the knots from these stressful last days. She could join the fight again—investigate Nevian, then bring back all the information she'd gathered to the family. She couldn't wait to climb the Dathirii Tower again and burst into Uncle Diel's quarters. If he had slept at all since her disappearance, she would be surprised. The sooner she returned, the better for everyone.

As Branwen imagined the tight hugs and apologies, Master Avenazar teleported to the middle of Nevian's path.

She flung herself out of sight, flat against the bridge. Her road crossed Nevian's, about fifteen feet above and at a sixty-degree angle, and she had an excellent view of the scene below. Good enough to twist her insides as the small wizard advanced on Nevian, mocking his apprentice's defence, preparing a spell of his own. Branwen's heart hammered against her chest as she leaned forward. Then Avenazar took a verbal stab at Varden—an Isbari friend with fire, who else?—and it climbed into her throat, beating faster. Her mouth went dry, and she squeezed her eyes shut as flames erupted from Avenazar's hands. Had he found out about Varden? Was that how he had known to look for Nevian? It made sense, but it implied consequences Branwen refused to accept. Nevian's screams made her imagine Varden's. Was he even alive? Did Avenazar know about her? Branwen's head spun as she wondered if he would come after her next. She fought the rising nausea and concentrated.

Avenazar had his fingers around Nevian's forearm, claws digging into the thin flesh. She couldn't tell what he was doing, only that the young man whimpered and struggled against the hold. Branwen's hand went to her knife. Her tiny weapon, brought with her when she'd followed Varden. It was all she'd had then, and all she had now.

A knife was more than enough when you knew what to do with it.

With an experienced flick of her wrist, she flung the blade, then threw herself backward. She didn't wait for the satisfying *thump* of knife in flesh and dashed for the nearest tower, crouching to be invisible from the bridge down there. Her boots gave a faint echo as they hit the stone, but Nevian's huffed breathing would cover it. She hoped. Either way, the angle of her throw revealed her general position. She didn't have long to escape.

She ran for the Little Square, a park close by, knowing she'd never reach the Dathirii Tower before Avenazar came after her. Even at this hour and in the cold, the small plaza would have a fair crowd. She could hide in it—*had* to hide in it. Branwen rounded a corner, scrambled up a flight of stairs. As long as Avenazar didn't know where she was, he couldn't materialize in her face.

Instead, he rose behind her, floating up with an expression stuck between boredom and pain. The dagger was buried in his shoulder to the hilt, but in the dim light, Branwen saw no blood. The blade kept it in, and his robes were already red. Was he even hurt? Perhaps Master Avenazar endured pain as well as he could dish it out. Her little dagger throw no longer seemed that good an idea.

"Would you look at that?" Avenazar said. "Both of Varden's protégés at once? It must be my lucky night!"

He definitely knew about the last week, then. Her heart sank, but Branwen dashed off. No time to dwell on it, not now. She had to get away first. Just survive the night. She climbed the stairs two by two, her hand trailing along the tower wall on her right as she went around. She tried to keep her wits about her, to control her breathing to avoid collapsing into a wheezing pile halfway through her escape. Inhale for three seconds, exhale for seven. And think of a way to buy enough time to slip out of sight. She reached a platform from which two arching bridges spanned and opted for the shortest of the two. The Little Square was right around the next tower.

Branwen took three strides before a rope of green energy snapped around her ankle and yanked. She fell, and searing white pain covered her sight as she smacked her chin against the solid stone. The rope pulled her, and Branwen's hands clawed for a hold as Avenazar dragged her off the bridge. She let out a surprised yelp, then swore as he dangled her above a significant drop. Magic was so unfair.

"Nevian decided he'd rather throw himself off the bridge. Want to follow?"

After everything she'd heard about Avenazar, Branwen wondered if it might not be a better idea. Before she could answer, he flung her into the nearby tower. Her back smashed into the smooth stones, and she slid down into a minuscule garden, pain flaring in every muscle near her spine. The impact nauseated her, but when her fingers closed around a handful of small rocks, Branwen shook her head to clear it. Avenazar landed farther down the bridge.

"Since Nevian is a bloody pile of broken bones, and dear Varden's mind collapsed earlier, I think you ought to be my amusement for the night. I do so need to vent my frustrations."

"Too bad." Branwen's voice was raw, breathless. She clenched the small rock in her hand. "I had something else planned."

She threw the stone at the knife still stuck in Avenazar's shoulder. It smashed into the hilt, drawing a surprised yelp of pain. Branwen scrambled up as the rope holding her flickered out. Avenazar glared, raising his palms.

"You little—"

Branwen flung another rock, clipping his forehead this time. He stumbled over the edge and she dashed away, not without a bit of pride. Her aim was as good as ever, but she'd only bought herself a few seconds. Avenazar could fly. If she didn't reach Little Square by the time he recovered ... better not to think of it. She put everything she had into her sprint, gritting her teeth against the pain running up her back with every long stride. She could bawl at the agony all she wanted once she was safe. Behind her, Avenazar's outraged screams became louder. His fall hadn't lasted. Branwen reached the pale tower and sprinted around, into Little Square and its disparate crowd.

The Little Square stood on a small platform halfway up the Lower City with a large elm in the middle and flowers arranged around the massive tree. Four pathways shot away from it, each with their own flowery decorations and a handful of benches to rest. On most days, it was a quaint refuge from the area's rundown stench. Tonight, it was also her only hope against Avenazar. Several people turned as she burst onto the platform and gave her wary looks before returning to their business. Little Square might be a nice park, but it was still located in the Lower City, and people knew better than to ask questions.

Branwen scanned the crowd for a potential disguise, never breaking her stride. She noticed a trash can—a rarity anywhere out of the Upper City—and headed for it. A young couple occupied a bench on her way, the man too absorbed by their kiss to pay attention to the crumpled hat beside him. Branwen snatched it, shoved her hair and elven ears into it, then flipped the collar of Varden's overcoat up. Her gait changed as she reached the trash can. She squared her shoulders to appear larger, hunched to the side, bent over the refuse, and started digging through it. Her fingers grazed slimy leftovers she didn't care to identify as Avenazar flew above the edge of the park.

He floated over the square, studying the crowd. Branwen focused on her search of the trash, tilting her head away. She smeared her cheeks, darkening them with filth, and hoped he wouldn't pay any mind to the vagrant digging for a meal. A cold breeze blew across the park, and she noticed the kisser patting the bench beside him, searching for his hat. *Go away*, she thought at Avenazar. *Find someone else to torment.* She regretted the thought as it crossed her mind. That 'someone' would be Varden. Branwen bit her lower lip, snatched some rotting bread from the trash, and busied herself scratching the mould off it. Her hat-lender whispered something urgent to his girlfriend. Branwen's heart thumped so loud in her ears, she was afraid it would give her away. Avenazar snorted.

"I guess Varden will have to pay for the three of you," he called out. "Just in case you're around, here's an idea of what awaits him."

Branwen's grip on the old bread tightened. She forced herself not to react, not to let it get to her. Several folks turned to Avenazar, and their eyes widened as electricity gathered between his palms. They gasped and screamed in alarm, and Avenazar unleashed the energy on the great elm tree in the middle of Little Square. It caught fire as the sparks reached it. Branwen dashed away, diving behind the bench once occupied by the kissing couple. She found herself kneeling right in front of the hat's owner and hushed him. On the other side of the square, Avenazar cursed and vanished.

As soon as he disappeared, Branwen removed the hat and extended it back to its owner. "Sorry." She wanted to add more, but her hands shook and her mind refused to come up with something witty. "Gotta go."

Branwen straightened up, shaken to the core. The great elm crackled under the flames. People shouted everywhere, calling for water buckets, rushing for safety. She covered her face, took a few deep breaths, then left Little Square and its burning tree behind. She was almost safe, but she dreaded the difficult climb to the Dathirii Tower. If only she could teleport home. Branwen had never longed for her family so much.

CHAPTER TWENTY-SIX

LARRYN would kill him.

Cal sprinted through the Lower City, cursing himself. He couldn't be late, not tonight. They had spent an entire week planning for this evening. Larryn had spied on the prison's guards for days, memorizing their schedule, bribing them to learn Hasryan's precise location, and gathering information on the special allowances made for the winter solstice. They had devised a dozen different approaches to sneak into the city guards' headquarters and break Hasryan out of their jail.

Calleran Masset, part-time priest of Ren, was at the centre of their final plan. Followers of the Unlady cherished the winter solstice, especially its long night. Many of Ren's legendary schemes had been carried out in the dead of the night, and on this particular night, Xe had tricked Evzen, God of Birth and Death, into a game of luck, winning over a sliver of Evzen's immortality and elevating Xirself to the rank of deity. Since then, people everywhere considered the solstice an excellent night for gambling and other chancy endeavours—perfect for a difficult prison break. Besides, Ren was the chosen patron of many thieves and scammers, and Xir priests were allowed to visit inmates and bless them, giving Cal and Larryn a legal reason to be inside.

Entering the headquarters this way removed half the obstacles. Once past the first guards, they could veer into the high-security area and seek Hasryan. Sneaking around made Cal more nervous. Unlike Larryn, he hadn't spent years training his discretion through frequent uninvited trips into the Dathirii Tower. He did, however, have incredible luck. When they had devised the plan, they had discussed Cal staying behind and keeping their cover up but determined he should come along. Happenstance always favoured him, and Larryn's skills might not suffice. Not to mention, Hasryan could be wounded and in need of Cal's meagre healing abilities.

No matter how he looked at it, Cal concluded he was a crucial part of tonight's scheme.

And he had overslept.

Larryn would definitely kill him. Hasryan, too, if he ever had the chance. No amount of running on his short, plump legs would make up for the lost time. All he had wanted was a nap, to be in better shape through the night! Cal took naps all the time, almost every single day. It was a habit he'd developed long ago, when he lived in the far south with his brothers. The heat there became so stifling, everyone slept through the late afternoon. Cal still did, despite moving to Isandor and complaining about the fast-approaching winter. His naps, however, never lasted more than an hour. Two when he was really exhausted, which hadn't been the case earlier. Yet somehow, on this special day, he had slept so late into the evening it would be more proper to call it a night.

Cal wanted to curse his luck, but he knew better. Ren wouldn't betray him like that. Xe never had before. Cal might not understand why he had overslept. He had, though, and he chose to see it as a sign. So he ran, hoping to arrive in time, or that his lateness would turn to their advantage. He had learned not to question his deity's flights of fancy and trust Xir. Ren had a reason. Xe always did.

It came falling from the sky, crashing on the bridge at Cal's feet.

He jumped back with a yelp, tripped on his feet, and landed on his ass. Cal rubbed the hurt flesh with a mutter before turning to what had surprised him. A long-limbed teenager had smashed on the bridge then rolled over. Blood splattered the stones under his head, stopping Cal's heart and mind. So much red. After a moment of shock, he scrambled back up, his heart racing, and rushed to the young man's side. He had to help. Now. With trembling hands, Cal withdrew his melted silver coin, knelt next to the teenager, and slapped his holy symbol on the kid's chest.

"All right, Ren. You brought me here. Don't let me down."

Cal had never been the best healer. He could fix immediate injuries—enough to save a life—but the intricacies of the art didn't interest him. Neither did they Ren, really, yet Xir soft laugh echoed in his mind as he focused on the spell, and white light spread from Cal's coin, swirling straight to the teenager's head and enveloping it.

The blood puddle ceased to widen, but Ren's presence grew distant almost right away. The glow flickered, then vanished. *Shit.* Cal tried to push the blood-soaked blond hair aside to inspect the damage, but he had no real idea how to evaluate this teenager's health. He could stare at the wounds for hours without ever knowing if it looked good. Why had Ren put him here? Cal wasn't who this kid needed! *Calm down,* he berated himself. *Do your best.* He'd figure out the rest after. Blood beat against his skull, but he set his palm over the coin a second time and managed to conjure another brief burst of healing.

Cal then sat back with a groan. Now he was exhausted, but he hadn't done much more than prevent an immediate death. Without a professional—someone who had an inkling of how to heal—this teenager wouldn't make it through the night. And if they stayed here, the cold might finish him off anyway. Cal grabbed him by the armpits, determined to pull him out of the way. His weak muscles managed to slide the teenager an inch or two before he had to stop, out of breath. Sweat covered his body, and the chill wind cooled it further. He was hot and cold, and convinced he wouldn't achieve anything on his own.

This time, he did curse his luck. Why did it have to be someone twice his height? Why now? He could never save this kid and reach Larryn in time. Cal stared at the youthful face. Squarish, contorted in pain that seemed at home there, with deep pockets under his eyes. How could someone so young have years of fighting etched into his very traits? Cal checked his heartbeat and had trouble even finding it. He was dying, losing whatever war he'd been involved in. But Hasryan's execution was in two days. They freed him tonight, or not at all.

Either a teenager died there, right before his eyes, or his friend hanged before the end of the week.

A disgusting choice, yet one that became more obvious with every passing second. Cal looked at the broken body before him again, then straightened up. "You stay right here, buddy. I'll get help for you."

Cal spun around and started back toward the Shelter. His small steps lengthened into strides, then he launched into a sprint. His lungs burned from the night's exercise, but now that he'd made his decision, a sense of urgency pushed him past his usual limits. He needed to save that kid. Why else would Ren have kept him in bed? Cal just hoped he would succeed, and fast. Once Larryn came back from the guards' headquarters, Cal would become a dead halfling.

∾

ARATHIEL studied the subdued atmosphere at the Shelter with worry. This place always bustled with activity, and the strange calm tonight didn't sit well with him. True, Hasryan's arrest had doused everyone's mood, but it hadn't stopped the locals from sharing in Larryn's food and creating lively melodies. At times Arathiel had wished it had. It had felt wrong—Hasryan had obviously loved the wild rhythm of wooden-spoon music, fingers jumping and tapping in sync whenever he didn't watch himself. He had smiled when Arathiel had pointed it out. Not his usual smirk, but a softer expression, more sincere.

"This is what home sounds like to me now," he had said.

Home still played, but Hasryan couldn't hear it anymore.

Larryn and Cal weren't around either, leaving Arathiel alone for winter solstice. He had hoped for another game with them, to keep himself distracted. Lady Camilla had invited him to join a small dinner with a few family members, and he hadn't had the courage to accept. Perhaps he was missing out on a pleasant evening and a chance to catch up with old times, but every day, it became harder to return to his previous life. The more he settled into the Shelter, the less he wanted to knock at the Brasten Tower's door and face his sister's ghost. Lindi so often hovered at the edge of his thoughts, as if she stayed with him, participating in his mind in this new life he was growing for himself.

Arathiel took a long swig of ale. The liquid flowed down his throat, but he couldn't tell whether it was warm or cool. Perhaps it tasted like piss, though Arathiel doubted Larryn would ruin his reputed meals with shit drinks. Not that he even remembered what it tasted like. After a while, certain memories had turned into blanks. Arathiel wished he could imagine the taste the way he sometimes mentally cast more vibrant colours on the towers outside. As if the projection could ever give him back his senses. He ought to stop and move on but couldn't. He remembered enough for the rest to cling at the edge of his consciousness, refusing to let go.

Arathiel set his pint on the counter and slid off his stool. A walk in the cold might improve his mood. After all, it didn't matter if others froze outside. He wouldn't feel it at all. Moving around would get his blood flowing and his spirits back up, however. Physical exertion always helped, whether through endless treks, a quick exhausting run, or training to improve his balance.

He had almost reached the door when it was flung open. Cal dashed inside, panting, and Arathiel caught him before he crashed into a table. Red streaks covered his cheeks, the marks deeper than exercise and cold should warrant. Had he cried? Cal's breath came in painful gasps, and he sniffled. Definitely cried, though from what Arathiel had no idea.

"Woah there. Calm down." Several heads turned to stare at them, and the sudden attention gave him goosebumps. Arathiel led his friend back outside, eager to escape the unwelcome scrutiny. "Let's go out. Breathe a little."

Cal wiped his tears and nose with his sleeve. His movements were shaky, but he managed to stifle his gasps as they exited. He wrapped his stubby fingers in the fabric of Arathiel's pants as if holding on for life. Cal lifted bright blue eyes to him. A long second trickled by in which he remained silent, and Arathiel felt himself being evaluated, as if Cal sorted through how much he could say, if anything. Apparently he passed because when Cal started talking, it surged out in a semi-coherent ramble.

"It's that teenager. He just fell—almost on me—and I tried to heal him, but I'm not good and I think he's going to die anyway, and I left him there on the bridge—just like that!—and anyone could come by and do something fatal to him, but I didn't have a choice. I couldn't move him by myself, not with these tiny flabby arms, so I ran all the way back here." He breathed deeply, then coughed. "My lungs feel like little balls of flames spinning and burning everything inside, my mind included, and there's no way I'll ever fix this kid and get to the guards' headquarters in time to save Hasryan and I ruined—"

"Wait, what?" Cal's entire story had been near impossible to follow, but Arathiel had handled it well until that last part. He couldn't let *that* slip uninterrupted. "Save Hasryan?"

Cal slapped a hand over his mouth with a horrified expression. "I said nothing! Especially not that!"

He had. Arathiel glanced around, making sure no one had heard them, or would. Cold dark nights did not prompt a lot of traffic, for which he was thankful. Arathiel put his hand over Cal's and squeezed. "It's all right. You can tell me. I don't like these accusations any more than you do."

Cal's wistful expression told Arathiel he was considering it, but he gave an emphatic shake of his head. "Nuh-uh, not twice. Forget you heard anything? Pretty please? Except everything about the dying teenager who really needs to be moved to safety?"

Arathiel bit back his questions about Hasryan, even though he'd rather know what was going on with him. In the few choice nights he'd spent with Larryn, Cal, and Hasryan, he'd grown attached to their trio, and to the dark elf in particular. Hasryan knew how it felt to be the outsider, the weird one others stared at, and it calmed Arathiel to have this kindred spirit, even if they had little else in common. Cal's pleading tone convinced him to hold back, however. Pushing a panicked friend for more information wouldn't be right. "Okay. Let's start by bringing your kid here. He can be in my room if you want."

"No need. The one across from yours is empty. I'll give him that." Cal craned his neck to look up at Arathiel, a forced smile on his lips. "Just lift and carry him, and I'll manage everything else. You don't have to trouble yourself further."

"It sounded like you had a lot on your plate two seconds ago." Arathiel kept his tone warm and inviting, but Cal shot him a warning glare, so he raised a hand in apology. "I get it. I heard nothing. Everything is perfectly fine, and you never mentioned a certain friend of dark elven descent. Show me the way."

He motioned down the street. Cal mumbled his thanks, then trotted off, taking two steps for every of Arathiel's long strides.

⟡

BY the time they arrived, Cal shivered and drew his winter cloak tight around his shoulders. The sweat from his long run must have cooled down, freezing him, and Arathiel wondered how cold it actually was. He remembered wearing extra layers of fur at this time of the year and regretted not throwing a cloak on. Walking through the city with a simple shirt had already earned him several weird looks, and he didn't want to draw more attention than necessary to his body. The disbelief and confusion in others' gazes reminded him of his own sense of disconnect. Arathiel ran a hand over his arm, as much a fake attempt to warm himself up as a gesture of reassurance. The pressure might be distant and barely noticeable, but the movement's familiarity grounded him. He was real, he had returned home, and he might still build a life for himself here.

"There he is!"

Cal's exclamation drew him from his thoughts. He pointed ahead and started running down the street. By squinting, Arathiel managed to make out a blurry humanoid form on the bridge. He thanked the moonlight for what little his destroyed sight perceived and approached. No wonder Cal hadn't been able to move him: despite his young age, the teenager was taller than even Arathiel. Something about his position seemed off, but when Arathiel noticed the weird angle in his leg, he understood. He touched Cal's shoulder to draw his attention on it.

"We'll have to see to the leg, too. It looks broken."

Arathiel knelt next to the young man and reached for his neck. He stopped himself before he could check his heartbeat, however. Even if there was one, it wouldn't bypass Arathiel's numbed sense of touch. He'd once tried finding his own with no success. Arathiel had never asked anyone to verify he indeed had one. He assumed he did, since he still bled when cut.

"You should check," he said. "You'll be able to compare with earlier."

Cal stared at him with a mix of worry and curiosity, lips pinched. He must have noticed Arathiel's withdrawal but decided not to question it. Instead, he applied his fingers on the young man's throat, and his concerned frown deepened.

"Well, he's alive, I guess." Cal brought his hand back and blew on his fingers. "I'm freezing, yet his skin is still colder than mine. If he stays outside any longer, it'll kill him. We need to bring him back so I can finish healing him somewhere warm. Or try to."

Arathiel swallowed hard. He'd had no idea the cold was this intense. Apparently, the temperature matched winter solstice's name, and a strong wind blew across the bridges, worsening the weather. The wounded teenager wore a long coat thrown over heavy robes, but it didn't protect him enough. Arathiel glanced at his own skin, its dark brown almost grey to his eyes. Not a single goosebump.

"Let's hurry," he said.

He slid his arms under the teenager's unwieldy body, then twisted one around to hold his head stable. Poor kid. How had he ended up falling? Above Arathiel, the bridge lines smeared together, the complex crisscross too obscured for his sight. He'd ask later but doubted he'd receive an answer. If Cal didn't trust him with tonight's plans for Hasryan, why would this teenager tell Arathiel his story? Everyone had secrets, and no one wanted to share them with the half-dead stranger who lived a step removed from this world.

Not that Arathiel shared his secret either. He walked in silence, trying his best not to look out of balance despite the heavy load he carried. He'd never practised hauling lanky teenagers! Every stride, he prayed he could continue to predict when his foot touched the bridge and how to best shift his weight to progress without falling. Arathiel hadn't been forced to be this calculating about walking in a long time, and it darkened his mood. Sometimes, he could almost distinguish the rough fabric of the cloak against his naked forearm, and the fleeting sensation left him wanting more. The return trek to the Shelter promised to be a constant string of reminders about his numbed perceptions. Arathiel gritted his teeth and kept moving. He was saving a life, and that mattered more than his discomfort.

"Aren't you cold?"

Cal piped up in the middle of the way back. He'd been staring at Arathiel for the past five minutes, perplexed. His teeth clattered despite his hands gripping his cloak tight and fur-lined boots keeping his feet warm. Arathiel wondered how long ago he had noticed Arathiel didn't have winter clothes on, and how difficult it had been to hold the question back. Cal always tried so hard not to launch into intrusive interrogations during their card games. Hasryan had been right about that much: he might like his gossip, but he valued people even more.

"No," Arathiel said, "I'm not."

"How come?"

Arathiel shrugged. There had been no point in lying about the cold, but he didn't want to explain either. "Who knows? You weren't supposed to be doing something involving Hasryan, and I'm definitely not walking around like I can't tell if it's hot or cold outside. The strange things happening tonight are all lies."

"That's not fair! I'd tell you, but this isn't my secret, and I'm not the one who'll suffer the most if it becomes known. You're just hiding!" Cal's eyes widened as the words crossed his lips. He gasped, then scrambled to explain, his hands flailing around. "I didn't mean that! Well, yes, but not ..." Cal stopped, pausing long enough to get his thoughts in order. Long enough for Arathiel to realize he was holding his breath, unsettled by this direct confrontation. "So many little things about you are different, and I know it's bothering you, yet you never tell us anything. I just wish you would. I want to help, Ara, but I can't if you hide."

Arathiel turned his head away. "I'm not hiding, I'm delaying."

His soft answer convinced no one, not even himself. Alone at the Shelter, he could silence his family name, conceal his dysfunctional body, and become one homeless man among many. A strange one, but the Lower City had its share of bizarre occupants. Live and let live was the norm, but it seemed Cal had had enough. Arathiel suspected his already difficult night had destroyed his friend's patience.

"So you don't feel cold, you can't taste, and you don't feel pain," Cal said. Arathiel's gaze snapped back to the halfling. How did he know the last one? "Hasryan told me. About how your feet were full of scars and you'd never notice cuts on them. He said, 'You're right, Cal, this one's got a story, but if you harass him for it, I'll punch you myself.' So I didn't."

"Yet here you are, asking questions."

A bitter smile twisted Cal's lips. "Hasryan can't punch me now, can he?"

Arathiel jumped on his chance to change subject, relieved at the opening. "Do they really want to execute him?"

"On some bullshit reason, too! It's so ridiculous. When they put him in jail, we thought he'd be back within a day. As usual! But all of a sudden they're saying he killed the prick's mother a decade ago? They have his dagger, and they're all convinced it's the one that did it, and just because his horrible boss said she'd given the weapon to him before the kill, not after, they're all 'oh yes, must be him.' Like she couldn't lie to cover her own ass! But Hasryan has everything against him—dark elven ancestors when she doesn't, and no powerful friends while she owns half the city. So they're all happy to pin the blame on the scapegoat and call it a day. It's just ... it's so unfair."

They reached the Shelter's door by the end of his rant, and Cal's voice cracked as he grabbed the handle. He turned it and entered, his tiny shoulders slumped.

"And you're certain it's not him," Arathiel said.

He'd never questioned the city guards' decisions before, but the time spent in Larryn's Shelter had changed that. Once you lived in the Lower City, you noticed them harass vagrants and presumed thieves on a daily basis. Would he be that surprised to learn they would execute someone without protection in order to solve a famous case?

"When I imagine Hasryan as a teenager," Cal said, "I see an insufferable smart-ass. Not a cold-blooded killer."

Arathiel wanted to point out no one envisioned their friends as murderers, but he couldn't picture Hasryan doing it either. Perhaps it was because of how vulnerable he had seemed, the first time Arathiel had met him. Like he was waiting for the inevitable insult from Arathiel to bail, and he had this dazed expression when it never arrived. Then he'd shielded Arathiel from questions at their first card games, and gone out of his way to include him in the following days. None of this meant Hasryan couldn't kill, not from a rational point of view, but Cal's obvious distress convinced Arathiel not to press the point. Nobody needed irritating logic after indirectly dooming a friend to hanging.

They traversed the common area in silence and entered the section with private rooms. Cal pushed open the door to room number seven, right across from Arathiel's. They set the teenager down on the hard bed and stared at him. At least they had accomplished that much tonight. After a moment, Cal examined his head wound and his bent leg, careful not to move him too much. His actions drew a groan from the young man.

"Don't you dare wake so soon," Cal scolded him. "You were dying."

Arathiel set a hand on Cal's shoulders and squeezed. He could hear the doubts in his friend's voice, the questions underlying them. What if he could have saved both him and Hasryan? Had he made a mistake? Chosen wrong and wasted Hasryan's only chance? Arathiel wished he had an answer to reassure Cal. A way to solve his problems, even if just as a thank you for the trio's warm welcome to the Shelter.

"You said he'd need a better healer. I know where I might find one."

Cal raised his head. Curiosity buried his doubts for a moment. "You do? How?"

"When I arrived, I thought everything I knew about this city would've changed. I was wrong. Some acquaintances are still here, and they'll help. Keep him alive until we return." Arathiel could almost hear all the questions on the tip of Cal's tongue. He turned to face him and smiled. "Listen, I can't explain now. I don't have the time, and neither does our new Shelter resident. But you were right earlier. Maybe it's time I stop hiding."

Revealing himself and detailing his past filled Arathiel with dread, but a tentative plan was forming in his mind. Camilla wouldn't hesitate to send a healer to the Shelter, and she might even be able to do more for him. First, however, he needed to ask her questions on Isandor's current methods of execution, the political weight of Hasryan's supposed crime, and how much of Cal's declarations about scapegoating relied on blind faith in Hasryan.

But even if Lady Camilla told him they were deluding themselves and Hasryan must have done it, Arathiel already knew he wouldn't abort his rescue attempt. He couldn't stand by and watch them kill Hasryan, no matter how irrational it seemed. Through a few games of cards and several understanding silences, Hasryan had provided him with the first brick to build a life independent from his past—to grieve, accept what he'd lost, and seek what he could have now. In a way, he and the others had gently been teasing him back into this world.

If Arathiel needed to leap fully into it in order to save Hasryan, he wouldn't hesitate.

CHAPTER TWENTY-SEVEN

L ARRYN usually directed his murderous urges at slimy nobles—arrogant pricks who flaunted their titles like a free pass to be horrible, or holier-than-thou hypocrites who gave a coin or two away to assuage their guilt but otherwise didn't give a rat's ass about the poor sod who carried their shit every day. Especially House Dathirii, who posed as champions for those in need but hadn't blinked at tossing his mother out in the street. His *lord* father could throw all the money he wanted Larryn's way, but they both knew the truth. The elven house fared no better compassion-wise than any noble family out there, and they despised the slums and their inhabitants.

Today, however, Larryn kept a special spot in his hating heart for a certain halfling and his empty promises. They would see how long his luck held once Larryn got his hands on that unreliable wretch.

Hasryan *needed* him to be there, and where was Cal? Nobody knew! Sleeping or gambling, probably, but most definitely not saving his friend's life. If Cal had a drop of wisdom, he would be running away because Larryn would be coming for his lying ass the moment he exited the headquarters' prisons.

At first, Larryn had thought he'd never get in without Cal to back their scheme with his magic. Plans could be changed, however. Larryn had his acolyte disguise and no qualms about deceiving guards. He strode straight to the ones at the entrance, clad in the simple outfit, and with a few fake words professing his faith, he was in. They didn't ask questions. They mocked him for wasting time on the scum in their cells, praised his devotion in a tone coated with derision, then escorted him inside the low-security prisons.

This, of course, wasn't where Larryn meant to be. Without Cal to distract the guard while Larryn took him down, he had to rely on a cruder and riskier method. He reached into his sleeve, touching his small bag of ground pepper, and hoped it would be enough. It had cost so much time and money to prepare, but Larryn hated lacking a back-up plan. Good thing he hadn't bet everything on an irresponsible twat. Once he made his move, however, he would have to be fast. Flawless. Larryn reviewed his mental map of the headquarters one last time. He could do this. He had to.

A single guard flanked him on his left, and it unnerved Larryn not to hear her steps, but he didn't need to. No one else was in sight. With a slight smile, Larryn smashed his elbow into her nose, then unleashed the bag of spice into her mouth. It choked her cry of alarm, turning it into a pained gasp. Larryn wasted no time hitting her temple and knocking her out. Her uniform would never fit on his slender frame, but he snatched her sapphire cloak and keys. The former might fool someone far away, and even without that no-good halfling, he might get lucky, and one of the keys would open Hasryan's cell.

Larryn stalked down the corridors. He knew his way around these prisons, had already been in these cells in the past. Guards laughed and kicked you, disgusting food came at irregular times, and wounds became infected and festered. Larryn remembered lying on the floor in a feverish daze, wondering how long he'd been there and why he still fought to survive. He must have been thirteen, skin stretched over flimsy bones, and they'd caught him stealing. Broken his fingers. Again. At the time, his days had cycled between starving and freezing outside, or the painful grind of prison. His only respite came in occasional stays at the haphazard collection of mismatched and rotten planks nailed together that Jim called a shelter. It had taken years for Larryn to recognize Jim's love and understand how the gentle welcome had helped keep him alive. Most of the time, he'd been determined to live through the day as an insult to his father.

Hasryan had survived the same way—out of spite. They'd talked about it one night, a discussion that had solidified their friendship. They'd passed a bottle of throat-ripping alcohol between them, sitting on the railing of House Lorn's biggest balcony. Neither of them were allowed there. They'd climbed Isandor's most prestigious family's tower, laughing at how convenient the vines covering it were for thieves, then sneaked inside and acquired a few pricey items. Their success warranted a little celebration. That night must have been the first time Hasryan revealed anything about his past. *Every day I live, I stick out my tongue at the shit-licking bigots who punched or spat on me for my black skin.* A sentiment Larryn had shared. Nobles kicked the street kids around for fun, and every time he survived their beatings had been a small victory. Hasryan had also muttered something about his mother in a soft voice, but Larryn hadn't dared to ask. They hadn't known each other long enough. After that night, however, they'd become fast friends. Two young men with shitty lives, surviving out of spite for the rest of the world.

Larryn had the Shelter now—people to feed and protect—and as far as he was concerned, Hasryan was one of them. If Cal didn't care enough to show up and break him out of prison, he could go drown in the Reonne. Larryn had no intention of letting this vile city execute his friend.

Larryn hurried back through the headquarters to the room where they kept evidence, dodging out of sight whenever he needed. The single guard inside never had a chance. By the time he noticed something wrong, Larryn had smashed the lights out of him. The trail of unconscious bodies made him uncomfortable. Larryn wished he could follow their original plan. It had been simple and less violent. Full of risks, yes, but with a priest of Ren by his side, he had felt confident in their luck.

In the end, sacrificing a single night to rescue a friend from an undeserved execution was too much to ask of Cal. Larryn couldn't quite believe it. How often had Cal been there for him? He had saved his life when Larryn had first provoked Drake, stayed by his side after Jim's death, taken care of so many cuts and burns, and kept his temper in check countless times. Larryn's fingers might be crooked because of how often others had snapped them, but without Cal they'd be unusable. Cooking wouldn't even be an option for Larryn.

Yet he wasn't there for Hasryan. His absence burned the bottom of Larryn's stomach, eating away at his patience and trust. He would never be able to rely on Cal after tonight. With a frustrated growl, Larryn searched through the boxes and bags for Hasryan's dagger. What would have taken five minutes if Cal had come to read the labels instead lasted half an hour. By the time Larryn left the room to find the high-security cells, his fists had balled up, and his mind reviewed the few choice words he'd throw at Cal once Hasryan was safe.

HASRYAN had no idea how long he had left before his execution. He'd lost count of the days since the trial. Not that he had tried hard to keep track. Less practical matters occupied his mind. He played with a small rock found on the dirty ground of his cell and flung it at regular intervals against the wall. Every throw punctuated an angry interrogation. He tossed the stone—how could Brune sell him out like this?—and it bounced back, rattling on the floor. Hasryan picked it up. He spun it between his fingers, wondering if another condemned soul had played with it. Then he threw again—had she ever wanted anything but a scapegoat from him?—and the rock returned. It never answered him. Hasryan sighed.

He had trusted her for protection, for support, and for a

continuous string of jobs that saved him from the slur-ridden series of meetings finding freelance work meant. She trusted him to get any contracts done. Or so he'd thought. For a decade, he had served as her best man, willing and loyal. They'd built her mercenary empire together. Yet she'd pushed him off the bridge to get more space for herself without the slightest hesitation.

Hasryan had believed she didn't care about his dark elven ancestry. What a mistake. Brune cared a lot. It made him the perfect scapegoat.

He never should have trusted her. Or anyone. Every time he let someone close to him, they betrayed or abandoned him. Hasryan had learned long ago people saw him as a tool to use and discard. He'd counted those he could call friends on a single hand. Brune, Larryn, Cal … perhaps even Arathiel, given time. Brune had been a lie, however, and he didn't know how the others would take these accusations. Sora had admitted Larryn had tried to visit, but he was liable to do so just to yell at him. Hasryan picked up the rock again when a hesitant voice called down the corridor.

"Hasryan?"

His heart jumped as he recognized Larryn. Hasryan scrambled to the thick wooden door and grabbed the iron bars of its tiny window.

"Larryn! You … how did you—"

It was the middle of the night. Hasryan struggled to form a coherent sentence. What risks had he taken to get inside the headquarters? Could that really be him?

"Thieves go where they want." Larryn's familiar tight-lipped smile, pointed chin, and hollow cheeks appeared in front of the door.

"They wouldn't let me visit through legal means."

"Yeah, Sharpe told me."

In a way, it had been considerate of her. This way Hasryan had known his isolation came from forbidden visits. He had still convinced himself they'd stopped trying once they discovered he was an assassin. Larryn and Cal knew he worked for Brune, but he'd always refused to explain what he did, calling it professional discretion. He'd also shared a few thieving escapades with Larryn, who had witnessed how he melted into shadows and could go unseen. He'd thought the two of them had drawn the line of what they considered moral at killing. Didn't everyone?

"How nice of her!" Larryn punched the wooden door. His righteous anger brought a smile to Hasryan's lips. "Let us thank the lords almighty she was courteous enough to tell you why you rotted alone in this disgusting cell while she pinned every unsolved crime in this city on your ass! We'll have to send her a card or something." Hasryan heard the jingle of keys, then Larryn inserted one in the lock. "My good friend the guard lent me her keys. Let's see if one is yours."

"You're breaking me out?"

"Of course I am!" Larryn tried to turn the key, and when it failed, he switched to another. "Why else would I show up in the middle of the night?"

It should have been obvious, but Hasryan couldn't believe Larryn was there yet, let alone about to save him. Another key stuck in the lock without opening it, and his friend moved on to the next with a grunt of frustration.

"I'm not sure how we'll escape yet, but you're not spending another night here."

"You came here without a plan?"

Hasryan snorted. He wanted to laugh and cry at the same time. This was so typical of Larryn. He'd rushed into danger because he *had* to, certain he could figure everything out as he went. Consequences didn't matter when the need to act overtook Larryn— which most often meant they piled up on him immediately.

"I didn't." Larryn kept trying out new keys, and every new failure drew a deeper grunt from it. "We had a great plan, with a good bluff and magical chance and everything! Perfect, except it relied on that worthless, half-sized bag of flesh and luck. I swear, once I get my hands on Cal, he'll wish he was out of reach behind these bars!"

Hasryan's legs wobbled, and he tightened his grip on the bars to hold himself up. Was the ground even under his feet anymore? He tried to focus on Larryn and ignore the painful hammering of his heart.

"Cal was supposed to be here too?"

"Forget him," Larryn said. "Friends like that aren't worth your time."

So Cal had ditched him. Hasryan wasn't worth the risk, even for the luckiest person in Isandor. He squeezed his eyes shut and rested his forehead against the door. How many friends had he been forced to forget before? Perhaps he shouldn't be surprised. For all his laughter and hugs, Cal's life had been riddled with lucky happenstance and trustworthy friends. He'd always thrived and couldn't understand the difficult grind of constant rejections, starving, and scrambling to survive. Not the way Larryn did. But Larryn had come, at least. He had to remember that. Cling to it.

Larryn rammed another key in the lock, and when this one didn't turn, he cried out in rage and flung the key ring down the corridor. A string of curses followed, and Larryn's colourful cussing brought a smile to Hasryan's lips—until an alarm bell interrupted it.

"Oh, piss on Allastam's old balls. They must have found the knocked-out guard. One of them, anyway."

Hasryan's insides twisted into tight knots as he realized their time was running out. He wished he could see Larryn better through the barred window. His friend crouched near the door, and Hasryan heard him pull something out of his sleeve, then slide a metallic stick into the lock.

"Larryn, they'll come here. You don't have time for this."

"I'm sure as hell going to try."

Hasryan didn't argue any further. Any attempt to convince Larryn otherwise was pointless. Instead, he knelt on the other side of the lock and pressed his ear to the wood. They stayed like that for painfully long seconds, Hasryan's mouth turning dry as he listened to his friend's handiwork. After a while, Larryn cursed, rattled the lockpick in frustration, then kicked at the door with such strength Hasryan scrambled back.

"Apparently a thief goes wherever he wants, except into a goddamn cell!"

"Stay here and you will. Just not mine."

The quiet in his own tone surprised Hasryan. His last hope had shattered with Larryn's pick. The twists and knots inside held tighter than ever, but he accepted he wouldn't escape. Larryn shouldn't share his fate. No one else believed in him, and Hasryan couldn't bear the idea it would get him imprisoned. He needed his friend to be safe and free, and to keep the Shelter alive.

"You have to leave," he said.

"Not without you." Larryn's strangled tone betrayed his doubts. Hasryan pictured him on the other side, fists tights, one tiny impulse away from unleashing his rage on the door. "I was supposed to have more time. This should have worked. Cal had promised, and I could take that lock down with a few more minutes."

"You don't have them." Hasryan returned to the window, a lump forming in his throat. What if he died tomorrow? How long did he even have left? He would never talk to Larryn again, and his friend couldn't linger. If Hasryan wanted someone to know the whole truth about him—to accept him and call him friend despite everything—it had to be now. Larryn was his only chance. But if he had even one person behind him when he dropped, a noose around his neck ... it wouldn't be as miserable. "Larryn, please, listen to me. About the assassinations—"

"You don't need to tell me. I know they're fake." Larryn gave the door's handle an angry shake. "How anyone can fall for this is beyond me. Calling the dark elf an assassin is the easiest ploy in the whole damn world. I know you better than that."

"Clearly you don't!" Hasryan's mind spun. He blurted the rest out before he lost his courage—before Larryn's dismissive assurance that he *wasn't* a murderer extinguished his desire for a clean slate. "I am one. Larryn, I'm an assassin. I kill people."

Sudden silence greeted Hasryan's words, and his admission hung between them, as much a barrier as the wooden door. Hasryan shoved his shaking hands in his pockets and braced himself for the rejection.

"You're not. No."

The tightness in Larryn's voice crushed Hasryan's heart. It was a silent plea for Hasryan's words to be an illusion, a misheard confession. Hasryan's fingers tingled, and he felt dizzy. He needed Larryn to be okay with this. If he didn't dare call him a friend after this, who would?

"I'm sorry. That's what I do—well, did—for Brune. Larryn, please—"

"Stop!" Larryn stepped back until he hit the wall on the other side of the corridor. "Do you have any idea what I did to get you out? Who I've yelled at or pleaded with? *I begged my father to bail you out.* Crawled back to him for help, promising they'd set you up. And now you're telling me I was wrong?"

Every single word was a dagger punched into Hasryan's heart. Larryn always refused to mention his biological father. They all knew he existed—and anyone who'd heard Larryn harp on nobles could guess at his social standing—but Hasryan wasn't aware they were still in touch. Begging and vouching for Hasryan's innocence must have cost him a lot.

He had cared. As long as he'd believed Hasryan had done nothing wrong, he had done absolutely everything he could, no matter how hard on him. Not anymore. Hasryan needed time to explain.

"Larryn, I—"

"Over here!"

A guard interrupted them, his voice coming from way down the corridor. Hasryan rushed to the tiny window to look at Larryn, but his friend refused to look back. Larryn's insistence on keeping his eyes on the ground said everything. Hasryan's last friendship had just slipped away.

"I didn't kill Lady Allastam, I swear!" Hasryan said. "Brune is using me as a scapegoat. She lied about the dagger. Larryn, please. I … I don't want to die like this."

"I need to go. They can't find me here. The Shelter …"

His voice was hollow. Defeated. Hasryan ached to plead for him to stay. He didn't want to be alone in this cell, to wait for his execution knowing everyone had abandoned him. For once in his life, he needed to be accepted. But Larryn had Isandor's entire homeless population to care for, and no desire to help the lying assassin he used to name a friend. Cold numbness slipped into Hasryan as he stepped back from the cell's door.

"Go," he said. "Don't get caught."

Larryn remained frozen on the other side, but a second call from a city guard shook him out of his daze. For a brief moment, he seemed about to add something, then he gritted his teeth and dashed down the corridor. Hasryan listened to his steps growing fainter until he could no longer hear Larryn. His last friend had come to save him in the middle of the night, risking everything, and Hasryan had said just the right words to drive him away. He'd hoped their shared hardships would be enough, that Larryn would understand why he'd gone down this road. In the end, however, Larryn had left him alone.

Hasryan leaned on the wall and slid to the ground. His hand found the small stone he'd been throwing about, now a familiar shape in his palm. Perhaps he shouldn't be surprised by this end. He'd endured most of his life alone. It was only fitting that in a few days, he would die alone, too.

CHAPTER TWENTY-EIGHT

ARATHIEL knocked at Lady Camilla's exterior door, relieved he did not have to enter the Dathirii Tower through the main gates. Most quarters didn't open directly onto Isandor's network of bridges like these, but Camilla's used to belong to an outsider. When her family had bought them, she'd claimed the rooms, arguing that she was the oldest and it would save her aging body the staircases. She'd resided there for two centuries—longer than Arathiel had been alive. Although most of their tea sessions together had been in public places, he'd visited before and knew how much the decor inside matched Lady Camilla's temper: simple flower patterns, soft colours, and an enveloping warmth.

Soon enough, the glow of a candle escaped from the nearby window. He heard the old lady shuffle inside; the door's lock clicked, and she opened it a crack. Her long greying hair framed a tired and worried expression, but her eyes widened as they settled on Arathiel. She let out a small 'oh!' and pulled the door farther before stepping back, giving him space to enter. A web of wrinkles appeared as she smiled, and the genuine joy his night visit procured eased Arathiel's nervousness. He doubted it would last once she heard his requests, however.

"Lord Arathiel, what a pleasant surprise." No sarcasm laced Camilla's smooth voice. She put a hand on his forearm and guided him into the living room. "I trust you'll forgive my nightgown. Would you like some tea? Biscuits?"

Arathiel allowed her to lead him and sat down, amazed at her unflinching hospitality. "Tea? At this hour?"

"You heard me." She moved to the kitchen, separated from her living room by a wide and delicate arch through which he could easily see the counter. "In my opinion, 'tea time' is a myth. There is no precise hour for tea. It's always delicious. Besides, you must be cold. Hot tea will set you straight."

Cold? Arathiel glanced down at himself. How had he forgotten the winter cloak again? Lady Camilla wasn't a fool. She must have noticed he wasn't even shivering. "I'm fine," he said in a low voice, "and I'm not sure we have time for tea."

A frown marred Camilla's expression. She set the kettle down, pulled her hair into a quick bun, then moved back to the living room to sit opposite of him. "You're ... even more concerned than usual. I'm sorry, I should have noticed. Please, forgive my overbearing hospitality and tell me why you came."

Arathiel couldn't imagine how anyone might resent her unflinching kindliness. He'd knocked at an ungodly hour and received nothing but smiles. In fact, Camilla's constant sweetness had brought him here. Arathiel counted on her to extend her welcome even further, or at least consider it.

"You promised you'd help me if I ever needed it. I'm aware you meant help with possible attempts to reintegrate House Brasten, but—"

"I meant no such thing." Camilla pulled her nightgown closer around her. "I do not specify my offers in such a way. When I say 'help', I imply any kind of support. Tell me what you need. If your requests transgress some personal moral law, I'm more than capable of refusing them. I hardly expect such things from you, however."

Her voice softened at the end. Lady Camilla's subsequent smile acted like a hot bath on tired muscles: warmth spread through Arathiel, easing his fears and removing the weight on his shoulders. Camilla had a tranquil strength that seeped into everything and everyone around her. Even knowing Hasryan's case might be touchy, he managed to stop wringing his hands and smile back.

"I have two of them, and doubt the first will cause problems." It was the second he worried about. One thing at a time, however. "We found a teenager in urgent need of professional healing. He fell off a bridge, and I know House Dathirii has dedicated healers on hand. Sending one down to Larryn's Shelter would save his life."

"Consider it done." A soft laugh escaped her lips. "I doubt you were nervous about waking me up to save a man's life."

"No." His sharp reply edge stopped her laughter. Camilla's eyes shone in the candlelight, intrigued. She waited for him to go on. Arathiel shook his head. He didn't want to speak about saving Hasryan until she'd sent someone to help Cal. "My second request will need more explanation, and perhaps a greater deal of convincing. It's not without political consequences."

"Mysterious."

Her smile had returned, and if she was concerned about the nature of his request, she didn't show. Camilla's hand tightened on her chair's arm as she pushed herself up. Arathiel rushed to help her, putting one hand on her elbow and the other on her back. The proximity made him wonder if Camilla had a particular scent—her, and the entire quarters. Something soothing, probably. His gaze found dried lavender in a pot on a small table. Yes, that fit. Lady Camilla was a lavender type of person.

"Thank you." She squeezed his hand, and he thought he could feel the fragile bones in hers. Or was his mind completing what he knew he should perceive? Sometimes, Arathiel doubted he distinguished between reality and memories. "I shall go and wake young Vellien. You might remember them? They were little more than a shy child when you left the city. Now they're quite a talented healer. Singer, too, but that's not what your teenager needs." As she spoke, she moved toward the second door to her quarters, this one connecting with the rest of the Dathirii Tower. "I'm rambling again. Milord, I entrust you with the tea while I send Vellien. Once that is done, we can discuss your second request with our minds at peace."

Arathiel's mouth quirked into an amused smile as she readied to leave. "I understand how crucial the preparation of tea is to you. On my honour, I won't fail."

Her light laughter filled the room for an instant, then Lady Camilla disappeared into the Dathirii Tower. Arathiel stared at the door, his mouth dry. Her good mood might not last through the night, let alone their friendship. Arathiel steadied his nerves with a deep breath and moved to the abandoned kettle. Unless Isandor's customs had changed, criminals were executed at Carrington's Square. The Sapphire Guard tied them to the arching bridge above the plaza and put an end to their lives with a quick shove. If memory served, several bridges passed above that area, close enough that he could leap down from them. Perfect for a surprise rescue.

Without Camilla's help, however, his desperate plan might become pointless. Hasryan couldn't return to the Shelter, and if his boss had sold him out, he might not have secure hideouts across the city. He and Arathiel would need somewhere to hide. A place above suspicions in which they could rest and figure out their next step.

Arathiel hoped Lady Camilla would agree. His own plan terrified him. Every noble of note would attend the execution, along with a thick crowd from the Lower and Middle City. The thought of so many staring at him as he exposed his resistance to pain paralyzed him. How would they perceive it? What would they say about him? Arathiel could barely hear the kettle's whistle under his whirling thoughts. He gritted his teeth and removed it from the fire before forcing his mind elsewhere: to the subdued mood at the Shelter, Cal's earlier panic, and the unwavering friendship between Larryn, Hasryan, and Cal. One they had started opening to him.

He might die rescuing Hasryan, as he should have in the Well. If the extra time given to him allowed him to save Hasryan, then he could take pride in his abilities and assign purpose to his failure. He hadn't saved Lindi—could never have, really—but he would not let a friend die. He could rescue Hasryan, and he would.

CHAPTER TWENTY-NINE

WHY Uncle Kellian bothered with guards at the main gates of the Dathirii Tower had always been beyond Branwen. Two soldiers wouldn't protect them from good thieves—the frequent disappearance of precious commodities and the piss on Garith's favourite rug one night had proven that. Nor could they stop dangerous enemies. Kellian's love of protocol had turned into a waste of personnel and a useless show of force meant to parade the family's ceremonial armour. He could have replaced them with mannequins with the same result.

Her opinion changed when she reached the Dathirii Tower that night. By the time she'd climbed to their door, every shuffling step lit Branwen's back with agony. Walking felt like shoving hot iron bars along her spine, her head swam, and tears welled in her eyes. Even blurred by them, however, the sight of the two guards encased in their decorative armour brought warm fuzziness to her heart. Home. She had survived her days at the Myrian Enclave, Avenazar's attack, and the climb through Isandor's stairs. Somehow.

Intense relief sapped away the last of her strength. She stumbled to her knees, tears streaming down her cheeks. Booted feet rushed to her, and within a minute strong hands lifted her back up. Mannequins wouldn't have done that.

"Miss Branwen! Are you okay, miss?"

The world spun around Branwen, but she used the woman's soft voice as a focus. She knew that guard, had always found her kind of cute. Branwen managed a smile and held tight to her shoulder.

"Don't let Kellian hear you call me that. You say anything but 'Lady Branwen Dathirii' and he'll give you night duty."

"I'm already on night duty."

"Oh." Branwen blinked, then burst into a short laugh. It rippled through her back and ended in a pained groan. "True enough. Would you escort me please? To Lord Dathirii?" She doubted she'd make it on her own.

"With pleasure. But first, you should be presentable." She gestured at her cheek and grimaced. Branwen gasped, then wiped away the trash's filth in a hurry.

"Better?"

"Beautiful." She hooked her arm with Branwen's, allowing her to lean into her. Every step inside her home breathed new strength into Branwen. She trailed her fingers on the wooden walls, marvelling at their familiar softness. Nothing like the rough stones of Varden's quarters. The tightness lodged in her stomach for the last week slipped out through her fingertips, freeing Branwen of her constant fears.

Despite her renewed energy, the climb to her uncle's quarters seemed to take forever. Branwen let out a low whine when the door came into view, even if it lacked Jaeger's usual presence. She'd made it. A web of pain crisscrossed her back, and her head throbbed, but she could tell Diel and the others she was safe. That, and so much more. Her heart squeezed as she thought of Varden and what might be happening to him. She trudged to the door and knocked twice. Familiar voices spoke to each other inside, and Branwen smiled. Uncle Diel and Jaeger. Of course they'd be together at this hour.

"I'll be fine, thank you," she told her guard as steps approached. The soldier wished her a good evening, disappearing around the corner as the door opened.

Jaeger stood in the doorway. His silky black hair cascaded over his shoulders and down his back in wild strands, an unusual sight for the tidy steward. A part of it had been braided on the side, however, the task clearly incomplete. An intricate hairstyle, which would require long hours of practice to master. The kind Diel used to apply to Branwen's hair when she was a little girl. Jaeger flung the door open when he saw her.

"Lady Branwen! You … I'm … Welcome home."

Branwen stared at Jaeger. He was so flustered he couldn't form a coherent sentence, yet he'd still used her proper title? Did he *ever* forget? His delighted stutter warmed her heart all the same. She took a tiny step forward, and he caught her arm, supporting her weight and leading her inside. An instant later, Diel's lighter voice followed.

"Did I hear—" Diel emerged from his private rooms and stopped short, his eyes widening. "I did!" Then he was running, bare feet hitting the ground in three long strides, golden hair flying freely behind him. Before she could say anything, he wrapped his arms around her and squeezed. The sudden pressure sparked sharp agony in her muscles, ripping a surprised scream out of her. Diel let go and stumbled back, confused and horrified.

"I'm sorry, Branwen, I didn't mean to—"

"It's okay. I'm okay." She struggled to calm her breathing despite the fire in her spine. Jaeger pushed a chair against her legs and applied pressure on her shoulder, forcing her to sit. Her calves thanked her for the relief, but she leaned forward, keeping herself clear of the chair's back. "My back feels like a dozen horses trampled it, but I'm alive."

"We were so scared."

His voice broke at the end, and Branwen studied her uncle. Now that his initial grin had dimmed, she noticed the large bags under his eyes and how thin he seemed. It had only been six days, but worry had eaten through Uncle Diel like moths through her best dresses.

"Me too. I thought I was dead. Several times." She ran her hands over her face with a shuddering breath. "I can't believe I'm here."

Before she could add anything, the room's door flew open. Garith strode in, golden hair in a ponytail and glasses on his nose—the work outfit. "A cute lady guard told me Branwen was here!" She turned as he stormed inside and offered a feeble wave. "And you didn't come to me first?"

"Thought you'd be in bed. With someone."

Also, reporting to Diel meant she could get the important things done immediately, before she ran out of strength and collapsed for good.

Jaeger gave a small, polite cough. "I daresay no lady has come and gone from Lord Garith's quarters since you vanished."

Her astonishment must have shown because her cousin winked at her. "You're the one true lady in my life. You should know that."

Branwen tried to laugh, but a tidal wave of emotion hit her, and she produced a stifled sob instead. He'd been too worried about her to flirt. All of them had thought her dead, or under torture, and she'd been one bad disguise away from it happening. Tears welled up again, and she cried before she could fight them back. Diel's hand squeezed hers, then she noticed Garith leaning in for a hug. Branwen stopped him, putting a hand on his chest.

"Don't. No hugs."

"No hugs? You disappeared for days—no, months! Years!—and I can't even hug you? What is this sorcery?"

Branwen wiped her cheeks, smiling despite her tears. Nothing said home like Garith's faked indignation and his willingness to exaggerate every detail to make a point.

"I got thrown into a wall. My back cannot endure your outrageous demonstrations of affection."

At first Garith laughed, but his mirth died as the meaning of her words sunk in. "Thrown into a wall? Who did this? I'll … I'll …"

"Ruin his day with numbers?" Branwen asked. "I can't wait to see that."

"Keep this up and I'll thank him."

He shoved a hand into her hair and messed it up, an act he was fond of when she'd spent hours preparing it, sometimes braiding the wild strands into a flower crown matching her dress. Branwen replied in her usual manner: she kicked his shin hard and forced him to hop back with a pained laugh.

"Six days didn't change you," he said.

"Why, thank you."

"That wasn't a compliment."

"You know it was."

Their gazes met, and a defiant smile curved her cousin's lips. Branwen knew what that meant. He had no intention of giving in so soon, and neither did she. She matched his expression with a proud grin, forgetting for an instant about the pain in her spine and the night's scare. Before Garith could continue what promised to become hours of endless banter, however, their uncle interrupted.

"All right, kids. That's enough." Diel tried to sound stern, but Branwen mostly heard tired relief and amusement. He was used to their antics and probably glad to witness them again. "You can have this important debate later, with Vellien as judge. Can you tell me what happened, Branwen? Did the Myrians take you? What did they do to you?"

"Nothing." Her damaged back said otherwise, and Branwen groaned as she tried to get her thoughts in order. Fatigue clouded her mind, but one thing mattered more than any others in this story. She started there. "Varden hid me in the enclave all week."

"That fire-happy religious maniac?" Garith's expression turned into an angry scowl. "If he touched you—"

"He didn't. Don't be jealous, Garith," she interrupted with a sly smile. "I'm allowed to have a platonic relationship with another handsome man, you know."

Stunned silence followed, Garith's lips moving without a sound as he worked on a witty denial. Branwen's smile widened at the proof she could still get her charming, honeyed-tongue cousin to fumble for his words with a few choice sentences of her own. She had no time to savour this small victory, however. Branwen turned to her uncle. She needed him to understand Varden's part in this.

"Varden is the sweetest man I've met in a long time. If anyone else had been in charge of burning the tailor's shop, I would be imprisoned in the Myrian Enclave with Avenazar tearing my mind apart for information." Nevian's screams still echoed in her mind. That could have been her. Branwen lowered her head, and her voice fell into a tight whisper. "Varden saved me from the fire and hid me until I could escape. He risked Avenazar's wrath to keep me safe."

She remembered his answer when she'd called him a coward—how his hands and voice shook as he tried to explain Myria to her. *In the end, if you make one false move, you are an uncouth savage to be disciplined, an object that can be thrown away. And Master Avenazar? He combines this mentality with incredible fickleness, a cruel sense of humor, and the power to rip your mind into tiny shreds.* During her stay, he'd once woken screaming in the middle of the night, then stoked the fire and stared at the flames until dawn returned, never uttering a single word. Tonight, his nightmares had turned into reality. Branwen raised her head and met her uncle's gaze.

"We have to help him. They caught him. Avenazar called me

Varden's protégé before he slammed me into a wall. That disgusting excuse for a human being knows he helped me." In reaction to her plea, she received a horrified look and a small squeeze on her hand from Diel. She reached into her bodice, withdrew the charcoal map of the enclave, and showed it to him. "Uncle, he didn't just save my life. He drew this for me and answered all my questions. He's an ally, a friend, and a good man. He needs our help."

Diel Dathirii was already shaking his head. Branwen's guts twisted. He couldn't say no. He wasn't. She refused.

"You can't do this!" She snatched her hand back from his, a hitch in her voice. "Not you. You're Uncle Diel. You can't leave him there."

"I can't get him out. I'm sorry, Branwen. I really am. We were preparing to attack the enclave for you but ... it would have meant so many deaths. Too many."

He moved to put a hand on her shoulder, but she slapped it away. She hated the defeated look on his face. So she had been worth that plan, but not Varden? How could he even say such a thing? Anger and disappointment roiled in her stomach. She couldn't believe she was hearing this from her uncle.

"I don't care. You don't understand. He was terrified to help because he knew if we didn't win, he'd pay for it and lose everything. But he did. Because it was right. Do you know what I told him? I said: my uncle never leaves anyone behind. My uncle can beat any odds. He always finds a way."

"Branwen ..."

"He doesn't deserve this!" She jumped to her feet, shaking so badly she should have fallen. A light hand grabbed her elbow to support her. Garith. The delicate attention almost triggered her tears again.

"I believe you, I do." Her uncle's voice had grown soft and hurt, and he stared at the floor, too ashamed to look at her. He knew he was wrong. "We owe him. I'll search for a solution, I promise. We're not giving up, but … we're just not rushing in either. We're all exhausted, and perhaps a solid night of sleep will help. Sometimes life needs time to provide an answer."

Branwen lifted her chin. Sleeping on it wasn't good enough. Not knowing the fate awaiting him. Her usual inclinations to compromise vanished, her resolve hardening. She would not accept this. "Varden doesn't have time. Do me a favor, Uncle: when you go to bed tonight, recall the torture you believed I was enduring. Bring the worst scenarios to your mind, all of them. This is what they're doing to him, right now, while you're trying to get some beauty sleep. Remember that. I certainly won't forget."

She spun on her heels, intending to stride out with dignified anger. Diel's crestfallen look hurt, but she refused to give in. Varden had to be a priority. Branwen managed two steps before her tired left foot caught on her right, and she stumbled forward. Garith caught her, avoiding pressure on her back, and helped her along. The floor shifted under Branwen's feet as he half-carried her out of Diel's quarters. Silent tears streamed down her face, and the moment they were out, she drew her cousin into a tight hug, almost collapsing into his arms.

Garith caressed her hair, allowing Branwen's maelstrom of emotion to run its course, then helped her to her room.

᧞᭼ᬽ

LADY Camilla hadn't expected her search for Vellien to send her climbing up and down the Dathirii Tower. Age stiffened her bones, and the shortened night of sleep sapped her strength. Despite regular exercise on the city's unending stairs, her ability to come and go as she pleased was waning. One day—far away, bless her elven blood—she would need as much help as the old people she cared for. At least her mind hadn't decayed yet. Tonight it was more awake than ever, puzzling over Arathiel's mysterious request even as she sought to find her nephew.

What complaints Lady Camilla had vanished once she learned why the youngest Dathirii was no longer in their quarters. Branwen was home.

The news breathed life into her tired legs, and she hurried back up to her niece's quarters. Camilla didn't knock, or even call. She knew Branwen wouldn't mind and went straight inside. Her niece's quarters were among the tower's smallest: they had been a single room with a second section split by an archway, but Branwen had installed a curtain of heavy cotton to separate her bed from the rest. A mannequin decorated one corner, and one of her walls was covered in a flurry of fabrics hanging from a pole at the top, as if she'd piled up a dozen different curtains. Some had bright plain colours, others sported soft flower patterns. Branwen kept her small desk with the sewing machine Camilla had given her decades ago in front of them, near the window. Sunlight would flood it during the day. After a week without access to it, Camilla would bet Branwen couldn't wait to sew again. She picked her way across the room, toward the curtain through which Vellien's young voice drifted.

"Say I needed you to avoid any activities possibly straining your back ... what would be my chances?"

"Next to none."

Until she heard Branwen's voice, Camilla hadn't understood how real her return was. Relief washed down her spine, lifting a weight off her heart, and while Branwen's tone held a worrying emptiness, she grinned as she pulled the curtain aside.

"Already defying your healer's advice, young lady?" she asked.

"Aunt Camilla!"

Branwen tried to push herself up from the bed, but Vellien forced her down with a hand on her shoulder. She lay on her chest, her back bared, its smooth skin bruised into a surrealist pattern of sick yellow, deep purple, and brownish red. She muttered unhappily about her cousin's quick reaction, which in turn made Vellien smile. The warm colours of Branwen's blankets and curtains highlighted the copper undertones in Vellien's hair, along with their freckles. They massaged the back of their neck.

"She shouldn't," they said without much conviction.

"And yet, we all know she will," Garith said. "No one ever listens to you."

Garith had dragged a posh chair to the other side of the bed and sat in it, holding Branwen's hand. Camilla wasn't surprised to find her grandson here. He and Branwen were inseparable, and she must have sent for him immediately.

"Everybody should," Camilla said, looking at Branwen and Garith in turn. "They're wiser than both of you combined even though they're several decades younger."

Garith scoffed, which earned him a shove from Vellien. It reassured Camilla that Branwen's serious wounds did not mar their usual dynamic until she noticed their mirth didn't reach Branwen. Her niece had plopped back down on the bed and stared ahead, waiting for everyone to be done joking. Normally, she would've been the first to jump into the banter. Worry constricted Camilla's heart. She stepped closer and brushed a strand of her hair aside.

"It's a relief to have you back, Branwen. We'll all have our first good night of sleep in a long time."

"I won't." Tears returned to her eyes. She sniffed, wiped them away. "How am I supposed to sleep while Myrians torture my friend for saving me?" Her voice broke at the end, and Branwen heaved a sigh. "It's just … all of it is so unfair."

Camilla caressed her hair, at a loss for words. She doubted any would help, anyway, and while Camilla wished to know Branwen's whole story, she decided to postpone asking for it. Her niece needed to rest, and Arathiel waited in her quarters. She let the moment pass, allowing Branwen time to wrestle with her feelings and acknowledging their validity by giving them space, then squeezed her shoulder briefly.

"Sleep finds a way. No matter how you look at it, you'll need to be rested to help your friend."

Branwen *humphed* but didn't argue further. Considering the state of her back, Camilla suspected exhaustion would crush her worries for a time. She turned to Vellien.

"I was looking for you when I heard about Branwen," she said. "Must you stay here all night?"

"Not at all. I've done all I can to heal her and dull the pain. Time and rest will finish my work. Why?"

"A good acquaintance of mine needs a healer." How much did Arathiel want her to share? He'd been so nervous about asking her, but his stress mostly emanated from this second, mysterious request. Camille opted to explain more. "He came to see me with news of a badly wounded teenager. I was told he might not survive the night without professional help."

A soft chuckle escaped Branwen. "Sure, Aunt Camilla. Steal my healer away, go ahead."

"I can find someone else. If Branwen needs you ..."

"If I have my way, my dear cousin will be snoring so loudly no one else in this tower will be able to sleep," Vellien said. "Don't worry about it. Tell me where, and I'll be off as soon as I can."

Garith snorted. "Sounds like I'd better get a book and spend the night here."

Camilla's gaze hovered from one cousin to the next. Hard not to be proud of them—Branwen, Garith, and Vellien, House Dathirii's youngest generation. They had learned to stick together and worked extra hard to carve their space in the family's business. Vellien had found theirs early on: even as a child, they'd had a powerful connection to the Elven Shepherd and had used Alluma's strength to heal wounded birds. Garith shared his father's love for numbers and had inherited the money keeper's job when Gallinos was slaughtered. Watching his talent develop had always been a source of pride and sorrow for Camilla. She had learned to cultivate the former and stop the latter from overtaking her. Gallinos' sudden death would forever remain a throbbing hole in her heart, but although her grief stayed, she no longer mourned him.

Compared to the other two, Branwen had struggled to find her calling. For a long time, she'd had no specific role and spent her days hanging out with friends or designing new dresses. Then one day, they'd discovered she always seemed to know Isandor's dirtiest gossip first, and Branwen found her place. Her love for sewing and theatre became a talent for disguise, and she trained her gift for earning a stranger's trust into skillful information gathering. Now Diel called upon one of the three cousins almost every day, and Camilla knew with utmost certainty that House Dathirii would always be in good hands.

She explained to Vellien how to reach the teenager and what little she knew. By the time she was done, Branwen had closed her eyes, her breathing steady. Camilla exchanged a knowing look with Garith and Vellien, then excused herself. As much as she wanted to spend the night watching over her niece, she had a special guest waiting in her quarters.

Camilla hurried down the wooden corridors of the Dathirii Tower. Ever since she had first shared tea with Arathiel, she had hoped he would shake off the torpor holding him hidden in the Lower City. Something had happened to him in the last century that blocked him from reaching out to House Brasten even though she'd assured him they were fine people and would welcome him in. Yet tonight, Arathiel seemed ready to break out of his shell. An event important enough to bring the young lord—no, not young anymore, though it was hard for her to think of Arathiel as anything else—to her door in the middle of the night warranted her attention. She meant to help, no matter the nature of his request.

CHAPTER THIRTY

L ARRYN pushed open the Shelter's door, his entire arm taut from restrained anger. Hours of dodging pursuit through Isandor hadn't burned out his fury, but if he stomped in, he'd wake everyone.

Inside, the tables had been set aside, and patrons curled on the floor, sharing blankets and trying to sleep while they were warm and fed. His people. They counted on him and this home, and tonight he'd almost lost them. Larryn wound his way through the labyrinth of bodies, one long stride after the other, sometimes struggling to find a spot for even the tip of his toes. His gaze never left his target: Cal sat on a stool behind the counter with a mug. The closer Larryn got, the paler the halfling became.

Larryn's jaws hurt from clenching in anger, his hands shook, and the blood hammering against his temple made his head spin. In two days, Hasryan would be executed. Isandor's great nobles would hang him above Carrington's Square and cheer at yet another Lower City scapegoat with which to wash their hands of their own massacres. Everything had gone wrong tonight, and all of it was Cal's fault. If he had been there, they would have saved Hasryan. There would have been no hurried confession through a cell door, and Larryn wouldn't have snapped like that. He would have had more time to let it sink in because they could *all* talk about it in the safety of a hideout. But no. Instead, that piece of shit was sitting on his ass in the Shelter, nursing a drink like no one had counted on him! Larryn meant to teach him a thing or two about loyalty, even if it involved his fists.

Larryn grabbed the front of Cal's shirt when he reached him, yanking him off his stool as Cal tried to speak. Whatever pathetic words were about to cross his lips turned into a surprised yelp, then Larryn dragged him out of the common room and into the corridor.

"You killed him." Larryn shoved him away the moment the door closed behind them. Cal stumbled and fell, his face scrunching up in a sorry grimace. "I couldn't get him out. Not without your help, I didn't have enough time! Where the fuck were you?"

"I was coming, I swear! I ran so hard my heart wanted to explode, and—"

"Don't lie to me!" Larryn advanced on Cal, and the halfling scrambled back. "I waited almost an hour for your ass."

Cal flinched, turning his head away. "I tried, Larryn. I'm so sorry, I really wanted to be there, but I couldn't."

Larryn grabbed him again, heaving Cal to his feet. "Then where were you, hmm? What could possibly be more important than saving Hasryan's life?"

Hasryan, for whom he had endured his hypocrite father and dared to plead for a favour. Hasryan, who had hidden the truth from them and been an assassin all along. Hasryan, always so scared of betrayal, who had finally trusted him with his secret only to have Larryn run away right after. The night's events sank in—the enormity of leaving Hasryan behind, truly alone—and guilt wrapped around Larryn's rage. He loomed over his smaller friend—no, ex-friend—and glared. Cal could have made it all better if he had come. No amount of pleading eyes would change that, but Cal tried anyway, gesticulating as an answer tumbled out.

"A teenager crashed on the bridge right next to me, and his skull was almost cracked, and I couldn't leave him there! He needed help. Immediate help!"

Larryn let go and stepped back, amazed. Cal had never been a good liar, and Larryn had heard ludicrous tales from others before, but this beat all of them. A teenager falling from the sky? Did Cal not even have the decency to tell him the truth? If he'd wasted the night gambling, Larryn at least deserved to know.

"You're the worst friend ever."

"You think I'm lying? He's in there right now!" Cal pointed at the door across from Arathiel's with a determined frown. Larryn stared at it, taken aback. Would Cal push the lie so far? If Larryn walked in there to find an empty bed … He glared at the '7' painted on the wood, knowing deep down that behind it rested a wounded teen. Cal lowered his hand. "He fell, but I was too small to move him, so I ran back here and found Arathiel, and now he's—"

"I don't care." Larryn tore his gaze from the door, turning his head to better hear Cal, a great lump in his throat. It didn't change anything, this teenager. "Nothing matters more than Hasryan. Nothing should have! When that rope tightens around his neck and snaps it, I hope you remember you chose some random kid over him."

"He'd just crashed on a bridge! I couldn't—"

"I don't give a rat's ass about your teenager!" Larryn threw his arms up. His anger coiled at the bottom of his stomach, like a snake ready to strike. "He can die for all I care."

The halfling blinked out tears, his guilty expression hardening into a scowl. He lifted his chin, defiance lighting his still-wet eyes. "Well, he's dying right now if that makes you happy!"

"Oh, because you abandoned us but didn't even save him?"

"You would know that if you'd let me finish a sentence. But no! You're too busy blaming me for everything, and being angry and— and mean! I can't stop thinking about Hasryan either and I don't need you to remind me of the consequences of my decision. I'm the worst friend ever?" His voice cracked, and the tears returned, but Cal finished in an angry snarl. "You should find a mirror!"

Larryn's fingers clenched into a tight ball, and his rage uncoiled all at once. His fist flew into Cal's face, who stumbled back with cry of pain. He held his cheek, eyes wide and confused. When Larryn strode forward, his head spinning from the sudden release of anger, Cal scrambled back. His tiny legs weren't fast enough to retreat, however. Larryn seized him. How dare Cal call *him* a bad friend?

Larryn had tried everything—an infuriating face-off with Sharpe, the humiliation of pleading with his father, the high-stakes infiltration in the headquarters. And what had Cal done? Sacrificed Hasryan. Larryn pulled him close and raised his fist for a second punch.

A small, sharp cough interrupted from behind. Larryn froze.

"I'm sorry, but I heard there was a halfling here, looking for a healer?"

Larryn spun on his heel, but the moment his gaze fell on the newcomer, his hot anger died, replaced by cold and horrified fury. Outrage, shame, and confusion rioted inside, and Larryn's entire world vanished except for the visitor. A young elf stood in the corridor, his hair short and messy. Although hastily garbed, his clothes exhibited the hallmarks of the richest castes: attention to detail, quality fabric, and with white areas clean as a bleached asshole. This elf's hair might have a tinge of copper in it, but the underlying golden colour screamed of one particular House. Larryn's throat tightened. Fantastic. A Dathirii noble was all he needed to conclude this most wonderful night. Next thing he knew, his pretentious father would step through the door and try to give him life lessons!

"Oh no," he said. "Absolutely not. You're not allowed here. Get out. Now."

He dumped Cal to the ground, shaking. He didn't want them here, not now, not ever. Larryn didn't deal well with nobles on a good day. Tonight, he would commit murder and end up sharing Hasryan's noose. This Dathirii needed to leave.

"I'm confused." The elf seemed uncertain what to say. "Isn't there a wounded teenager?"

"Yes!" Cal scrambled to his feet and stepped forward. He cast Larryn a determined glare before turning to the elf. "He's in room seven, right there."

Larryn grabbed Cal's shoulder and pulled him back. "It doesn't matter. This is my Shelter. Get out."

"Like hell he will." Cal slapped his hand away. "I'm not letting the kid die because of your issues. Follow me, Mister Healer."

Cal entered room seven without another glance at Larryn, his head high. Silence stretched in the corridor as Larryn stared at the Dathirii, daring him to go any further. The elven lord looked young, and he shuffled from one foot to the next, rubbing one of his arms. His deep-set eyes never left Larryn, however. There was a hint of confused recognition in them, like someone coming across an old acquaintance and trying to remember where they'd first met. After an awkward pause, he seemed to give up.

"I'm not sure what I did wrong, sir?"

Of course he wasn't, Larryn thought. They never knew. They went about their life like a stroll in the park, oblivious to the harm they caused, to the suffering hanging right under their nose. Nobles didn't see the begging men unless it was to piss on them.

"You don't know what you did wrong." Larryn didn't bother to hide his bitterness as he repeated the words. "Did you not notice the dozens of homeless folk huddled on my floor while you stepped over them? Or did it never cross your mind that your fur-lined cloak and its pretty golden thread is worth more than the entire building? I could sell it and feed everyone here for a week. I'll tell you what you did wrong, *milord*: you exist."

An outraged expression flickered on the young noble's face, quickly replaced by a saddened frown. Their shoulders slumped, and they looked back toward the common room. Then the Dathirii unclasped their cloak, stepped forward, and offered the garment to Larryn.

"You're right. I should have seen it. I'm sorry for that," they said. "I'm not going to apologize for existing, however. I came all the way here to heal a perfect stranger despite the ridiculous hour and despite having a cousin in great need of help, too. Since this makes me such a terrible person in your eyes, though, I won't linger. I'll save his life and get on with mine."

When Larryn didn't take the cloak, the elf dropped it and pushed past him. Larryn grabbed their forearm, digging his fingers in. "I hate you people. Don't you dare act like you're some sort of benevolent saviour for this. You … you don't get to claim that you care because you dumped your cloak on me."

Then he let go. The elf moved into the room without another word. For the longest time, Larryn remained rooted where he was, trembling. He stared at the fur-lined cloak, tried to block out Cal's broken and accusing voice from inside. This was the worst night. Everyone and everything hated him—Cal, Hasryan, the entire damn city. Larryn's breathing hitched and sped and refused to slow down, to turn back into something normal. His mind zipped from one shattered piece of his life to another until he couldn't find anything right with it anymore. Or … almost. *The kitchens.* He still had that— his haven away from the cloak, the complete disaster this night had been, and the anger roiling inside him.

∾✕∾

WHEN the door opened behind Cal, he wiped his tears in a hurry. Now was not the time to be crying. He could do this—he could remain calm and professional. His nose and cheek throbbed and his heart felt like it had shrivelled and hid, but he breathed in deeply, smacked a smile on his lips, and turned around. His gaze met the young elf's, and he motioned for the bed where the teenager rested. This kid had better thank Cal a thousand times for his troubles.

"He's right here," he said, as though it wasn't obvious. He needed to fill the silence, to act like he didn't hurt so much. "Sorry about all that, um … sir."

"Vellien. No sir, and I prefer 'they' to 'he,' if possible." Vellien made their request in a soft voice, couched in a mix of worry and irritation.

"Of course!"

With a brief smile, the young elf moved to the bedside and crouched. "Good. Let's forget your friend outside and do what I came here for. What can you tell me?"

"Not much." Cal walked up next to Vellien. He had to push aside Larryn and Hasryan for now. If they couldn't save this one life, all his pain would be a waste. "He fell—smashed his head on the bridge right beside me. I'm a priest of Ren, but no healer. I dumped all the energy I could in his skull to stop the bleeding. Oh, and his leg is broken, I think?"

Vellien let out a thoughtful 'hmm', then lifted the head in a slow movement, their fingers spread around the teenager's forehead.

White energy enveloped their palms, but it didn't fan out. It shimmered, its intensity wavering. Cal held his breath and prayed to Ren he had done enough for this kid, that this better healer had arrived in time. Vellien's face grew darker as the seconds elapsed. They set the head down with a concerned frown, then moved their palm over the twisted leg. A soft hiss escaped them. Vellien removed their hand, the light vanished, and they rubbed the back of their neck. The thoughtful expression aged their youthful traits.

"It's a good thing you sent for me. Your initial judgment was right: I doubt he'd make it through the night without professional help." Vellien drew a chair closer to the bed and sat down. They smiled at Cal, as if to comfort him, and the unnecessary consideration did soothe his nerves. Vellien set their index finger near the dried blood on the teenager's skull. Their white light appeared again, undulating over the head like water, slowly working on the damage. "Proper healing is more than shoving divine energy in a wound. When you do that, you risk stitching it up wrong and causing permanent harm."

Vellien's tone was devoid of reproach, but shards of shame stabbed at Cal's heart nonetheless. Had he done anything right tonight? Would Ren not give him a tiny amount of respite? He wrung his hands together.

"I just wanted him to live."

"A good reflex. Bleeding out is no better, and I think you bought him enough time for me to arrive." Vellien seemed about to add more, but instead snapped their attention back to their patient, lips parted. "What the … someone did *something* to his mind."

They snatched their hand back and murmured a few words, shifting the focus of their healing. The white light rose above the teenager's body as a bright blue sphere, illuminating the room. For the first time, Vellien examined *who* they were treating, rather than what. Their eyes narrowed.

"Those are Myrian clothes," they said. "He's from the enclave."

Cal perked up. He hadn't thought much of the robes earlier. But House Dathirii was at war with the Myrians, though, wasn't it? And Vellien's snazzy outfit, calm demeanour, and golden hair all pointed toward that noble family, or Larryn wouldn't have threatened to throw them out so fast. Cal bit his lip, his throat tightening.

"Please heal him anyway? He doesn't deserve to die because his robes say he's with your enemies!"

"No, of course not." Vellien kept staring at the teenager, however, as if working through a puzzle. "One of their wizards attacked my cousin tonight. I was taking care of her wounds earlier, and she said she'd been defending an apprentice. Apparently, he threw himself off the bridge. Were you in the Lower City?"

Cal's eyes widened. It *had* to be him. He nodded eagerly. "Yeah, I was!" His smile returned a little. "Which means he's not even on their side, so you can absolutely heal him without remorse."

Vellien chuckled, unbuttoned their sleeves and pulled them up. "I would have tended to him either way. This does explain the terrible state of his mind, however. Master Avenazar attacked it earlier. The burns are probably from him, too. I'll do what I can to fix the damage, but … this kind of work demands precision and time, and I've had no practice with it. I guess we'll know when he wakes up?

Chances are I'll be dealing with this until sunrise."

When Cal heard the doubts in Vellien's voice, he reassessed them. Freckles covered their nose and cheeks, and their face was rounder than most elves. They couldn't be much older than the teenager they were healing—not in relative age anyway. How much experience did they even have? How many nobles did Arathiel know? The answers hould have been none, considering he had a room here in a shelter dedicated to the poor. Another piece of the puzzle for their already very mysterious friend. One that would have Larryn kicking him out if he learned, too. Cal had no intention of telling anyone. He reached for his stinging cheek and sighed. He wasn't sure he'd even talk to Larryn again anytime soon.

"Thanks for coming," he said. "I'm Calleran Masset. Cal."

"It's nothing. I'm glad I arrived when I did. If you need me to look at your cheek …"

"No." Cal wished he could forget about it instead. He'd helped Larryn through so much in the past, he couldn't quite believe his friend had turned on him like that. He'd known Larryn would be pissed, but 'Larryn would kill him' had always been an exaggeration. Cal never thought his violent impulses would ever touch anything except objects, let alone him. "I'll be fine. Just ignore Larryn. When he's furious, he could set the whole world on fire and not care."

Most of the time Larryn had excellent reasons to be pissed. He just got carried away. Tonight was no exception. Hasryan had depended on Cal, and he'd failed him. Reminding himself there had been another life at stake didn't wash Cal's guilt away. He could apologize a thousand times without changing one hard fact: they would hang

Hasryan because he had stopped for this teenager. While Vellien worked on healing the apprentice, their fingers shining from the white light, Cal rubbed his eyes and sighed. He wanted this day to be over. Gone and forgotten forever.

After a while, Vellien withdrew their hands with a shuddering breath. It couldn't have been more than fifteen minutes, but they already seemed exhausted.

"Are you okay? Can I help with anything?" Cal asked.

"I would appreciate it if you could stay through the night and bring me water. I'll need frequent breaks. His head is like a battlefield after a clash of mages. Everything is ruined, and I'm not even sure how and what to put back together." Vellien rubbed their face. "I'll rest for a few minutes, then fix his leg before I spend all my energy trying to save his mind."

"Sounds rough."

Cal wondered how much it would hurt if everything was that broken. What kind of terrible person could do this to anyone? Plus, this teenager was probably a really sweet guy who didn't deserve any of this pain. Cal hoped so. It helped him feel better about Hasryan to think he had saved the gentlest of souls.

"Without a doubt. What a horrible experience." Real concern tinged Vellien's voice, and they squeezed the apprentice's forearm as if they'd been friends. Perhaps trying to heal someone's mind formed connections. Vellien sighed and turned to meet Cal's gaze. "Can I ask you something? About Larryn."

Cal tensed. Even though Larryn had punched him not an hour ago, the thought of answering a noble's questions about him

bothered him. Nothing good would come out of that. Larryn hated
them all, and the Dathirii even more than others.

"No, I'm sorry. You can't." He wrung his hands, and found
himself explaining. "He has a history with nobles, but I don't think I
should share."

"All right." Vellien bent over the kid's legs, and the strain returned
to their voice as they snapped the knee back to its original position,
hands shining once more. When he focused, Cal could feel the
power flowing from them. Vellien's connection to Alluma, the Elven
Shepherd, seemed so different from his own with Ren. Cal's luck
followed him everywhere, as if Ren never left his side, but Cal
struggled to call upon Xir power for long. In comparison, Vellien
could bring their deity's divine energy into sharp focus without
pouring their entire concentration into the act. "He just seemed
familiar, and so young to own a place like this."

"People age faster on the streets, or they die."

An awkward silence followed Cal's answer. Vellien finished their
work on the knee then straightened up again. "Can you make sure he
doesn't kill me if I come back? I'll know more in the morning, but I
might not be able to do everything tonight."

"I'll ... I'll see what I can do." Cal had no idea what would happen
the next time he spoke with Larryn. He preferred not to think about
it. "Please don't hold it against Larryn. He has good reasons, and
we've all had a tough night."

"I noticed." Vellien offered him a reassuring wry smile. "Don't
worry. He seems to be doing a lot of good here. Not to me, but I
don't want to get in his way."

Cal thought of Drake Allastam, who had done nothing but that since they'd met him. Vellien was so different from the entitled lord. Instead of throwing insults at them, they tried to understand and went out of their way to heal a stranger. This calm and kind elf didn't match what one expected, listening to Larryn rant about them all the time. But they all knew something personal lay there. Perhaps Cal shouldn't be so surprised—if Arathiel had friends within House Dathirii, then they couldn't be that bad.

"Well, Larryn will appreciate that sentiment, for sure."

Vellien laughed—a tiny sound punctuated with an occasional snort, which Cal found both amusing and adorable. His smile returned. He was glad not to stay alone through this awful night. Vellien needed someone to keep them company? He would be more than happy to oblige and chat his worries away. After all, none of his problems would vanish before morning came.

CHAPTER THIRTY-ONE

HE guards' headquarters had been on high alert all night. Soldiers rushed about, opening cells and counting prisoners, checking every corner. Hasryan listened to the panic with a slight smile, impressed by the chaos Larryn had left in his wake. The urgent search through the headquarters eventually morphed into confusion as it became more and more obvious that no one had escaped. Dangerous criminals still waited for their punishment in their dank individual cells while petty thieves quarrelled in the largest ones. Hasryan played with his smooth rock until his door creaked. He smiled but continued staring ahead. He didn't need to look to know Sora Sharpe had come for a visit.

"Ma'am, I have a complaint. My neighbours are noisy, and they keep me awake at night. Couldn't sleep."

"I'll make sure to warn them," Sharpe answered. "I have to admit,

334 ~ CLAUDIE ARSENEAULT

I'm surprised you didn't move out."

Hasryan shook his head with a bitter smile. "Not for lack of wanting," he said, even though the words now felt like a lie, "but I seem to have lost the keys to my own door. You wouldn't happen to have a spare?"

This drew a short laugh from her. "Afraid not. Since you were awake, you might be able to answer a few questions? Has a thief attempted to break into your glorious home during the night, by any chance?"

Hasryan doubted the use of 'thief' was accidental. If she'd looked into Larryn—and Sharpe would have—she would have found him in their records. Guards had even nicknamed him Bonebreaker, mocking Larryn's last escape method: breaking the bones at the base of his thumb to slip out of his shackles. Hasryan scoffed at the thought. He'd seen the bend in his friend's fingers and knew soldiers had snapped them more often than Larryn himself. He threw his rock at the wall.

"One prison break and you're convinced it's about me. This borders on obsession."

"You are a high-profile prisoner, I haven't heard from your very insistent friend since your sentence was made public, and your precious dagger is missing from the evidence room."

High-profile. What a nice way of saying a lot of political weight rested on his execution. Hasryan stretched to pick up his rock again, his heart squeezing at the idea that Larryn had gone through the trouble of retrieving his weapon. He played with the stone for a moment, then looked at Sora. She never ceased to impress him with her ability to size up people. As far as he knew, she had only met Larryn once, but she had guessed he wouldn't leave it at that.

"Seems like he's not as good a friend as you thought, then." Hasryan lowered his gaze. He'd meant to sound amused, but bitterness drenched his tone. "Whoever came left me in my cell. Brune might've wanted the proof of her lie back, for all you know. Don't harass Larryn. He does a lot of good for people who otherwise don't get any help."

Sharpe crouched next to him. She stared at Hasryan for what seemed like an eternity, and he made sure never to look back. The longer the silence stretched, the tighter his throat became. He wanted to be left alone.

"It was him, wasn't it?" she asked softly.

"Why would I tell you?" His fingers clenched around the stone— too obvious an admission for someone brilliant like Sora. "I'm not talking to you."

"It seems to me no one else wants to talk to you anymore."

"Yeah. I get it. I'm alone. Pretty used to that part by now."

She was still studying him; he could feel it. He hated that scrutiny, which forced him to wonder what she saw in him. A cold monster, probably. Hasryan wished he could tell her to disappear, but he didn't have the strength to shoo away the last vaguely friendly contact he'd have before his execution. Sora sighed and straightened up.

"You deserve that noose. My brain knows you do." She sounded annoyed. Hasryan's eyebrows shot up, and he forced himself to look her way. The irritated crease in Sora's forehead hid a softer expression. "I dislike hanging others, but with you it's worse than ever before. I wish you hadn't killed anyone."

"I am so sorry I'm not the heartless killer you wanted me to be."

"Yeah. So am I." Sharpe sounded sincere, at least. Funny how the one person who would regret his death would be the same one who put the noose around his neck. She strode to the door and added, "Your food will be along shortly."

"Thanks."

He leaned his head against the cold stone wall as she closed the door, a shudder running up his spine. Perhaps the broth would bring him warmth, but he suspected his shivering had nothing to do with the actual temperature. As time passed, Larryn's brutal departure became more real. More draining, too. Hasryan's exhaustion went beyond the sleepless night, the hard floor, the piss stench or the lousy food of the last week. He didn't have the energy to fight this life anymore. Soon enough, he'd have a noose around his neck, and a quick shove off a bridge would put an end to his pointless struggles. This world had pushed him down and betrayed him since day one, and Hasryan was finally ready to admit defeat.

⌖

THE rising sun found Diel Dathirii curled against Jaeger on a large sofa, awakening from a fitful sleep. After Branwen had left them, he had stood in his office, stunned and wordless, unable to process what she'd yelled at him. He couldn't handle having Branwen's shattered hopes thrown in his face in such a fashion. Her anger ripped through his heart and stomach like a dozen shards, leaving confused shock behind. Jaeger had been at his side in an instant, a comforting hand on his shoulder, but Diel could only stare at the door his niece had slammed.

A man she cared deeply about was being tortured. Diel had met High Priest Varden Daramond before on diplomatic occasions. The priest had remained distant, guarding his thoughts behind pleasant words. Diel had assumed he was silencing the worst of his worldviews when it had been the other way around. What was the man truly like? Diel hoped he'd meet the real Varden one day. But for that, he would need to conjure a miracle. Diel had heaved a sigh and leaned into Jaeger.

"I hate letting them down," he had said.

He despised disappointing anyone at all, but Branwen's promise he would have a solution worsened it. He wished he could provide. How often had he fixed her problems for her to assume he could resolve any issue?

"You can't save everyone," Jaeger had said. "She's tired and distressed. Give her time."

Time. The one thing Varden didn't have. Weary to the core, Diel had gathered every piece of information they had on Myrian or Dathirii funds and manpower. "Let's go through everything again."

And they had, deep into the night, without finding their miracle. Before long, Diel was half-sleeping on Jaeger, muttering the occasional idea while his steward verified the actual numbers. Diel didn't even remember falling asleep, but when the door was flung open the following morning, he jerked to his feet with a start.

Yultes strode in without a pause, giving him and Jaeger a slightly irritated look, like he couldn't believe they were cuddling at a time like this. Which was quite ridiculous—Diel needed Jaeger's warmth now more than ever. He raised his chin and shot Yultes a warning glare. His brother-in-law enjoyed slinging subtle insults at Jaeger, but Diel wouldn't tolerate his dismissive banter.

"Knocks are always appreciated," Diel said.

Behind him, Jaeger had decided to remain sitting, his back straight as a plank. How unusual for him to disregard etiquette. After last night, however, Diel could understand. It was Jaeger's way of indicating he cared little for Yultes' intrusion.

"Someone broke into the prison yesterday and tried to free Lady Allastam's assassin."

Yultes flung his news at them in a matter-of-fact tone, and Diel struggled to retain his calm. His head throbbed, although to a lesser degree than his heart, and he had no patience for Yultes' sense of self-importance. He needed to get this over with before he exploded.

"Tried?" Diel asked.

"They failed."

"Pray tell, Yultes, why a failed attempt matters so much it couldn't wait another hour, or even the few seconds of a knock?"

"Because I think the one who tried ..." Yultes' voice trailed off, and his eyes widened, panic flickering through his expression. He pressed his lips together. "We don't know who it is."

Diel frowned. How was that proper justification? And why did Yultes seem so horrified with himself? Diel pinched his nose and wrestled with his desire to throw Yultes out and force him to come back later. He had a House to lead, a priest to rescue, and a war to win. He couldn't afford to lose control of his shaky emotions.

"Out with it, Yultes. I have too much on my plate to guess at your half-truths. Whatever you're not saying, spill it and be done with it." Yultes cast his gaze down but remained silent. Diel stared at him, hoping against experience that Yultes would talk. They hadn't had a heartfelt conversation in years, and Diel no longer counted the number of unfinished sentences Yultes left hanging, as though he'd almost spilled a terrible secret. He yearned to know what. More than anything, he wished they hadn't grown so far apart, and that Yultes himself hadn't become so arrogant. Impenetrable silence met Diel's request, however. "Fine. Whatever. Keep your secrets. How is Lord Allastam?"

"Disagreeable." Yultes squared his shoulders, and his glacial bearing returned. "Your last visit left quite an impression on him. Congratulations."

Although Yultes' face was the perfect mask of neutrality, his tone dripped with contempt. Diel glared at him. "A statement I find quite mutual. Keep placating him, and let's pray he was pulling my strings when he spoke of joining the Myrians. He's more arrogant than he is greedy, and a deal with them now would be admitting he should have done so sooner. Play that against him as much as you can, and do remind him I was right about Branwen. We need his reluctant neutrality."

"I know my job." From the sound of it, Yultes believed no one else in the room did. Diel almost wanted to agree—between Lord Allastam and Branwen, he had run from one disaster to another. Jaeger's discreet cough behind him staved off his doubts. Yultes cast the steward a disdainful glare. "Enjoy your lazy morning while I keep us afloat. And please pass my good wishes to my niece."

Pass his good wishes? Diel scowled. What was it with Yultes? When Branwen was born, he'd been so excited to have a niece, he could barely hold it together. He had told everyone he couldn't believe his little brother was building a family, and insisted on touching Diel's sister's belly every day. Just in case something special happened. Yultes' enthusiasm had been contagious, yet time had passed and he'd grown distant and pretentious—unbearably so. Today, he couldn't even be bothered to see Branwen after she'd been kidnapped.

"She'd love to hear it from you, Yultes. If you don't care enough to tell her yourself, I'm not sure your 'good wishes' are worth passing on." Yultes' jaw dropped in surprise. Diel pressed on before he could regain countenance. "She *is* your niece, and we're your family. Some days it's like you forget this is more than a business arrangement."

Yultes closed his eyes, and for a long time, he let Diel's words hang unanswered. The silence itself surprised Diel, but not as much as his shifting expressions. Under the expected disdain flickered guilt and sadness. Diel's curiosity flared, along with a pang of worry. Perhaps the old Yultes still hid under there.

"Yultes ..."

"Don't." He raised a hand and met Diel's gaze, his eyes cold and hurt. "It's all so simple for you. Don't you dare talk about family to me."

For the second time in less than a day, someone turned their back on Diel, strode out of his quarters, and slammed the door. Except this didn't hurt like Branwen's departure. It left a slew of questions—a small crack in Yultes' mask that Diel despaired of widening. His memories of the excited, soon-to-be uncle were too vivid for him to accept the snide noble he spoke to every day.

"He's hiding something."

Jaeger shifted behind him, staring at Diel instead of the door, his mouth a hard line. "Whatever it is, we are best off not knowing."

CHAPTER THIRTY-TWO

A HOT iron spike through his mind greeted him as he returned to consciousness. He moaned, and his hand crawled to the top of his head, as if the touch of cool fingers could soothe the pain and allow him into the jumbled mess behind. His thoughts. *Nevian's thoughts.* The name felt right, but he struggled to associate anything with it. He opened his eyes, hoping his surroundings would trigger some remembrance. Nothing familiar around him. Was that normal? He stared at the ceiling—decrepit wood instead of smooth stones—and grew convinced he had never seen this place before. Good. A new location, even to his faulty memory. He had no blankets, and sunlight plunged into his room from the window on the left. Was it early morning or late afternoon? How long had he been here?

Nevian closed his eyes again and fought to keep his breathing steady. He tried to dig out his most recent memories despite his throbbing head. Images trickled through—the night sky obscured by spires and vines, a snide cackle, a hand on his forearm. *Avenazar.* Master Avenazar of the Myrian Enclave. His mentor. Tearing his mind to shreds. The memory drew a whimper from Nevian. Some things were better forgotten. Like rolling off the bridge to escape, through death if necessary.

"I'm ... alive?"

His voice was coarse. He'd screamed a lot the previous night. He knew that much. His cracked and weak question received an immediate, enthusiastic answer.

"You're awake!"

Nevian glanced sideways toward his exhausted-sounding watcher. A halfling scuttled to the bed, not more than three feet high, with ear-length blond hair and plump cheeks, one of which was bruised. Plump lots-of-things, really. He climbed onto a chair next to the bed and leaned forward with a large smile. His happiness irritated Nevian. He clacked his tongue and returned his attention to the ceiling, which at least didn't spin like the floor had.

"Maybe I sleep talk. Where am I?"

"Safe."

"That does not answer my question," Nevian said, "and I highly doubt the veracity of it."

His retort was met by a pout. The halfling crossed his arms. "This is Larryn's Shelter. We found you dying on a bridge. You almost fell right on top of me. I'm Cal, by the way."

Nevian wished he had crashed on him. It would have broken his fall, and perhaps diminished his headache and nausea. Although Avenazar's attacks might be as much to blame as the brutal landing. Nevian closed his eyes again, trying to focus. Even *thinking* demanded all his energy, as if his mind had grown dull and lazy. Had he lost his talent for rigorous logic and coherence? Fear squeezed his insides. He needed to get back on his feet and figure out what Avenazar had taken and how much of him was left. Whenever he tried to remember more of last night, however, the pounding in his head became splitting agony.

"Never heard of this place. If you want to live, you'll let me be."

"Absolutely not."

"Don't mess with Avenazar. Don't."

Nevian's voice turned pressing, and he heard in it the visceral panic gripping his heart. Don't anger Avenazar. A rule he just knew and did not question. He had triggered the night's assault by making his master furious. Always a terrible idea.

"I don't care who I have to mess with!" Cal threw up his hands, then caught Nevian's gaze and stared him down. "I had important things to do yesterday, real important. One of my friends might die because I stopped for you, and the other slammed his fist in my face and won't talk to me. You don't get to shoo me away, and no Myrian wizard gets to kill you on my watch. I refuse."

Cal's voice morphed halfway through the tirade from an angry rant to a broken whisper. Tears welled in his eyes, and he wiped them away. Nevian focused on the ceiling, ill at ease with his intense reaction. Was he supposed to comfort him? It wasn't his decision if Cal had stopped! He shouldn't have to deal with his feelings! It would be hard enough to piece his memories back together, if at all possible, and he did not want the burden of someone else's problems. Nevian pointedly looked away until the little crisis had passed.

"Your healer left about an hour ago, but they gave me instructions." Cal sniffled then withdrew a crumpled piece of paper. "These are questions. They might jog your memory. Vellien said your mind was destroyed when they got there. They salvaged the core from the wreckage, which apparently meant preserving your inability to express any form of gratitude, but let's ignore that for now. They'll be back tomorrow. Until then, these are supposed to help."

"Questions." He didn't bother to hide his doubts. A powerful wizard had demolished everything inside Nevian, blocking or destroying entire aspects of his life—and Nevian couldn't tell which! Avenazar would return to kill him sooner or later, to put a definite end to Nevian. And their solution was *questions*. "You think questions can give me my memories back? That questions can protect me?"

His breath hitched, and his vision swam. The walls closed in, pressing down on him and stifling him. Nevian tried to slow his frantic heart. He had to calm down and pull himself together. Something of incredible value was locked away in his mind. He knew it, and he'd fight for it as long as he lived. Small fingers landed on his hand, startling him.

"It's a start, no?" Cal said. "Vellien knew what they were doing. They saved your life and fixed your leg. If they say this list can help you, I believe them. Give them a chance, at least."

Nevian propped himself on an elbow—a position he held exactly two seconds before his nausea overtook him and he collapsed back to the bed. Now that Cal mentioned it, Nevian noticed the distant sting of his left leg. Nothing that compared with the pain ensnaring his head, however. He was such a mess, but perhaps staying busy would help him.

"Fine. Ask."

Cal's big grin made Nevian regret his decision immediately. Too late. Cal brandished his list and read off it.

"What's your name?"

"Nevian."

"And you were an apprentice with the Myrians. For a long time?"

Nevian massaged his temples. How long? He tried to stretch his memory and come up with an answer, but it only made his headache worse. After a moment, Cal moved on.

"Do you remember how old you are?"

"Seventeen?" It sounded right. "Yes. Seventeen."

Images of his birthday with another wizard surfaced. A woman. Sauria. His first master, before Avenazar. She had given him a dozen books to read and joked that he would be done within three months. He'd finished in twenty-four days. Nevian smiled a little.

"Wow, you can actually smile!" Cal exclaimed. "I take it the questions are working! Do you know where you are?"

"Larryn's Shelter. Or so you said."

"No, I mean … as a more general thing. Where are you?"

Nevian lacked an immediate answer to this one. He struggled to conjure a hand-drawn map of the world in his mind, ignoring the growing headache to pinpoint his location on it. Not west, in the sprawling Myrian Empire. His focus shifted to a snaking river in the northern hemisphere, but still south of Mehr. Nal-Gresh, the Stone Egg, the greatest port city on the east coast, thrived at its mouth. But that wasn't it either. "We're ... in Isandor, along the Reonne River."

"Great!"

Cal clapped. Nevian winced at the harsh sound and glared at him, which caused Cal to slap a hand over his mouth. The brief silence didn't last, and they went back to work. His questions exhausted Nevian. Every answer brought its share of memories, but while he could attach some to clear moments of his life, many just floated around his mind, unhinged. Nevian tried to piece the puzzle back together. As time passed, however, his energy declined. Even listening to Cal was becoming harder, let alone focusing enough to give an answer. Nevian eventually snapped.

"Is that all?" he asked, interrupting the next question. "Or are there a hundred more on your list?"

For a moment, Cal only stared at him with wide eyes, his mouth hanging half open. Then he folded the list—a silly precaution, considering how crumpled it was. "Just one more. Do you need anything? Food? Water?"

"Silence."

Water, too, but Nevian refused to admit it. After such a long discussion, he wanted nothing more than sweet silence. The sun had moved farther up in the sky, shifting light away from his room, which felt stuffy and hot to him. He needed to rest and recover, to let everything he'd learned sink in. Pieces of his time in the enclave had come back, but through it all, Nevian had noticed one thing missing: his knowledge of magic. He could remember entire nights studying, putting together spells that Master Avenazar refused to teach him, but no matter how much he tried, the spells themselves remained a mystery. The frustration, fatigue, and stress had stayed, yet the result of his hard work was gone. Vanished forever.

"Okay, fine. I get it." Cal slid off his chair, his smile stiff. "You want me to leave. No more annoying halfling. Never mind that he saved your life."

"It doesn't matter." Nevian turned to stare at Cal. "You were too late. Everything important is gone. I don't thank people for salvaging an empty husk."

"You should. At least you have an opportunity to fill it back up. Not everyone gets that chance."

Cal crossed the room, slapped the list of questions on a minuscule desk barely big enough to hold two tomes, then stalked to the door. He slammed it as Nevian focused his attention on the ceiling, and the loud noise sent a sharp pain through his mind. At least peace returned after.

Nevian closed his eyes and grasped once more at his memories, as if it would change anything. Perhaps the healer could help. Nevian would make them try. He hated giving up. Besides, Cal had a point: it wasn't over. Not yet. Even though Nevian doubted Avenazar would allow him time to pull himself back together. Once the wizard realized Nevian had survived, he would find him again, and it would only become worse. No one escaped Master Avenazar. That, at least, Nevian hadn't forgotten.

CHAPTER THIRTY-THREE

A THIN sheet of sweat covered Arathiel's body, but none of his muscles ached from his exhausting physical training as he returned to the Shelter. The last hour of climbing trees and jumping down would leave only the best athletes in good shape. Even considering the healthy training regime he had kept as House Brasten's weapon master, he should be hot and tired, straining from his heavy breathing, and ready to collapse. A century had passed since his last serious routine, and he'd barely slept last night.

His talk with Camilla had lasted until the sky greyed over. She confirmed executions still happened at Carrington's Square, and several bridges above would allow him to drop close to Hasryan. Which meant he needed to learn to land. He used to be able to tuck himself into a ball and soften any fall, but that technique involved responding exactly when his feet hit the ground. Hard to do when you no longer *felt* it. So Arathiel had waited for the rumour mill to confirm Hasryan was still imprisoned, then headed out of Isandor and into the nearby woods, east along the Reonne River, where no indiscreet eyes would catch him during practice. He'd climbed countless trees, springing down and trying to roll with the landing from visual cues.

It didn't go well. Arathiel stopped halfway through the morning. His feet didn't hurt—of course not—but a normal step left him off balance. He suspected he had pushed his muscles to their limit. If he strained or broke something, there would be no rescue. He could always try again later today and tomorrow, after a short rest. For now, he wanted to examine his feet with Camilla's mirror to ensure no wounds would ruin his plan, then he could check on Cal and the teenager they'd saved yesterday. Perhaps Larryn would even have breakfast left for him.

When Arathiel stepped back into the Shelter, he found it deserted. A few patrons huddled near the fire—had it been cold?—and a strange, heavy atmosphere filled the place. He tried to pinpoint the source of the malaise, and the pervasive silence hit him. No music played in the Shelter, and the hushed conversations of those present remained inaccessible to Arathiel's ears. He traversed the common room and pushed open the door to the side corridors, leading into the tower with the private rooms.

An Isandor guard waited at his door, her arms crossed. She had straight dark hair, a serious and round face, and was of obvious Tuenese descent. How uncommon for anyone from the Peninsula to travel so far north. Her rumpled uniform and the bags under her eyes signalled a tiring night, but as soon as he stepped into the corridor, she straightened herself and approached him.

"Mister Arathiel? I'm Lieutenant Sora Sharpe, investigator for the Isandor Sapphire Guard. I need to ask you a few questions."

Arathiel had no illusions about her chosen topic. Sharpe was in charge of Hasryan's case, and there had been a suspicious prison break during the previous night. Others must have told her he participated in Hasryan's card games. Arathiel nodded to her, opened his door, and let her in. If he refused to answer her questions, she would know something was up. He had to risk it.

"Ask away," he said.

Sharpe didn't, not right away. She scanned the room, her alert eyes stopping on every detail. She lingered on the handheld mirror but didn't comment. Instead, she turned to him and offered a reassuring smile.

"Where were you last night?"

Arathiel hesitated. Careful now. He might never have gone to the prison, but his friends had. If only he'd spoken with Cal before, he would know when to lie and when to tell her the truth. The best might be to stick as close as he could to what had happened. "I moved around a lot, so I hope you're not busy," he said. "I was sitting in the Shelter's common room until midnight, or about."

Her gaze narrowed. "After that?"

"Cal arrived. He was panting and panicked, so I asked what was going on. A teenager had crashed on one of Isandor's bridges in front of him. He wanted help moving him. If you've seen Cal ... well, he's a halfling. He couldn't drag a human all the way here."

He hoped his calm tone convinced her, and that Cal and Larryn hadn't invented anything ridiculous to protect themselves. A single contradiction could blow their cover, and if it also put Arathiel in trouble … He would never save Hasryan with Sora Sharpe watching over his shoulder.

"You went?"

"We got Larryn first, then went, yes." His heart sped up, but he didn't hesitate. How else could they convince her Larryn had never been around the guards' headquarters? At least now if patrons hadn't seen him at the Shelter, he had a plausible justification. Arathiel repeated to himself it was a logical lie, one Larryn could come up with on his own. "It took a long time. I'd say we might have returned about two in the morning? Hard to tell. Then I left again, to find a professional healer."

"What did you carry? Head or legs?" Sharpe asked. Arathiel's confusion must have shown, because she clarified in an irritated tone. "You and Larryn moved him. Which end of this teenager did you hold?"

"Oh! The head." Arathiel looked down and tapped his chest where the teenager's blood had stained his shirt. "His head was in a terrible state."

"You went outside on the night of the winter solstice with nothing else but a light shirt?"

Arathiel tensed. He had been so focused on involving Larryn in his story and telling it right, he'd forgotten how little he wore. Certainly nothing warm. He pressed his lips together.

"Yeah … I was in too much of a hurry. Didn't think of it before we were halfway to this kid, and then it didn't seem right to risk his life for a coat."

"And at no point during this period did you leave Larryn's side? He was with you at all times?"

Her anger and disbelief seeped through the tightness of her voice. She had wanted different answers. Something to confirm her suspicions. Arathiel struggled to maintain a neutral expression even though her frustration relieved him. He might do it—he might get through this without giving everyone away, leading the Shelter's heart into prison and destroying Hasryan's last chance.

"Not until I left to fetch a healer," he said, careful not to mention the Dathirii either. Perhaps he ought to push for another topic. He allowed himself a little frown. "Lieutenant, can I ask what this is about?"

"You can ask." With a wry smile, she proceeded to ignore the question. "How long have you known Larryn, Cal, or Hasryan?"

There it was. Hasryan's name had finally entered the conversation. Arathiel tilted his head to the side and met Sharpe's gaze. Probing to see if he'd lie for them, was she? He smiled. Of course he would, but she couldn't know what he'd trained for all morning. Sora Sharpe had no way of understanding how much these three friends and the Shelter meant to him now.

"I shared a handful of card games with them. Cal greeted me when I arrived some twenty days ago—he's the waiter here sometimes. They invited me to join later on, but we haven't played since Hasryan's arrest. I do miss it. I don't get out much otherwise."

Sharpe had tensed a little at the mention of Hasryan's arrest. Her dark eyes bore holes into Arathiel as though she could sift through the lies by staring hard enough. She must know they were all lying even if she couldn't find the crack in it, and Arathiel wondered if she would drag them to an interrogation room anyway. Down here, no one had the power to stop her. After a long silent scrutiny, Sharpe huffed.

"Very well. Thank you for your time, sir."

Arathiel withheld a sigh of relief. He nodded before opening the door for her, his shoulders squared and his chin raised high. He had nothing to conceal, after all—or so he wanted her to think. As she strode through the doorway, Sharpe turned.

"You don't seem like you belong here. If something keeps you hidden and you need help, you can come to me." She even offered a smile with her proposal, though it didn't last. "And if you remember any strange behaviour from Larryn while you were with him yesterday, I would like to know."

Arathiel's insides twisted. He didn't belong. A single interview with Sharpe, and she could already tell as much. He rubbed his forearm, digging his thumb in hard enough to feel it, wishing she had said nothing of the sort. But she was also wrong. He might always be the odd one, whether in the Lower City or among other nobles, but he no longer intended to hide. She would have a solid surprise in two days. He returned her brief smile.

"Thank you, Lieutenant Sharpe. I will keep that in mind."

Sharpe wished him a good day and hurried down the corridor. Arathiel had an urge to run to Larryn and make sure they had their story right, but he didn't trust his hearing. He waited until well after the sound of Sharpe's boots had vanished to slip out of his room, then headed toward the kitchens. Larryn spent most of his days there, even more so when he had strong feelings to manage. After last night's failed attempt, Arathiel didn't doubt the Shelter's owner would busy himself cooking enough food to last the week.

❧

COUNTLESS stories circulated around the Shelter about Larryn throwing out people who dared to enter his kitchens without knocking, but Arathiel pushed open the door and strode in without a pause. He needed to talk with him whether he liked it or not. The room stretched before him, long and narrow, with wide counters on each side and a strong fire at the end. A large pot rested over the billowing flames, and Larryn stirred the mixture. Fatigue and disappointment hunched his shoulders, but he spun as the door closed with a creak. Drops of hot stew splattered the walls around from the sudden movement. Larryn ignored them, glaring at Arathiel, his head slightly turned to the side.

"Get out of my kitchen."

Arathiel stopped short. The bitter anger in Larryn's voice took him by surprise. "We need to talk first. Lieutenant Sora Sharpe was just in my room, asking questions about my whereabouts last night."

"Don't mind her." He was clutching his spoon so hard his knuckles had turned white. "She's looking for new crimes to pin on Hasryan and build her career."

Arathiel met Larryn's gaze. Was he not even aware of what

Sharpe wanted? "I don't think Hasryan was her target this time."

"Are you saying I should also prepare to be arrested on false charges?" Larryn leaned against his counter with a mirthless smirk. "How grand."

Arathiel moved closer, trying to decipher Larryn's mind. Cal had broken down from the stress yesterday, and Hasryan's upcoming execution was bound to affect Larryn just as much. Add the Shelter's upkeep and a failed prison break to his load, and he couldn't be in a good state.

"They wouldn't be false, though," Arathiel said. "Did you intend to use me as a cover story and send her to me? Because next time, I'd appreciate some warning. I told her you were with us when we saved the teenager. I said Cal came to the Shelter panicked, talked to me, and I fetched you. We went together and carried him back—I had the head, you the feet—and then I left again. You're safe for about two hours, starting at midnight. Please tell me that covers most of your prison break and matches your story."

Larryn's eyes widened when Arathiel mentioned the prison break. "How did you—?"

"Know? Cal told me." Arathiel rubbed his face, amazed at what he was hearing. "So you believed I had no idea? You risked that I would cover your ass and lie to an investigator without a clue of what I thought of your illegal expedition?"

Larryn set the spoon down on the counter and pushed himself off. "Yeah, I did. People lie to the guards all the time around here. That's what we do. We have each other's backs, no questions asked." A flame lit in Larryn's eyes, and he strode up to Arathiel. "But you're right. Wasn't very bright of me to include you like this."

It took all of Arathiel's willpower not to back away. Every one of Larryn's muscles seemed taut, ready to spring. He had always been quick to anger and react, but this was different. Worse. Neither Cal nor Hasryan could defuse his building rage and bitterness with a simple joke. Instead it swirled, on the very edge of being unleashed, and Arathiel was the closest target.

"I don't get you." Larryn tapped Arathiel's chest with his twisted finger, pushing hard enough for Arathiel to feel. "You're not one of us. You never were." Larryn scoffed. "You sent a noble—a Dathirii, of all the shitheads out there—down to *my* Shelter to heal that kid. I can't believe you acted all poor and downtrodden on me. Ask your rich ass friends for help next time. You sure are more like them if you can just profit from this place without second guessing yourself."

"I didn't—"

"Yes, you did." Larryn shoved him, then his hands curled into fists. He looked as though he wanted Arathiel to fight back. "Vacate your room before the evening is out. I can fit three kids on your bed, and they can't ask pretentious Upper City residents to house them."

Arathiel's mouth went dry. He needed two more days in the Shelter. He didn't want to involve Camilla in this more than she already was. She risked a lot on his account, and the harder it became to see the link between her and Arathiel, the better it'd be for everyone.

"I'm not ..." No point in arguing. Arathiel squeezed his eyes shut, wrestling with his feelings. "Perhaps you're right. I don't belong here. I don't belong anywhere, not anymore, not since I left the city a hundred thirty years ago. Let's just make sure we all have the same story for Sharpe, and I'll be gone."

Larryn scoffed. "Yeah, whatever. I heard you the first time. Cal arrived at midnight, and I grabbed the feet, and so on."

"His leg was broken," Arathiel said. "Make sure you mention that. And he's a tall teenager, with short blond hair."

"I'll visit him. Once that elf noble isn't stinking up my Shelter anymore." Larryn shot Arathiel a very meaningful gaze. "With any luck, all the undesirables will have vanished by sunset."

The implied insult hurt more than any real punch could have. Arathiel gritted his teeth together. "I get it. I'm gone. Never discussing any of this again. Let's hope you don't wind up in prison because you were too angry at me to work out the details properly. You don't want to leave Cal with the cooking."

Cal's horrible cooking skills had been a frequent topic of mockery during their games. He apparently had a knack for burning eggs to a crisp. Larryn stifled a bitter laugh and shook his head.

"You don't want to leave Cal in charge of anything," Larryn said.

"He saved a life last night."

Larryn turned away and returned to his stew. He stared into it, his voice falling to a whisper. "And sacrificed another."

"It's not that simple."

"It is. Now leave."

Arathiel held back a sigh. He wanted to tell Larryn not to worry about Hasryan, that there were other ways than a prison break, but he didn't dare. Larryn and Cal would be the first suspected of helping him in this, and he would rather keep them in the dark. Besides, the tightness in Larryn's voice and the clench in his jaw told Arathiel this argument had already happened between him and Cal, and it hadn't gone well.

"I'm sorry I tricked you," Arathiel said. "It wasn't my intention. I'm glad I can at least have your back on this matter, as a thank you."

Larryn's only answer was a small grunt. Arathiel decided he would get no better than that small acknowledgment and left the kitchens. He returned to his room to pack what little he owned right away. He could sleep in the forest for a night or two. The cold wouldn't affect him if he could avoid frostbite, at least. As Arathiel wrapped his handheld mirror in a dirty cloth, he caught sight of his white hair, and his heart squeezed. This was him now. He had to accept that. But Sharpe and Larryn had both agreed he didn't belong. Arathiel felt like the world was pushing him back, telling him to stay out of this matter, to linger on the fringe and never participate. Not anymore. In two days, he would be leaping back into Isandor's politics whether the city wanted him to or not.

CHAPTER THIRTY-FOUR

LARRYN didn't leave his kitchens until late afternoon. He didn't dare, not with his anger still simmering, ready to explode at the first person to provoke him. His thoughts whirled, a hurricane of frustration and regrets with Hasryan at its centre. Miserable Hasryan, alone in his cell, condemned. Curse it all, why had Larryn fled so fast? He should have stayed. Even with the lies, he should have stood by his friend and freed him. Who else could have? He'd been Hasryan's last chance, and he'd wasted it by letting his anger and fear take over. The possibility of returning to jail—of shackles around his wrists and boots crunching his fingers into hard ground—had frozen his mind. It didn't seem fair to be cooking safely in the Shelter while his friend prepared to die, but there was nothing else he could do now. They would never sneak into the headquarters a second time. Hasryan was doomed, and

Larryn never wanted to see Cal's face again. The Halfies Trio was broken.

All for a Myrian who had fallen off a bridge, splitting his skull and shattering Larryn's friendship with Cal. Larryn stared at door number seven, his hands curled into fists. As much as he tried to remind himself this wasn't the Myrian's fault, he couldn't contain his bitterness. Couldn't he have smashed his head an hour later? Cal would call it a fated encounter, saying Ren had timed the fall and didn't want him to die. But as always, it seemed luck was not on Larryn's side, and now he had a wounded stranger to watch over.

Larryn turned the doorknob and entered without knocking before his willingness to have a peaceful talk with this Myrian ended. His gaze went straight to the bed to rest upon the teenager. One of his long legs dangled over the side, out of proportion with the apprentice's height, as was so often the case with boys his age. He had a tuft of down-like blond hair, and sleep smoothed his otherwise squarish features. Looking at him now, Larryn realized the boy couldn't be all that old. Cal *had* said he was a teenager, but the information settled in Larryn's mind. He hadn't been listening, not really.

This kid didn't deserve his rage. Someone had tried to kill him, pushed him off a bridge. Last night might have been as enjoyable as sloshing shit all over his clothes, but Larryn refused to unleash his pent-up anger on a wounded teenager. He cleared his throat, loud enough to wake him. The Myrian jolted up, wide-eyed, tucking his lanky limbs into a tight ball. Larryn recognized the terror in his gaze—how often had he sprung to his feet after being shaken awake, fists curled and ready to fight?

"Hey, hey," he said. "Sorry. I didn't know that'd scare you. You're all right. You're safe."

The teenager raised a hand to his mouth, leaned over the bedside, and vomited. Not a lot, as his stomach must have been almost empty, but Larryn winced at the retching sound. The bitter smell overcame the Lower City's latent stench right away. The boy groaned, wiped his mouth, then flopped back to the bed.

"Thanks for provoking that," he said.

"I'll clean it, don't worry." Larryn had seen worse than a puddle of vomit. Once you'd found yourself lying in a pool of shit and piss, half-conscious from a thorough beating, a little puke didn't seem so bad. "I'm Larryn."

"The owner."

"Yeah."

He studied Larryn in silence. After a moment, his tongue made a small clack of disapproval.

"You're too young to be the owner."

"Look who's talking! You're just a teenager."

"And you're not?"

"Not anymore." No one needed to know it hadn't been a month since he'd turned twenty. Besides, the birthday evening seemed so long ago now, so impossibly serene. He'd never have one of those rooftops chats with Hasryan again. "I wanted to ask you a few questions."

"Again?" Nevian propped himself on an elbow. "What is it with you people and questions? I answered a billion of them this morning.

Can't you just talk with one another?"

"No." Larryn had considered reaching out to Cal, but he wasn't ready. He wasn't sure he ever would be. "I can tell you're from the Myrian Enclave. What's your name, and can you go back there?"

"Nevian." He scoffed, then stared straight ahead. "I can return if I want a brutal and painful death, perhaps. And when they learn I survived, they will come for me. It won't be pretty."

Larryn wondered if they would attack the Shelter, too. Was Nevian nothing but problems waiting to happen? That would be just like Cal, to dump more trouble on his shoulders. "So you have nowhere to go. Any money or means to earn some?"

Nevian's sickly shade of green turned even paler as he shook his head. Did this bother him more than being hunted? He wouldn't be the first to struggle with helplessness. Larryn sighed. A part of him had come looking for an excuse to throw Nevian out, to get back at him for causing Cal's lateness. He couldn't do that, though. He would never dump another kid on the streets.

"So you're now a homeless teenager too sick to stay on your feet. I guess you qualify for this place."

"I'm not homeless." The distinct disgust in Nevian's tone made Larryn's hair stand on end. "I'm a young wizard. I can work, I'm serious and disciplined, and I'd never waste entire days burning my gold on alcohol and loitering."

"Oh, I'm sorry." Larryn voice dripped with acid. What revolting shit had he just heard? "You're right, Nevian. You're nothing like the rest of us. We know what it's like to struggle every day for our most basic needs, and we're grateful for what protection, food, and warmth this place provides. You, however, are just an asshole." Larryn sneered and moved closer to the bed. "Lucky you, though, you're an asshole who has no home and no income. You are homeless, but you'll never have to live through the shit the others do because you smashed onto the right bridge at the right time. I don't throw people out, not when they have nothing else. If you ever say anything like that again, though, I'll make an exception for your ass and boot it out with great pleasure. Those good-for-nothing folk you just trashed? They are my people, and this Shelter is dedicated to them. You don't get to profit from this place and talk shit about them. Is that clear?"

Nevian had stiffened as Larryn neared the bed, leaning as far back as he could, shifting his right arm away again. Controlled fear. Larryn stayed a safe distance from him, hoping it would help. Threatening a physical hit was not the goal, but he needed Nevian to understand he wouldn't accept words like these.

"Now, this once-homeless kid"—Larryn tapped his own chest—"is going to clean up your vomit and bring you something to eat. Why don't you use the time to rest and think about how wrong you are?" This time, Nevian scowled and seemed about to protest. Larryn hushed him. "Let it sink in first."

He left Nevian in his bed, not caring in the least if the apprentice hated him. This was his Shelter. He made the rules, and he intended to keep the place safe. Enough people spat on street folk every day already. Nevian would have to change his mind or endure their presence and learn to shut his mouth.

◠◡◠

VARDEN stepped into his cell and collapsed to the ground.

How had he even managed to walk from Avenazar's torture room to his new home? He didn't remember dragging himself but knew only that he had, somehow, through sheer willpower. Guards could flank him all they wanted. He refused to let them carry him. Not until he couldn't stand any longer.

Not that this tiny defiance would last. Varden shivered, the stone's cold seeping through his ruined garb. They had taken away all torches from the corridor, all sources of fire and warmth. Even after the Long Night had ended, he had stayed cut off from Keroth. Severed from Their power and wisdom, from the comfort of Their presence nearby. Or perhaps he simply no longer felt the Firelord—perhaps They had abandoned him.

No. Varden pushed the idea away. He couldn't let himself go down that road. He needed to think straight, to consider his position. If only he could …

Hours of torture had turned his brain into wet logs, and Varden no longer managed to strike any kind of fire from it. He curled up, unable to feel anything past the pain radiating from his back and the exhaustion in his confused mind.

Avenazar had rifled through his entire life, leaving no memory untouched. Nothing was sacred to him. Not his parents' death, not Miles and their time together, not Varden's peaceful meditation, sitting in Keroth's brazier. Certainly not anything concerning Branwen and Nevian. He tainted it all, forcing Varden to relive his past in flashes, jumping back and forth depending on Avenazar's interest. By the time the wizard's crushing presence left his mind, Varden was completely disoriented, unsure he'd escaped his memories. Even now, his most solid grip on reality was the notable absence of Avenazar's snide comments and the horrible needling pain across his shoulder blade.

Varden doubted Avenazar had meant to ground him when he'd materialized a fire poker in his hands. *To mark the passage of days*, he had said. *Because prisoners always lose track.* Avenazar had pinched the poker's tip, and the metal had glowed red, then white. Varden knew too well what had followed, but his mind slid over it, blocking the searing agony. One Avenazar would have no trouble inflicting upon him again, whether through memories or another strike.

This was his life now, and he was terrified. How long could he withstand Avenazar's torture before he lost track of himself? How many times could he hop through his past before he no longer knew what had happened when and how these experiences shaped who he was? He couldn't allow this. What else did he have, if not himself? He refused to surrender it, to let anyone twist it. He had held true and helped Branwen and Nevian despite the risk. Now he would endure, test his resilience, and trust in Keroth's will and his own self-love.

And when he put it that way—when it was his inner strength and Keroth's support against Avenazar's evil—Varden had no doubts he would survive.

∽⚬∽

BRANWEN hissed as the needle pricked her finger and set her current work down. The faint ripples of pain running up her back distracted her, slowing her work. It would help if she slept more, too, but anxiety and nightmares plagued her nights. Nothing to be done about it, except save Varden. She wouldn't rest until she knew he was safe.

At least she was doing something to help. Branwen spread the rough fabric of her project on her workdesk to evaluate its progress. She had an excellent memory for clothes and remembered the outfits worn by Keroth's acolytes down to the details. Reproducing them was another matter, but Branwen trusted her ability to create an appropriate disguise. She would infiltrate the enclave and get him out, even if she had to do it alone.

Branwen leaned back, tears blurring her eyes, her hands shaking. She couldn't remember ever crying so much, but the floodgates had opened during winter solstice, and she'd never found the energy to close them again. Every time her mind wandered back to Varden, she found tears streaming down her cheeks and had to take a moment to wrestle control over herself. It never failed. Except on one occasion.

Shortly after her return, Diel had called a meeting between several House leaders, to discuss a Coalition between them. He had asked Branwen to share the last ten days with them and reveal the extent of Avenazar's ruthlessness and plans. Moving about triggered jolting pain along her spine, but she had agreed. Anything to give Varden a chance.

She had picked an open-back dress for the occasion, one in which she felt absolutely gorgeous. Branwen knew she would need the confidence, and she wanted to expose the ugly purple and yellow pattern of bruises Avenazar had left her. She had hoped they could shock the nobles into action, force into them the realization that they could no longer stand by and watch.

She should have known better.

The lords and ladies of Isandor offered Branwen their sympathies and wished her a prompt recovery. They expressed dismay over the state of her back and the violence of Avenazar's actions, and promptly condemned the use of such brutal force. So far, so good, Branwen had thought, standing in front of the assembled group, her heart swelling with hope. Though they couched their words, their disgust and fear seemed real.

Then again, one had said, and Branwen immediately understood the excuses would follow. *Then again*, House Dathirii had provoked the Myrians. *Then again*, this battle didn't concern Isandor as a whole. *Then again*, the fate of Varden Daramond was a matter of internal affairs, and they should not interfere. *Then again*, if Lord Dathirii had found the soldiers he kept promising, Branwen might never have been hurt, and he could guarantee nothing bad would happen to the other nobles, either.

Over and over, they told her she would receive no help—and neither would Varden, not from them.

Diel had stood in silence, growing paler with every rebuttal. Branwen tried to argue, burning off her urge to cry with furious indignation. The soulless bastards didn't care. About her, about

Varden, about Isandor's future.

But so be it. She would not wait to act—not for her health to fully return, not for the support of other Houses, not for Diel's non-existent miracle. Come what may, she would complete her disguise, go back to the Myrian Enclave, and save her friend.

CHAPTER THIRTY-FIVE

A CROWD would gather long before Sora Sharpe arrived at Carrington Square with Hasryan. She had noticed the flow of residents when heading to the prisons to collect him and delayed as much as she could before escorting him out. More time for the Sapphire Guard to assume their position and less time for attempts to free him. Security measures. That was her excuse. It had nothing to do with lessening Hasryan's exposure to those ready to cheer at his death.

Ever since Brune had pushed the blame solely on him, Sora found it hard not to think of Hasryan's reaction. She couldn't get his stunned expression out of her mind—how the defiance had drained away, leaving behind a bitter shell. This execution didn't sit well with her. She scolded herself. He had killed several others aside from Lady Allastam, and whether or not Brune had framed him didn't matter.

The weight in her stomach didn't move. She knew Hasryan was not the problem. Today's hanging belonged to the political circus of Isandor, and in the process, they would kill their best source of information on the Crescent Moon's activities.

She hated how often the demands of the powerful tied her hands. Lord Allastam and Brune wished to see Hasryan dead, and so he would hang today. Just like a Dathirii protected Larryn, preventing her from a thorough questioning. She could have nailed him for the prison break if she had tried harder, but her superiors had ordered her to back off from 'Bonebreaker'. They had wanted her both to keep Hasryan imprisoned, and to do nothing against those who had tried to free him.

Admittedly, she didn't care about Larryn if he stayed out of her way. A quick investigation of the Shelter revealed how much he helped others around. Sora had bigger targets, people who bypassed laws without breaking a sweat, eating Isandor from inside and ruining lives. But to get to them, she needed to climb through the ranks of Isandor Sapphire Guard, to play their game and forge alliances until no one remained untouchable for her. In a city corrupted to the core, it would prove a long and arduous road—one in which distasteful high-profile executions such as Hasryan's became a necessity.

It didn't alleviate the weight in her stomach as she extracted him from his cell and walked him out of the headquarters. He flinched at the sunlight, and the small movement provoked a ripple of tension in the guards escorting them. As if he could escape against the massive number of troops in place today. As if he had the will to try. Sora doubted it. Prison had hollowed his cheeks and sapped his energy, but his silence weighed on her more than anything. No more quips or smirks. As if he was already dead inside.

No. Sora pulled her thoughts away from there. He had killed others. People with families and friends, people who had deserved to live. She'd proven that long before Brune intervened, and Hasryan didn't even deny it. How had she grown attached to such a man? She couldn't get sentimental over this.

Sora Sharpe didn't celebrate another death, but she wouldn't mourn it either.

⚬✖⚬

CAMILLA Dathirii could not remember a time when she had enjoyed executions, and she had a few centuries of memories to draw from. Why would anyone delight in watching a man be pushed off a bridge, only to have a noose break his neck or choke him? Putting Carrington's Square, built in honour of one of Isandor's founding Houses, to such use was barbaric. Luscious gardens filled the park, which nestled in the middle of the city's towers, and four elegant arches reached upward, meeting twenty feet above the centre. This central point formed a smaller circle with a hole sufficiently wide to drop a man through. The body would hang high above the statue of Lord Carrington in the middle of the park below and the large hydrangea bushes surrounding it. Part of the crowd often stood right under, amidst the flowers, eager to see this gruesome spectacle from as close as possible.

Today, however, the ambiance differed from the usual. Commoners packed the gardens and nearby bridges, but no cheers or excited screams came from them. They stared in relative silence, a buzz of hushed conversations drifting up from them. They used to be the loudest crowd, unruly and chaotic, but their enthusiasm had been doused. Camilla studied the group, curious. The poorest huddled with solemn expressions, some even holding black flowers to display their grief. Arathiel had said he'd met Hasryan at a shelter for the homeless, and she imagined these were the patrons who had appreciated him. They had come to pay homage to a comrade, not cheer at his death.

Unlike the nobles, who wanted to celebrate. They occupied the bridges above Carrington's Square, which offered a great view of the criminal before he dropped. Members of lesser Houses lined the handful of stairs winding up the surrounding towers, halfway between the gardens and the top of the arch. Sometimes, these spots were empty, and residents of the Middle City could climb on them to witness executions, but not today. Almost every family of note in Isandor had sent someone to watch, most of them with a bright lily, symbol of a celebration. House Allastam had been granted places close to the central hanging circle, at an angle where the city guards would not block their view. Even young Mia Allastam had come despite her frail health. A light blue scarf wound around her neck and over her pale blond hair, and she wore fur-lined gloves to protect herself from the cold.

Diel stood behind her, his golden hair whipping in the wind. He had chosen somber attire, held no flowers, and wasn't smiling. This was an obligation, nothing more. Only a few Dathirii had come: Kellian to congratulate Miss Sharpe, Hellion and his friends—all relatives for whom Camilla bore no love—and Yultes. They chatted with other ambitious nobles who had gathered to praise House Allastam for finally solving the mystery behind Lady Allastam's murder. Camilla noted Lord Freitz among them. Of everyone assembled, he had the most legitimate reason to rejoice: this arrest had cleared his name of a crime for which House Freitz had suffered Lord Allastam's bitter wrath. His presence surprised no one, and he even seemed of a mind to talk with Lord Allastam. Perhaps their families could at last start to mend the deep wounds between them.

The stage was set, she thought, and in the middle of it was their infamous assassin.

Camilla stood not too far from the guards surrounding the middle circle, and she had an excellent view of the young Hasryan. They had shackled his hands behind him, and three soldiers flanked him. More waited on each bridge spiking out, crossbows at the ready, their gaze never leaving the assassin. The longer Camilla watched, however, the more ridiculous these precautions seemed. Dirt clotted Hasryan's thick white hair, and his shoulders hunched in defeat. He had scanned the crowd below earlier, but his eyes glazed over everyone, and now he stared at his feet, so close to the drop.

He seemed so young, yet already broken. Ready to die.

Her heart clenched. How could he not be? Nobles jeered at him, called for guards to give him the final push early. He had been burdened with one of the city's most heinous crimes and framed by his boss. Camilla remembered Arathiel's slow explanation. He had tried so hard to be factual, but he had no proof Hasryan hadn't done this assassination. He just *believed* it was all false, and Hasryan mattered enough to draw him out. As Camilla stared at the young man standing above Carrington's Square, empty eyes set on his feet, she couldn't help but agree with Arathiel's assessment. It wasn't fair for him to die. Criminal or no, she didn't have the heart to let it happen.

She spotted Sora Sharpe among the guards close to Hasryan and made her way through the crowd. People gasped and ruffled as officials finished tying their hanging rope to the central circle under Hasryan's feet. They pulled on it to test the strength, and she knew from experience they would have the noose around Hasryan's neck within a few minutes. Then they only needed to read the list of his crimes and give him the final nudge. Her pace quickened until she reached the line of city guards behind which Sora stood, holding a heated discussion with one of her superiors. Camilla glanced at the bridges above. She spotted Arathiel, waiting, ready. She wasn't sure she would ever be. Camilla hadn't done anything so dangerous in decades, but she couldn't deny the flutter of excitement in her stomach.

"Miss Sharpe!" Her call drew Sora's attention. She excused herself from her current debate and moved closer to Camilla, pushing past the guards. This was perhaps her least favourite part of the plan, but it gave Arathiel an honest chance to reach Hasryan. "I never had the opportunity to congratulate you for—oh!"

Camilla had extended her hand to shake Sora's and pulled on her own purse in the process. She dropped it as subtly as possible, and the contents scattered among the guards' feet as it crashed on the ground. A few objects rolled over the bridge's edges and fell below, drawing surprised exclamations when they landed on Carrington's Square's crowd. The soldiers stepped aside and crouched down, trying to gather what they could. Camilla apologized over and over, then moved through them to help, further disrupting their line. Sora put a hand on her shoulder.

"It's fine, milady, let us. We'll take care of it." She squeezed Camilla's shoulder in reassurance. "Hurry up, boys."

A pang of guilt overtook Camilla as she straightened up. She had enjoyed Miss Sharpe's great wit over several tea conversations, when the investigator and Kellian had collaborated. An arrest as important as Hasryan's would launch her career. This case mattered, and while Camilla didn't favour the outcome, tricking Sora felt wrong. Too late now.

"Thank you, Sora," she said.

Then Arathiel's lithe form landed on the bridge behind them, sword drawn. His feet hit the stone a little hard, but he moved right away. He smacked two guards with the pommel while they spun around, confused and surprised, and parried the first attack. Camilla forced an expression of horror on her face. The chaos of bodies shuffling on the narrow bridge pushed her, and her faked fear became real as she stumbled back. A bad fall to the gardens below would shatter her bones. Sora caught her and helped her up.

"Quick, Lady Camilla, you ought to get out."

Her heart hammered against her chest, and she met Sora's gaze. Miss Sharpe seemed more concerned about her safety than about the man crashing through the guards behind her, parrying attacks as he advanced toward the centre. Their distraction had worked, but as Camilla's wrinkled hand squeezed Sora's, the elven lady wasn't thrilled about it. She hoped Sora could forgive her if she one day realized it had been intentional.

"I'm sorry," she said. "Thank you again."

Then she was moving back into the crowd, melting away as Arathiel proceeded with their plan.

⟳∞⟳

ARATHIEL'S fingers dug into his palm as he watched Camilla approach Sora Sharpe. Part of him wished she had no part in this plan, that she had stayed safe in the Dathirii Tower. The other thanked her courage and willingness to help, no matter how little. He had woken up nauseated and exhausted, and although excitement now coursed through his body, Arathiel could barely focus. Everything seemed miles away from him, muffled and withdrawn. He hadn't felt so isolated from the world since first walking through Isandor's docks, desperate to smell the stench of fish.

Today, his numbed senses would be his blessing. Today he stopped hiding, stopped pretending his body worked perfectly, and just accepted it didn't. Most days brought new struggles, small but draining. Even today, Arathiel was as likely to fail as he was to succeed because of it. What if he failed his landing and flattened himself pathetically on the bridge? What if he couldn't overpower the guards down there, and they captured him before he reached

Hasryan? But he had to try, for Hasryan's sake and his own. If he stepped back and watched now, Arathiel would always remain a ghost.

The contents of Camilla's purse scattered across the bridge below, and so did his thoughts.

Jump. Now.

Arathiel's stride lengthened. He sprinted until his path crossed over Camilla's bridge, where guards scrambled to kneel and pick up her things. In one fluid movement, he drew his sword out and leaped down.

His heart slung into his throat, and for a moment it felt like flying—breaking free from the doubts and fears holding him back. In a single jump, he had turned his life around and flung himself in front of everyone's gaze. Arathiel landed hard. Shouts surrounded him, surprised and dismayed. Elation coursed through him, pushing a grin to his lips. He'd kept his balance and crashed through their line without breaking any bones!

A handful of soldiers blocked his path to Hasryan. Arathiel slammed his pommel into the two closest soldiers, side-stepped the third's slash, and advanced through their ranks. He did not feel the impact of his sword stopping the next attack, parrying then striking on instinct. Years of training flowed back through his muscles, and although he needed every inch of focus to break through the numbness of his senses, Arathiel intercepted each slash with ease, countering them with the flat of his blade.

Even rusted, his skills surpassed these guards'. They outnumbered him and managed superficial cuts, but Arathiel ignored the growing number of wounds and progressed at a steady pace. They didn't hurt, and with every new stride—every slam of his sword in a guard's face—he approached Hasryan. It didn't matter how many wounds he collected in the process. He would get there, and he would save his friend.

⟨✕⟩

HASRYAN closed his eyes as guards passed the heavy rope over his head. It weighed on his shoulders, brushing against his throat whenever he moved, a reminder of the fate that awaited him, minutes away. At first, he had searched the crowd for Larryn, Cal, or Brune. Would they come to see him die? Perhaps it was best not to know. What would it change? He wouldn't be any less alone. Better to forget them, to accept he would die on his own. The guards next to him joked about some party last night, how one of them had jumped into the icy river and almost frozen. Hasryan wished he could trade lives with them, become so accepted that even the most careless stunts would earn him cheers. Not that he regretted how he'd lived his. He'd done a lot of bad things and wouldn't apologize for any of it. He was who he was.

The first surprised shriek came from his left. Men grunted from pain, blades clanged with a resounding sound, gasps emerged from the crowd. Hasryan's heart jumped.

"Stop him!" nobles screamed. "Push the dark elf off!"

His eyes snapped open. All but one guard had left his side.

Hasryan searched the confused mess of armours for the intruder causing this chaos and froze. *Arathiel?* Arathiel the would-be friend, the one with whom he'd shared immediate understanding, the potential relationship cut short by an arrest. He parried attacks from all directions with amazing ease, ducked under a blow, and kicked at the guard's steel-covered legs with his thin leather boots. Hasryan cringed, certain that must have hurt, before recalling the deep cut in Arathiel's sole on their first meeting. Perhaps it didn't. A sword cut through Arathiel's shoulder as he pushed past another guard, but he didn't wince. He moved on with nothing more than a glance at his new wound, and soon he was out of the thick of soldiers, sprinting toward Hasryan.

The guard nearby swore and turned to Hasryan. "You're dead."

"Oh no." Someone had come to save him. Someone *cared*. "No way."

Hasryan dropped into a crouch as the soldier reached for his back, intending to shove him off the bridge. He flung his weight into his opponent's legs, and the man crashed down hard. The guard rolled away, almost to the edge of the circle—a dangerous fall. Close enough to spark doubts, and he backed off to wait for reinforcements. Arathiel's strong hands helped Hasryan up. One grabbed the rope around his neck and yanked it off. Hasryan touched his throat with a deep breath, then turned to his unexpected saviour. Arathiel smiled.

"Ready? We're not out of this yet."

Guards were closing in on their small circle. They raised

crossbows, and a salvo of bolts followed. Arathiel jerked as one clipped his hip. He swore and gave the wound a cursory look. He seemed tense, perhaps even worried about it, but Hasryan knew he should have been on his knees, legs buckling under the pain. Instead, he wrapped the rope around his right arm, slipped the left one around Hasryan's hips, then pulled him close.

"Hang on tight!"

Arathiel leaped off the bridge, not giving him time for an answer. The rope yanked as it reached its full length. *Snap.* Hasryan's throat tightened as he imagined it around his neck. *Snap.* A friend had saved him from that awful fate, one he'd never dared to count as such. They swung above Carrington's Square, Hasryan clinging to Arathiel, his eyes watering. Why would Arathiel risk it? What had Hasryan done to deserve this kind of trust? The wind of their speedy descent wiped his tears away. They accelerated fast, and as they passed the lowest point of their arc, Arathiel let go of the rope.

The crowd under them jostled in a panic to get out of the way. They screamed and ran, trying to take cover from the crossbow bolts that would soon fall. Hasryan thought he heard a few cheers. Perhaps he had imagined them, or perhaps people just loved a thrilling escape attempt, even from a hated criminal. The ground rushed toward them. It had seemed terrifyingly high from the bridge above, but now it was way too close for Hasryan's liking.

"This is bad."

"Less than death, no?"

Hasryan grinned at the wild amusement in Arathiel's tone. A

neck-breaking swing from a high bridge and a chance to stick it to Isandor's guards and Brune? Of course it was better than death! He let go of Arathiel as they landed in the flower bed and tucked himself into a ball as soon as his feet touched the ground. Pain coursed up his legs and spine as he rolled through the bright-pink flowers, breaking most of his fall. He managed to straighten up despite the hands tied behind his back and sprinted away, eager to put distance between the guards and himself.

"Where to?" he called, turning to the side.

Arathiel wasn't with him.

Hasryan skidded to a stop and spun around. Arathiel struggled in the flowers still. He tried to step forward, but the moment he put his weight on his left ankle, it gave in, and he crashed down. He'd landed wrong, broken something. Hasryan ran back and crouched nearby. Above them, guards yelled and pointed crossbows in their direction. Bystanders had cleared the park, leaving the two of them as easy targets.

"We've got to move," Hasryan said.

"Heh. I knew I'd mess up a landing. At least it wasn't the first."

Arathiel didn't even sound hurt. Irritated and worried, certainly, but he pushed himself up and took a careful step. Hasryan watched his expression as he put his full weight on his ankle. No sign of agony distorted his features. Chills coursed up Hasryan's spine. This went way beyond tolerance to pain. Arathiel had dozens of small cuts from his run through the guards, a bleeding wound near his no-doubt smashed hip, and a deep slash in his shoulder. None of them bothered him in the least. None except his twisted ankle, and only because he had trouble walking. Hasryan struggled with several questions but decided not to ask any of them. Not now. Arathiel had just saved his life.

His friend shoved a paper in Hasryan's palm. "Go there. It'll be safe."

"I'm not leaving you here! You can't walk."

"I can." Arathiel grabbed his ankle with both of his hands. He jerked it back at the right angle in one sharp movement. The sudden pop and the sounds of bones grinding one against the other made Hasryan's insides shoot up. He gasped, his mind refusing to wrap around what Arathiel had just done. Without flinching. Arathiel pushed himself to his feet, balanced for a moment, then smiled.

"See? Now run."

Hasryan only stared. "What ..."

"I don't feel pain, or much else for that matter."

Arathiel answered the unfinished question in a soft tone and looked away. Hasryan swallowed hard and captured Arathiel's gaze.

"Thank you. Thank you so much." Shouts from above warned them they didn't have time to linger. The next bolts wouldn't miss them. It might not kill Arathiel, but Hasryan would be done for. "May Cal's luck be with you."

He spun on his heels and sprinted away, the paper crumpled in his hands. Arathiel's chuckle followed him, and the sound wrought crushing guilt through Hasryan. A shout to fire resonated from above as he reached the edge of Carrington's Square, and he ducked. A bolt whizzed past his arm, narrowly missing him, and he kept moving. It wasn't a serious wound, and for the first time since Larryn had ditched him in his cell, Hasryan wanted to live. Experience told him not to trust Arathiel, that he was running into a trap—something darker and trickier. But why would he, when Hasryan had been about to die? He needed to believe, to give this strange painless man the last of his faith. Everyone else had abandoned him, and Hasryan clung to the idea that one person had risked it all to see him through.

As soon as he was out of sight, he crouched, put the paper on the ground, held it with his foot and checked the address. Silly Arathiel should have found a better way, one in which handcuffs wouldn't be a problem. Not that Hasryan had room to complain. The address was somewhere in the Upper City. Perfect. They would expect him to run into the shadiest part of town, not among the nobles' bridges. Hasryan ripped the paper in two and kicked the pieces off the street and into the wind, trusting it would be enough to cover their tracks. Then he sprinted up, watching for signs of pursuit as he took a winding path through Isandor. The guards seemed to grow more distant, and it had been a while since he'd heard the whistle warning he'd been spotted.

He arrived at the indicated address, and as he lay eyes on the door that was supposed to be his safe house, his stomach sunk. It was a small white door encased in the side of a high tree-shaped spire. The Dathirii Tower. Home to Isandor's elven House, friends of the Allastams, Larryn's most hated nobles. How could this be safe? If an elf found him in there, he would be back to Carrington's Square by nightfall. Hasryan swallowed hard. This wasn't the main entrance, and no guards stood around. He could hear shouts from a squad of soldiers below him. Someone could run past his bridge and spot him at any moment.

He had no other choice. They would tear the Shelter down looking for him, and Brune knew all his hideouts. If he meant to trust Arathiel, he had to go all the way.

Hasryan twisted around to turn the unlocked doorknob, then slipped inside, unseen.

CHAPTER THIRTY-SIX

A WALL of legs formed around Cal as he tried to push his way toward Carrington's Square.

"Let me through!" he called. "Come on, I need to reach them!"

Except everyone had to go somewhere, and for most of them that somewhere was in the opposite direction. The panicked crowd didn't care about his shoving and pleading. People from the Lower City had entered a confused rampage as soon as the first volley of crossbow bolts had flown. Cal understood. They couldn't afford to get hurt—no one would be there to heal them. But he wished they would let him through anyway.

Cal had been watching from a connecting bridge, nauseated and distant, like his mind refused to believe in Hasryan's hanging. Until Arathiel's lithe form jumped from an upper bridge. Screams and grunts echoed down, but his viewpoint was too far below, the angle all wrong for him to see what was going on. Everyone froze at a standstill, holding their breath. Cal prayed harder than he ever had, half choking on his whispered pleas to Ren. Then the first bolts fell, and Arathiel had swung down, carrying Hasryan. Blood stained Arathiel's clothes, and small drops followed their rapid descent. He would need a healer. Cal rushed for the Square, desperate to help.

The bodies around Cal blocked his view, and he couldn't tell what was going on anymore. Had Arathiel landed? Were his friends safe? How wounded was Arathiel? He needed to move faster, but he was so small, and it seemed all he could do was get buffeted left and right.

A hand grabbed his collar and yanked him out of the thick crowd. Cal yelped as Larryn dragged him to a tower out of everyone's way, then glared at him. An expectant lump blocked Cal's throat, and he avoided looking at his friend, instead trying to peek at Carrington's Square, half-hidden behind the building. Larryn knelt and grabbed both of Cal's shoulders, frowning. Fear coursed through Cal. Would he yell at him again? Hit him? They hadn't talked since their fight on the solstice, and thinking of Larryn's punch made his cheek throb.

"What's the plan?"

Judging from his tone, Larryn was trying hard to keep his anger in check. Cal bit his lower lip.

"What plan?"

"What do you mean, 'what plan'? Your weirdo friend just landed in the middle of city guards and freed Hasryan! Don't act like you're not involved in this mess. You lying dipshits have a strategy, and I want to know what it is."

"What? No, I don't know." Cal wished he did. Arathiel had never said a word about this. He had asked how Nevian fared, then vanished from the Shelter, thrown out by Larryn. "He planned this on his own. Hard to talk to me when you kicked him out."

Larryn didn't take the bait. He let go of Cal's shoulders with a slight push. "Gods, you're useless."

Cal fought against his rising tears. Larryn's relentless insults were acid down his throat. But he'd had enough. He refused to endure this unfair treatment for the sake of a friendship Larryn no longer cared for. Cal grabbed Larryn's shirt and pulled it down. He blinked out his tears and met his friend's grey eyes.

"You're wrong. Without me, no one would've come for Hasryan and he'd be dead. Who do you think convinced Arathiel he was innocent? Who talked to him about the friend we knew instead of the scapegoat they want us to see? Who first invited him to our card games at all?" Cal pointed at himself, then released Larryn. "I'm so useless I managed to save both Nevian *and* Hasryan! For once in your life, Larryn, shut up. We need to help them now."

Larryn scowled, and after the solstice's night, Cal's instincts took over. He recoiled and raised his arms to block. No strike came. They remained there, standing in silence, Cal holding his breath. Larryn stepped back, his expression morphing into horror. He cast his gaze down, his shoulders hunched, his fists unwinding. The obvious shame acted as a balm over Cal's heart, but it wouldn't calm his frantic heartbeat or erase the pain now etched in his soul. Larryn, once his best friend, now scared Cal.

"You're right," Larryn said. "Cal, I'm ... I didn't think it through. You're ... so often right."

Cal stared at him, stunned into silence. When did Larryn ever admit being wrong? The most he'd ever gotten out of Larryn was a 'how can I make things better?'. Despite Cal's resolution not to let Larryn off the hook easily, his heart swelled, and he managed a smile.

"Yeah, I am. I'll want to hear that again later."

For a brief instant, Larryn seemed irritated, but he nodded. Cal decided to take that as a promise. "I saw them split," Larryn said. "Arathiel had some scary wounds. We should search for him."

"Lead the way."

Cal followed him toward the now-deserted bridges, noticing for the first time the bow on Larryn's back. What had he meant to do? What kind of awful idea would Larryn have gone through with, if not for Arathiel's intervention? Cal still couldn't wrap his mind around Arathiel's stunt. When he'd spilled his heart, he hadn't thought to convince him. He had just needed to let it all out. How and why Arathiel had planned this didn't matter. He had landed above Carrington's Square, fought his way to Hasryan, and escaped with a fantastic jump off the bridge. They all owed him, and now Arathiel was hurt. He needed Cal's healing, and Larryn's uncanny ability to avoid authorities.

Once the four of them were safe, they could talk at length about Larryn's apology.

∾

ARATHIEL never even left Carrington's Square. When Hasryan had turned heel and run, he had tried to do the same. His ankle didn't comply. The weird angle voided all his walking and running practice. He couldn't tell when his feet hit the ground, and his usual timing didn't account for the broken bones. Jerking the ankle back into place had helped, but Arathiel put deliberate care in each step. The next volley of bolts rained down soon enough, and one struck his calf. The impact threw him to the ground.

Arathiel let out a soft swear and rolled over. Focusing became more difficult the longer blood oozed out of his shoulder, hip, and now leg. He swallowed hard, staring at the growing red stains on his clothes. Exhaustion was catching up to him, wrapping around his mind, thickening the blur that was already his world. He dragged himself to a bench and leaned against its side. Maybe he was dying. Was that even possible for him? He'd never tested his limits since the Well. But if he was alive now, then surely he could die, too? Darkness slipped at the corners of his consciousness, chipping at it. He was dying. The blood loss was killing him like it would anyone else—an oddly comforting thought.

A shape obscured part of the sunlight. Arathiel lifted his head and squinted until he identified Sora Sharpe. She had a crossbow aimed at his heart and stood over him.

"You're under arrest."

Her voice was strong and clear. Much more distinct than everything else. Arathiel used it as an anchor into this world.

"I know."

She didn't move. Her expression was stuck between fear and

confusion. Indecisive, unlike her tone. Had he scared her too? Hasryan's stunned horror when Arathiel had snapped his ankle back had crushed his heart. Perhaps only shock had caused him to recoil—he had seemed to recover quickly from it. Arathiel might never know how disgusted Hasryan was if Sharpe continued to stare without moving or helping.

"I don't feel pain," he said, "but I think the blood loss will kill me."

"Are you expecting an apology? You freed a high-profile assassin on the day of his execution. Of course we shot you down."

Arathiel chuckled, then he put his hand over the shoulder wound and pressed as hard as he could. If he could staunch the bleeding, perhaps a healer would get there in time. Without pain and other signals, he had no idea how long he had left. Arathiel hoped Hasryan had reached the Dathirii Tower. It would be a shame to die and have failed.

"No, I understand. I was hoping for some healing, actually."

"Healing."

Sharpe seemed to hesitate, and Arathiel lifted his head a little higher. Perhaps she didn't want to help a monster like him. Or she was too angry. He couldn't tell. He tried to decipher her solid mask, but his sight was growing blurrier. He closed his eyes, attempting to clear the rising fog in his mind. Sora would come through. If she let him die, she would lose her best link to Hasryan's new hideout.

"All right," she said after an eternity. "Let's get you patched up and—"

"Back off! Step away or I'll shoot!"

Arathiel's eyes flew open when he recognized Larryn's voice. He withheld a curse and tilted his head to the side until he spotted two familiar shapes at one end of the Square. It took some time before he could make out the contour of a bow in Larryn's hands. They were threatening Lieutenant Sharpe with a weapon. His insides recoiled, and he gritted his teeth. If Larryn shot her, he could kiss his Shelter goodbye. Whether Arathiel was welcomed there or not didn't matter. The unique haven at the bottom of the Lower City couldn't fall. Arathiel gathered his strength to speak loud and clear.

"Larryn, don't," he said. "It's okay."

"And let her lock you in a cell? No way this is happening again. I protect my own."

His own. A bitter smile reached Arathiel's lips. Two days ago, Larryn had thrown him out, making it clear he wasn't part of the Lower City and didn't belong. How quickly he could change his mind ... and at the worst time possible, too. Arathiel shifted his weight to better see Larryn, earning a warning glare from Sharpe. She'd aimed her crossbow at the half-elf now, perhaps guessing Arathiel wouldn't have the strength to do much.

"Larryn, you were right about me. My full name is Lord Arathiel Brasten, and I am a noble of this city. Was. More than hundred years ago." Arathiel had almost withheld House and title, but there would have been more Dathirii at the execution today, and he was convinced one of them would have recognized him. The time for hiding was over. That had been the point all along. Sora hissed when she heard him, realizing the extra complications this meant for her. He ignored her. "Lower your bow. Don't lose the Shelter on my account. I'm ... I think I'm dying anyway."

It was becoming harder to keep his voice from slurring, and his sight had grown so dark he couldn't tell if Larryn put his weapon down. At least he wasn't cold or in pain. It was like the world around him was moving further away than it already had in the Well. He heard Cal's heavy but rapid footsteps across the park's cobblestone pathways, then Sora's sharp order.

"Stay where you are!"

The running stopped, and a pleading voice rose, very close to him. "I just want to staunch the bleeding! Please, Miss Sharpe, he's my friend."

In the silence that followed, Arathiel forced himself to look at Cal. He was just a few feet away, his hands in the air, watching Sora with a desperate pout. She pressed her lips together.

"One false move, and I'm arresting you too."

"Thank you!"

Cal threw himself on his knees next to Arathiel and fumbled for something. His half-melted silver coin. How often had Arathiel noticed Cal touch it and wish for luck? His friend placed the burned side over the shoulder wound and began a soft prayer. Arathiel twisted his head to see. He didn't feel any kind of relief—no more than he felt pain—but the blood flow slowed, and the cut closed itself. Sweat rolled down Cal's forehead, and he grew pale. Should it be this hard? Arathiel put a hand on his forearm to stop him.

"Fix the hip and let go," he said. "As long as I live to get to the guards' headquarters, I'll be fine."

"You can't go there. Something's wrong, Arathiel." Cal's voice cracked. He moved his melted coin to the hip, and the wound started to heal too. It didn't last. Cal quickly snatched his hands back, confusion plain on his face. "This is wrong. Please don't go to prison. You can't."

Sharpe cleared her throat. "He is coming. You're lucky I don't drag everyone in with him."

"It's okay, Cal," Arathiel added. "I've been in worse places than a cell."

Cal leaned back. He seemed on the verge of crying, and from the bags under his eyes, Arathiel doubted he'd had much sleep since the solstice. They had all been convinced Hasryan would die. Arathiel picked up his friend's hand and squeezed it.

"Thank you for the card games, Cal, and the warm welcome. Keep being nice to strangers like that."

"Don't talk like this is goodbye!"

"Yeah, don't." Larryn had come up behind Cal, his bow slung over his back. He put a hand on Cal's head and stared at Arathiel. "You say you're a noble. Politics will save your ass."

Arathiel wasn't so certain. They would keep him alive, yes, but freeing Hasryan had set half the city against him, if not more. He shrugged, not too concerned about his fate. Not as long as Hasryan was free. The very thought brought him a strange elation. He should have died in the Well, yet instead had come out with this new body and extra time in their world. How long had Arathiel hung to the side, a spectre watching events unfold, uncertain he deserved to participate? Not anymore. In a single strike, he had changed the course of Isandor's politics and announced his return. It wouldn't be possible to hide anymore. He had jumped in with both feet, given history a big shove in one direction, and proved he still had a role to play. Maybe he didn't feel pain or touch or warmth, but he was very much a part of this world, and he had saved a friend.

Guards started to surround them, none of them bringing good news for Sora. Hasryan was gone. They were still searching, but every new soldier arriving did so empty-handed. Sharpe gave all three of them a long glare, then took her handcuffs out.

"Don't think you've won yet," she said.

She pulled Arathiel to his feet. Two men came to hold him up, and the cuffs clipped around his wrists—locked him into this new, exposed life. Cal and Larryn had been forced to back away, but he nodded in their direction. He managed to smile despite his dizziness and the fog over his brain. Sora was right, of course. Even if he lived through the day, he would face endless interrogations about Hasryan and himself. It didn't matter. He'd finally made his peace with the strange turn his life had taken and decided to make the most of it. Arathiel couldn't remember when he had last been so content.

AFTER Arathiel's arrest, Larryn hung around Carrington's Square for a while longer. He hoped and dreaded to hear more about Hasryan, but the guards and nobles slowly cleared out, and soon it became obvious he wouldn't learn more. Cal had stayed by his side. Neither said anything to the other. Larryn couldn't bear to look at him for more than a few seconds at a time. Memories of the winter solstice resurfaced without fail, bringing bitter anger and shame with them.

A petty part of him wished Cal hadn't been right—that he'd made a mistake by saving Nevian—and he tried to stomp it out. He didn't want Hasryan dead just to prove a point. Not in the least. He just hated being wrong. More than that, he hated how he'd hurt Cal. Being right might have made it a sliver better.

Maybe.

Larryn doubted it. He glanced at his hand, flexed the fingers with which he had punched his friend. Nothing *could* make that better. And the truth was, Larryn wasn't sure he wanted to yet. Anger still overrode his guilt whenever he looked Cal's way. He needed more time. Still, when it became obvious there would be no more news, Larryn turned toward him.

"C'mon. Let me get you a meal."

Hope passed through Cal's expression, and Larryn avoided his gaze. They headed out in silence, and he wondered if it seemed as heavy to Cal as it was to him. They used to talk all the time. Mostly Cal, really, but Larryn contributed a rant or two every now and then. Yet they made it all the way to Larryn's kitchens without a word. He let Cal in after a slight hesitation, and dragged a chair inside for him to sit down. Cal climbed into it, then stared at Larryn, his legs dangling. Expecting something.

Larryn cleared his throat, hurried to his pantry, and retrieved several types of cheese from it. He had bought so many yesterday, and it would be delusional not to admit guilt had played a big part in it. He had no intention of cooking with this much cheese, and everyone knew of Cal's undying love for it. He picked a solid block of *Windfoot* from Aberah Lake's southern shore—Cal's favourite—and handed it to the halfling without looking at him.

"You bought me cheese."

Cal's dumbfounded tone wasn't as pleased as Larryn would have hoped. His throat thick, he picked up the small wheel of *Kessyr*, a softer goat cheese from Mehr. Cal took it, but his frown deepened.

"You know I can't refuse cheese."

With a faint smile, Larryn rubbed the back of his neck and showed him the last type: a strange, squeaky cheese that roasted rather than melted when put above fire. He lit his oven then gathered a few herbs and a slice of cold pork. He didn't have time to launch into a full-blown meal, but he had promised Cal something, and even this bit of cooking soothed him.

"So what are you trying to do?" Cal asked. "You think if you just feed me, I'll forget?"

Larryn stiffened and squeezed his eyes shut. He was glad he hadn't been looking at Cal. "No. I don't want you to forget." Shit. That's not what he meant. Larryn groaned and slapped the pork onto a plate. "I'm still angry."

"Of course you are."

The hard edge in Cal's tone surprised Larryn. Cal had always softened the blows and accepted his spikes of anger. It had been like no matter how often he lashed out in frustration, Cal endured to help. But Larryn had obviously crossed a line now, and he knew that, and he wished he could make it a bit better somehow.

"Cal, I—"

"Don't bother." Cal's shuddering breath wrung Larryn's insides. "I can tell you're trying, but if you're not going to utter the words 'I'm sorry' in the next, like, five minutes? I'm leaving. With the cheese. And you will still owe me a meal."

Larryn couldn't help a slight smile. Of course he would take the cheese. Then again, he deserved it. Larryn turned around and forced himself to meet his gaze. He had to apologize. He knew he shouldn't have hit Cal. It didn't matter how furious and confused and terrified he'd been for Hasryan. Larryn licked his lips, but the words refused to leave his throat. They bundled together, glued inside by his latent anger, until only a low growl came out. Larryn's fists clenched, and he whirled around before he could see too much of the tears filling Cal's eyes.

"I thought so," Cal said. "Some other day, maybe. I'll spend some time at my place instead of here and only return to check on Nevian. It'll do the two of us a lot of good."

Larryn heard him climb off the chair. He gripped the counter. "Wait." The familiar shuffle of Cal's steps stopped. One last chance. "I …" Larryn tried to swallow, but he was parched. "I shouldn't have. Hit you, I mean."

"Yeah. You shouldn't have."

No need to turn around to notice the obvious efforts Cal made to keep his voice steady. A short silence followed—his friend waiting for more—then the kitchens' door creaked. Larryn stared at the beginning of a meal in front of him, his excuse for a conversation with Cal. What was the point when he couldn't even utter two simple words? It shouldn't be this hard! But they wouldn't come out, and somehow Larryn doubted they would anytime soon. Not as long as Hasryan was out there somewhere, and Larryn wasn't certain he was safe.

With a final grunt, Larryn shoved the pork away and turned to his pantry. He had half the Lower City to feed and no more time to waste on Cal's hurt feelings. He started bringing out the ingredients he needed for the evening's meal, doing his best to ignore the nagging voice in his head, repeating over and over that when it came to Cal's friendship, 'waste' was not a term he should ever use.

CHAPTER THIRTY-SEVEN

H ASRYAN pushed the door closed with the tip of his foot. The moment it clicked into place, he leaned against it and slid to the floor. Immense relief spread from his stomach, climbing up his throat in slow waves until Hasryan had to choke down a sob. He brought his legs close and wished his hands weren't cuffed behind his back, to cling to his pants while he calmed himself. Instead, he let his fingers slide through the entrance's rough rug. The door muffled sounds from outside, and after the crowd's cheers and the guards' whistles, the silence was stifling. The whole city would probably hear the one thought always cycling to the front of his mind.

He was alive.

He could still feel the rope against his neck, and his legs ached from the rough landing with Arathiel. His frantic heart hurt, as if a hand squeezed it hard, but he was alive. Someone—not Brune, not Cal, not even Larryn—had cared enough to save him. It didn't matter if Arathiel had this weird inhuman pain resistance going on. He had more heart than anyone else Hasryan had trusted so far. More guts, too. What a dangerous rescue plan. Hasryan hoped he had managed to escape on his broken ankle, but he would know soon enough. Arathiel would be coming here once he'd shaken everybody off his trail. If they were lucky.

Hasryan forced himself to take a few deep breaths and calm down. The crushing relief from unexpected freedom started giving way to the realization he wasn't *safe* yet. He needed to get a grip and scout the place.

Hasryan raised his head and scanned the area. He sat in a large room that encompassed both a kitchen and a cozy living room. The sweet scent of baked goods hung in the air. Hasryan used the door to prop himself up on his feet. He couldn't wait to get these manacles off. Perhaps there would be a tool in the kitchen. He moved toward the dark counter, and when his eyes fell over a plate of small cookies, his mouth watered. He hadn't eaten anything but dull oatmeal mixture since his arrest. They looked delicious—round and golden and soft. Hasryan pressed his lips together. Grabbing one would prove a challenge with his hands behind his back, and now was not the time to devour cookies. The entire city guard hunted for him, and he was relaxing in some part of the Dathirii Tower. He had to stay focused.

He moved through the kitchen, registering every detail he could: the tea pot at the ready, the numerous glass jugs of dried herbs behind it, the flowery apron on a hook, and the open notepad filled with slick handwriting. Hasryan crouched and blew on the edge of the pad to flick through the pages. He stopped to read every now and then but only found grocery lists and recipes. Nothing special there. One page had a series of names with a specific dish next to each of them. Some had been crossed off, though there was no apparent pattern to it. Hasryan wished he could get more information on whoever lived here. A woman, probably. He straightened up and moved to the living room, the scent of cookies trailing behind him.

A two-seater rested against the wall next to a thin and tall bookshelf. Almost every tome seemed handmade, all in different sizes and shapes. Most had no titles on the spine, but those which did were recipe books. Hasryan's mouth quirked into a smile. Whoever lived here loved cooking, that was for sure. Was that why he had immediately concluded it was a woman? Sora would be angry with him.

As Hasryan imagined the scolding Sharpe would give him, voices reached him from a nearby room. Hasryan froze and turned to the only closed door. He suspected it led into the Dathirii Tower itself. On the other side, two servants discussed what remained to be cleaned. The conversation grew louder at first, then faded away as they walked past. Hasryan swallowed hard, his mouth dry. He had to free his hands. As long as he was cuffed, he wouldn't be able to defend himself.

If the owner really was a woman—and a noble, too—she might have jewels he could use. A solid brooch pin would let him work at the manacles, at least. His lock-picking skills didn't come anywhere near Larryn's, but it seemed better to try than to sit still and stare at the plate of golden cookies, waiting for his fate. He made for the third door in the apartments, pushed it open, and smiled at the flower pattern on the bed's blanket. Definitely a woman. She even had a desk with her makeup and perfume on it, along with a small mirror. His gaze settled on the box with an ornate pattern on the lid. Jewelry, for sure.

He should grab everything and disappear. Leave this place before the owner returned, before Hasryan discovered Arathiel had betrayed him, too. He would have enough money to get by if he escaped Isandor. No ships or caravan would take him, so he would have to manage on his own in the wilds for a while, but if he had survived it at ten years old, he could do it now. He *could*. He didn't want to. Hasryan loved people. Just thinking of being alone and shunned again made his throat thick with emotion. He had believed he'd escaped his years of constant vigilance, always putting survival first. He wanted friends he could trust, and the only one he dared put his faith in right now was Arathiel.

Which didn't mean he had to wait with his hands cuffed behind his back and nothing to defend himself.

Hasryan grabbed the jewelry box from behind and up-ended it on the bed. The contents spread on the cover, and he turned about to examine them. The dim afternoon light pierced through thin curtains, making some of the rich apparel shine. Hasryan's gaze stopped on a sturdy brooch—small enough to fit in his manacles, thick enough not to break. He pushed everything else out of the way with his elbow before patting the bed until he found the brooch.

Great. Hasryan moved farther up the bed and out of the jewelry pile, settled on the pillows with his back against the wall, then tried to insert the brooch's pin in the keyhole. He couldn't wait to be free.

The lock-picking tested his patience sorely. The afternoon light grew dimmer as he worked on the lock, wondering how long he would need to break it open. He wished Larryn was around. He would have been done within minutes even without seeing what he was doing. He always said to listen to the sounds. Hasryan didn't hear a lot more than metal on metal, and his occasional hiss of pain when he pricked his fingers. He dropped the brooch and had to try from the start again, and by the time the manacles clicked open, his arms and shoulders hurt from the awkward position. He sighed, slipped out of the hold, and brought his hands before him. His wrists and fingers tingled as blood rushed back in. At last.

Hasryan jumped off the bed and made a few large circular movements with his arms, pushing blood into them as he left the bedroom behind. Sunlight's steep slant gave the kitchen and living room an even cozier appearance. As though he could settle down on one of those sofas, eat the cookies and drink tea, and time would stop and let him breathe. Hasryan shook his head. Illusions. He knew better than to get caught in such fantasies. First, he needed a weapon. He recalled the knives on the counter and headed there. The cookies almost glowed in the afternoon light, and it seemed to Hasryan that their scent had only grown more powerful. Everything was so peaceful, so welcoming—like the entire room demanded his surrender.

"Never," he whispered.

He drew the biggest knife from the rack and tested its edge. Blood pricked at the tip of his finger. Sharp. Good. Now to get away from those damnable cookies. Hasryan strode out of the kitchen and back to the door leading outside. She might arrive from the entrance to the tower itself, but he could sprint across. He crouched, ready. His confidence had returned with his free hands. He didn't need help. He could survive by himself, had done so for almost two decades now. No matter who came through that door, he could handle it.

The doorknob next to him turned. Hasryan jumped to his feet, holding his breath and tightening his grip on the knife's handle. A lithe form appeared as the door opened, dark against the afternoon sun. Hasryan leaped forward, grabbed the front of her dress, and pulled her in. He kicked the door closed as he pushed her against the wall and pressed the knife at her throat.

"Oh!"

The small exclamation came from an old lady, grey hair threaded with golden strands. She kept it tied in a bun, making her pointed ears quite obvious. Hasryan searched his memory for an elderly Dathirii, but he had never paid the family much attention. He knew to watch out for a young, brown-haired elf with wits—their spy— but that was it.

"Don't move," he said.

She held her hands up and froze, but she smiled despite the precarious position. "Good evening, Hasryan."

Hasryan's throat tightened. Of course she knew who he was. The entire city did. She would try to sound soft and harmless, to catch him off-guard, but she couldn't fool him. Age didn't matter. Everyone could be vicious. Even an old elven lady who had obviously baked cookies the previous night. Even Arathiel's supposed trusted friends.

"What's going on?"

She seemed confused by his question and tilted her head to the side. Her pale blue eyes studied him, and Hasryan's heart quickened under the intense gaze, stripping away layer after layer of invisible protection to look inside him. He didn't want her to! A shiver ran up his arms, and he pressed the knife harder, his hands shaking.

"Tell me!"

His voice cracked. Hasryan wished it hadn't, wished he was in perfect control of himself. But the more this lady stared at him, silent but smiling, the bigger his panic grew. It swirled inside, reminding him of the rope around his neck, of the dozens of guards wanting to kill him, of all the people who had betrayed his trust before. The slow confidence he'd built as he freed his wrists evaporated. He needed to know if he was safe here, but how could he ever be sure? The elven lady started lowering her hand, and his heart jumped.

"No, I told you not to move!"

She did anyway. She had to realize he had killed before—cold, calculated murder. Yet she set her wrinkled fingers on the blade, her gaze never leaving his, and pushed it down. Hasryan could feel it slice a little into her old skin, but she neither grimaced nor flinched. He let her, caught up in her clear eyes and her sad determination.

"This is my home, and you are my guest. You don't have to be afraid of me."

"I'm not afraid! I just don't trust you."

He would sound more convincing if he could stop shaking. His palms were sweaty, his muscles tight—ready to spring, as if faced with a dangerous threat.

"Distrust is only one facet of fear." She tried to meet his gaze again as she pushed the knife farther away, but Hasryan lowered it. He noticed the thin red lines on her fingers. "I think you've had plenty of opportunities to experience that already."

Despite her soft voice, the comment was a punch in his stomach. How often had people refused to talk to him? To give him their names, or to offer him a contract? Even when he'd been a kid, others had avoided him on sight. They said they didn't trust a stranger, but he'd known they feared the dark elf. Stories of dark elven raids outside of their walled lands had burned a specific imagery in their mind: ruthless, merciless killers. That was his heritage: he had 'do not trust me' painted on his skin.

He had learned to use the reputation early on. As a kid, he would hang in the dark to appear taller and utter threats, forcing people to give up their gold and food. They believed him to be a monster, and he played with that to get what he wanted. In time, he had also rolled with their other expectation: that he could kill without remorse. All dark elves were assassins, weren't they? Why not? He needed the money, he loved the challenge, and when he received a contract, someone was *trusting* him to get a job done. Brune had even trusted him to help build her mercenary empire.

Or so he'd thought.

Trust could be an illusion. Sometimes, it appeared as a magical dagger gift to seal a solid and blooming relationship. He had to make sure he would not be tricked again, that Arathiel wasn't laying another trap for him.

"What do you want?"

"Right now, I admit I'd love to sit down with a cup of tea. I had a rough day." She smoothed out the front of her dress where Hasryan had held her. "So did you, but I suspect that's not what your question meant."

"It's not." Her calm disturbed him. What was he supposed to do about it? Usually when he put a dagger at someone's throat, they tended to become some variation of terrified.

"I'm not expecting anything in return," she said. "I do hope you will stay with me until we can dig deeper into Brune's game, but I will not force you to." She reached for his shoulder, but Hasryan jerked out of the way and stepped back. She withdrew her hand with a sad smile. "I doubt I'll have the resources to help you while the Myrians assault us. You should know, however, that these quarters will always remain safe for you. There are even magical protections against divination spells."

Hasryan reeled, his mind unable to accept what it heard. They had stepped right into the realm of impossibilities. "Anyone could walk in here and find me. Someone will, and it'll be over again, and none of this makes sense. You don't know me. You don't have any reasons to help me. I was about to be hanged for murder, and I put a knife at your throat!"

He shouldn't jump from one fear to another, and he didn't make much sense either, but he couldn't settle on what bothered him the most. He tightened his grip on the knife, raising it. The old woman's gaze flickered in its direction, and she licked her lower lip. So she was scared after all.

"You had a rope around your throat a few hours ago. I understand your impulse to defend yourself." She touched her small cut. "Arathiel believes you were framed, and I find it difficult to see anyone get hanged. I will shamelessly admit that I agreed to this for Arathiel's sake more than for yours, though that might change."

"Arathiel ..."

"Yes, Arathiel." She decided to ignore his knife and moved toward the kitchen. As she continued to talk, she filled the kettle with water, lit a fire and put it over to boil. "I tried to convince him to reintegrate into his family, to tell them he was alive despite all odds. Nothing got to him. He was scared, I think, because of how different he is today. Then one night, he knocks at my door and asks help to free you, even if it meant—and these are his words—showing everyone what he'd become. I couldn't refuse. I had promised support if he wanted it, and I wouldn't go back on my word."

"I just played cards with him."

She stared at him for a moment, then soft laughter escaped her lips. The sound stirred a comforting warmth at the bottom of Hasryan's stomach. It was so at odds with these past two weeks.

"Really? He must have enjoyed it a lot, then."

"Cal let him win the first few times to make sure he would stay."

Hasryan remembered sitting at the table, exchanging dumbfounded glances with Larryn as their friend lost one play after the other with exaggerated exclamations, shoving the copper pieces toward Arathiel. They'd joked about it, telling Cal that his divine help had found a new favourite, but they all knew he did it on purpose. He'd done it with Hasryan too, two years before. The memory felt like claws digging in his heart, and he pushed it away. Mulling over broken friendships would only hurt him. He had to think of himself and this weird position he'd landed in.

"So this isn't about me. Not really."

"It wasn't," she said. "If I can help you too, I will."

"What *is* going on with Arathiel? He smashed his ankle and snapped it right back without flinching!" Hasryan moved closer to the counter and set down the knife. He didn't understand why, but knowing she hid him for Arathiel's sake eased his doubts. No one wanted to help him, sure, but Arathiel deserved it. "It was scary."

"I don't really know." She selected two glass jars and opened them, throwing some of the dried herbs into her teapot. "I'm not sure Arathiel himself understands. From what I gathered, most of his senses have been altered, including his ability to feel pain."

"That's so weird." Hasryan ran a hand through his hair. He shouldn't have implied that to Arathiel, though. "I hope he's all right. I thought he'd be here by now."

"So did I." Camilla heaved a sigh. "He asked not to worry about him, to protect you instead. I can do both at once."

"I don't *want* you to take care of me." A bitter laugh escaped his lips. How ridiculous. He wasn't a child to be adopted. "This might be normal to you, but my life isn't made of sweet tea and cookies. It's all murder and betrayal. I can't stay here. I don't even know your name!"

"I'm Lady Camilla Dathirii, but you can keep it short. Camilla is enough, or even Aunt Camilla if you prefer."

Aunt Camilla. She wanted him to call her 'Aunt'. He must not have heard that right. Or it was a joke. She toyed with him because she could sense how desperate he was for a solid relationship.

"I'm not going to call you anything."

He strode to the two-seater and dropped into it. Camilla's lips pinched in a disappointed frown, but before she could comment, the kettle whistled. She poured hot water into her prepared tea, set the top on, and brought both the pot and small cups to the table of the living room. Hasryan followed her movements without a word. When she returned with the plate of cookies and set it down next to the tea, however, his stomach grumbled. Camilla looked up.

"Eat one," she said. "You seem famished."

"I'm not. They give you food in prison."

He didn't want to eat her cookies. They had been taunting him all afternoon, daring him to dig in and accept her hospitality. If he ate one, he surrendered to Camilla—and he didn't trust her enough yet. Even if she didn't sell him back to the guards, she could do worse. Perhaps she meant to give him to House Allastam so they could do whatever they pleased with him, away from indiscreet eyes. Although … that would be betraying Arathiel. He had to remember she was doing this for him, too.

"If you want to call it food. I doubt it tasted anywhere near as good as these cookies." She snatched one for herself and sat on the seat opposite Hasryan. "I was up all night baking them. Your execution had me too nervous to sleep."

"That makes two of us. Why don't you go rest in your fancy bed and leave me, then?"

Alone, he might manage to sort through his jumbled thoughts and make the right decision. He refused to jump from one prison to another without questioning it. Even if this one had tea and cookies.

"Oh no, not yet." Camilla poured them two cups, then bit into her cookie. Hasryan stared at her as she ate, wishing she would swallow and explain already. "I asked for a tub of hot water at dusk. They're great to relieve oneself of filth and stress. I suspected you'd have gathered a lot of these two things while in a cell. So I'll stay until I can answer the door for you."

A bath. A hot bath. A luxury he'd only enjoyed once before. Even the Lower City hadn't put as thick a layer of grime on him as prison had. Something about the cell's damp ground, the unwashed corners, and the sweaty nights had clung to him. He had to stink, though he no longer smelled it. Camilla hadn't mentioned it, but the stench alone might give him away from the corridor. Hasryan needed that bath, and if he was going to accept it, why not the tea? Why not the cookies?

"You win." The words were a disgruntled whisper. "I'll stay."

He didn't know how long yet, but he could stick around until he'd cleaned up at the very least. Besides, he had no better options. The Shelter—no, the entire city—would be under surveillance. He leaned forward and picked the biggest cookie off the plate. He caught the pleased smile on Camilla's lips as he bit into it, which turned into a chuckle when he couldn't hold back a satisfied 'mmm'. The hint of salty butterscotch tickled his taste buds and made him crave more. Larryn could take lessons from these. Camilla poured him some tea as he munched down the rest of his cookie and picked up another. He savoured that one for minutes.

Then he stopped.

Something about those cookies was *too* good. Too ... home-made. Full of care and love. And they had been made for him, after a fashion. She had known he would come and spent her night baking for his arrival. Hasryan brought his legs to him, a sudden rush of sadness climbing into his throat. Camilla had prepared her quarters for him the way you did for honoured guests. He stifled a sob, then clenched his fists. It was just a cookie, damn it! He wasn't going to cry over a cookie. He wiped his cheeks and tried to ignore how much his hands shook. Five hours ago, he'd had a rope around his neck, and people were cheering for him to be hung. He had thought he would die there in front of everyone. The day's grand spectacle. Instead, he was sitting in a cozy living room, and the late afternoon sun warmed his back as he stuffed himself with cookies and waited for a hot bath. Comforts offered by an old lady who cared neither for his dark elven blood nor for his crimes. Believing in such a safe haven was too dangerous, but it was just *there*. In every butterscotch bite, in the sweet aroma of tea, in Camilla's patient smiles.

Hasryan jumped to his feet. All his emotions threatened to burst, and he didn't want anyone to see.

"I have to go. Warn me for the bath."

His cheeks hot with shame, Hasryan strode past her before she could protest. He sprinted to her bedroom and slammed the door behind him, curling on the floor right on the other side. Hasryan didn't know if he could handle this place. It was too perfect, too much of everything he'd longed for. How could it last? Nothing ever did. Leaving now would hurt less than losing this again. If Arathiel didn't return tonight, he would have to escape. The taste of butterscotch lingered on his tongue, and Hasryan prayed to every deity out there his friend would come back soon.

CHAPTER THIRTY-EIGHT

ISRA'S third attempt to turn her skin into bark fizzled out, her magic evaporating before it could so much as stiffen her arm. She cried out in rage and stomped before positioning herself for another try. Frustration tensed her muscles and tightened her lips, and Jilssan recognized the storm brewing under her staunch refusal to stop. Isra would never have the concentration to finish the spell in her current state.

"Enough," Jilssan said.

Isra's shoulders slumped, and she glared at Jilssan. "I can do it! I've cast more complicated spells!"

"I know you can, but not today." Jilssan motioned toward the large elm at the back of their courtyard—the very one Isra had spotted Nevian on. "Why don't we talk?"

Isra's anger deflated, and she threw the tree a haunted look. Jilssan knew she'd spent a great deal of last night staring at it. She had watched Isra from a distance, the two of them freezing outside while Varden's screams rang out of the prisons' basement. Hard not to empathize with Isra. Jilssan remembered too well how guilty she'd felt betraying her first rival, and throwing him to the wolves. And he had deserved it, unlike Varden.

They moved to the tree, and Isra sat down with a pout. "I don't see what you want to talk about."

Jilssan's eyebrows shot up. "You know."

She left it at that, certain Isra would come around. She needed time to sort through her feelings and decide what to share and what to keep to herself. Jilssan settled next to her apprentice and leaned back on the solid trunk, closing her eyes. Cold already seeped through her skirt and tights, and the afternoon sun did nothing to warm her. Isandor's winters always chilled her to the bone, but she suspected the day's shivers also came from the latest turn of events.

"I miss him," Isra said.

"Varden?" Jilssan couldn't believe such words from her. They had never gotten along, to say the least, and even if she felt guilty, she wouldn't miss him.

"No. Nevian."

That surprised Jilssan even more. Why would anyone miss Nevian? He never did anything but complain or study, and Isra's determination to spend time with him had always confused Jilssan. Maybe she was desperate for someone her age, even though Nevian acted decades older than he really was. Still. Nevian's absence would make the enclave more dangerous. An imprisoned Varden wouldn't hold Avenazar's attention forever.

"That's sweet of you," she said, lacking more encouraging words.

"I don't understand. Why didn't he say anything? I offered him a chance—he knew I'd spotted him! He could have told me the traitor wasn't Varden."

"And you would have kept silent?" Jilssan turned to face Isra, worried. "Isra, you see what happened to Varden because he protected Nevian. Don't make their mistake. Master Avenazar is not an opponent you want to fight."

"Varden hid a Dathirii," Isra protested. "It's not the same."

"It would have been." Jilssan picked up Isra's hand and squeezed it. "Listen to me. You are not responsible for what happened to Nevian and Varden. They made their decisions and put themselves in that position. You did what you had to. It's not easy, and you won't feel better about it anytime soon. But until we have full control of Isandor, we're stuck here with Master Avenazar. The best we can do is obey and make it through to the other side."

Water filled Isra's eyes. She reached for her amber amulet and sniffled. "I hate this city. I wish Father was here."

What wouldn't Jilssan give for Master Enezi's presence, too? His reputation in Myria carried a power even Avenazar would have a hard time ignoring, and his mastery of transmutation spells made him an incredible adversary, should it come to that. "Me too, Isra. Me too."

No point in daydreaming, however. It didn't matter how much Isra wished Nevian had survived, or whether Jilssan regretted never having a chance to stop Varden. They would both have been caught, and it would take a miracle to save Varden now.

ᥱᢞᢙᥱ

DIEL stood on the balcony outside his rooms, his gaze drifting to the city below. He had thought things would be calmer after today, that the lords of Isandor would put aside their squabbling. This execution, distasteful as it was, should have marked the end of a decade of feuding. Lord Freitz had come to speak with Lord Allastam, a first since Lady Allastam's murder. Diel had hoped to drum up a desire to collaborate from this new united Isandor. He had to make them see that for all their infighting and competitions, their collective success relied on the city's status as a major independent trading post. And there was nothing independent about a Myrian Enclave controlling half the Houses sitting around the Golden Table.

His new campaign was only possible thanks to the capture of one assassin. Or rather, his execution.

In less than twenty minutes, Lord Allastam had accused Lord Freitz of orchestrating the dark elf's escape, and the hostilities were on again, harder even than in the last few years. Freitz had taken personal offence and returned to his tower. Neither man was willing to talk. Diel had sent Yultes to Lord Allastam, praying his stepbrother's glib tongue would smooth out part of the situation. He didn't have high hopes, not in the current state of their relationship with the Allastams. Even though Diel was convinced Lord Freitz had nothing to do with the sudden escape, reason seldom worked on Lord Allastam. Despite his best efforts, he had no soldiers to include in his Coalition and no House willing to join. Branwen's return had only cemented their reluctance to get involved. Once again, he needed a new plan.

Familiar footsteps scuffed the ground behind him, discreet and welcomed. Simply knowing Jaeger approached sufficed to make Diel smile. Then a hand ran up his back, warm and reassuring, and squeezed his shoulders. No need to tell Jaeger how exhausted he was. His love would have guessed from the slump of his shoulders and decades of companionship.

"It's him, isn't it?" Diel asked.

"Lord Arathiel Brasten." Jaeger moved to his side and set his hand on Diel's. "We have received word from the guards' headquarters. He confirmed it himself upon his arrest and said he used to live here a hundred thirty years ago. Your eyes were not deceiving you."

"He changed, though," Diel said. "Even if the last century hasn't otherwise aged him ... watching him move ... I can't explain. He felt different. It could be an illusion, not the real Arathiel."

"Do you think it is?"

Jaeger's voice was soft. He was withholding his own opinion, knowing how much Diel would rely on it to form his. The little trick brought a smile to Diel's lips. He wondered when in their decades of interactions Jaeger had noticed how often Diel asked for his advice and developed ways not to give it right away.

"No," Diel said after a moment. "My gut tells me it's really him."

"Passing as Arathiel would be a very convoluted lie, requiring knowledge of minor events that happened too long ago. Isandor struggles with remembering anything before Lady Allastam's murder. I doubt anyone recalls the young lord from a modest family who left searching for a cure for his sister."

"Anyone but us." Diel leaned on the railing. "Arathiel must have known we would recognize him. I don't understand any of this, Jaeger. He's *human*. How can he still be alive? What happened to him in that century? When did he return, and why would he do this?"

Diel ran a hand over his face. He would need to speak with Arathiel himself. Regulations around visits would be strict at the headquarters, but he was Lord Dathirii. He could get through. He wanted to ask Arathiel so much. His actions brought up as many questions as those surrounding his past.

"I'm guessing Lady Brasten denied any involvement in this mess?"

"Yes."

"Send word that we do the same," Diel said. "Just a quick note to declare that our family had no part in today's events, but that we recognize Lord Arathiel Brasten and support his claim to the title. There is no point in denying it. It would look suspicious, and I can't afford to have the other Houses against me at this time."

And yet ... whenever he closed his eyes, he saw Arathiel drop among the guards, parrying and dodging, moving with amazing ease. He had always been a skilled fighter, but the way he ignored every hit as he progressed toward Hasryan had stolen Diel's breath. Given the element of surprise, Arathiel had bested a dozen soldiers at once.

"If you could find Kellian, I need to ask him a few questions."

"Yes, milord." Jaeger squeezed his shoulder again, strongly enough to make Diel turn. His gaze met Jaeger's deep-set eyes, and the trust and understanding in them was like a blanket around his heart. Jaeger knew what he was thinking. Didn't he always? The steward smiled. "It's a dangerous idea, but it might be worth it."

Then Jaeger walked away to take care of his duties, Diel watched the balcony's door close behind him, lightheaded. Even after more than a century, Jaeger's approval stirred powerful warmth in his chest. Diel trusted his lover's opinions and instincts more than he did his own—Jaeger had the same solid moral compass, and none of Diel's tendency to panic and get carried away.

He doubted Kellian would appreciate his idea as much as Jaeger had. How could he breach the topic with his guards' captain? Kellian was loyal to a fault, and Diel wasn't worried about betrayal—they were a family, had toiled together for decades—but Kellian could get tempestuous and would heartily disagree. No wonder. If Diel decided to go ahead, Kellian and Yultes would bear the brunt of the extra work, appeasing Lord Allastam and protecting House Dathirii. Diel returned his gaze to the towers around him, glowing bright red in the setting sun. Even the greenery covering most of the Upper City had an angry colour. The white spirals of House Allastam's tower seemed bloodthirsty in this light. Diel knew Lord Allastam would never be satisfied until someone paid for his wife's murder with their life.

The sun had almost vanished by the time Kellian joined him on the balcony. His smaller cousin frowned, and Diel couldn't help but think he looked exhausted. He had spent his weeks running around, trying to organize the few guards and mercenaries they had to keep their trade partners safe. The entire family was worn thin by the constant fight against the Myrians.

"Long day, wasn't it?" Diel asked as a greeting.

"Sora's was worse. We thought she'd have some time off after the execution, but she can kiss that goodbye."

Diel tried not to smile at how 'we thought' implied they had eagerly planned to use that time to see each other. Under the circumstances, Kellian's fondness for Miss Sharpe would be a hindrance.

"You witnessed the escape, didn't you?" Diel waited for Kellian's confirmation even though he had no doubt his cousin had been somewhere in the crowd. "What can you tell me about Arathiel's fighting skills?"

"His skills? Why?"

Diel glanced at Kellian, then pressed his lips together. It might be better not to explain too soon. The silence stretched until Kellian gave in.

"He's good, as he always was. Quick and fluid, brilliant at dodging. He used to have some of the best footwork in the city." Kellian stepped up to the railing and stared at the closest bridge. Diel wondered if he was reliving the fight in his mind. "But Diel, you saw him too. He's unnatural. He doesn't notice when he gets cut, and his movements are more calculated than improvised. Sora said he broke an ankle and snapped it back into place without flinching. He admits to feeling no pain, and I'll venture there are a lot of other things he no longer feels. The way he walked and ran made me suspect he couldn't sense the ground beneath his boots."

Diel's stomach sank as Kellian explained what he could. What had happened to Arathiel to change him this way? Was he all right? They had been good acquaintances, sharing social circles and meeting at events often enough for Diel to develop a huge crush. He hoped nothing too horrible had affected Arathiel.

"No physical pain, then," he said. The adjective seemed an important distinction.

"None."

"Kellian, we both watched him take on a squad of Isandor's guards and free a high-profile assassin alone. Provided with a small elite team, how would you evaluate his chances of infiltrating a powerful wizard organization to liberate their prisoner?"

"What?" Kellian spun on his heels, glaring with disbelief. "You want to send him into the Myrian Enclave?"

Diel gripped the railing and nodded. Could anyone else succeed at something like this? Arathiel had just proved he had the skills for it.

"You can't. He just freed Hasryan. He has to stay in prison until he tells us where the dark elf is."

"That's not an answer to my question, Kellian."

Silence stretched on, as if Kellian believed he could avoid providing one if he waited long enough. Diel didn't budge. "He suffered terrible wounds from which he has yet to recover, so no, he can't do anything like that. He can't even run on his twisted ankle, let alone fight." Kellian crossed his arms. Exhaustion deepened his angry scowl. "This is ridiculous, Diel. You might be able to pull enough strings to get him out of prison, but you'll have the entire city against you. What good is this rescue mission if we lose all our allies?"

Diel closed his eyes, his throat tight. He knew that. Lord Allastam would consider it a betrayal and say he'd sided with the enemy, with his wife's killer. The wrath he had directed at Lord Freitz for years would fall upon House Dathirii at a time when another powerful player was trying to take them down. Not to mention that if Arathiel succeeded, Master Avenazar would only become more aggressive. He needed Lord Allastam as a proactive ally, not his enemy. Approaching Arathiel as anything other than a criminal would be a horrible strategy. There was no rationale that justified it.

"What is the point of running the Myrians out if we allow them to torture whomever they please? I started this conflict to protect a teenager from undeserved pain. I can't ignore the man who defended Branwen from a worse fate. I promised her I would try—that if I had a solution, I would do it. Arathiel is our solution."

Kellian fell silent. Branwen had been sullen and irritable these last few days. She had refused to speak with either of them, except to follow Diel at the second Coalition meeting, and her eyes were often red from crying. Diel missed hearing her laugh and tease everyone, or having her burst into an important dinner to show off the last dress she had modified with Camilla's help. She had grown serious and angry, and without her energy, he felt empty.

"You'll ruin our family to save one man," Kellian said. "Even if we make it through, we'll never have the same political strength."

"We won't," Diel agreed. "But if it lets me rescue Varden and return Branwen's smile, then I'll be content."

Saying it out loud made it concrete. He would do it. It was the right thing to do, and he could feel it to the core of his bones. As the decision sank in, the sun vanished. Bioluminescent flowers lit up the city, wrapped around railings or hanging from balconies. As usual, lively colours covered the Upper City while the Lower City was plunged into darkness. He wondered where in those shadows Hasryan had hidden.

"I guess you were right, Kellian. I am this family's greatest peril."

Kellian's strong hand landed on Diel's shoulder, and he squeezed. Their gazes met, and though Kellian was still frowning, Diel knew the guard would have his back. *Family sticks together*, he thought. Every Dathirii would stand behind him in this decision, and so would Jaeger. They would always be there for one another.

"No, Diel. You're our greatest challenge."

CHARACTER GUIDE

THE following is a full list of characters featured in the City of Spires trilogy with short descriptions, to help readers navigate the story. The titles are meant to poke fun at them—don't take them too seriously.

House Dathirii

Diel Dathirii (Lord Dathirii), Eternal Idealist, he/him
Head of the Dathirii House, loves political fights and people, but none more than Jaeger.

Jaeger, Stalwart Steward, he/him
Diel's personal steward, the logistics behind the passion, a stickler for titles even for his long-time love.

Branwen Dathirii, Master of Disguises, she/her
Dathirii spymaster, her heart is as big as her multi-gender wardrobe.

Garith Dathirii, Number One Flirt, he/him
Dathirii coinmaster. Has ladies over at irregular hours, beware.

<u>Vellien Dathirii, Anxious Healer, they/them</u>
Dathirii priest of Alluma, youngest cousin. Would sing more if it didn't focus everyone's attention on them.

<u>Camilla Dathirii, Tea of Kindness, she/her</u>
Diel's aunt, has retired from wilder years to grant tea, cookies, and wisdom to those in need.

<u>Kellian Dathirii, Stiff Guard, he/him</u>
Captain of the Dathirii Guards, spends many hours wishing people would stop taking huge risks.

<u>Yultes Dathirii, Professional Impostor, he/him</u>
Main Dathirii liaison to House Allastam. Diel's step-brother and Larryn's father. Is great at lying to himself and others.

House Allastam

<u>Lord Allastam, Bitter Crusader, he/him</u>
Head of House Allastam. Would watch the world burn to get his way and avenge his murdered wife.

<u>Drake Allastam, High on Privilege, he/him</u>
Lord Allastam's son, heir to the house leadership, typically responds to 'no' and 'fuck you' with violence. Long history of harassing Larryn.

Mia Allastam, the Discreet Daughter, she/her

Lord Allastam's daughter, often kept away by chronic pain and the family's overbearing protectiveness. The only person Drake listens to.

The Shelter

Larryn, Anger Stew, he/him

Owner of and cook at the Shelter. Rages against the machine (and everyone else, really). Member of the Halfies Trio.

Hasryan, Assassin Seeks Friends, he/him

Once Brune's favourite assassin. His sass is as deadly as his blades. Member of the Halfies Trio.

Cal, Luck's Generous Hand, he/him

Priest of Ren, the luck deity. Lover of cheese, quick to develop friend crushes and act on them. Member of the Halfies Trio.

Arathiel Brasten, Drifter from the Past, he/him

Stayed trapped for a hundred and thirty years in a mysterious Well that drained his senses. Returned to Isandor recently.

Efua, Genius Letter Girl, she/her

Orphan living at the Shelter. Larryn's unofficial little sister. Works as a letter delivery girl.

Jim, Hard-Working Father, he/him

First owner of the shelter. Adoptive father for Larryn and Efua. Dead.

The Myrian Enclave

Master Avenazar, Destructive Ego, he/him
Head of the Myrian enclave. Ruthless and powerful mage who avenges every slight.

Nevian, Stubborn Pupil, he/him
Avenazar's apprentice. Determined to learn magic despite his master's constant abuse.

Varden Daramond, Gentle Flames, he/him
High Priest of Keroth, leader of the enclave's temple. Talented artist, loving soul, powerful fire-wielder.

Master Jilssan, Ambitious Pragmatic, she/her
Transmutation specialist and Isra's master. Always ready to do what it takes to survive.

Isra, Privileged Princess, she/her
Jilssan's apprentice. Loves shapeshifting spells and dragging Nevian along her dangerous ideas.

Other Figures of Note

Sora Sharpe, Unapologetic Law Enforcer, she/her
Investigator for Isandor's Sapphire Guards in charge of finding Hasryan. Hates political games.

<u>Brune, Ruthless Mercenary Leader, she/her</u>
Leader of the Crescent Moon mercenary, powerful mage, Hasryan's boss. Has hands in every pockets. Loves the colour brown.

Noble Families of Isandor

<u>House Allastam</u>
Second biggest family in Isandor. Its rise to power can be attributed almost entirely to the current Lord Allastam.

<u>House Dathirii</u>
Founding family and the only elven noble house.

<u>House Brasten</u>
House of medium importance. Has managed to retain a seat on the Golden Table despite the family's often deadly hereditary illness.

<u>House Freitz</u>
Targets of a bloody campaign from House Allastam after their leader was accused of assassinating Lady Allastam. One seat at the Golden Table.

<u>House Carrington</u>
Founding family that fell from power after a botanical spell gone wrong infected and killed half their family. Still sits at the Golden Table.

House Serringer

Small house that has a fur monopoly. One seat at the Golden Table.

House Almanza

Minor Isandor house. One seat at the Golden Table.

KEEP READING...

TURN THE PAGE for an exclusive short story set more than a century before the events of *City of Strife*. Travel through time and learn how Diel and Jaeger first met...

THE DIVE

AN ISANDOR SHORT STORY

NAKED river dives were Lord Ade Serringer's favourite summer endeavour. He called upon friends several times a week to leap off a cliff and into the cool waters of a tributary of the Reonne. Half a dozen naked young men swam nearby—muscled or fat, pale as snow in winter or rich golden brown—but Jaeger did his best not to look. He was in charge of lunch and privacy, and peeking at the soft curves of Lord Seymour Lorn or the solid six-pack of House Brasten's weapons master would be failing this second duty. So he stood guard, his back to the river, as the lords splashed behind him. He didn't mind. Two decades of service had taught Jaeger discipline and patience, and he'd much rather stare at willing, *interested* men than steal glances at nobles above his rank.

Or so he thought, until one of them trampled through the underbrush, only to stop some thirty feet away from Jaeger and exclaim, "Why, that must be the most ill-drawn map I've ever received! Even the simplest streams would lose their way to the Reonne by following it!"

Jaeger bristled at the suggestion. He had drawn the map and

knew it to be a model of cleanliness and precision, devoid of any colour codes he could have messed up. He straightened, dignified offence clipping his tone as he cast his voice. "Perhaps it is the holder who, after having one drink too many, can no longer make sense of top and bottom."

A melodious laugh answered his call, flitting through the leaves like a butterfly. "Come see for yourself, my good friend, and you'll find yourself as distraught as I am."

"I assure you, I know my maps and the quality of my drawing," Jaeger countered, and he started in the direction of the voice. Many nobles would have called him presumptuous, but he found it difficult to associate snobbery with the playful man. "You are obviously in need of a—"

This must be the last of Serringer's friends, arrived more than an hour late. Jaeger hurried around a large trunk.

The other elf's striking beauty stole his word.

Lord Diel Dathirii stood in the middle of the clearing, and the dappled sunlight turned his long golden hair into a cascade of glitter. He held the map high above him, two delicate hands crumpling its edges as he squinted at it. The intense colour in his eyes caught Jaeger's attention even as he tried to parse which word was right for it. *Green*, most likely. He'd always struggled to differentiate it with red, but he supposed *red* was too unusual an eye colour. Jaeger stared as Diel shifted in his direction, eyebrows shooting up, an amused smirk playing on his lips.

"A …?" he asked.

"Guide." Jaeger choked the word out. The humid day had suddenly become much warmer, as if the full sun beat down on his dark hair instead of the shade from the trees.

Diel Dathirii lowered the map, studying Jaeger with obvious interest. Not many elves inhabited Isandor, and although everyone knew of House Dathirii—they were one of the founding members of the city—Jaeger suspected Diel rarely saw elves not related to him by blood. He withstood the scrutiny despite his adolescent need to smile back. Lord Diel Dathirii might have a failing sense of direction, but he also possessed the most dynamic and beautiful face Jaeger had ever seen. What an unfair advantage, he thought: a single second had sufficed to conquer Jaeger. He'd never been prone to lovestruck foolery before.

"Come closer and show me," Diel said, his husky tone a contrast to the earlier crystalline laugh. "If you would."

Jaeger obeyed without hesitation. Three long strides and he stood next to the noble elf, and the strong scent of pines made his head spin. *Tree perfume*, Jaeger thought, laughing. Lord Diel Dathirii, an elf living in a gigantic tree-tower, had chosen conifers as his smell.

"Is something funny?" Diel asked, and under the humour, Jaeger heard a hint of worry.

"Who would ever guess an elf would lose his way in a forest?"

"Me. I can find my way around several layers of bridges, but push me out of a city and I'm lost within ten minutes. My sense of orientation has the same quality as the mix we fling down the shitslides."

"Oh, so it's not my map, then." Jaeger flicked the paper and allowed himself a victorious smile. A precise drawing of Isandor's surrounding lay on it. Lord Ade wanted every guest to have one, which meant Jaeger had drawn the exact same thing almost thirty times. Always with the same care.

Diel Dathirii lifted his gaze from it, and his playful smile melted Jaeger inside. "Indeed. I'm afraid you'll have to walk me through the entire forest next time. I'm liable to go due east instead of west."

He forced his arm into Jaeger's, picked a random direction, and started off. For an instant his proximity obliterated all rational thought, then Jaeger realized he'd gone the opposite way of Lord Ade and his friends. "Wrong way, milord," he said, and although he did his best to remain serious, Jaeger couldn't contain his amusement.

"Is it?" Diel stopped. "You suppose I mean to go toward the river."

"Well … yes, of course." What else? But before Jaeger could voice his question, his eyes caught Diel's. Was the lord suggesting he'd meant to stay alone with him? Jaeger's heart leaped, its rhythm irregular enough that the steward scolded himself. He had duties to attend to, and positions to respect. "I—*I* must go back, at any rate," he managed to say. "If the shame of your lateness is too much to bear, I'm afraid you will have to find Isandor on your own."

Diel Dathirii laughed again, and the sound sent Jaeger's heart spinning. He pulled a light-headed Jaeger back the other direction and they shared a blissful minute of silent walking during which Jaeger struggled to ground himself and control the ridiculous level of his crush. He was a steward in one of Isandor's smaller houses, and Diel would inherit the leadership of one of its oldest noble families. Social barriers could be ignored for a time, but this had no future. Besides, all Jaeger truly knew about Diel was that he couldn't bother to arrive on time and he'd rather blame a perfect map for his failures.

And he was very beautiful.

"Don't you swim?" Diel asked as they neared the tiny cliff once more. "It's too hot a day to spend it out of water."

Jaeger stopped in his tracks, words failing to form in his mind—all but one, which he blurted out. "Naked!" Way to impress. Jaeger flushed and he fumbled for a coherent sentence. "I cannot bathe naked with his lordship! It would be beyond improper."

"Really?" Diel pouted, then examined Jaeger from head to toe. Jaeger's mouth dried under the stare, and he breathed in relief when Diel shrugged and moved on. "That's a shame, but I won't insist."

The lord began unbuttoning, peeling off his shirt without the slightest hesitation.

"Did I hear Diel?" Lord Ade Serringer called from the water.

"Late as usual!" added another—Lord Arathiel Brasten, if Jaeger was right. "We should tell him to arrive an hour early!"

Diel laughed, flung his shirt over the closest branch, then attacked his pants' laces. "I'm an elf! We have an entirely different conception of time."

The lords snorted and laughed. "Jaeger is never late! Ask him—I bet he thinks it abhorrent."

Diel turned to him and grinned. Summer had tanned his skin, yet he had the wiry body of someone without much exercise. "Jaeger, isn't it? Be careful not to get heatstroke, standing like this all day."

He didn't wait for an answer, instead pulling down his pants and running toward the cliff. The last Jaeger saw of Diel Dathirii was a perfect, skinny ass leaping off and into the water.

DIEL checked the contents of his basket for the hundredth time, his stomach twisting with the certainty he'd forgotten something, *anything*. He listed off every component of his carefully planned meal in his head—three different types of cheese, grapes from southern Alloria, a local baker's fresh bread, honeyed pate, and a sweet wine to top it off—then looked at his pocket watch. Two minutes to go. He covered his basket with the beautiful blanket provided by Aunt Camilla, then cast his gaze around the room. How he wished it had a looking glass! Diel had run here, and he knew the two simple braids holding his hair back had come partly undone. He'd aimed for perfection, and failed, and now butterflies buzzed around his stomach, nauseating him.

Then the door clicked open behind him, and the butterflies flew away. Diel spun to face the newcomer, an easy grin reaching his lips as Jaeger stopped in the doorway, stunned and uncertain. "Milord? I did not think Lord Ade Serringer had an audience planned."

"No, no! I'm here for you, of course." Why else would he wait in the servant's quarters? "For dinner. Don't you finish in two minutes?" Diel raised his basket, and Jaeger's cheeks turned an adorable pink.

"In theory … but there are always more tasks."

"Can't they wait for tomorrow? Just this once. I even arrived on time!"

Diel added pleading eyes to his words and a smile cracked Jaeger's face. It lit his serious expression, smoothing his high cheeks and brightening his dark eyes. Diel's heart swelled. No day would ever be as lucky as the one he'd first laid eyes on this beautiful mapmaker, all dignified outrage at being blamed for Diel's lateness, his wit as quick as the red of his cheeks. *Jaeger.* The name had struck bells within him, and Diel had immediately decided no one would ever become such a profound part of his life. He might love hundred others at the same time, filling his heart with a constellation of amazing people of all genders, yet he knew without the slightest doubt Jaeger would never leave. Aunt Camilla had tried to reason with him, and while a tiny rational part of Diel admitted he barely knew Jaeger, his faith in this crush remained unchanged.

"I can't let such a miracle go to waste," Jaeger conceded. "But is this wise, milord? We're not … We're different."

Different *how*, Diel wanted to ask, but he'd heard the inflection Jaeger set on his title, and he knew what lay between them. He *hated it*, and couldn't help the sneer crawling on his face. "Let others deal with titles and hierarchy. I care for nothing but your unwavering talent for drawing plans and making me laugh."

"Yet it is not whether *you* care that will matter in the end," Jaeger said, and although Diel knew it to be true, he refused to stop there.

"We're far from the end," he pointed out. "We can deal with that when it comes. I offer only dinner—not even private naked swimming lessons!"

Shyness infused Jaeger's next chuckle, as if he couldn't believe Diel's brazenness. "Is that a promise?"

"It is." Diel brought the basket over his heart. "Only dinner."

"Then I accept."

Three words and Diel's chest suddenly felt ten times larger, his body a hundred times lighter. Only dinner, along with his too-full heart.

⬨

JAEGER did not remember the last time he'd talked so much. Words spilled out of his mouth, prompted by the occasional question from Diel, encouraged by the strangest feeling of *safety*. Jaeger stayed guarded around nobles, watching everything he said for potential offence and keeping his own thoughts private. Not today, not with Diel, and he didn't regret an instant of it. Diel listened with obvious interest, as if every word Jaeger offered was a precious jewel, a gift to treasure.

As time passed and the amount of cheese and grapes and bread diminished, the distinct impression of oversharing crept on Jaeger. The sun crawled down, its light barely peeking through the tree leaves, its heat ever-present. A spell of hot and humid days had gone unbroken for over a week now—gorgeous sunlight but stifling weather. They'd weighed on Jaeger all week, but he'd forgotten all about it over dinner, as if Diel had the power to drain difficult days away. What foolish thoughts! Jaeger scolded himself and tried to regain composure, but Diel melted his resistance with a single grin.

"You've lapsed into silence," he said.

"I am not usually this talkative," Jaeger replied, only to regret his admission immediately.

Diel's smile widened and amusement lit his eyes. "Then Alluma has truly blessed me. You're wonderful."

Jaeger didn't answer, but this time it was because Diel's blunt compliment had stolen his words. He blushed, snatched a piece of bread, and dug at its inside while leaving the crust intact. "You're smitten," he countered, "and no longer know what you're saying."

Diel laughed, sending Jaeger's heart spinning and tumbling. He *loved* the sound, how easy it was to bring about, how honest and simple. As Jaeger struggled to keep his wits about himself, he wondered which of them was the most smitten.

"I'm hot, too, and you're only half the reason."

Jaeger stammered, growing every bit as hot as Diel must be, although embarrassment played the biggest part in it. "You promised—"

"I know. The shade's fuller down by the river, though." Diel pushed himself up and extended a hand to Jaeger. "We could dip our feet in, if you're done eating."

Jaeger shoved the last piece of bread in his mouth, refusing to set it back down. He hated wastefulness. Decades had passed since he'd pretended to eat at work to convince his parents to have dinner themselves, but he'd never forget how it felt to starve. Would the noble now offering a hand to help him up ever understand? Would he care? When had nobles ever cared, really? Years as a steward for House Serringer had brought financial stability, but never understanding.

"I am. We should pack everything and keep it out of ants' reach, so we can give it away later." Jaeger's tone stayed casual, but his heart hammered in his chest. If Diel scoffed or laughed or dismissed the idea ... well, better to shatter any illusions now, before his ties to the elven lord turned into more than intense desire, natural comfort, and a love for his laugh.

Diel's tilted his head, his expression puzzled. "Give it?"

"You brought enough for five. Surely we can feed three more."

"Oh!" His face lit up. "That's brilliant. Of course." Then he laughed, awkwardness trickling into the usually clear sound. "Did I really bring that much? I'm sorry, I never do this and had no idea how much would be enough. I'm …"

Jaeger exhaled, more relieved than he cared to admit. "Let me handle that next time."

"Absolutely not! I don't want you to work for—wait, next time?" His early protest turned into a hopeful question. Diel grinned, then grabbed Jaeger's shoulders. "I get a next time?"

Of course, Jaeger wanted to say, but instead he picked up Diel's wrists and slowly removed his arms. "Only if you help me clean up."

"I'll do even better: let me handle this, and head for the river. I promise not to make a mess of everything."

Jaeger tore his gaze from Diel and examined the leftovers. He should by all means trust the other elf to clean up properly, but he knew too well how little his own employer ever did by himself and couldn't help but worry. Only once satisfied that nothing required complex care did he nod.

"Don't get lost on the way," he teased, even though the river passed less than a rock throw away, down a steep slope.

Diel's honest laugh followed Jaeger as he picked his careful way to the rocky riverbed. He rolled up the cuffs of his pants and found a suitably flat stone to sit upon, glad for a chance to cool both his heels and his mind. Jaeger planted his toes in the riverbed, revelling in the cold water curling around his ankles. A simple pleasure, without complications or consequences. Just his feet and the freshness of water on a hot summer evening.

Jaeger closed his eyes and focused on the sensation, pushing aside the vivid memory of Diel's hands on his shoulders, of his laugh, and the hope in his *I get a next time.* Every minute together transformed Jaeger's infatuation with who Diel could be into love for who he was.

Too fast for comfort, but the shivers desire Diel's touch and smile gave him made it hard to slow down. He ought to consider more carefully what was happening.

Nobles and commoners didn't get to love each other. Their worldviews did not align enough for lasting relationships. This was a fluke, or it would be. Yet Jaeger found he didn't *care*. Whether this lasted a month or a decade, it added wings to his heart and sent it soaring. Not even the cool water could compare, despite all of its simplicity. If a relationship with Diel meant a dangerous leap off a cliff, Jaeger wanted nothing more than to run to its edge and take that dive. And if he couldn't learn to fly in time, then he would deal with the crash when it came—and who knew? Perhaps it never would.

⤎⤏

DIEL took longer than he should have to return. Either he'd needed space for himself or wanted to grant Jaeger some. Still, by the time he scrambled down the slope and toward the river, Jaeger had another map quip ready.

"Not a word," Diel interrupted, forestalling the teasing. "I had worldly needs to take care of. Very romantic, I assure you."

Jaeger snorted. "Better a tree than upriver from our feet." Hard to believe Diel would even *mention* peeing. Some lords preferred to act like they never pissed or shat, as if they didn't pay commoners to carry their refuse to the shitslides.

Diel grimaced at the idea and hurried next to Jaeger. Instead of sitting down, he gestured at a string of larger stones advancing into the river. They ended in a flat rock more than large enough for the two of them. "I'll be over there, where I can get water up to my knees, instead of here where my ankles are lucky to get any."

He grabbed his shoes, threw them away, then leaped to the closest rock with practised ease. Jaeger watched Diel skip from one stone to the next, balancing his wiry body, and enjoyed the show. Although Diel lacked the muscles of more athletic men, he moved with beautiful grace and his golden hair caught the warm light of the setting sun as it flew about. Diel reached the flat rock without ever slipping, then spun about to grin at Jaeger.

"You're welcome to follow whenever you want," he said. "Or do you need a map of which rocks to step on?"

Jaeger recognized the challenge, and silly though it was, he hurried to his feet. His gaze travelled the path he needed to take, registering the moss and humidity covering several of these stones. How had Diel almost danced from one to the other? Jaeger's confidence wavered, but one glance at his date's smirk pushed him onward. He strode to the first rock, then leaped to the other. The moss's softness surprised him, and Jaeger almost lost his balance. He extended his arms, regained his footing, and looked up.

Diel was still grinning.

With renewed determination, Jaeger moved from one rock to the next, eager to join Diel on stable, flat ground. He hurried along and soon found himself rushing, feet slipping under him, convinced he'd fall the moment he stopped. Diel must have noticed, because when Jaeger reached the next-to-last stone, he extended a hand. Jaeger reached for it, glad for the help. His fingers clasped around Diel's, and the firm grip pulled him home.

Diel's expression shifted, mischief sparkling in his eyes and curling his lips. He tugged harder, bringing Jaeger close to him, then wrapped both arms around his body. Using the momentum of his arrival, Diel stepped back and let himself fall backwards, into the river, dragging Jaeger down with him. His clear laugh buried Jaeger's surprised exclamation, then they crashed into the water.

The river rushed around them, swirling, muffling sound. Diel's back took the brunt of the hit when they slammed into the riverbed—the shallow water didn't allow for a deep dive. Diel could've hurt his head, Jaeger realized, all for a wet prank. He slipped out of the embrace and pushed himself to the surface, panting from his run across the rocks and the sudden fall. Diel reemerged a second after him, laughing.

"You promised—" Jaeger sputtered.

"No naked swims, yes. I said nothing of clothed."

He sat there, water to his chest, the current carrying the tips of his golden hair away, grinning. He'd planned this! From the very moment he made his promise, he'd aimed to shove them both into the river, and now that he'd succeeded he radiated smug, playful pride and—

He was just *so goddamn desirable.*

Jaeger flung his dark wet braid aside, grabbed Diel's collar, and pulled him into a hard kiss. The warmth of his lips contrasted with the cold water, sending a wave of longing down Jaeger's spine. Diel melted into his arms, one hand reaching through the stream for Jaeger's waist, and all Jaeger wanted to do was to lean into the embrace and feel Diel's body against his.

There would be time, he told himself. Many other occasions. For now, he had revenge to take.

Jaeger broke the kiss to smile and meet Diel's gaze—a pause to let him read, if he could, the signs of what was coming. "With apologies, milord," he whispered. Then he pushed his lordship back under the water, holding him down long enough to savour his victory. When Diel came up gasping, Jaeger gave him no time to catch his breath: he kissed him again.

⟡

DIEL'S deft fingers worked at Jaeger's scalp, massaging it as they split the silky black hair for a braid. After a week of clouds and rain, the sun had finally dared to peek out. Its rays had lost their full summer force, and although the tree leaves hadn't turned, the first autumn chill settled over Isandor every night. Soon it would encroach over the days, too, and his time lazing outside with Diel would come to an end.

Jaeger sighed, refraining from leaning back into the other elf and hindering his work. Summer had been slow for House Serringer, and Jaeger had found himself with a lot of free time to share. He'd seen Diel almost every day, in the forest where they would be left alone and where Diel's eyes seemed to grow even greener for all the leaves around. Business would pick up soon, however. House Serringer specialized in furs, and as the winter cold returned, so would potential buyers. Jaeger often wound up working late into the evening to keep everything in order. They were running out of time. Sooner or later, the soft bubble of this summer would burst, and they'd barely see each other.

The thought left an empty hole in Jaeger's stomach. Diel had proven to be playful, easy-going to the point of being unreliable, but also deeply caring, for Jaeger and everyone else. When they'd brought the basket of leftovers to a popular refuge after their first date, Diel had inquired to the lady in charge about what else could be done, and within a week he'd brought not only money, but spent time working with them. It'd changed their dynamic—Diel asked more questions about what other problems they didn't see up in their towers, and how he could help fix them. They alternated between volunteer work and private dates, and Jaeger didn't know which of these contributed more to how deeply in love he became. He'd jumped into this relationship convinced he could survive the fall should it fail, and now he knew it'd leave him shattered. Even the next months of limited time with Diel would leave him ragged, strung out for more.

"Jaeger?" Diel's soft voice drew him out from his reverie. The fingers no longer moved through his hair, either, and Diel took a deep breath, as if amassing courage. Jaeger tensed. "Come work with me."

The request froze Jaeger in place. He stared ahead, his mouth dry, the words bouncing around his head. *Work with me.* "I-I can't!" he stammered. Heat climbed to the very tip of his ears and he spun around to stare at Diel, his braid be damned. Wide and confused eyes met him. "Work for you? We—aren't we ... that would be improper and—"

Diel put a finger on his lips and stopped him. "Propriety can go to hell," he said. "You're the most competent aide in the city, and I cannot bear the thought of not having you by my side."

"You don't understand, milord." Jaeger wanted to close his eyes and retreat, far away from the intensity of Diel's gaze, the rawness of his desire. They *both* wanted this, so much, but Jaeger couldn't accept. He couldn't, and it hurt. "Some lines should never be blurred. You cannot be both my lover and my boss, and I know which I prefer."

"But Jaeger ..." Diel's fingers moved to Jaeger's cheek, holding it. The touch sent a shiver down his spine and twisted his stomach. Jaeger had always feared what the class difference could do to them. He'd dreamed of an opportunity to spend all his time with Diel, but this was a terrible idea.

"I cannot tie my financial security to a relationship. What would it do to us? Any disagreement—any fight—and I'd have to wonder if I would lose my job in addition to you. Gold ... once you've run out, it never leaves your mind. It twists things."

A smile stretched Diel's lips despite the shadow in his eyes. "You think we'll disagree," he teased.

"We are disagreeing right now," Jaeger replied.

"What if you had a contract with House Dathirii? One without my name on it, with clear indemnities covering your departure. Enough to live a long time if you *somehow* couldn't stay." Diel clasped his hands over Jaeger's and squeezed them. His voice tightened, a hint of despair crawling into it. "I want a partner, Jaeger, in every sense of the term. You're ... brilliant, generous, ridiculously beautiful, and you taught me so much. I used to hate the idea of becoming Lord Dathirii—of dealing with the city's crass politics and constant trade deals. You showed me how much I could do with such a position, what I could change. We have centuries ahead, and I know I'll love and mourn many others, but you'll always be there."

The trees around them seemed to close down on Jaeger. He felt nothing but Diel's hands squeezing him and the warmth spreading from them and into him. The cool ground had vanished from under him, swallowed by the tide of Diel's intense love and the heady sensation of floating forced him to close his eyes.

Even with a contract the risk was huge, but Diel hadn't even hesitated. Beyond his brief teasing, he'd found no insult in the idea Jaeger needed reassurance, or that this proposal of his required a safety net to work. Jaeger knew he'd be given whatever he asked for. "I'll want my room, too," he whispered. "A space for myself."

"Of course! Anything, really, please just say yes."

"You'd think you're asking to marry me," Jaeger joked, his voice weak from raw emotion.

"Would that be simpler?"

Jaeger laughed, but heat rushed to his cheeks and his heart stumbled past a few beats. "No, no!" He preferred their love quiet and private, and the prospect of a wedding terrified him. Diel would lead one of Isandor's oldest Houses, which would make it a grand and public affair. Jaeger couldn't bear the attention. "Just a contract to sign, milord," he said, "although you're allowed to seal it with a kiss."

"Am I allowed to put 'never calls me by my title ever again' in it?"

Jaeger's mouth quirked, and he fought against his urge to smile. "And disrespect you in front of other important nobles? I would never."

"No one else is around," Diel pointed out.

Jaeger leaned forward until his lips hovered inches from Diel's ears. "Then make me stop."

Diel's clear laugh filled their small clearing, but only for a brief moment, after which his lips found Jaeger's. The beautiful sound and subsequent passion washed away Jaeger's lingering fear. What did one gain without risks? Diel had always made him feel safe—listened to, cared for, and loved for who he was. In his company, Jaeger vibrated with life. Accepting meant enjoying that peace for the foreseeable decades.

Jaeger would take that contract—that was his true dive off a cliff, to swim stripped most protections and live this relationship fully—and even if it shattered him in the end, it would have been worth every second of passion and love.

Want More?

The second book of the Isandor series, *City of Betrayal*, came out October 22, 2017!

Follow Claudie's works and new releases by signing up for her newsletter at her website, **claudiearseneault.com**!

If you enjoyed this read, please be sure to leave a review wherever you bought it. Every review makes a world of difference, in addition to keeping the writer thrilled and happy.

You can also pick up Claudie's first book, *Viral Airwaves*, in which a reluctant noodle-lover stumbles upon a government conspiracy and must expose it with little more than friends and a hot air balloon!

Finally, be sure to check out Claudie's publisher, **The Kraken Collective**, an alliance of indie writers of LGBTQIAP+ speculative fiction for more amazing stories!

ACKNOWLEDGEMENTS
REMERCIEMENTS

THE more I write, the more people I find I want to thank for their support. *City of Strife* is my first all-indie novel, the beginning of a long and promising adventure, and the result of years of an universe simmering in my mind and evolving. I like to start my acknowledgments in my own tongue, in French, for the wonderful people in my local life, but first I want to share the tale behind this novel and what it means to me to finally have it published.

Isandor is how I started writing. It wasn't a novel at the time—I was Dungeon Master for a sprawling roleplaying game that stretched on for over three years and was dedicated to a single player. I'd never played around in my imagination, created characters, storylines, and whole universes that way before! Soon I was writing short scenes happening out of my player character's sight to complete the unfolding adventure. That, really, is where my first thanks for Isandor should go: to Bobby Moran—you told me once I should be a writer, and sparked a fire that has since engulfed my life.

Things have changed a *ton* since these characters first emerged in my mind—I've changed a lot! This story is truer to myself, tighter than any roleplaying game needs to be. Even after my original game died, I kept playing these characters in other circumstances, and they evolved with me. And the wonderful thing about that? These precious babies have *so many more things to live*. I can only hope that as I continue to grow, so will Isandor, and that it will continue to live on with me.

[English will be back later, don't worry!]

Je voudrais donc dire merci d'abord à mon ami Jonathan, à qui ce livre est dédié, qui a suivi les aventures de ces personnages et leurs changements depuis les premiers balbutiements. Ta loyauté, ton rire facile, ta créativité et ton immense gaieté de coeur me seront toujours précieux. Merci aussi à Marianne et Audrey, pour les heures incalculables de roleplay et l'inspiration et les rires constants qui en ont découlé.

Merci encore à ma famille, mes amis proches, mon merveilleux copains, Eric, pour le soutien, les belles soirées, les rires--particulièrement à ma soeur, qui continue de produire des couvertures à couper le souffle pour mes histoires. Je vous aime tous.

[And look, we're back!] Speaking of thanks to support circles: I have met so many amazing people through social media. Shira, Elena, RoAnna, Ren, Lyssa, Jaylee and so many more: your enthusiasm, love, thoughtfulness, and talent are a constant joy to behold. And please, if you are not directly on this list, know that you *are* included, and I value our exchanges greatly.

I need to thank more specifically the people who worked on this book with me. Marianne (again!) who reads and loves everything I write and gets to see it all in its roughest form. Brenda and Katie, who saw first drafts and helped shape Isandor into the solid novel it now is. Ren, Jaylee, David, Nicole and Amy, who all to some extent commented on *City of Strife* and made it better. Special mentions go to Jess R. Sutton, without whom my prose wouldn't be so crisp and polished, to Lyssa who keeps designing my interiors, and to Gabrielle for the cover. You're all amazing.

Frankly, I hope this novel finds its way into the hands of a great many asexual and aromantic spectrum people. Your support and enthusiasm as we neared publication helped me through writerly self-doubts. I have found great solace and fun in stories that featured aromantic and asexual characters, and which focus had little to do with romance and desire. I hope you enjoy(ed) this new one as much as I loved writing it.

Merci à tous, and here's to the start of a wonderful series!